M000307340

Heart
and Seoul

Copyright © 2019 Erin Kinsella

All rights reserved. No part of this publication may be reproduced,
distributed, or transmitted in any form or by any means, including
photocopying, electronic or mechanical methods, without the prior
written permission of the publisher or author, except in the case of brief
passages embodied in reviews. For permission requests, write to the
publisher at the email address hello@tychismedia.com.

ISBN 978-1-988931-04-3 (Paperback Edition)
ISBN 978-1-988931-03-6 (E-Book Edition)

All characters and events in this publication are fictitious. Any
similarities to real persons, living or dead, businesses or organizations is
coincidental.

Edited by Sasha Knight
Front cover art by Odette.A.Bach
Book design by Eight Little Pages

Printed and bound in the United States of America
First printing, 2019

Published by Tychis Media
https://tychismedia.com

Heart
and Seoul

ERIN KINSELLA

TYCHIS
MEDIA

Content Warning

Tropes: marriage of convenience, found family, cohabitation
Representation: LGBTQ+ leads (panromantic, demisexual, bisexual), mixed race lead, Korean lead
Content Warnings: sexual situations, anxiety, panic attacks, PTSD, mentions of child abuse

Chapter 1

Tessa

Tessa woke in the dark, completely disoriented. The espresso she'd consumed after getting off the plane had kicked in hard, dragging her through the day in a caffeine haze. Eventually the crushing weight of her jet lag had pulled her under. Her phone screen blazed with light, and she squinted against the glow.

4:00 a.m.

The apartment around her was heavy with silence and scented with sesame and ginger from dinner. She peeled back the curtain to reveal the glittering sea of lights bisected by the serpentine form of the Han River. The road below was a steady stream of white and red as cars travelled around the colossal city of Seoul.

Her stomach rumbled. She fished out her remaining cookies and peanuts from the flight and ate them while tucked under the curtain like a cat on a windowsill. She remembered nothing from the last time she'd been to Korea since she'd only been a toddler, but there was still that link, a small piece of her heritage that anchored her here.

Fiddling with her phone, she checked the time back home. Noon. Tessa dialed her mother's number for a video call.

"*Meu amor*, what are you doing awake?" Her mother's mahogany curls were tucked up in a bun, emphasizing the soft heart shape of her face, both traits she shared with Tessa.

"Just jet lag, *Mamãe*."

Her gut swirled with nerves, unsettling the recently consumed cookies. Seeing her mother in the bright sunshine of their kitchen solidified that she really had just crossed the ocean. She was in Seoul, the capital of her paternal grandmother's homeland, and staying with her best friend who'd moved to Korea years ago. In a few days she would get to visit the set where a studio was going to turn her book into a drama.

"How was the flight?" Her mother propped the phone against the wall to free up her hands.

"Boring, but not so soul-crushingly long as when we visited all the fam in Brazil."

Her mother laughed. "That's why I only go back to see my parents every five years."

The sound of pops and sizzles intensified, her mother stirring something in a pan on the stove.

"Mamãe, you're getting splatters on the camera. Move me over." Tessa waited while the view changed, the phone shifting away from the stove. "What're you making?"

"Garlic noodles and shrimp."

Tessa's mouth watered. It was her father's favourite dish. "How's *Appa*?"

"It's a bad pain day for him." Her mother wilted. "He was up most of the night, and he was supposed to cover a class today. He'll be disappointed about having to miss it."

"Cheering him up with food?"

Her mother nodded.

"He'll appreciate it." Guilt twisted in Tessa's chest. "I feel bad for leaving."

"Meu amor, no. This is good for you. It wouldn't change things if you were here, and you deserve a break. I want you to be able to get out and live your own life."

"You're part of my life," Tessa instantly defended.

"That's not the same. Appa's pain isn't going to go away, and you can't while away your entire life helping us."

"I wouldn't mind." She'd written her books while doing just that.

"Meu amor, you're twenty-seven." Her mother's face turned stern and unyielding. "I know how much you love us. You've proven it a thousand times, and I promise that neither of us will think otherwise if you start living your own path. We're still going to be here, no matter how high you reach or how far you go. You've done so much for us, and believe me I don't mean to sound ungrateful at all, but you need to take some time for yourself. Your lovely assistant Amelia is around for any emergencies, and the nurse will be checking in. You don't need to worry. Just enjoy yourself."

"I'll try."

The sound of rustling in the cutlery drawer was followed by the echo of flatware settling on the counter. Her mother piled two plates with the shrimp and noodles.

"Take advantage of this trip. You're there for a few weeks, and there are going to be plenty of beautiful people running around. Kelly would be over the moon assisting with a fling if you wanted to break out of your bubble a little."

"I think we both know I don't do flings."

Her mother laughed. "First time for everything."

"Mamãe, please." Tessa groaned.

"Just try to have fun. For goodness' sake, your book is becoming a drama! You're free as a bird in a foreign country with your best friend. Go soak in every exciting moment of this."

"Consider me a sponge." Tessa grinned. "I swear I'll do my best."

"You'd better." Her mother tucked the phone under her chin, carting it and the two plates up to the room where her father was resting. He was awake when she flicked on the bedside lamp and gave a tired smile, accepting the food and a kiss. The image went wonky while her mother resettled on the bed.

"Hi, Appa!"

"Hi, Peanut." He waved and shoved a bite of food into his mouth.

"So, tell me about the drama. Do you think they'll do your book justice? Goodness, if it were me, I'd be too excited to even notice any flaws. You told me this company has pretty good productions, right?"

"Mhmm, they do. They made that one historical you loved and cried over for a week."

"Ah, yes. They don't often steal my heart like my telenovelas do, but I'm sure yours will make me cry just as much."

"I hope not." Tessa laughed. "A lot less people die in mine."

"Still, I'm glad all those people like your story as much as I did." Her mother beamed. "I'm so proud of everything you've accomplished."

"I'm proud too, but I have a mouth full of noodles." Her father's cheeks were puffed up like a chipmunk.

"You're both too sweet."

"I'm biased because I'm your mother, but I'm allowed to praise my favourite author." She winked, and it warmed Tessa down to her toes. "So, tell me more. When do you go to the studio?"

"I'm not sure yet. I'm still waiting to hear when they want me. I imagine it'll be sometime this week since they start filming soon, so I should get to see the set and meet some of the actors before that. I was just going to hang out with Kelly and check out Seoul until then."

"What sort of place doesn't have that planned in advance?"

She shrugged and propped the phone against the window. "Kelly said it's pretty common for a lot of things to be last minute. It's not like I have anywhere else to be when they tell me what's happening. I gave them my flight details, so I guess they'll figure it out from there."

Her mother frowned. "You'll keep me updated?"

"Of course."

"Is your lovely assistant excited to have full-time hours while you're in Seoul?"

"Totally. Amelia's saving up for a trip, so she was jazzed. I'm trying to let her take care of more so I can focus on my next deadline. You can call her—"

"If we need anything. Yes, I know." Her mother grinned. "Don't worry so much, meu amor."

Tessa blinked rapidly, exhaustion sneaking up on her.

"You should get to sleep." Her mother smiled softly.

Tessa sighed, pressing her cheek to the window. "I'll attempt, but I make no guarantees. I love you both."

"I love you too," her parents chorused.

They hung up, and Tessa burrowed into the blanket Kelly had covered her with when she'd passed out on the couch hours before.

Beams of sunlight seared her eyeballs. Tessa groaned and buried her face into the pillows.

"Good morning, sunshine."

Kelly had her hair pulled into a braid, deep violet fading into bubblegum pink at the tips. Her pale face was sans her usual makeup, and she was still in a set of cozy flannels.

Tessa tried to sit up but let out a whine and slumped back down. "I can't move. I've aged five decades overnight."

"It'll only get worse if you keep laying on our awful couch. Go have a shower, and I'll handle breakfast." Contrary to her words, Kelly draped herself over Tessa, squeezing her into a hug before releasing a sound only dogs could hear.

"I can't believe you're here! I'm going to find you someone perfect to go on a date with so you can fall in love, and then move here so we can be best friends in proper proximity!"

Tessa snorted into her pillow. There was no way she was going to meet anyone in the few weeks she was visiting, but she didn't want to burst Kelly's bubble. Her best friend's delusions of grandeur when it came to Tessa moving to Korea, and her love life for that matter, had always been a little out of hand. She never minded since she'd entertained the thought of moving more than once before but hadn't quite worked up the courage to leave her family and uproot herself.

Kelly's husband, Min Joo, emerged freshly showered, dressed, and groomed. He wandered into the living room, adjusting his tie, and looking so much like Tessa's mental expectation of a professor that she couldn't help but smile. Shining black hair swept over his brow, brushing the top of his round glasses. The pair of them lived simply in a small apartment in Itaewon, though they made decent money through Kelly's vlogging channel and Min Joo's job teaching business English at one of the local universities.

"Good morning, Tessa-*ssi*. Did you sleep well?" His face softened considerably when he lifted his gaze from his tie to the tangled pile of Kelly and Tessa.

"I did! Minus some jet lag, it was pretty good."

"We can start your review of Korean business terminology tonight if you're feeling awake enough for it." Min Joo fixed the buttons holding his tie in place.

"You're the best." Tessa tried to wriggle free of Kelly. "I've been reviewing, but I learn a lot better from people."

"It's no trouble." Min Joo smiled. "I'd have offered to start last night, but you were out like a light."

Tessa blushed. "Sorry about that."

"You only drooled on him a little bit." Kelly snuggled in closer.

"You're fine, Tessa-ssi. You didn't drool."

Tessa's stomach growled obnoxiously.

"Hungry?" Kelly sat up and pulled Tessa with her.

"Starving."

"Go wash up so we can eat." Kelly pushed Tessa off the couch, and towards the bathroom.

Tessa stood under the blistering hot spray until her protesting body limbered up, emerging from the shower squeaky clean and considerably more awake. Kelly waved her over to assist with breakfast by setting the table, so that they could eat together before Min Joo had to venture off to work.

Tessa inhaled her rice, tofu, and eggs, placating her ravenous stomach.

"You two have a good day. I'll see you tonight for dinner." He kissed his wife, slipped on his shoes, and off he went. Kelly smiled wistfully at the closing door.

"You're too cute, Kel." Tessa poked her friend in the ribs.

"Can you blame me? I love him so much."

"Oh, trust me. I'm aware." Tessa laughed. "From the moment you met him you made sure I knew exactly how much you were into him."

"That was almost ten years ago. I was a young'un."

"It was sweet then, and it's still sweet now. I'm glad that you're so happy with him."

Kelly's bluebell eyes glinted with mischief.

"No," Tessa said.

"No?"

"I know that look. No."

"I can't imagine what you mean." Kelly fluttered her eyelashes innocently.

"Just because I'm single doesn't mean you can start thinking about fixing me up now that I'm conveniently located."

Kelly pouted a pink lip. "That's how things work here though. You meet cool people through your friends and friends of friends. I wouldn't set you up with anyone bad."

"Kel, please. I'm demi, and you *know* how stupid people can be about it."

"Not everyone will be stupid. If they respect you, they'll roll at your speed. Regardless, I'm not gonna set you up with a fuckboy." Kelly gazed at Tessa imploringly. "Please consider it? Maybe you'll make new friends."

"But I don't plan on living in Korea, so what would be the point of dating?"

"You can date without intending to marry. Just have some fun. Everyone is going to be vetted, and I will sic Min Joo on anyone who upsets you."

Tessa snort-laughed at the thought of straight-laced Min Joo starting a brawl for her in his button-down shirt and dress pants.

"Fine, but at least let me get used to the time change before you start throwing people at me."

Kelly looked so excited she might burst. "So, what're you feeling, men or women?"

"Whoever you think would be good is fine. I'm open to anyone."

"Cool." Kelly squeezed her cheeks, her smile overwhelming her face. "I know a couple people you might like. Let me contemplate. I'll figure out some double date stuff later in the week."

Tessa rubbed her fingers over her scalp, trying to loosen the tension. "Don't make me regret this."

"Never ever," Kelly promised.

They were picking at their lunch and deep in planning what to see around the city when Tessa's phone pinged.

The readout said it was an email from Elite Studios, the production company making the drama. She held her breath and clicked on it, scanning over the orderly *Hangul* characters. The nerves returned, swirling in her gut.

"They want me to come to a meeting this afternoon."

She'd missed her chance to review business language with Min Joo, but her conversational fluency would hopefully be enough.

"Already? Jeez, they work fast." Kelly snatched the phone. "Hmm, the address isn't too far from here. I can take you over."

Tessa was loath to trade her pajamas for actual clothes, but she could hardly show up to a meeting in cat-patterned flannel pants. She decided on black skinny jeans with knee-high leather boots, paired with a red cardigan. It turned into a three-quarter-length sleeve on her, wrists and forearms bare though she'd bought it full length. Her arms were too long to fit most off-the-rack clothing properly. She chose to focus on colour, rather than fit, which meant it was red and gorgeous with her bronze skin and dark hair. It was a little confidence boost she desperately needed.

Hours later Kelly drilled her on local custom as they rode the subway. "They'll most likely have a work dinner after this. It would be super rude of you to refuse to go, and they'll probably all drink tonight. If someone offers you a drink, you have to take it unless you have some kind of health or religious reason to decline."

"Why?" She'd never gotten used to drinking, and wasn't eager to acquire familiarity. So many customs had never come up with her grandmother that she'd have to contend with now that she was in her homeland.

"Tradition?" Kelly shrugged and continued rattling off etiquette to help Tessa avoid embarrassment. "If all else fails, play the dumb foreigner, and they'll give you a pass."

"Does that happen to you a lot?"

"Not as much anymore, but let me tell you, it's saved my ass a few times. You'll be fine though. I think. You're obviously not from here so they should be pretty lenient."

They moved with the crowds off the subway and up to the street where a sleek office building glinted in the sun. A stiff-faced man in uniform opened the door for them when they arrived.

"Hale Tessa-ssi?" A petite woman approached them, heels clacking against the floor. Her hair was cropped to her shoulders, and she was dressed in a smart black blazer and pencil skirt combo.

Tessa nodded.

"My name is Kim Ha Yun. Welcome to Elite Studios." She introduced herself in rapid Korean. "Oh—" she switched to English, "—I forgot to ask. Will you be needing an interpreter?"

"I don't think so? I'm mostly fluent, so I should be fine."

"Excellent. That will make things much smoother." Ha Yun turned her attention to Kelly. "Will you be joining us?"

"No." Kelly shook her head. "I just brought Tessa. She's staying with me while she's in Seoul."

Ha Yun nodded briskly.

Kelly nudged Tessa forward. "I'll head home. Call if you need anything."

"Stay?" Tessa whispered, already panicking.

"I can't go to a business meeting with you when I have nothing to do with the drama. That would be like taking your mom to a job interview." She gave Tessa a tight squeeze. "You're going to do awesome. Love you, Tess!"

Anguish roared through Tessa as Kelly retreated from the building, leaving her with this stranger. Worry over her ability to hold her own in a professional setting gnawed at her gut, but she leaned towards optimism.

Her stomach twisted into knots, and she shoved shaking hands into her pockets.

The interior of the building was immaculate and intimidating, shining marble floors, tall windows, and high ceilings. Ha Yun waved her along and led her to the elevators. They rode up to the top level and disembarked into a pristine white hallway. Cast photos of previous dramas lined the walls, and Tessa recognized more than a few faces.

"This way, Tessa-ssi," Ha Yun urged her onwards.

Tessa followed obediently, emerging into a room where every eye turned towards her. She scanned the attendees, noting the plethora of suits, before getting to a few more casually dressed people. One of them turned towards her and stopped her heart instantly.

Holy. Shit. It's UpBeat!

Chapter 2

Tessa

He sat there, watching her, with his perfectly swept and styled black hair, flawless pale skin, and full lips that she definitely needed to stop staring at. Right. *Now.* She dragged her gaze up, zeroing in on golden-brown eyes she knew too well. They were framed by thick lashes that made her envious in insecure moments. He'd been her bias, her absolute favourite idol of any K-pop group, for the better part of eight years.

Somehow he was even more beautiful in person.

Her pulse buzzed in her ears, a steady drone that narrowed the world down to him.

"Hale Tessa-ssi." Ha Yun's voice snapped her back to attention.

Tessa's fingers itched to text Kelly immediately, to express some of the silent scream rapidly building in her throat.

Ha Yun went around the circle, introducing the staff, director, producers, and designers before moving on to the actors. "This is Brooks Lily-ssi who will be playing our female lead, Bridie Murphy."

Lily smiled at Tessa. Her sandy hair was cropped by her ears, blue eyes bright with excitement.

Tessa's eyes burned dangerously. Lily exactly matched what she'd imagined for the character. Her name was unfamiliar, but then it wasn't entirely common for white actresses to get leading roles in Korean dramas.

Tessa turned to the idol, scarcely able to breathe.

"And this is Baek Eun Gi-ssi. He will be playing our male lead, Lee Do Yun," Ha Yun said, pointing out the man responsible for Tessa's internal crisis.

She'd seen all the names in the email they'd sent her once casting was confirmed, but she'd never in a million years thought it was *that* Baek Eun Gi. At best she'd assumed it was an up-and-coming actor whose information had been drowned out on her searches by the idol's popularity.

Baek Eun Gi, or UpBeat, as he was more commonly known to his fans, had the voice of a goddamn angel. She'd discovered his music during a particularly difficult period of her life and had followed his career ever since. She loved all of his group, 24/7, as was only proper, since they were all talented, hardworking, and beautiful. But UpBeat... He was special, and being face to face with him now eroded her ability to be a reasonable human being.

"Hale Tessa-ssi, are you well?" Ha Yun set a gentle hand on Tessa's shoulder.

Tessa bowed quickly and muttered an apology, accepting a glass of water from one of the assistants. She sipped it carefully, hands shaking.

"Thank you for joining us, Hale Tessa-ssi," the executive producer said, organizing a stack of papers. "Was your flight pleasant?"

She had grown up speaking Korean with her father and grandmother, but exhaustion and jet lag had her brain working overtime to decipher the words.

"Yes." Tessa nodded. "It was, thank you."

"You said you had no concerns with the script when you read it. Is that still your opinion?" the executive producer asked.

"The script is fine," she replied. "The writers did a wonderful job."

He nodded, apparently satisfied.

Other voices mixed together, discussing the fine details of what was to come. Tessa wasn't all that familiar with most of the business vocabulary and missed too much to get a grasp on what they were talking about. She caught *filming* and *Busan*, vaguely recalling that there would be on-site filming in the southern city long after she'd arrived back home. Ha Yun said something about emails and schedules, but the explanatory words eluded her.

Yawn after yawn was stifled. So much ice water had been consumed to keep herself alert that her bladder threatened to burst. She blinked her burning eyes rapidly, trying in vain to be fully present, to overcome the jet lag. It was a losing battle as she listened for her name just in case, but after an hour or so of it not coming up, she got less diligent. Every time her attention drifted she noticed UpBeat all over again, and it sent a spike of adrenaline zipping through her.

They toured the studio with Tessa trailing behind her leads. She'd never been to a film studio before, and stared in wonder at the intricate lighting and camera systems. Several sets had been constructed, including the trade ship interior and the inside of a *hanok*.

Ha Yun kept close to her side, so she didn't have a chance to pull out her phone and spam Kelly. The overhead lights blazed, seemingly growing brighter the longer she was there. She rolled her shoulders to release some of the tension there, but it didn't help.

UpBeat paused in front of the costume rack. *Hanbok* and Georgian-style clothing hung in neat rows of bright silks and sturdy, plain cotton. His gaze flickered back to her, and she froze, heart whipping like a pinball. Tessa wanted to talk to him, to smoothly introduce herself, and have a story to take back to Kelly, but every time she worked up a fractional amount of courage, her tongue turned to lead in her mouth and nothing came out.

She was hopeless. The opportunity of a lifetime stood in front of her and she couldn't even form a sentence.

If she had a little less dignity, she might have managed, but she decided that silence was infinitely safer than making a fool out of herself. She wished Kelly were here. Her bestie had no barriers at all to this sort of thing and could have helpfully paved the way to Tessa having an actual conversation.

Tessa imagined it in her head. She would offer a charming smile, warm and sweet. He would be intrigued, asking her about her home and her writing. She'd provide witty commentary, and he'd laugh. She loved his laugh.

A low, pulsing sensation climbed up the base of her skull, interrupting her fantasy.

Her dreams of avoiding a migraine were dashed. She should have expected it with the jet lag and the stress, but somehow she'd hoped it would skip tormenting her, just this once. Nausea and more pain than she could tolerate would come along in a timely manner, as it always did with her migraines. It distracted her from UpBeat's proximity, which was likely for the best.

"Reservations for dinner are in twenty minutes," the executive producer said as they reached the end of their tour. "We can all walk over together." Everyone moved to follow him, and Tessa focused back in a moment later when Lily rested a hand on her shoulder.

"Not quite over the time change?" she asked, blessedly in English.

Tessa shook her head. She wanted nothing more than to tip over and fall asleep on the couch. "Not quite."

Lily chattered away in her charming British accent while Tessa half-listened, following along with the group as they headed down the street to a restaurant.

Tessa checked her phone and sent a message to Kelly.

Tessa:
I AM WITHIN TOUCHING DISTANCE OF MY BIAS AND I'M DYING

Kelly:
WHAT?? WHERE? WHY? HOW? Did you ACTUALLY touch him? I need details!!!

Tessa:
He's playing the LEAD! I'm going to get to see him every time I'm on set and I'm so awkward. We're heading to the work dinner now and I just want to nap. My head hurts :(

Kelly:
Min Joo looked very concerned over the sound I just made XD
I NEED TO KNOW EVERYTHING! They'll keep you out late, but call if you need anything <3 I'm expecting a much better update later so be prepared to spill every single impression!

The endless supply of rice, pork belly stew, and *banchan* side dishes perked Tessa up a little as she mechanically lifted her chopsticks to her mouth. Unwilling to appear rude, she accepted a drink of *soju* from Ha Yun who sat to her left, and then another as Lily refilled her glass. She shoved down her natural reaction to shudder as the tang of liquor bathed her tongue, leaving warmth blooming in her chest.

UpBeat passed her another shot, and she smothered a pitiful sound as their fingers brushed one another. She kept stealthily pinching herself under the table to be sure, for the hundredth time, that he was actually right there.

Maybe next time she saw him it wouldn't be so embarrassing.

The evening lasted for three more hours, and several more shots, before people got restless about needing to head home. Most of them packed up quickly, eager to leave. Tessa was considerably more intoxicated than she'd have liked. She picked up her purse and excused herself to use the washroom, using chairs along the way to balance herself. The pulsing sensation in her head had slowly grown to a throbbing ache that squeezed her entire skull. Migraine auras flooded the periphery of her vision, an insistent swirling that blurred the world into static. She stumbled when she reached the doors and slipped inside, bracing her arms on the sink.

Her stomach heaved, and she lurched into one of the stalls, emptying her dinner into one of the toilets. She whimpered. A waste of amazing food. Staggering to the sink, she splashed cool water on her face and dried it off carefully to avoid smearing her makeup. The gloss of pain and fatigue was heavy in her reflected gaze.

Tessa fished through her purse for her painkillers. She cursed, remembering they were useless to her anyway since she couldn't take them after consuming alcohol.

A yawn cracked her jaw, and she swayed on her feet.

Tessa turned back to the door, heading into the restaurant as a wave of nausea and lightheadedness knocked her flat.

Chapter 3

Eun Gi

Eun Gi stepped out of the men's bathroom and tripped over an ornamental plant when someone collided with him. He steadied himself on the wall, one arm wrapped around the person's shoulders to keep them from tumbling to the floor.

"What on earth? Hey." He jostled the writer a little. "Are you okay?"

She didn't answer, instead sinking to her knees, her hand pressed to her mouth. He kneeled next to her. There was sweat on her brow and no response save a quiet groan when he gently shook her.

He hoisted her up bridal style and peeked around the room to find that the rest of their party had vacated the restaurant.

"I was gone two minutes," he grumbled. "How did they all leave so fast?"

He sighed, shifting the writer in his arms.

What am I supposed to do with you?

Eun Gi flagged a waiter and awkwardly maneuvered the writer's dead weight. "Can you find her a spot to rest for a few minutes? I have a car service on the way already."

The waiter bustled off to do just that. The restaurant was empty, and the waiter arranged a line of chairs for Eun Gi to lay her down. Eun Gi checked her phone and found it unhelpfully password protected.

He phoned Kyung Mi. Their manager was a terrifyingly efficient woman, but Eun Gi had long since outgrown being intimidated by her. Female managers in the industry were extremely rare, and Kyung Mi took her job *very* seriously.

"Eun Gi, what's wrong?"

"Why would you think something's wrong?"

"You don't call me unless it's important."

"I need to find out the writer's address."

"Do I want to know?"

Eun Gi flushed when he realized how creepy that must have sounded. "She's with me right now, but not well. I have no idea where she's staying."

"Let me do some digging, and I'll get back to you. Stay safe."

"Thank you." Hanging up, he noticed that the car he'd ordered had pulled up. He shook the writer's shoulder.

She peeled open one eye.

"Are you okay?" he asked again in English, figuring she might be too out of it for a foreign language. "Do you need to go to the hospital?"

"Migraine, and maybe drunk," she mumbled. "I'll be fine, just...need sleep."

She dropped off again.

He chewed his lip. His home wasn't far from here. If she didn't need a hospital, and Kyung Mi couldn't find out where she was staying, then he could always take her there. The car beeped its horn.

Eun Gi muttered a curse.

He carted the writer into the backseat and wrangled the seat belt into place. Eun Gi stared up at the starless sky in exasperation. Theoretically, it should be safe to take her home until he could get her to where she belonged, but he hated not being sure. She had clearly recognized him, but he was used to that. He'd been expecting her to do something, anything, but she'd mostly avoided eye contact, and hadn't spoken a word to him directly. Surely the studio would have warned him if she were a *sasaeng*.

His phone rang and he melted with relief when he saw Kyung Mi's name.

"Did you find it?" he asked.

"No one I contacted knows the name of the person she's staying with, and she's not booked into any hotels that we can find. Ha Yun said she arrived with a woman, but they never collected her information."

"Great. I guess I'll just take her home for a while then. I can't leave her unattended like this."

"Why do you have to get into trouble when I'm out of town?" Kyung Mi sighed.

"I'm not in trouble. It'll be fine, probably. I'll keep you posted on how things go."

Eun Gi slipped into the backseat and told the driver his address. He kept his gaze firmly out the window, and when they arrived, he sighed quietly before wrestling the writer's uncooperative body out of the vehicle. She curled into his arms, fingers latching onto his shirt. He steadfastly ignored the warmth of her body against his. Ruffled and cranky, he hoisted her up and carried her inside, nodding to the doorman.

The elevator ride seemed to last forever. He elbowed the doorbell, and his roommate answered.

Hwan's eyes widened as he took in the woman in Eun Gi's arms. "What's going on?"

"Out of the way. She's getting heavy."

Hwan stepped aside and closed the door, following Eun Gi into their apartment. After kicking off his shoes, Eun Gi crossed the white-carpeted living room and set her on the couch, draping a blanket over her before digging out her phone again. There was a single text from someone named Kelly, but he couldn't reply to anything. Eun Gi diverted to the kitchen, opening then closing the fridge after seeing nothing he wanted.

"Well." Hwan crossed his arms, moving to lean next to him. "Are you going to explain?"

Eun Gi did, briskly, agitation growing as he paced. Anxious energy buzzed through his body, and he shook his hands, as if it would shake out the energy too. He turned back to the couch. The writer's dark-brown curls were a riot around her head, and thick lashes fanned over freckled cheeks. Her full lips parted softly with her even breath.

Hwan scanned her, hands on his hips, glasses balanced on his nose. His black hair was slicked back and styled to perfection. "I'm sure someone will be searching for her soon enough. If not, she'll wake up, and then you can send her on her way. The studio should have made sure she got home safely."

She stirred, and both men froze, but she only rolled over and settled more deeply under the blanket.

Hwan looped an arm around his shoulders. "I get that you're not comfortable with her being here, but you were a good person helping out someone in need."

"I guess." Eun Gi glanced at the clock on the microwave. It wasn't too late yet, but he was drained. "Are you guys out tonight?"

"Yeah, but I can stay home if you want. We're going to a club. I'd say you should come along, but I don't think either of us want her to wake up here alone."

"It's fine," Eun Gi said. "I can stay. You go have fun with the others."

"You're sure?"

Eun Gi nodded and shooed Hwan away from the couch. "Have you eaten?"

"Sung Soo ordered take-out and I stole some." Hwan grinned, a dimple adorning each cheek. He pulled Eun Gi in, smacking a kiss to his cheek. "I need to figure out what to wear tonight. You have fun babysitting."

The writer's phone rang a while later and Eun Gi realized he'd just been staring blankly at his script.

"Finally." He picked up the phone. "Hello?"

There was silence for a moment and then a woman snapped, "Where's Tessa?"

"She's asleep and safe."

"Bullshit. Tell me where she is and who the hell you are."

"My name is Baek Eun Gi. Tessa-ssi and I work together on the drama. Who are you?"

"B-Baek Eun Gi? *The* Baek Eun Gi from 24/7?"

"Yes."

"Why is she with you?"

"Why don't you tell me who you are so I'm not providing information to a stranger?"

"Right, sorry. I'm Kelly Walsh, Tessa's best friend. She's staying with me while she's in Seoul." Another pause. "Now, answer my question."

Eun Gi explained the situation and the subsequent difficulty in finding any useful information to get Tessa home.

"Why did she collapse? Why didn't you take her to the hospital?"

"She said she had a migraine, and she also had a fair amount to drink at dinner, but she said she'd be fine and just needed to sleep."

"I want to see her. I'm going to call back on video and if you don't answer... so help me God—"

"Okay."

Kelly hung up, and the video call came through. Eun Gi saw her face shift as she realized he wasn't lying about his identity, then he rotated the phone to where Tessa was curled up. He lifted the blanket for Kelly to see that her friend was untouched and clutching one of the pillows.

"Tess? Wake up so I know you're safe."

Tessa cracked an eye open, but closed it again and turned over. "Sleeping."

"Shit. The subway is already down for the night. I'll wake up my husband. We can take a taxi to come and get her."

Eun Gi turned the screen to face himself. He wasn't entirely certain he wanted this strange woman to have his address and come into his home. The clock on the microwave told him it was after one in the morning.

"She can stay until morning if it's too much trouble. The others won't be back tonight."

"Who are the others involved here?"

"Hwan is the only one here with me. Sung Soo and Min Jae have a separate apartment, but either way, they're all out for the night."

Kelly scrutinized his face through the screen. "If anything happens to her, I will find a way to make you pay for it."

"Noted." It wouldn't be difficult for her to do so. The fans could go either way, supporting or destroying him if someone put forward allegations. "You have nothing to worry about. I just want to sleep, but I was waiting for someone to wonder where she was."

Kelly puffed up her cheeks. "Okay, fine. She can stay there, but let me know as soon as she wakes up."

"Of course."

Emotions flickered over Kelly's face before she settled on acceptance. "Thank you."

They parted ways after he provided his phone number to her so they could keep in contact. He could always get a new number if she leaked it. It wouldn't be the first time he'd had to.

Eun Gi slipped into his room and tried his best to ignore the sleeping woman on his couch. He pulled the blankets up to his chin, hoping against hope that his nightmares would give him the night off with a stranger in his home.

"*Hyung*, wake up!"

Eun Gi ignored the familiar voice on the other side of the door. Maybe its owner would leave him in peace for a few more moments of sleep.

The sound of a body thumping against the door had Eun Gi rolling over to stare at the ceiling, but exhaustion kept him pinned.

"I'm awake," he called out.

"Prove it!"

Eun Gi smiled. "Doesn't speaking prove I'm awake?"

The door cracked open. "No! I need to see your face."

A pink-haired bullet launched into the air and landed on the bed, flattening Eun Gi into the mattress. The air whooshed from his lungs. He struggled with the ball of energy that was Jeon Min Jae, the *maknae* of their group, nearly landing face-first as he scrambled off the bed.

Min Jae grinned. "Now you're up."

"I told you to wake him, not crush him." Sung Soo, the eldest of their group, stood by the door with a bowl in hand. He shook his head, an indulgent smile on his face. Strands of blue-tinted hair escaped into his eyes, and he pushed them back with his arm. "You two are ridiculous."

"Don't pretend you don't love us, Hyung!" Min Jae shouted to Sung Soo from the bed.

"I don't even know yoooou," Sung Soo sang as he made his way back into the kitchen.

Eun Gi groaned and wandered bleary-eyed into the living room. "What're you all doing here?"

Usually they ate in Sung Soo's suite since he had his own kitchen set up just so, and was the only one of them who actually enjoyed cooking.

"We were curious about your guest." Sung Soo added the egg mixture to a pan.

Eun Gi froze when he saw the writer still nestled on his couch.

"Oh. Right."

Tessa

Tessa woke to a blazing sunbeam piercing through the large window. She grumbled and tried to burrow under her blanket, away from the light. Her head ached like the devil, but at some point she'd have to open her eyes. Voices were nearby, and it took a few moments to process that they were male and speaking Korean.

She pulled the blanket down a little and was met with a sight she didn't recognize at all.

Tessa sat up carefully, her weight sinking into the leather couch. Another equally sumptuous couch sat perpendicular to her, and a huge television was mounted on the wall. Her head swiveled toward the stainless-steel kitchen where the voices and the scent of omelets were coming from. Tessa froze.

Holy shit. It's 24/7! Why are they here? Why am I here?

Hwan noticed she was awake and motioned to UpBeat. He approached, arms crossed over his chest, and Tessa fought the urge to hide under the blanket again.

"How do you feel?" UpBeat sighed when she didn't immediately answer. "English?"

"Yes, please." She was grateful to be able to use her native language while her head was throbbing. "Where am I?"

"Our apartment," UpBeat said before explaining how she'd ended up there.

Tessa's cheeks flamed. "I'm so sorry."

"It's fine. Do you need anything?"

"Painkillers?"

UpBeat made the request in Korean, and Hwan disappeared for a minute, returning with a small pill bottle and a glass of water. Tessa accepted them without a word.

She was in the home of her favourite performers in existence, and had to figure out how to avoid making a fool of herself. Easy, right? Her tongue was a lead block in her mouth. Hwan watched her intently. She needed to say words.

"Thank you."

Hwan blinked at her before the English words registered. He grinned, his dimples fluttering to life.

Inside, Tessa was screaming, but outside she remained neutral, weighed down by exhaustion.

"Sorry, he doesn't speak English," UpBeat said.

"Just Korean and Mandarin." Tessa's eyes widened, and she slapped a hand over her mouth. "God, I'm sorry. That's so creepy. I promise I haven't memorized your blood types or the names of your childhood pets."

UpBeat gave her a chagrined look. "That's a relief."

Jeon Min Jae, or Jaybird, as Tessa knew him, loped into the living room and jumped onto the couch opposite her. "Good morning!"

Tessa stared at him, agape. She reeled her shock in and pasted a smile onto her face.

"Jae, don't bother her." UpBeat shooed him away.

Tessa swallowed down the pills and the water, wishing desperately for a toothbrush. She tried not to think about how her hair and makeup must be faring after fainting and sleeping it off on a stranger's couch.

"Thank you for keeping me safe last night."

UpBeat nodded. "You should call Kelly. She was worried."

Tessa cringed at the litany of missed texts displayed on her phone screen. She sent a quick reply to tell Kelly she was awake and safe and would be heading back at the earliest opportunity.

"Do you want breakfast before you go home?" Sung Soo asked from the kitchen.

Her stomach heaved at the mere suggestion of food.

"I don't want to be a bother." Tessa winced. "More than I already have been, I mean. I'll eat when I get back to Kelly's. It's not far from here, or at least I don't think. What district are we in?"

"Gangnam," UpBeat answered. "I'll call a car for you."

If she'd been feeling well and meeting them under better circumstances, she might not have been so cripplingly awkward, but alas. The only thing she wanted right now was for the floor to open up and swallow her.

She crossed her legs, squirming in a vain attempt to thwart the desperate need to pee.

Hwan sat on the other couch and pointed toward the hall opposite the kitchen. "Toilet."

"Thank you." Tessa nodded, regretting the movement as a fresh wave of throbbing hit her. She slipped away, hiding out in the bathroom, washing up as best she could without any supplies. It wasn't as bad as she feared. The makeup Kelly had put on her had mostly held in place instead of turning her into a raccoon.

Witchcraft.

Water tamed some of the frizz, but overall her hair was a bit of a lost cause. She emerged tentatively after wasting as much time as she could.

UpBeat was fussing in the kitchen, likely eager to have her out of the way. His phone rang before she could sit back down.

"The car is here. I'll take you down."

Tessa thanked them for the hospitality and grabbed her purse, pulling on her shoes at the door. "My coat?"

"You weren't wearing one when you collapsed. I may have left it at the restaurant." He fished one out of the closet and handed it to her. "We start filming soon. You can bring it back to me then."

Tessa nodded slowly, dying inside over the concept of wearing her idol's clothes. She was being ridiculous, because it was *just* a coat... but, it was *his* coat.

She slipped her arms into the blue garment and buttoned it up.

Do not, *and I repeat, do* not *sniff.*

She could smell his shampoo, or something equally fragrant lingering on the fabric.

Coconut? Oh my God. Stop it. You're a grown-ass adult.

The trip down to the front doors was silent and awkward. Tessa wanted so badly to be charming, but she felt like trash. She was in too much pain to be witty, to put on a bright smile and give him some reason to think of her past this moment.

"Have a safe trip back," he said, pausing at the exit doors of the apartment building.

"Thank you, again." She forced her lips into an upwards curve, but she wasn't certain whether it came across as a smile or a grimace. The doorman cast her a speculative look as she slipped past him and settled into the black sedan waiting out front.

The Han River glittered in the morning sun as they crossed it, traveling from Gangnam to Itaewon. Tessa thanked the driver upon arrival and was declined when she tried to pay. UpBeat had already covered it.

Kelly was at the doors when Tessa got out. "You're here! How are you feeling?"

"Like a pile of ass. I'm sorry I worried you. I should have come home before dinner, but I wasn't sure how to excuse myself when it was the first time meeting everyone."

"It's okay. Let's get you upstairs. I know your migraines knock you on your ass, so you can have some food and then you're going back to bed."

"Okay."

"Be prepared to love me because I made you *canjica*. I ordered in the maize so I'd have it when you were here. I figured it would be easy on your stomach and at least get some food into you."

"You're a goddess."

Inside, Tessa changed into pajamas while Kelly ladled out a bowl of the sweet maize porridge. With a satisfied stomach, Tessa climbed into Kelly and Min Joo's bed with the curtains drawn.

"I'll check on you later," Kelly said. "I'm going to film some videos while you rest. Just some vlogs so you don't have to listen to me clanging around for a cooking one. Sweet dreams, Tess."

Tessa nodded, waiting to succumb to sleep. Maybe when she woke she'd find all this humiliation had been a dream.

Chapter 4

Eun Gi

"Well, that was certainly interesting." Sung Soo portioned their breakfast onto plates and passed one to Eun Gi.

"Hyung, I'm starving!" Min Jae sat on the couch with Tessa's blanket draped over his shoulders like a cloak. "I'm tired from the club, and I've only had soju and peanuts."

"That's what we've all had. Set the table please."

Min Jae flopped over in protest. "She has nice perfume."

"Don't be weird," Eun Gi's snapped at the maknae.

"I'm just saying!"

Sung Soo rolled his eyes. "Jae, this will go faster if you help instead of watch."

The maknae huffed and stood, still wearing his blanket cloak as he fished out bowls and chopsticks.

The four of them sat together at the coffee table, the remaining active members of the wildly popular idol group,

24/7. They were in a strange sort of limbo with three of the seven members fulfilling their military service, which left the rest to navigate the challenges of keeping the group going. Sung Soo would be next in two years, then Eun Gi and Hwan in four, and lastly Min Jae in five years. One by one their careers would be put on hold under the mandatory draft just before they reached the age cap of thirty.

"You start filming next week, right?" Sung Soo asked.

"Yeah." Eun Gi blinked, having lost focus staring at his food.

"Don't sound too excited," Sung Soo teased.

"I can't tell if I *am* excited." Eun Gi sighed and chewed his rice. "It doesn't feel the same without the others, and I guess acting is as good a distraction as anything. I don't have the motivation for music that I used to."

"It's weird for everyone," Hwan pointed out. "We can't let our careers go though. Yoon will be back this summer, and we have to keep up the hype for the comeback."

"What if there isn't one?" Eun Gi whispered.

Sung Soo laid a hand on his shoulder. "What do you mean?"

"It's a lot of pressure. We're losing so many years and we won't be a full group until Min Jae is done with his service. There's so much up in the air."

Stop it.

The slope down a wicked spiral of anxiety was crumbling under his feet.

"There's not going to be military reform before we have to deal with it ourselves. We just have to adapt," said Sung Soo pragmatically. "There's no way for any of us to get out of it."

Eun Gi squeezed his chopsticks, knuckles white. "I *know* that."

Their inevitable separation was a brick wall, and he was careening towards a collision that he feared would destroy him.

"Hey." Sung Soo scooted closer and looped an arm around Eun Gi. "We still have each other even if we're not all together."

Appetite gone, he pushed away his bowl. "I'm going for a run before I have to head out."

They knew enough to keep any protests about meal-skipping to themselves. After he burned off some of his energy he would try eating again.

The treadmill in the building's gym whirred under his feet. He ran until his lungs burned, and slid off the slowing belt, panting. He tried not to let his anxiety get the better of him, but success was sporadic at best. Forcing himself into physical exhaustion was the most effective method he'd found so far. Fortunate, considering the commonality of that state in the industry he'd chosen.

When he re-entered the apartment, Min Jae smacked a kiss onto each of Eun Gi's cheeks. "Feel better?"

"I guess," Eun Gi murmured. His food was still there waiting for him, and he dug in after popping it into the microwave. They rejoined him around the coffee table.

Hwan settled next to him. "I know you theoretically already know, but I'm reminding you anyway. There's a lot of good to focus on. You're the lead in a drama, Sung Soo is working on a solo album, I'm working on the Mandarin translations of our last album. Min Jae is existing."

"Hey!" Min Jae shoved a socked foot into Hwan's ribs, toppling both men against Sung Soo.

Hwan walloped Min Jae in the head with a couch pillow. Sung Soo crawled to safety and pulled the table and food out of the way as the maknae line descended into chaos. He fetched a spray bottle from under the sink and proceeded to take aim, nailing them in the face. Yelps and flails broke out as they scrambled away from the onslaught.

"Can we have one meal together without you three rolling around on each other?"

"Hyung," Min Jae whined, "you're just jealous because you're too old."

"I am *not* old." Sung Soo hurled himself into the pile. They flattened, the couch sliding back from the impact, sending them sprawling.

Min Jae dissolved into laughter. "You're so easy, Hyung."

Sung Soo draped his dead weight across them.

"Hyung, I can't breathe." Hwan shoved at Sung Soo.

"You should have thought about that before you allowed Min Jae to call me old. My bones are too brittle to get up. You all must suffer."

"Jae, apologize," Hwan squeaked out.

Min Jae sighed and rolled his eyes. "Hyung, I'm sorry. You're the most youthful and vigorous, the most loved and respected hyung in history."

Sung Soo rolled off them, and Hwan sucked in a grateful breath.

"I'm the one who's getting too old," Hwan complained. "I can't handle being crushed by your giant butt, Hyung."

"Excuse you, everyone loves my butt. All the fans say so."

"Well, go crush one of them with it." Hwan laughed and climbed up onto the couch.

"I'm going to meet Lily-ssi at the studio to run lines after I shower," said Eun Gi. "You should all get some sleep."

Sung Soo nodded. "No argument here."

When they finished eating, Eun Gi helped Sung Soo clean up.

"Hyung, do you think this is the right choice for me?"

Sung Soo looked up from loading the dishwasher. "I'm not sure how many more times you plan on asking me that question, but my answer is still yes. It'll be good for you to try out something different for a while, then you can come back to music refreshed."

"I'm just still unsure."

"Well, it's not so different from when we became trainees. There's never a guarantee of success. You have to put in the effort and hope you stumble across the right choices to make it all work. We're here for you no matter what happens."

Sung Soo poured himself a glass of water and drank it leaning up against the counter. He watched Eun Gi over the rim.

Eun Gi frowned. "I'm bad at being a failure."

Sung Soo snorted into his drink. "You've been many things over the years, but failure isn't one of them. You can do this. I believe in you completely."

Eun Gi hesitated.

Sung Soo patted his back and pushed him out of the kitchen. "You know what they say. 'Even monkeys fall from trees', so if this ends up with you falling, you'll just climb a new one. You've got this. Now, stop pouting, and get to the studio."

Lily sat across from him with a soft smile on her face. *Ships in the Night* by Tessa Hale, which Eun Gi had read before accepting the part, was a tale of bravery, travel, and romance; a young Irish girl in Georgian times escaping poverty by dressing as a man to join the sailing trade routes that eventually brought her to the Kingdom of Joseon.

"Lee Do Yun, I don't want to get back on the ship. I've been so focused on escaping my old life that I didn't realize I'd already found a new one. I wasn't running, I was searching for home." Lily beamed at him, entirely out of character as she rattled off her lines in Korean. "I just wanted a place to belong."

The script writers had added more soap opera flare to the lines than he remembered from the actual book. While he wouldn't admit it out loud for the sake of his job, he secretly preferred the original version.

"Joseon is nothing like where you come from. How can you feel like you belong here?"

"The difference is part of the beauty," Lily said. "Everywhere I've been is different from where I've come from, but it helped me learn who I am and where I want to be."

"What is it about Joseon that makes you want to be here?"

"Wow, this guy is obtuse." Lily laughed, breaking character again. "Lee Do Yun, how can you ask me that?"

"I'm not accustomed to speaking my feelings. I wouldn't want to presume what may be between us."

"You presumed correctly when you kissed me last night." Lily winked at him.

Eun Gi sat up a little straighter in his chair. "We don't have to practice the kiss now. Just lines, right?"

"Whatever you prefer."

Eun Gi stood awkwardly and addressed her in English. "I'm going to get a drink. Do you want anything?"

"I'd love some water. Thank you."

They'd been running lines for the better part of two hours. He sipped his water and flipped through his phone, scrolling through pictures of cute animals to de-stress before venturing over to the news headlines.

Eun Gi choked on his drink and fumbled his phone, dropping the cup but catching the device before it clattered to the floor. He set his phone on top of the water cooler, heart hammering. Grabbing a fistful of paper towels, he knelt to mop up the mess, mind churning.

Lily joined him to help. "Is everything okay?"

"I'm not sure."

Dread climbed in his gut as he picked up his phone again and clicked into the article. He swallowed, hard. It was never a good thing when any of them showed up in the news. Most of the pictures were fuzzy, but a couple were clear enough that anyone familiar with the group would be able to recognize him. He scrolled, searching for details. Her name was nowhere to be found. Maybe they didn't know who she was? That would be even better.

Further on were pictures of her leaving the building in the morning alongside an older picture of him wearing the same coat. There was speculation as to who she might be and what their relationship was, but no actual information. The double-edged sword of relief and regret plowed into him. Maybe without her identity exposed she wouldn't get dragged into a mess, but that didn't help him at all.

Then he found the comments.

He shouldn't have looked.

Mixed in among the genuine curiosity was a hearty helping of vitriol, tainted with any and all horrible names the commenters could come up with to describe the apparent mystery woman.

Eun Gi forwarded the article to Kyung Mi, adding a brief explanation as to his relationship, or lack thereof, with Tessa Hale.

The response was instant.

Kyung Mi:
I'll keep an eye on it from here.
I'm heading back tonight, but I've sent it on to the company.
Please don't do anything stupid.

"Too late for that," he muttered.

Eun Gi:
When do I ever?

He couldn't see her, but he knew she'd be sighing deeply.

Soon enough another dozen articles from various sources featuring the pictures were published. Unable to focus on his practice with Lily, he opted to cancel the rest of it. He squeezed the phone to keep the trembling in his hands under control. Pictures were bad. Pictures led to scandals and scandals ended careers.

Stop it.

His phone rang.

"Hello?"

"They want to do a press release to nip this in the bud." Kyung Mi's voice was sharp.

"Is that necessary? You can hardly tell it's me in the pictures."

"The comments say otherwise. I know you don't want to do this, but we have to."

"But none of the articles list her name. If we do a press release we'll have to reveal it and expose her. I don't want the writer to be under scrutiny for nothing."

Kyung Mi was silent for so long, Eun Gi lifted the phone to be sure the call hadn't dropped.

"Talk to this woman and get her prepared for a release if necessary. I'll do what I can, but we can't have this affecting your reputation."

"Wouldn't it make more sense for you to talk to her?" Eun Gi asked.

"No, no, no. That's not how this is going to work. I'm cleaning up as much of this mess as I can from my end. You're cleaning things up from your side. If you tell me there's nothing, then that's the angle we'll work with, but whatever your relationship with this woman is—"

"There's nothing, I—"

"*Whatever* your relationship with this woman is," Kyung Mi repeated, "you are obligated to handle this like an adult. Talk to her."

"Fine."

They hung up, and Eun Gi shoved his phone into his pocket.

Reminding himself to never be nice again, he paced restlessly in front of the doors of the studio until his car service picked him up and carted him back to his apartment.

Circular arguments swirled in his head, and he slammed down on them. He'd already helped her, and there was nothing to be done about it now except to try to mitigate the potential damage.

Shoving a hand through his hair, he tapped out a message he dreaded a response to.

Eun Gi:
Kelly-ssi, can you please pass my number along to Tessa-ssi?
Have her call me?

Chapter 5

Tessa

"Tessa!" Kelly threw herself onto the couch where her friend was curled up resting and reading. "Tessa, Tessa, Tessa! Guess what!"

She lowered her book. "What?"

"Guess who wants you to call him!" Kelly beamed a megawatt smile at Tessa.

"Who?"

"Your favourite iiiidol," Kelly sang.

"Oh God. Why?" A blush flooded Tessa's cheeks, and she tucked the book back in front of her face to hide.

"Why don't you call him and find out?"

"I can't call him. I've already embarrassed myself plenty. I don't need the opportunity to do so again."

"Come on, live this dream for me." Kelly poked her in the ribs. "Your idol bias is giving you his phone number. This is the stuff of fairy tales. Maybe you made a better impression than you thought."

Tessa groaned and slunk down, burying herself under one of the couch pillows. "I'm pretty sure that's not the case. Passing out from a drunken migraine is about as bad as it gets, short of throwing up on him."

"Well, you're at least a step above the worst." Kelly snared Tessa's phone off the side table and shoved it into Tessa's hands. "Call him."

"Please don't make me."

"Girl, stop being a chicken. This is your chance to redeem yourself to this guy. Don't you want him to have a more positive memory of you?"

Tessa huffed. "Fine. What's his number?"

Kelly squeed and immediately sent the number to Tessa's phone.

Tessa unburied herself and stared at the screen with dread. Her fingers shook as she pressed the link and jacked up her call volume so Kelly would be able to hear. Speaker-phone would sound obvious, but she wanted the backup just in case.

"Hello?" UpBeat answered in his smooth Korean.

"Hi, um, Baek Eun Gi-ssi, it's Tessa."

"Ah! Thank you for calling."

Tessa relaxed a little. He didn't sound upset, which went a long way to loosening the ball of nerves in her chest.

"Have you seen the news?" he asked.

"The news?" Tessa looked quizzically over at Kelly who popped open the search engine on her phone. Kelly's mouth dropped open, and she turned her phone to Tessa.

"Oh my God! We— we're in the news." Tessa's stomach clenched.

"Yes," he replied, "but only my name."

"Well, that's..." she paused, unsure how to respond, "...good?"

"For you, yes. I've discussed what to do about it with my manager."

Tessa stared wide-eyed at Kelly. "Um, forgive my ignorance, but why do we need to do anything about it?"

He sighed softly.

"The rules surrounding relationships in this industry are incredibly strict. Some companies are worse than others, but the media is never to find out about relationships for the safety and sanity of all involved."

"But we're not in a relationship."

"You know that, and I know that, but the media decided there's something there. The company wants to do a press release. If we do that, your name will become public."

"What happens if I say no?"

She desperately hoped he would let her say no.

There was silence and hesitation on his end for a few moments. "I'm not sure. If we keep quiet, they may keep searching for you. If we don't do a release, then the media will continue to speculate. Scandals are easy to create and hard to make disappear, especially when there are pictures."

Tessa pressed her forehead to her knees. "What do you think I should do?"

"I've dealt with scandals before." His voice gentled. "It's the company you'd upset, not me. If you don't consent, I'll handle them."

She wondered if that was actually the case or if he was just being nice to spare her from whatever was to come. Would he get into trouble if she didn't cooperate? Nerves clenched her chest again.

Tessa muted her mic and turned to Kelly. "Vote?"

"That depends on if you want your name associated with him or not. The fans and press can be pretty relentless." Kelly squeezed her cheeks, grinning. "It's a shame you guys don't have something going on. How cute would the lead actor and the writer falling in love be?"

Tessa snorted. "Oh please. That's never going to happen."

Kelly grabbed Tessa's phone and unmuted it before putting it on speaker-phone. She joined the conversation in Korean.

"Baek Eun Gi-ssi, it's Kelly. Have the company and studio discussed protection for Tessa if she gives her name?"

Tessa hadn't even considered that aspect. She'd seen enough mentions of sasaeng incidents in the news to know that some fans took things way too far.

"Normally people in these situations have access to security, door monitors, and a team of people to help them," Kelly continued. "Tessa doesn't have that."

"A fair point," he agreed. "I'll talk to them, and we can discuss the matter again."

"Thank you for being so patient with this, and for taking care of Tessa."

"Kelly, quit it!" Tessa lunged for the phone, but Kelly held it out of reach.

"It's no trouble," UpBeat assured. "I have to go, but I'll keep you updated."

"Thank you," Tessa said.

They bid one another goodbye, and Tessa cast pleading eyes at Kelly. "Why do we need security?"

"I just want to be prepared."

Tessa kneaded her scalp.

Kelly placed a hand on Tessa's knee. "You okay? You're not getting a migraine, are you?"

"No, I don't think so. This is all so ridiculous."

Tessa spent hours reading over the articles that were out, staring at the images of herself plastered across the internet. She hunted down past scandals and issues with sasaeng fans, trying to pick apart enough details to judge what might be ahead of her.

Kelly finally took her phone away when Min Joo arrived home with several bags of food.

"Fried chicken and beer!" He smiled brightly, setting the bags down on the table.

Tessa welcomed the distraction. She leapt up to get plates and glasses, and they sat at the table together. Kelly filled her husband in on things between bites.

"Oh!" said Kelly. "In all the excitement, I completely forgot that I found you a date. Technically two dates, so you can meet both or either."

"Or neither," Tessa added.

"Come on, you promised."

Tessa sighed. "Fine."

"Good, now, they both work with Joo at the university. Ae Ja is a first-time sessional teacher. She's a bit of a newer friend, but she's pretty and loved your book. Pyong Ho is a little bit younger—"

"How old is younger?" Tessa asked.

"He's twenty-three."

"Kelly, he's practically a baby."

"Twenty-three is hardly a baby. It's only four years difference and he's super nice," Kelly insisted.

"How old is Ae Ja?"

"Twenty-three, as well."

"Baby."

"Oh, for the love of God. Tessa, they're not babies." Kelly swallowed down half her beer. "They're adults who've expressed an interest in you."

"But I'm awkward, and dating is literally hell for me."

"Dating is hell for *everyone*. Your mom asked me to push you outside your comfort zone while you're here. New country, new experiences, all that jazz. I promise it won't be so bad. You get to hang out with me and Joo in addition to your date."

"Why do you hate me?"

Kelly laughed into her plate. "I do *not* hate you. I love you. You can make some Korean friends, and then I can use them as leverage to convince you to move here."

"Ah, the ulterior motive emerges." Tessa munched her chicken.

"It was never hidden. Besides, I'm allowed to want you to be closer. An eleven-hour flight makes it very difficult for us to be maximum besties. I can't use me for leverage, I'm the one who came over here. I gotta get you hooked on the locals."

"I don't know you well enough to speak to your compatibility," Min Joo piped up, "but I know them, and they're good people."

"Min Joo, not you too."

He looked emphatically down into his beer. "You did promise Kelly."

Tessa pouted. "Fine. I'll meet both."

"Aww yiss." Kelly pulled out her phone and sent the potential dates a note on KakaoTalk. They pinged back a moment later. "Sweet, we're scheduled with Pyong Ho for tomorrow and Ae Ja for Sunday."

"Oh Lord," Tessa grumbled, stuffing a bite of rice into her mouth. "Don't get too excited."

"Too late!" Kelly grinned. "Excitement has been achieved. Embrace it. Fear it."

Min Joo smothered his laughter behind his hand before giving up altogether and pulling Kelly into his arms. He murmured an "I love you" against her temple.

She sank back against him with a contented sigh, holding his arm across her chest. "I love you too, Joo."

"Quit being so nauseatingly cute," Tessa teased. "You're making me lonely."

"No can do. We're precious at all times. It's a rule, and you just need to adapt."

Eun Gi

Eun Gi skimmed his phone before getting out of bed. There was nothing new on the potential scandal situation, and both the studio and company were sitting on their hands as things appeared to be calming down.

He climbed out of bed and dipped into the bathroom.

Hwan was toying with his hair in the mirror. "Are you excited to start filming today?"

"I think so."

"Sung Soo said we'll go see you for lunch."

"If you guys make trouble, you're going to get kicked out."

"Trouble?" Hwan batted his eyelashes and unraveled a length of floss. "Me? I am hurt that you'd ever think I'd make trouble."

Eun Gi rolled his eyes and hip-checked Hwan over so he could reach his toothbrush. "I have to shower. Get out."

"I'm flossing."

"Out."

Hwan rolled his eyes and took his floss. "Fine, be a bathroom hog."

"There's a mirror in the hall," Eun Gi said as he closed the door in Hwan's face.

Eun Gi scrubbed down in the hot water, standing under the steady stream to let it clear out the last of the mental cobwebs. Nerves were a snake in his belly, coiling to the point of nausea. He set his forehead against the cool tile and willed away the queasiness. Music had been his life, solace, and strength for so long that he sometimes wondered if he could actually do *anything* else.

When he'd accepted the acting job, he had naively assumed he might get to enjoy a little lighter schedule, but Kyung Mi had had the opposite idea. He was still expected to maintain all of his obligations while acting. None of them ever had a ton of free time, so it wasn't unusual. It would be a schedule with an intensity like when they were touring, which was…somewhat sustainable. He wouldn't be acting forever, so he could manage. He hoped.

His phone pinged while he was drying off, and he checked the read out.

Eomeoni:

I see you're in the news again.
I'll be needing double this month.

The urge to throw the phone overwhelmed him, but he forced himself to turn away from it. He debated blocking the number, as he had contemplated a hundred times before, but experience had taught him to answer his mother quickly.

Eun Gi:
Fine.

His savings would have to take the hit to accommodate the request. Again.

"Hyung wants me to make sure you eat breakfast," Hwan yelled from the kitchen when Eun Gi vacated the bathroom.

"I'll grab something on the way."

"Coffee doesn't count. You're supposed to go by their apartment before you leave."

When he was dressed, Eun Gi and Hwan swept down the communal hall where the sweet, nutty scent of *yachae juk* rice porridge seeped out of the apartment the others shared. Min Jae opened the door before they even got there, and Sung Soo was already ladling out bowls. He waved Eun Gi over to take the first one.

"I'm declaring it good luck for us to be there on your first day," Sung Soo said.

Eun Gi paused in his eating to smile. "I look forward to it. I think I'm starting to get excited."

"Good!" Hwan swung an arm around Eun Gi. "You have to enjoy the process so I feel less bad about teasing you when we watch the final cut."

They indulged in a group hug before Eun Gi ran down to catch the car that was waiting for him. Traffic was dense, but he'd made it out with enough time to get to the studio with a couple minutes to spare. Kim Ha Yun was waiting, rushing him into makeup the moment he stepped through the door.

There was a buzz in the air that came from the beginning of a fresh project; a bright newness sitting on the edge of possibility. Eun Gi saw Tessa out of the corner of his eye, perched on a chair wearing a red dress and black tights with his coat folded over her arm. She looked so much healthier than the last time he'd seen her. Ha Yun interrupted his walk towards her, shoving him along so he didn't have time to stop and chat.

The face that greeted him when he sat down at the makeup chair was like a swift punch to the gut. Kim Hye Jin was petite and perfect. Jet-black locks were tamed into a French roll, not a hair out of place. Her makeup was as soft as the sweet round face it adorned, with a pink blush across her cheeks that highlighted her alabaster skin. She had once worked for EchoPop Entertainment. A dating scandal had ended with her quitting her job, and he hadn't encountered her in years. He hadn't known she'd been hired with Elite Studios.

She smiled at him, the same affectionate, immaculate expression he remembered.

Her beauty was what initially caught his attention, but her obvious talent and delight in her skills was what had intrigued him enough to ask her out.

"I wish you were here for a music video," she told him as she picked up her tools. "We could have so much more fun with your makeup."

She wasn't awkward at all around him, and there he was stewing in anxiety. How was that fair?

He caught sight of the writer in the mirror. She fiddled with his coat, clearly unsure if she should approach.

"Good morning, Baek Eun Gi-ssi," she said in polite, fluid Korean.

"Good morning." He nodded slightly, careful not to disrupt Hye Jin's work.

She held out his coat, but then realized he was otherwise occupied. "I brought back your coat. I just wanted to say thank you."

Hye Jin glanced between them. "I'm surprised at you, Eun Gi. You're usually so discreet, but this was all over the media."

"We're not together."

"Uh huh." She turned to the writer. "I hope you haven't been getting hassled. If you need any advice for how to deal with it, feel free to come talk to me."

Not everyone can quit their job and run away.

"Oh, no. It's been fine," the writer said.

"We're not together," he insisted again.

"If you say so. It certainly looks like you are. She's returning your clothes."

Eun Gi empathized with the startled expression on the writer's face. His hackles rose. He didn't owe Hye Jin an explanation of why anyone had been at his place.

"You don't have to hide it from me."

His cheeks warmed at her words.

"I'm more than familiar with how to be discreet when it comes to the affairs of idols."

Not discreet enough.

His gaze swiveled back to the writer in the mirror. Someone may as well have tossed cold water in her face. If she was a fan, she might recognize Hye Jin's name from when the company had swept the scandal under the rug in his youth.

"This is hardly the place to discuss that, Hye Jin." He didn't *want* to discuss it. He wanted to go back to pretending it had never happened.

Hye Jin winked. "I won't say a word, don't worry."

"There's nothing. Just drop it."

"Oh, calm down. You were always so uptight."

The writer looked mortified as she fled the room. Eun Gi made a mental note to apologize for Hye Jin's lack of tact.

Tessa

The coat was still in Tessa's hands, forgotten in her haste to get away. She'd come across that particular scandal in her obsessive search to assess their current situation, but there had been no information about what had become of Kim Hye Jin. Now she knew.

She hung around the edge of the set quietly until UpBeat emerged from makeup and Lily appeared to start filming. When the director called action, Tessa pressed her fingers to her lips, heart racing as she saw the words she'd written come to life.

It was eerie. UpBeat slipping into the role of a performer changed the entire set of his body, his face, how he moved. He was much better than Tessa had expected, not that she wasn't confident he could pull off anything artistic he wanted to do. She'd seen glimpses in behind-the-scenes footage and knew about the clear distinction between UpBeat and Eun Gi. It was so much more interesting to experience it happening in person, to see Eun Gi get tucked away and replaced with Lee Do Yun of the Kingdom of Joseon.

Tessa was utterly fascinated. They embodied the characters so well, bringing them into existence in a way she never imagined being able to see. Barely breathing, she stood enraptured until the director called cut and the historical personas disappeared in an instant.

They paused for water, rearranged the people and the camera angles before reshooting the scene. The buzz of Tessa's phone in her pocket startled her.

Kelly:
Call me when you have a moment <3

Tessa slipped outside, not wanting to disturb the production. The burst of chilled air hit her, and she pulled on UpBeat's coat. She dialed Kelly's number and sat down on the steps leading into the studio.

"Hey, what's up?" Tessa asked.

"I wanted to make sure you were available before I left. How's filming going?"

"It's the most surreal feeling." The smile on Tessa's face leaked into her voice. "It's so, so amazing."

"You're too cute. I'm on my way now, it'll take me about half an hour to get there, and then we can go for lunch. Sound good?"

"Absolutely," Tessa agreed. "Hey, Kel, do you remember a few years ago when UpBeat and a woman named Kim Hye Jin were all over the fan forums?"

"Yeah, why?"

"She's working here."

"Huh. How is she?"

"Beautiful. I dunno. I kind of panicked and bailed out."

"I'm curious. The scandal was hushed up fairly quickly, but it was big for a while."

"How is everything related to dating here a scandal?" Tessa snuggled deeper into the coat. "Let adults date. Honestly."

"Oh, I agree with you, but it's bad for marketing. I've seen idols deny relationships right up to the altar to temper the backlash."

"I kind of get it, like, I still had moments of *God I wish that were me* whenever it came up in the media, but I just want them to be happy."

Kelly let out a little squeak. "Quit being so cute! Talk to you in a bit. I'm getting on the subway. Bye!"

Tessa shivered in the breeze.

"Tessa-ssi!"

She turned towards the voice.

Lee Hyeong Hwan was heading up the steps towards her, followed by Park Sung Soo and Jeon Min Jae. Tessa forgot how to breathe. They were instantly recognizable with Sung Soo's and Jaybird's blue and pink hair, respectively, and Hwan's perfectly swept black hair.

"Are you feeling better?" Hwan asked in Korean.

Jaybird held out his hand. "This is how foreigners say hello, right?"

It took her a moment of staring before she put her hand into Jaybird's for a handshake. Sung Soo observed her silently.

"Yes, to both of you," she replied.

Jaybird grinned. "I'm glad you speak Korean. I never got the hang of English."

"It's definitely difficult to learn," Tessa said. "Halmeoni used to complain all the time about why it couldn't just make proper sense."

Jaybird's eyes lit up. "You're Korean?"

"Uh, part? Only a quarter."

"What's the rest of you?" Jaybird scrutinized her face.

Sung Soo kicked him in the back of the leg. "Don't be rude."

"It's all right," Tessa cringed. "People ask me all the time, so I'm mostly used to it. I'm mixed; Mamãe is Brazilian, also mixed, and Appa is half Korean, half English."

"We went to Brazil on one of our world tours," Jaybird told her. Tessa knew, of course, because she was all too aware of the entire musical history of 24/7. She'd wanted to attend one of their concerts in Rio, but it had coincided with her grandfather's birthday, and she'd stayed in Fortaleza for that instead.

An icy wind whipped over them.

"Let's get inside. I'm cold." Sung Soo pushed them toward the doors.

They waited quietly, albeit impatiently. When the director called for a break, the three of them flooded onto the set, throwing themselves bodily at UpBeat in a riotous hug. He squawked and disappeared amid arms, torsos, and excited voices.

"You're lucky it's lunch-time, or I'd have to admonish you for ruining my work," Hye Jin teased as she snuck up on the boys.

"Hye Jin!" Jaybird abandoned the pile and squeezed the makeup artist into a hug. "I haven't seen you in forever."

"You've been busy touring the world." She stuck out her tongue. "I've been here painting faces. We don't cross paths often anymore."

"You should come to lunch with us," Jaybird insisted.

"I don't think Eun Gi would like that."

Jaybird snorted. "But I would!"

Hye Jin smiled and cupped his cheeks. "Thank you for the offer. If he says I can come, then I'll join you. If not, there's lunch here, so don't feel too bad for me if he says no."

He turned to Tessa. "You should come for lunch too."

She reeled in her deer-in-headlights response as best she could. "I'd love to, but I'm going to lunch with Kelly."

"Is she a writer too?"

Tessa shook her head. "She's a vlogger."

Jaybird's eyes lit up and he tapped away on his phone before turning the screen to Tessa. "Is this her?"

"I, uh, yes, it is. Do you watch her channel?"

"Sometimes, when I have time. I like watching people cook, and she does those fun *mukbang* episodes. You should bring her."

"Sure, I'll text her." Tessa smiled. "She'll love that you've seen her videos."

UpBeat showed up out of costume, but still with his hair and makeup. "Where are we going?"

"There's a noodle house a couple of streets over that has great reviews," Sung Soo offered.

Jaybird turned imploring eyes to UpBeat. "Hyung-*nim*, can Hye Jin and Tessa-ssi come to lunch too?"

"You can't guilt me with honorifics." UpBeat glared at the maknae. "If I say no, are you going to harass me about it until I give in anyway?"

"Yep." Jaybird grinned widely.

UpBeat sighed. "Fine."

The maknae pumped his hand in the air, victorious. "Tessa-ssi, text your friend and tell her to meet us at the noodle place. We'll save her a seat."

She looked to Sung Soo for guidance, and he nodded. She'd known that Jaybird ran roughshod over them because he was the baby of the group, but it was still a bit strange to see them buckle to his whims so easily.

Surreal didn't even begin to explain the situation as Tessa sat down to lunch surrounded by the idols.

When Kelly arrived, the table was already laden with bowls of translucent *japchae* noodles and a variety of banchan side dishes. Tessa had tried to prepare her via text, but it was impossible to not be a little starstruck coming face-to-face with four excitable idols.

Sung Soo, Kelly's own bias in the group, chatted with her about her work. Jaybird seemed able to focus on three conversations at once, offering commentary to Kelly on his favourite videos, while still dividing his attention between Tessa and Hye Jin.

"Tessa-ssi," Jaybird said, "how long are you in Seoul for?"

"A month."

He frowned. "That's not very long."

"Well, it's only a vacation. They don't need me on set or anything, so there's not much sense in staying. If she got her way, Kelly would have me moving here."

"You should!" Min Jae said. "Seoul is great."

Kelly high-fived him. "Hell yes. Another one on my team!"

The concept sent a thrill up her spine, but she couldn't quite tell if it was fear or excitement at the prospect of relocation.

"You're in charge of telling my parents I'm leaving Canada then," she said to Jaybird. "Mamãe might hunt you down for suggesting it."

"I'm far away. Plenty of time to hide." He stuck out his tongue.

UpBeat filled the periphery of her vision, slurping up his japchae. It annoyed her that he managed to still look perfect while inhaling noodles. It shouldn't be humanly possible.

"Ow!" UpBeat jumped, startling her. He glared at Sung Soo. "What?"

Sung Soo looked from UpBeat to Tessa expectantly.

Tessa stared at the two of them, wondering if Sung Soo had kicked him under the table.

UpBeat set down his chopsticks and turned to her.

"What do you think of the drama so far, Tessa-ssi?"

A grin stole over her face. "I love it. You've been amazing. Not that I didn't expect you would be."

"I'll take that as the highest of compliments." UpBeat smiled and consumed another mouthful of noodles.

Sung Soo nudged UpBeat. "It's not easy to impress a creator with their own characters."

"You're perfect for the part, honestly," Tessa said. "I mean, I didn't write him with you in mind or anything, but I couldn't think of anyone better to play Lee Do Yun."

UpBeat gave her a long look. "Thank you. I was a little worried about taking the role, but I feel better that you think I'm doing it justice."

"I kept telling him he'd do great, but I'm pretty sure it means more coming from you, Tessa-ssi," Sung Soo said.

Her cheeks warmed. "Happy to help."

Sung Soo paid for the group, despite protests, and shuffled them back toward the studio. Tessa burrowed deeply into her coat when a honk sounded behind them.

UpBeat snared an arm around her waist and whipped her towards him scarce moments before a delivery motorbike zoomed past on the sidewalk. The handlebar lashed the skirt of her dress, and she'd have tipped backwards if not for him keeping her upright. She shrank against him, and his grip tightened. Tessa stood there in his arms, heart thundering.

"Are you okay?"

Tessa nodded dumbly. His brown eyes were wide and concerned, and she couldn't help but stare. Her palms were still pressed to his chest, and she sheepishly withdrew them, stepping back. Every gaze burned on her, but more than that was the unexpected heat where his arm had been, where her hands had rested. She almost wished something else would zip down the sidewalk so he'd touch her again.

"You okay, Tess?" Kelly asked.

"Yeah." She tucked her head down to hide her blush. "What are they doing on the sidewalk?"

Kelly shrugged. "I've stopped noticing them by this point. Every flat surface is a road to them so they can make their delivery deadlines."

Tessa tried not to think about UpBeat's arm around her waist.

She sighed and hunched her shoulders against the breeze.

Ha Yun was waiting for them when they arrived, shuffling UpBeat and Hye Jin back to work. Sung Soo, Hwan, Jaybird, and Kelly stayed on to watch some of the production. They were all infinitely charming in their enthusiasm for UpBeat's career, even if it didn't involve them at the moment. Every time the director called cut, his face lit up seeing them there cheering him on. It warmed Tessa's heart to see them there for him as much as it did to see Kelly there for her.

They ended up whiling away the entire afternoon until things wrapped up for the day.

"Ready to head back?" Kelly looped her arm through Tessa's.

"Yeah. Let me make sure UpBeat actually goes home with his coat." Tessa slipped away to fetch the garment off the chair next to hers and beelined towards the idol with it outstretched in her hands. "Thank you again. I'm sorry to be such a bother."

He took the coat and popped a brilliant smile that made her heart thump. "You're never a bother, Tessa-ssi."

Get a grip, Tessa. He's just being nice.

Her heartbeat disagreed. It was the first time she'd seen his smile in person.

"Take care of yourself." He bowed his head and wandered over to the other members.

"Uh-oh," Kelly said as Tessa returned to her.

"What?" Tessa squeaked.

"Don't get overexcited."

"Well that's the pot giving the kettle instructions neither of them knows how to follow. I'm trying not to." Jittery, Tessa zipped up her coat a little too vigorously and clocked herself in the face when it got stuck part-way.

Kelly laughed and finished zipping it up for her. "I can't decide if spending more time with him would cure you of your crush or make it infinitely worse."

"He's too much."

"What did he do?" Kelly re-looped their arms as they made the short trip to the nearest subway station.

"He just...exists? God, it's so stupid. I have no idea what to do or think around him. He's not even doing anything in particular, but whenever I see him I get this feeling in my chest. Crushes are awful."

Kelly laced their hands together. "I'd help, but I have no idea what advice to offer. If he were a dick, it would taint what the music means to you, but him being nice when in actual proximity has to be confusing. I don't envy you one bit. Keep reminding yourself that he's a regular person no matter how talented and pretty he is."

"You're not helping." Tessa side-eyed her friend.

"I said I didn't know how, so I'm rolling with this in an amusing fashion."

"Let's roll with it a little closer to home. I'm starving again, and I want to curl up on the couch for a while."

"But you can't couch. We're meeting one of your dates tonight."

"Oh God, why?"

Kelly pulled Tessa onto the train that would take them back to Itaewon. "Because you love me."

Min Joo had changed out of his work clothes and was waiting quietly in a grey cashmere sweater and dark jeans.

"We're not going too far," Kelly said as the three of them left the apartment building.

It was cool outside, but not intolerable with some extra layers added.

"So, what info do I need about this guy?"

"He's very smart and super nice. I've basically adopted him as a little brother."

"Does Benji know he has a Korean replacement?"

Kelly laughed. "I can have and love more than one brother. Benji likes Pyong Ho. They've met over video call a couple times."

Min Joo checked his buzzing phone a block from the restaurant.

"Pyong Ho's arrived."

"Min Joo, why did I let you two talk me into this?"

He steadfastly looked away, and Kelly snickered, sidling up to her husband.

"You're just meeting one of our friends. Try not to focus on the romantic potential too hard if it freaks you out. Oh, also remember no touchies on the first date or you're going to give him some serious signals."

The BBQ house wafted the most delicious scents into the air.

Min Joo waved when they got inside the restaurant. Pyong Ho had an undercut with the swept top dyed blond, and thick-rimmed glasses that suited the strong planes of his face.

"Tess, this is Choi Pyong Ho," Kelly introduced with a smile.

He stood to greet them, and Tessa realized he was significantly shorter than her. Not that most people weren't, but she'd never had a guy agree to a date with her knowing she was the taller one in the equation. She didn't personally mind as long as they weren't being a butthole about it.

He grinned at her and pulled out the seat next to him.

Tessa sank into her chair. Maybe it wouldn't be so bad?

Kelly guided a lot of the conversation at the start, and it turned out Pyong Ho had read Tessa's book.

"I'm always curious how foreigners approach our history," he said, "though it happens infrequently. I focus more on Goryeo than Joseon, but they're both fascinating."

"You're a historian?" Tessa asked.

"Almost." Pyong Ho nodded. "I'm still studying. I did my two years of military service as soon as I was able so I could focus on my education without interruption. I'll go for my Master's degree as well, but I'm hoping to get some practical experience at the National Archives when I've graduated."

"That's great!" Tessa sipped at her peach-flavoured soju. "I love history."

"I gathered as much by the subject matter of your book," Pyong Ho teased. "Where did you get the idea for it?"

"I was reading a book about women who disguised themselves to join the military and other ventures. I wondered what it would be like if someone did that to follow the trade routes and see the world."

Kelly ordered another bottle of soju for the table. They were small and didn't last long when split between four people, but even so Tessa grimaced. She'd set a hard limit for herself of only two drinks, and she could already feel the pleasant hum of the alcohol in her blood.

They chatted about school, travel, history, and current events, moving fluidly between Korean and English. Pyong Ho kept up easy conversation regardless of where the topic strayed. Meat sizzled on the grill between them, and they stuffed themselves full. Tessa had relaxed considerably by the end of the evening, but then she was also tipsy. She was too warm and every emotion simmered right under the surface with nothing to temper them.

"My sister is actually a fan of your book." Pyong Ho pulled out his phone to show Tessa an image. "She sent me this when she found out we were meeting."

It was a painted piece of her main character in the streets of old Busan. Tessa teared up, hugging the phone to her chest.

"Oh my God! Your sister is the sweetest person in existence. I can't believe she made this! It's so beautiful. This must have taken her forever!" Tessa sniffled. "Can you send it to me?"

"Of course!" Pyong Ho took back his phone and opened up KakaoTalk. "Put in your number."

Kelly unsuccessfully hid her grin behind her glass as Tessa punched her number into the phone.

"Another round?"

Pyong Ho looked a little queasy at the suggestion, but he nodded. "If you'd like, *Noona*."

"None for me," Tessa pleaded. She draped over Pyong Ho, staring at the painting on her phone screen. His whole body froze for a fraction of a second before he leaned into her. "It's so cute that you call her Noona. She doesn't let me call her *Eonni*."

"That's because I'm only six months older. I can't be your eonni, but I can be his noona." Kelly nudged her friend with her foot. "Tess, you're kind of all over Pyong Ho."

"My head feels funny," Tessa complained, resting her cheek against his head.

"When was the last time you drank?" Kelly nudged a glass of water toward her.

"Um, your wedding? No wait, at the work dinner. There was so much soju. I forgot."

"Sheesh. Okay, well we should get you home. Get off Pyong Ho, please. You can't be touchy with new people here."

"He's not new people. He's old people. To you."

"Okay, we're leaving. Pyong Ho, let me know when you're home safe." Kelly looped an arm around Tessa's waist and hoisted her up. "I forgot you're such a lightweight."

"It's *not* my fault. Soju is sneaky."

Tessa happily hugged her date goodbye. Min Joo paid for the dinners and saw Pyong Ho off while Kelly walked Tessa outside.

"Girl, he's going to think you want to marry him after that." Kelly laughed half the walk home.

Tessa was equally giggly as the soju pumped through her system.

"Did you have fun?" Kelly asked.

"I did! I didn't think I would, but he's nice."

"I told you."

When they got home, Kelly put her on the couch and set a trash container nearby.

"Sleep it off, and I'll check on you in the morning."

Tessa conked out, and woke hours later in a haze to a dozen messages on her phone. Most were from Pyong Ho, but there was one from UpBeat that tripped her heart.

UpBeat:
Call me.

Chapter 6

Tessa

UpBeat answered on the first ring. "Hello?"

Tessa made a soft sound of contentment when she heard his voice. "Hey, it's Tessa."

"Have you read the news?" he asked.

"Mm, no? I just woke up."

"EchoPop wants a meeting with you. As soon as possible."

"Okay. Yeah, um, yeah, sorry, I'm a bit hungover," she mumbled. "I need to shower first. Where do I go?"

"I'll text you the address."

"Cool." Tessa hung up in a haze and contemplated going right back to sleep.

Kelly wandered in, dressed in her cozy flannels. "Good morning, sunshine. I wasn't expecting you awake yet."

"My phone was too buzzy to sleep. I have to go to a meeting. Who has meetings so early? I'm supposed to be on vacation and sleeping in." She struggled to her feet. "Need shower."

Kelly forced a glass of water on her before she was allowed to disappear into the bathroom. The shower helped a little, but she'd forgotten her clothes. She poked her head out the door and saw Kelly fixing breakfast with Min Joo at her side.

"Look away, Min Joo!" Tessa dashed over to her suitcase and grabbed an outfit. She emerged a few moments later in purple jeans and a snug black top. "I kind of feel better, but my head hates me."

"Grab some painkillers. They're in the corner cupboard." Kelly scrolled through her phone while stirring an egg scramble. "Holy shit."

"What?" Min Joo peeked over her shoulder.

"*Are Hale Tessa and UpBeat of 24/7 dating?*" Kelly read. "*With numerous pictures on multiple occasions, we finally have a name for the face. Hale Tessa is the author of best-selling novel, Ships in the Night. News has surfaced that Hale is in Seoul to view the filming of a drama based on her book. The cast will be led by Baek Eun Gi of 24/7 fame and newcomer Brooks Lily. The drama is being produced by Elite Studios.*"

Tessa paled and swayed on the couch. "How did they get my name?"

"Tessa-ssi, is the meeting today about this?" Min Joo asked.

"I don't know. He said something about the news, but I was barely awake." She put a hand to her head, and nausea churned her gut. "Fuck my life. Am I in trouble? Is *he* in trouble? What do I do?"

"First, breathe. Second, eat." Kelly loaded up the plates, and they all sat at the table together.

Min Joo set his hand atop Tessa's wrist. "The meeting is probably to discuss how to deal with it. They can hardly get mad at you when you've done nothing wrong."

He had always reminded her a bit of her Appa, in that they both had a soothing presence that never failed to make her feel safe.

The knots in her stomach loosened a little.

"If they get irate you can pretend you're a dumb foreigner who doesn't understand the culture," Kelly suggested.

"Well, that's not wrong."

"Eat," Kelly ordered as Tessa pushed her food around on her plate. "You can worry later."

"Tessa-ssi, if you'd like, I can walk you to the nearest subway. I have to leave for work in a few minutes."

"That would be great, thank you."

He nodded. "Give me the address for the company, and we'll figure out your route, or we can catch you a taxi." He rinsed his dishes and set them in their tiny dishwasher while Tessa shoveled her breakfast into her mouth.

Min Joo kissed his wife. "I love you."

"I love you too, Joo."

Tessa gathered up her things and waved to Kelly as she followed Min Joo out the door. They rode the elevator in comfortable silence and stepped off into a lobby crowded with people.

One of them caught sight of her as they emerged. "That's her!"

The group turned as one and rushed forward, shoving microphones into her face, grabbing her arms, twisting her towards different cameras.

"Hale Tessa-ssi! What's your relationship with UpBeat?"

"How long have you been involved?"

"Hale Tessa-ssi!"

The voices jumbled together, yelling her name, shouting questions. Min Joo shifted, moving in front of her, arms snapping out to block them.

"Back. Up," he growled, and the reporters froze, shifting away uneasily. Min Joo acted quickly, hitting the elevator button and backing Tessa inside. "I won't let them follow you."

Tessa punched the button for Kelly's floor and rode it upwards. She plugged in the door code and slipped inside. Her whole body was shaking when Kelly approached.

"Hey, what's wrong? What happened?"

"Reporters."

"Fuck." Kelly turned the deadbolt. "How did they find out you're here? God, we need better building security."

Tessa pressed her forehead against the door.

"Hey, it's okay." Kelly led Tessa to the couch and pulled out her phone, tapping away at the screen. "I'll let UpBeat know. Let me check in with Joo first."

Kelly sighed, sinking onto the couch.

"Joo says he's called into work and will keep an eye on the crowd for a while. Pyong Ho should survive teaching his morning classes."

In the time it took Kelly to get Tessa a glass of water UpBeat had replied to say that the company was sending a private vehicle for her.

"We need to sit tight for a while." Kelly plucked Tessa's frantically buzzing phone out of the purse Tessa had abandoned by the door. "Are you going to answer Pyong Ho?"

Tessa took her phone from Kelly.

She sipped her water and scanned the messages. Most were simple well-wishes, asking after how she was feeling, whether she'd eaten breakfast that morning, and a plethora of other innocuous questions and commentary that she had learned from Kelly to expect when dating a Korean. It was the questions that came in most recently that had her chewing her lip.

Pyong Ho:
Are you safe? Min Joo-hyung told me he's missing class because of reporters? Please let me know if you need anything. I saw the article. Is it true?

Tessa put the phone face down on the couch.

"I have no idea what to say about all…" she gestured towards the door, "…that. Do I have to respond right now?"

"Well, no," Kelly said. "Only if you liked him enough to see again. Timeliness is important with this."

"I don't have the brain power to respond *and* deal with all those stupid people downstairs."

"I'm putting a pin in the stupid downstairs people for a minute since they're locked out and you're kind of leaving my baby bro hanging here. The messages can be a lot. I was overwhelmed with Joo at first too, but you get used to it when you're dating here," Kelly assured. "Pyong Ho likes you and is showing it. Even if you don't want to start things up with him, since I agree this is not a great time for it, you have to tell him."

Tessa's hands shook when she picked up her phone, and her eyes blurred with tears. "Can you talk to him for me?"

"Tess, if you don't like him, just say so." Kelly wrapped an arm around Tessa's waist.

"It's not that. Pyong Ho is cute and very nice, but I'm too overwhelmed to think about anything with all this chaos going on."

"Tell him you're not able to talk right now and will be available to message later."

Tessa rubbed her eyes and tapped out a quick message.

Tessa:
I'm so sorry, I can't talk right now. Things are crazy, but I'm safe.
Thank you for checking in :)

Two guards came with the vehicle to pick up Tessa, and Kelly let them in when they knocked on the door.

"Good luck at the meeting. I'll keep an eye on the hoard and see what I can do about getting them out of here before you get back," Kelly said.

The guards reminded Tessa of secret service agents. They weren't at all inconspicuous, but at least they looked intimidating. Nestled between the two men, Tessa pushed through the throng of reporters. She covered her face with her hands and ducked to avoid the reaching microphones.

By the time they got to the car she was beyond frazzled. She sat sandwiched by the guards, while a driver took them to EchoPop Entertainment. They were tailed by more than a few vehicles, but upon arrival she was hustled inside and the doors were locked behind them.

UpBeat was waiting in the lobby and waved her over. "Are you okay?"

"I've been better." A blush flooded her cheeks despite her building anxiety.

She squeezed her hands together to stop the shaking. He nodded and guided her towards the elevator. Hovering on the edge of tears, she leaned against the reflective walls. He was staring at her, his eyes warm and concerned. She bit her wobbling bottom lip.

He reached out, hand stopping part way to her, before he let it fall between them. "I'm sorry about this."

"It's not your fault." She cringed at the squeak in her voice.

"I should have been more careful." He puffed out a sigh and settled next to her. "I'm not certain what their plan is in this meeting, but I want you to know that you've got an ally going in with you, okay?"

Tessa sucked in a breath. "Okay."

They rode up to the top floor where a sleek woman in a tailored suit greeted them in crisp Korean, fresh off the elevator.

"Baek Eun Gi-ssi, Hale Tessa-ssi. I am Kim Gyeong Suk."

"The vice president," UpBeat whispered to Tessa.

"Thank you for coming so quickly." She nodded to them both.

They followed her to a meeting room where the rest of the executives were waiting around a long oval table. A woman in her forties with short-cropped hair and sharp brown eyes approached them, dressed every bit as impeccably as Gyeong Suk.

"Tessa-ssi, this is my manager, Sun Kyung Mi," UpBeat said, introducing the woman.

Kyung Mi ushered them to seats next to one another, then sat on the other side of UpBeat as the president of the company turned his frown upon them. Gyeong Suk stood behind him, staring them down.

"It's been some time since you've caused a dating scandal for us. We're disappointed, Baek Eun Gi." The president's brow furrowed.

"There's no dating part of this scandal," UpBeat insisted. "We're not together. This is a misunderstanding."

"Public sentiment says otherwise." The president clasped his hands in front of him. "She has been photographed being carried into your apartment building by you, wearing your clothing when leaving the next day, in the company of the other members, and with your arms around her on a separate occasion. If it had been a single instance, it would have died out."

UpBeat sighed deeply. "So what am I supposed to do? Should I just never be in public with anyone except the other members?"

The president was entirely unperturbed by UpBeat's words. "You knew the obligations of your role when you signed on with us. You are not forbidden from entering into romantic relationships, but you are obligated to be discreet. Sun Kyung Mi, you also bear responsibility for this indiscretion."

"It's not her fault," UpBeat interrupted before his manager could speak. "She was visiting family when this happened. It's entirely my doing."

Gyeong Suk and the president stared at him, displeasure plain on their faces.

"Regardless, I will do whatever I can to assist with the recovery of the scandal," Kyung Mi added. She patted UpBeat's hand in a sympathetic gesture.

Tessa pressed her palms against her knees, sorting through the words, trying to ignore the rising panic vibrating through her.

The president turned to her. "Hale Tessa-ssi, we're sorry that you've been caught up in this. Unfortunately, you are not associated with us, and your protection is not one of our concerns. Today was a courtesy to get you here so this matter could be dealt with."

UpBeat's hands clenched into fists. "That's not fair."

The president continued, ignoring him. "This has been picked up by too many outlets, and the fan forums have exploded."

"You can't disregard her safety," UpBeat snapped. "There are reporters hounding her where she's staying. You have to do something."

"This is your scandal, Baek Eun Gi." The president's eyes narrowed. "If you are concerned, then perhaps you should be in charge of her security."

"What?"

Gyeong Suk stepped up, smoothing her hands over her black pencil skirt. "We discussed everything before your arrival, and the level of intimacy in these photos can't be disregarded. Tessa-ssi, are you familiar with the standard of public relationships?"

"Um, no?" Tessa squeaked.

"Fans are under the assumption that you two are in a long-term relationship to explain the closeness and multiple occasions. I realize the international fan community has different ideas about these things, but our national fans do not. If you come out and say there is nothing, a different assumption will be made, and it could damage the reputation of Baek Eun Gi and the group as a whole. Fans do not want their idols to be seen taking liberties."

"I wasn't," UpBeat protested.

"It would be safest on all accounts if you two agreed to the rumors. Come out and say that you're together and that you're serious to deflect the worst of the criticism. We've agreed an engagement would offer the most flexibility for the situation. There would be no question of your devotion to one another within the context of these pictures, but it prevents additional criticism for not having been honest with the fans about a wedding having taken place."

"A w-wedding?" Tessa choked out. She grabbed the edge of the table, lightheaded.

"What?" UpBeat burst out.

Kyung Mi put a hand on his shoulder. "Surely there's some alternative?"

The executive stared at them all, deadpan. Gyeong Suk spoke. "This is an issue of your own making. The ineptitude of handling this situation by the three of you has created this problem, and we are offering a solution."

"I'm sorry," said Tessa, "but I don't understand. What are you asking me to do?"

Gyeong Suk frowned. "The reputation of 24/7 is our priority. You are an anomaly. If you care at all, then you will agree to going public with a relationship. An engagement to protect them."

Tessa pressed a hand to her chest. "You want me to pretend to be engaged? To Baek Eun Gi? I, um..." Each set of eyes in the room burned into her.

UpBeat put his hand on her wrist, and she turned her panicked gaze onto him.

"You don't have to do this." His voice was firm, and he glared at the executive. "They can find another way."

"Hale Tessa-ssi, what is your opinion on the matter?" Gyeong Suk asked. "We do require your consent before we put out a press release."

Words. Say words.

Her heart buzzed at dizzying speeds.

"I don't know."

UpBeat's fingers twitched against her arm. He was looking at her so intently, sympathy and panic alight in his eyes.

She took a breath, as slow and steady as she could manage. "I mean, I don't understand. Isn't this excessive?"

Gyeong Suk calmly laced her fingers together. "Tessa-ssi, are you familiar with the group Essence?"

"Um, not really."

"Exactly. A similar situation arose with the group several years ago. Photographs, intimate assumptions, but they refused to cooperate with our measures. There was a turn in fan approval. The member in question was banned from events at fan request, and was eventually removed entirely. The rest of the group did not recover. They became unprofitable, and there was nothing to be done to salvage the situation. Their contracts were not renewed. Do you wish the same fate to befall 24/7?"

"Of course not, but I was planning on going home in a couple weeks. We don't even live in the same country."

"We've thought of that too. Your passport currently allows you to be in the country without a visa for six months. We can handle the sponsorship after that."

UpBeat stood up from the table. "You can't ask her to do this. She has family and a job. You can't expect her to just drop all that to make things easier on you."

"We're not expecting her to," said Gyeong Suk, "but we *are* asking. It's a simple matter. We'll do a press release, provide photographs of your wedding, you'll live in the suites we own, and in a year, after your drama has finished its run, you can file for divorce."

Tessa sat in shock, sifting through what they were saying. Stay in Korea, live with her idol, *marry* her idol, and then divorce him.

"It plays to our advantage that you're a foreigner," Gyeong Suk continued. "Divorce won't be considered unusual, and you'll be able to go right back to your own country, avoiding any scrutiny here. The fans are opinionated and vocal. This is to protect the group, and we only require a year of your time.

A year. Tessa trembled.

"But my parents…"

"Will be thrilled. A whirlwind romance resulting in a picture-perfect wedding." Gyeong Suk had an answer for everything. "We'll set up a photoshoot so fans feel like they've been a part of the celebration. It would be soon; engagements here tend to be quite short, and we'll file the paperwork with the government so the press can do all the digging they want without worry."

A young man stepped forward and put a small box into Gyeong Suk's hand.

"We anticipated agreement with this and already had a ring prepared. A lot of Koreans forgo them, but we're bending to the expectations of you as a foreigner."

Kyung Mi chewed her lip. "Could I please speak with them in private?"

Gyeong Suk nodded, and Kyung Mi took them both outside the room.

"You have to stop them," UpBeat said immediately.

Kyung Mi frowned. "My boy, I'm a manager, not a miracle worker. What do you want me to do when they've convinced themselves of this path?"

"Something. Literally anything."

Kyung Mi turned to Tessa and put a gentle hand on her shoulder. Tessa towered over the petite woman. "Are you all right? You're quite pale."

"What am I supposed to say?" Tessa settled against the wall, pressing her palms to the cool surface.

"I am *not* going to let them do this to you. You can tell them no, and I'll deal with it." UpBeat spoke with such conviction, and she wanted to believe what he said. *Badly*.

"Eun Gi," Kyung Mi said softly. "It's not a bad suggestion. I agree it's not ideal, but there are certainly worse ways to resolve this."

"You can't be serious?"

Tessa deflated. Her options were disappearing in rapid succession and this insane engagement was a trap closing around her ankle. How could she possibly handle the guilt of saying no if 24/7 collapsed because of her?

Kyung Mi ignored UpBeat and focused on Tessa. "If you choose to go along with this, you will be compensated. I'll make sure of it. Eun Gi is a good man. I realize this is a sham marriage, but I'm certain he will do his best to care for you during the arrangement. If he does not…"

She turned to him, the threat hanging unspoken in the air.

Tessa shivered. "I don't know…"

An agreement was on the tip of her tongue. She swallowed hard. Marrying him was a thought that had crossed her mind more than once over the years, but always in the vein of impossible wishful thinking. Accepting under the pressure and scrutiny of EchoPop's executive board was not how things were supposed to go.

"How about this," said Kyung Mi. "I propose a trial period. They'll need some time to prepare for the wedding. If by then you find the situation unbearable, simply reach out to me. We'll deal with the repercussions then knowing we've tried it their way. I don't believe they'd enforce their wishes if you were truly miserable."

Tessa wasn't so sure. Gyeong Suk would feed her to a crocodile if it improved the company bottom line.

"Okay." Every other word froze in her throat.

"Fine," UpBeat bit out.

Kyung Mi brought them back inside and nodded to Gyeong Suk.

The vice president passed the ring box to Tessa. "Baek Eun Gi, put the ring on your future wife and get to the studio for filming. We'll draft a press release. Felicitations on your upcoming nuptials."

Chapter 7

Tessa

"Let me see it again." Kelly held out her hand expectantly until Tessa dropped hers into it. "God, they went all out on this rock, didn't they?"

A chunk of emerald-cut diamond set in platinum sat on her ring finger. A glittering shackle.

"Do you think it's real?"

"It looks real, but it felt rude to ask." Tessa pulled her hand back and tried to focus on packing.

"I still can't believe you're moving in with UpBeat," Kelly repeated for the fifth time that day.

Tessa scurried around the apartment, rounding up her belongings. "I can't believe it either."

"Nineteen-year-old you would be so freaking jealous." Kelly laughed. "You're living the dream. I know it's a lot more serious than that, but it's exciting."

"It's awful." Tessa buried her face into the shirt she'd been folding. "My parents are going to freak out. *I'm* freaking out. God, what do I even tell them? 'Hey, Mamãe, Appa, I've been pressured into a fake marriage by a huge company and have to live with a stranger, and oh, by the way, I can't come home until the drama is finished airing, and then I'm getting a divorce.'"

"Whoa there, girl. Take a breath." Kelly squeezed her tightly. "It'll be okay. Focus on the good parts of this. UpBeat seems nice. You said he defended you and tried to get you out of this whole situation, right? You guys can be a team against the world."

"It's not that easy. He doesn't want anything to do with all of this and I have so much to try and sort out. They emailed me a bunch of papers to sign, and I'm waiting to hear back from my lawyer to see if they're screwing me over. Amelia is on full time hours for a while, but it's still a lot to handle. I don't know how I'm going to deal with all of my work during this."

"You'll figure it out. I have every faith in you." Kelly took the shirt from Tessa and tucked it into the suitcase. "Try to go into this with an open mind. If it goes well, you get to be friends with your idol, and if it goes poorly, they've given you an out to go home."

"I guess. I feel like it's all my fault this is happening. I shouldn't have gone to that work dinner, should have turned down the drinks, done literally anything besides what I did." She flopped onto the couch and screamed half-heartedly into the cushion.

"You can't control when you have migraines. It's not your fault." Kelly put a gentle hand on the back of Tessa's head, scratching softly.

"Yeah, but I was expecting it. I was jet-lagged and stressed. It's the basic ingredients for one to start up, and then I drank anyway and couldn't take my pills. God, what if he loses his job because of me? What if they all do? I would never forgive myself. It's not fair. I don't want to get married, but they all mean too much to me, and I can't just do nothing."

Kelly snapped her fingers in front of Tessa's face. "Hey! You stop that thought spiral right now. There's no sense in feeling guilty about getting sick. If these efforts don't work out then we'll deal with that when it comes, but right now you're doing a hell of a lot more than nothing."

"Why are you so calm about all this?"

"You and I both know how you get when you dwell on the shitty parts of things. There's no way I'm adding to the dwelling. You're stuck with super positivity until you find good things in your own time. We'll get through this, Tess. I've got your back."

Tessa smiled. "Thank you."

"Now, you go have a rest so you don't stress yourself into another migraine. I'll finish up your packing. Go climb into our bed and pull the curtains."

Eun Gi

"How the hell did you end up engaged?" Min Jae asked through a mouthful of chips.

"We're not engaged, we're just…trying it out."

Eun Gi had been avoiding thinking about it. He was furious with the company and every time he let his thoughts drift in that direction, he wanted to scream.

"Yeah, but like, she's going to live here, isn't she? Where's she even going to sleep?"

"On the couch." Eun Gi shrugged. He'd offer his bed, but that was somehow far too intimate.

Please stop making me think about this.

His stomach twisted.

"You can't make your fake wife sleep on the couch," Sung Soo added. "Especially not if she ends up staying for the year. There are other units the company owns on this floor that won't be used for a while. Hwan, why don't you move into one of them?"

Hwan looked horrified by the idea. "I can't live alone! I don't know how to function as an individual."

"We could move into the three-bedroom unit. The others won't be needing it until they're back from the military, and we can figure out something more permanent then."

"That could work," Hwan said. "More space for all of us."

"I could live alone," said Min Jae.

"That's bullshit and you know it." Sung Soo chuckled. "You'd get antsy after the first day."

"I could get a dog."

"You're not getting a dog. I'm not letting you be in charge of an animal. I'll email Kyung Mi to see about switching units."

Eun Gi sank onto the couch, pushing back his panic. She'd be here tonight, and he had no idea what to do with her. "How am I supposed to live with a woman?"

"The same way you live with us?" Min Jae suggested.

Hwan burst out laughing. "I don't think she'll appreciate him playing video games in his underwear."

Min Jae glanced up from his chips. "Maybe she has an appreciation of video games?"

"Or Eun Gi in his underwear," Sung Soo teased.

"Can we *please* not make this any weirder than it already is?" Eun Gi curled up around one of the couch pillows, preventing himself from wandering to the fridge and finishing off the soju bottles in there. "I don't want to live with a stranger."

The cushion dipped next to him as Sung Soo sat down. "She won't be a stranger for that long, and Kyung Mi wrangled you an out if you need it. We'll all be down the hall, so the only thing that changes is that Hwan is a few more steps away than he was before."

"When's she arriving?" Hwan asked.

"Sometime tonight. She hasn't answered my last message."

"That doesn't sound like a good sign," Min Jae said. "Is she mad at you?"

"Why would she be mad at me? I didn't do anything."

"You *are* kind of moody." Sung Soo nudged Eun Gi. "Did you make her feel like you didn't want her here after she agreed to this huge favour?"

Eun Gi squeezed the pillow, hard. "I think my being moody is completely justified given the circumstances. We all know I'm terrible at this."

"Understatement of the year." Hwan lifted Eun Gi's head and set it on his lap. "But you're both kind of stuck. No sense in making things more miserable than they need to be. She seems pretty nice so far. Maybe it'll be fine."

Eun Gi's phone buzzed. He peered at the screen over the pillow's edge, as if it could act as a shield. "She's getting ready to head over with her two friends and asks if there's anything we need."

"Tell her to bring fried chicken!" Min Jae threw himself over Eun Gi's shoulder to grab the phone, but Eun Gi wrestled it away and tucked it under himself. Hwan snatched it, typing out a quick message.

Eun Gi lunged for it and opened the app to check what Hwan said. "Just your beautiful self. Hwan, what the fuck?"

"I'm being welcoming!"

"Be welcoming on your own app."

"Well, I don't have her number, so how could I possibly do that?"

Eun Gi groaned and rubbed his forehead. "Why me?"

"We'll order fried chicken for dinner," Sung Soo said. "What does she like?"

"How should I know?"

Sung Soo snapped his fingers in front of Eun Gi's pouting face. "Stop being so cranky. You're engaged, now be an adult and shake this off. Go for a run first if you need to. I'll order dinner, and you three get this place cleaned up. Hwan, pack up some things so you can sleep at our place."

"But my bed!"

"Fine, we'll talk to her when she gets here and see if she minds you staying the night."

"I can be a chaperone," said Hwan.

"That's a good idea," Sung Soo agreed.

"I don't need a chaperone," Eun Gi insisted. "Nothing's going to happen."

"It's for her comfort, not yours," Sung Soo pointed out. "We're trying to be considerate. Plus, Kyung Mi would hang you out to dry if you don't put your best foot forward with this. Now, get off your ass and start cleaning."

Tessa looked as tense as Eun Gi felt when she walked through the door. Her wide eyes met his and the knots in his stomach lessened a little. At least he wasn't the only one freaked out. Kelly and a man Eun Gi didn't recognize followed Tessa in.

Sung Soo stepped up to greet them, and Eun Gi let out a relieved breath.

"Lovely to see you, Tessa-ssi. I remember Kelly-ssi from lunch. Who's your other guest?"

"This is her husband, Lee Min Joo. I was staying with them before…"

Eun Gi watched the exchange with anxious interest, still rooted to the spot. Kelly's cheeks were bright pink, but she schooled her features and succeeded at words on her second attempt. "Where's Tessa staying?"

"We're still working on sleeping arrangements, but I assure you the couch is quite comfortable until that gets sorted." Sung Soo flashed a cool smile. "Can I take your bags, Tessa-ssi?"

She gave him a slight bow. "Thank you, Park Sung Soo-ssi."

"Kelly-ssi, Min Joo-ssi, could I bother you for some assistance in the kitchen? Kelly mentioned at lunch the other day that you both enjoy cooking. We ordered in, but I'm prepping some side dishes, and you can keep an eye on things while Tessa-ssi gets better acquainted with the others."

"Sure, we can do that." Kelly nodded.

Sung Soo gathered up the two rolling suitcases that were nestled behind Tessa, and tucked them next to the couches, glaring at Eun Gi as they passed.

Min Jae jumped forward and swung an arm around Tessa's shoulders. "Welcome, fake sister! Can I call you Noona?"

"Get off her." Eun Gi pulled the maknae away.

Tessa blinked rapidly and took a step backwards. "Um, sure?"

Eun Gi recognized her body language from this morning, the edge of panic in her voice and the subtle wobble of her lip. Swallowing his own discomfort, he moved closer, leading her into the living room to sit. He fetched her a glass of water from the kitchen and sat next to her in silence as she chugged it in long gulps.

Min Jae dropped down next to her. "Noona, how does it feel being engaged to Eun Gi-hyung?"

"Oh, but we're not."

"I told you," Eun Gi mumbled. "Min Jae, leave her alone."

"I'm making up for you being unsociable."

Hwan snuck up and grabbed Min Jae in a headlock, leading him away. "We're sorry, Tessa-ssi, he's a bit of a puppy with new people."

"She's not new people." Min Jae struggled with Hwan, yelping and wriggling. "She's a new sister. Noona, help! Noona!"

Tessa's whole body and expression shifted. "Lee Hyeong Hwan, let the maknae go."

Hwan's eyes widened in shock, and his arms released. Min Jae dashed back to hide next to Tessa. He stuck his tongue out at a narrow-eyed Eun Gi.

"Thanks, Noona!"

Eun Gi felt prickles of sensation on the back of his head and turned to see Kelly watching him like a hawk. Her hand moved smoothly, chopping green onions, but her attention was almost entirely focused on him. Nerves twitched in his belly.

The buzzer sounded, signaling the arrival of dinner.

Eun Gi nudged Tessa's water closer whenever the wildness started to creep back into her gaze. He wasn't sure what else to do. If he knew her better he'd have taken her hand, but he had the distinct impression that doing so would make things worse. Kelly's intense focus piqued his nerves. He *knew* Kelly was only being protective, had gathered it was an intrinsic part of her personality after their brief phone calls, but he hated every single second of it. He struggled enough with his own anxiety, but now everyone around him was on edge and he was a proverbial sponge, soaking it all up until it felt like insects crawling under his skin. Min Jae and Kelly chattered away through dinner, relieving Eun Gi of the burden of maintaining conversation. Small blessings. Hwan observed everyone, collecting information with an unwavering vigilance. Min Jae looped Tessa into talking as much as he could, but Eun Gi knew she was as overwhelmed as he was.

"Tessa-ssi," Eun Gi said. "Would you like some air?"

"Yes, please."

He pushed his chair back from the table and waited for her to follow, then guided them both out onto the balcony.

Tessa leaned on the railing, sucking in the crisp evening air. In place of stars there were thousands of headlights and windows aglow in towers all around them. Neon signs lit up the storefronts, and streetlights illuminated passersby.

"You looked like you could use a break." The knots in his chest released their frantic grip when she smiled softly.

"Thank you for noticing. It's been a lot to take in, and I'm struggling a little more than I thought I would."

"You and me both." He relaxed next to her. "I'm sorry, again. I feel like it's all my fault."

Tessa sank deeper against the railing, rubbing her temples. "I don't blame you for it. I'm pretty sure it's my fault anyway, even if we just got pulled along in the current of public opinion."

Eun Gi laughed awkwardly. "Story of my life."

Goose bumps covered her arms, and she was shivering, but she showed no signs of moving. She stared down at the vehicles and pedestrians, eyes unfocused.

"Come on back inside. Your friend might push me off the edge if I let you catch a cold out here."

Tessa smiled. "I'd save you."

The table was cleared when they returned and everyone stared at them as they entered.

"Tess, we've got to head out," Kelly said. "Will you be okay?"

"I think so. I'm adjusting."

Kelly snared her into a hug. "Good."

Min Joo stepped in front of Eun Gi, face unyielding. "I assume you'll do your best to make sure Tessa-ssi is well cared for while she's here."

Eun Gi swallowed hard. "Yes, sir."

"That goes for all of you." Kelly's bluebell gaze snared them each in turn. "I may be put under an NDA, but I will find a way to fuck shit up if she gets hurt on your watch."

Sung Soo stepped between Eun Gi and Min Joo. "I assure you we'll all be keeping an eye on things. I have both of your numbers if anything comes up. I promise you have nothing to worry about."

Kelly pursed her lips. "You'd better be right." She pulled Tessa into another hug. "Call me if you need *anything*. I mean it. Day or night, you phone and I'll be here in a heartbeat."

They all moved to the living room when Kelly and Min Joo departed. Tessa curled into herself on the corner of the couch. Eun Gi passed her the small blanket draped over the back, and the extra pillow from the opposite end. She took them gratefully, holding the pillow against her chest as everyone settled around her. Pillow shields were apparently something they had in common. Her phone buzzed incessantly on the side table.

Min Jae peeked at the lock screen. "Who's Pyong Ho? Why don't you want to talk to him?"

Tessa went rigid, and Eun Gi glared at Min Jae.

"Don't be rude." Sung Soo poked the maknae.

"It's fine," Tessa assured.

Nothing about her expression made Eun Gi believe it actually *was* fine.

"He was my date."

Eun Gi sank into the couch.

Great. I've fucked up her life and ruined her relationship.

"Date?" Min Jae sat back, confused. "But you're engaged to Eun Gi."

"Well, I wasn't engaged last night."

Eun Gi couldn't discern what her tone meant. Exasperated? That edge of panic was audible again too.

"What are you going to do about him?" Min Jae leaned closer.

Tessa shrugged and curled around her pillow. "There's nothing I *can* do. It's not like I can go out with anyone."

"Why did you agree to this if you were dating someone?" Eun Gi asked.

"The first time we met was last night. He's very nice, and Kelly wanted me to get involved with someone so I'd consider moving here, but it looks like she got her wish anyway, in a roundabout way."

Eun Gi squirmed in his seat.

"You can still meet him," he offered, "if you want."

"Even if I wanted to put myself through the hassle of dating, now would certainly not be the time to do it." The panic melted away a little, her features firmly set, eyes clear. "We might not have a real relationship or even be friends, but I agreed to this to protect you. I'm not jeopardizing this to try to date someone I just met. I don't even like dating."

"But you went out anyway?" Hwan asked.

"Sometimes people suffer through inconveniences for the sake of friends."

Tessa's phone rang, and they all turned to her.

Eun Gi led her towards his room so she could take the call.

"Sorry, I'll be quick," she muttered to him before answering. "What's up?"

"Can you *please* talk to Pyong Ho?"

Eun Gi could hear every word from his spot next to the door. He recognized Kelly's voice and leaned a little closer.

"The press release about you and UpBeat went out," Kelly said, "and he's confused. What am I allowed to tell him?"

"I don't know what to tell him either," Tessa replied.

"Talk to UpBeat and figure it out? Oh, and don't forget to phone your parents. What did his parents say?"

"You ask this like I'm gonna have an answer. I know nothing. I'm just along for the ride right now."

"I guess that's fair. Did they stay nice after we left?"

"Yep. We're chilling. I'll text you later."

Eun Gi heard Kelly's bright laugh. "Okay. Have a good night! Love you."

"Love you too."

They were watching her expectantly as she rejoined them.

"Who was that?" Min Jae asked.

Sung Soo rolled his eyes. "Jae, stop bothering her."

"I'm not bothering, right, Noona?" Min Jae turned his most perfect puppy dog expression on her.

She wavered, and Eun Gi was relieved they weren't the only ones susceptible to that face.

"Of course not." Tessa offered Min Jae a soft smile that he returned with a bright grin. "It was Kelly. She forgot to ask me some stuff."

Eun Gi blinked when she turned her attention to him.

"What am I supposed to tell people?"

"Who do you need to tell?"

"Well, I need to say something to my parents, and Pyong Ho." Tessa set her chin on her palm. "I guess I could tell them we'd broken up and you did a surprise proposal. Who could say no to Baek Eun Gi?"

He frowned, stomach clenching. *You'd be surprised.*

"I couldn't lie to my parents even if I wanted to. Mamãe knows me way too well."

Eun Gi offered a shrug, grasping for internal purchase as his anxiety spiked.

"I need you to have more of an opinion." Tessa narrowed her eyes. "If this has any chance of working, then you have to be invested in keeping it contained. What are you saying to your parents?"

"I..." he hesitated, "...nothing."

"Hyung!" Min Jae gasped. "You can't let your *eomma* and appa find out through a press release!"

Sung Soo's expression pinched. "I agree. You've done a good job of keeping them hidden all these years, but reporters could still find out. It won't go well if they're approached for a statement and they know nothing about it."

"I haven't talked to them for so long."

His mother's occasional texts demanding additional money were the only communication they tended to share.

"No time like the present," Tessa added.

"Tessa-ssi, I don't... We're not..." He tripped over his words, trying to impress upon her that he had zero desire to make such a phone call. Tension snared his muscles, panic climbing up this throat. "There are reasons I don't talk to them."

"If you don't want to tell me why, that's fine."

"Thank you."

"You still have to update them," Sung Soo said. "This is a delicate situation. A two-minute phone call will save you a headache later."

"Or cause one now."

"Eun Gi." Sung Soo's tone allowed no protest, and Eun Gi sank down in his seat.

Tessa

Tessa watched in silence as he slipped away from the table to make the call to his parents. The shouting from the other end of the line was audible through the closed door. It was shrill and furious, piercing the waiting silence while they stared at the door.

She chewed her lip. Guilt over bringing it up swirled in her belly.

"Eomeoni, I'm sorry. Yes. I'll be in Busan in a few weeks." Things went quiet, and UpBeat came back out looking miserable and disheveled. Sung Soo got up and pulled him into a hug.

"Hyung." UpBeat released a small sound of distress and buried his face against Sung Soo's shoulder. The older man squeezed tightly, and Tessa sat by helplessly. Hwan and Min Jae joined the hug and nestled a cocoon around him.

Tessa's mother had snapped at her before, raised her voice when she got upset, but she had never screamed at her like Eun Gi's mother had done. Anger and frustration were understandable, but what she'd overheard and the reaction it evoked seemed like more than that. She loved her parents, and the thought of ever *not* wanting to talk to them… It made her stomach queasy.

UpBeat's shoulders drooped, and his mouth stayed in a frown even after he wriggled free from the group.

"I'm tired."

Exhaustion tinged his voice, but also sadness. He was deflated. Tessa itched to hug him, but stayed where she was, knowing it wouldn't be appropriate.

"I'm going to sleep."

He walked away without another word and left Tessa with the other men.

Hwan awkwardly scratched the back of his head. "I guess that's our cue to clear out?"

"Keep an eye on him," Sung Soo told Hwan.

"Always."

"Min Jae, let's go."

"But, Hyung, he needs company. He always gets so cranky if he goes to bed upset. I'll go grab my PJ's and make sure he's okay."

The maknae returned barely a minute later dressed in a set of blue striped pajamas. He disappeared into UpBeat's room. There were sounds of a tussle, and Min Jae yelled out "Let me love you!" before things settled down again.

Sung Soo sighed and pinched the bridge of his nose. "Let me make sure Jae hasn't been smothered by a pillow."

Tessa's curiosity overwhelmed her as Sung Soo cracked the door, an indulgent smile enveloping his face. She wanted to peek into that room desperately, but she was committed to being a reasonable human. Instead, she occupied herself by quietly packing up the garbage and dishes from dinner with Hwan's help.

"I can promise you'll never be bored being fake married to Eun Gi." Hwan smiled at her as he rinsed the rice bowls. "I'll get you some blankets, and we'll figure things out tomorrow. I'd offer you my bed, but I'm selfish and my mattress is perfect."

Every time she thought she might have adapted to being around the idols she'd hit a new loop on the emotional roller coaster.

"It's okay. I don't mind the couch."

Sung Soo came to help them finish tidying. "I'm sorry about Eun Gi. He tends to retreat when he's upset."

Tessa nodded, filing that information away.

"We all have our coping strategies."

Sung Soo lingered to the point of awkwardness.

"Hyung, do you want to stay here too?" Hwan asked.

The oldest member looked so relieved Tessa had to bite her lip against the rise of laughter.

"I'm bad at staying places alone."

"We have two couches," Hwan pointed out.

Sung Soo turned to Tessa. "Would you mind if I stayed?"

Tessa's brain did a little static shock at the thought of sleeping a few feet away from one of her idols, but she covered it up by drying the bowls. "Of course not. You can sleep wherever you'd like."

Half an hour later Tessa was staring wide-eyed at the ceiling with the lights of Gangnam glittering outside the window. Sung Soo was already asleep, and there was silence from the bedrooms. She shifted around, trying to get comfortable, and while the couch was certainly that, she was still antsy.

Tessa glanced over at Sung Soo, who'd turned himself into a burrito in his blanket and wedged his head between two of the pillows. Jet lag and her nap earlier were thoroughly kicking her butt, but she eventually nodded off.

In the morning sunlight streamed across her face and made sleeping impossible. Sung Soo was still knocked out under his pillows, but Tessa was painfully awake. She stretched and basked in the pristine silence for a few moments, taking the opportunity to get washed up before anyone else was awake.

When she emerged she was ravenous, but didn't want to wake Sung Soo by rustling around in an unfamiliar kitchen. She was tired, and quietly dreaded having to think and speak in Korean so early, but only two of the four men could speak English so there wasn't much choice. Consistent exposure would probably prod her memory enough that it wouldn't bother her after a while. She hoped.

Settling in to wait, she unlocked her phone intent on popping a book open, but noticed an email from Muriel Brown Esq. with an invitation for a video call. Tessa replied and waited for it to be seen. She disappeared into the bathroom when her phone rang.

"Ms. Hale. Are you doing well?"

"Mostly. Have you had a chance to look over the paperwork?"

Muriel nodded. "It's a standard non-disclosure agreement, and the prenuptial agreement is remarkably well thought out. Both of your assets are entirely secure, which will make any potential separation an easy process. All assets gained after the marriage by either of you remain the sole property of the earning party. I do still urge you to review the documents yourself again before signing, but in terms of my professional view, there are no issues."

Relief melted through her body, and Tessa sat down on the edge of the bath. "Thank you."

"Congratulations on your engagement. Will you be needing any assistance navigating immigration? It's not my personal specialty, but I can recommend some individuals."

"That's okay. My—" she forced the word out, "—fiancé's company will handle the initial visa requirements, and I suppose I'll deal with it next year."

Not wanting to occupy any more billable hours, Tessa bid the lawyer goodbye and dove into a book to distract herself. She read for almost an hour before Hwan emerged from his room.

His hair stuck out in every direction, and he wore nothing but a pair of boxers as he shuffled blindly across the living room to the kitchen. Somehow, he managed to go through the motions of preparing coffee without actually opening his eyes. The scent of the brew percolating filled the apartment, and Hwan gave a pleased sigh as he poured himself a cup and sniffed the fragrant steam.

Tessa gaped, unable to look away. When he turned back to the living room with coffee in hand, he froze dead in his tracks. Their twinned panicked gazes met across the room, and Tessa swore she could see his soul shrivel and leave his body entirely.

"I forgot you were here," he said, still rooted to the floor.

Breaking from her trance, Tessa grabbed a pillow and shoved her face into it, giving Hwan a few precious seconds to bolt back into his bedroom.

The slamming door jolted Sung Soo awake. "W-what? What's happening?"

Tessa peeked out from behind the pillow. "Nothing, it's fine. Go back to sleep."

Idols with bedhead shouldn't have been as cute as it was. She hid her grin behind the pillow.

He rubbed his hands over his face and sat up. "Too late, I'm awake. Good morning, Tessa-ssi. Are you hungry?"

"Starving."

Hwan poked his head out of his room. He was considerably more awake and a lot more dressed. Sung Soo gave him an odd look when his cheeks flared pink under Tessa's scrutiny.

"I'm going to go get a few ingredients from our apartment. Tessa-ssi, could you wake up the others?" Sung Soo asked.

After crossing the room, she knocked lightly, but there was no response. She cracked the door open and peered inside. The only illumination was bits of sunlight breaking through the edges of the curtains and the beam of light from the door. UpBeat was fast asleep with Jaybird draped over his chest, a puddle of drool under his cheek.

I guess I should start using their names if I'm staying here.

She soaked in the scene, and although she didn't want to disturb them, she was also hungry. The heat of Hwan's body appearing next to her made her jump out of her skin.

"Sorry," he whispered. "Min Jae gets lonely easily and likes sleeping next to someone. Eun Gi is the same, but he thinks he's better at covering it up."

"Will it be weird living in separate homes now?"

Hwan shrugged. "Yeah, but we're together a lot anyway. I miss the dorm days sometimes, when every night was a sleepover, but I miss it more with Yoon, Ju Won, and Jin in the military now."

"We don't have compulsory service at home," Tessa said.

"Your country has also not been on the brink of war for almost seventy years," Hwan pointed out. "I wish we had a more peaceful history, that it was all different, but it's not."

Tessa's phone rang in the living room. "I'm so sorry. I should get that."

She was expecting Kelly, but it was her mother's number that flashed on the screen.

"Hi, Mamãe!"

"I have to find out from Kelly that you're an engaged woman?"

Guilt slammed into her. She couldn't tell if her mother was upset or amused. Probably both.

"I'm sorry. I meant to call earlier."

"Don't worry, meu amor. She explained everything. Is this the boy you had the poster of in your room?"

Tessa cringed. "There was more than just him on there, but yes."

Her mother laughed on the other end of the line. "So, will you try to win him over while this is all going on?"

"Mamãe, that would we weird. I'm only doing this to help."

"Mhmm. Well, you'll have to forgive your Mamãe if she doesn't believe one word of that. I never understood it, but I know they all meant a lot more to you than you ever said. If it turns out he's a genuinely good person, then what would the harm be?"

"Mamãe, please."

"I'm just saying! I give you my motherly approval if you like him. Appa wouldn't say anything, but I'm pretty sure he'd be secretly thrilled if you got together with someone Korean."

"Mamãe, why—"

"You're no fun." The pout in her voice was obvious, and Tessa couldn't help but smile.

"I'm not obligated to be fun about this topic. In fact, I'm calling for an end to it right now."

"Why don't you let Mamãe have her fun? When was the last time you dated? I never get to be entertained over your love life. Don't steal my joy!"

"Too late, joy stolen. I've got to go wake up my fake fiancé."

"If you insist. Does that mean you don't want to talk to Appa?"

"You're a guilt monster. Put him on."

"I love you, meu amor."

"I love you too, Mamãe."

Her father came onto the phone. "How's married life, Peanut?"

Tessa was relieved when she heard the smile in his voice. Worry over him was a constant, quiet whisper in the back of her mind, but today sounded like a good day for him. She was grateful for that since she wasn't home to help.

"Appa, it's a fake engagement. I'm not married."

"Well, you update us when that changes. I'll need to make sure I don't take any substitute shifts at the school."

"Why are you both like this?"

"I've spent thirty-one years married to your mother. It rubs off. She started crying when Kelly called."

"Oh God."

"Good tears. She was so excited. Oh, wait, you're going to hate this. She's sending you a picture in a minute. Anyway, we're heading out for dinner with the neighbors right away. I just wanted to hear your voice. Love you."

"Love you too, Appa."

After she hung up the phone beeped. Tessa groaned and opened up the picture her mother had sent. She'd dug out the old 24/7 poster Tessa had had on her walls in early university. She held up a peace sign and grinned brightly.

Mamãe:
Can't wait to meet my future son!

"Is that your eomma?"

Tessa jumped and hastily covered the phone so Hwan couldn't see.

Why is he so damn stealthy?

"Yeah, that's her."

He smirked. "Is that us next to her?"

"...Maybe."

"Don't be embarrassed. The posters are made to be purchased. Let me see." He wiggled his hand at her.

Tessa frowned and passed the phone over.

"Wow! This is our debut poster. We're so small." He laughed. "I haven't seen this in so long. So, you've been a fan for a while?"

"Is that bad? I feel like it's weird that I'm a fan."

Hwan shrugged. "I'm happy to meet people who like what we do. That's kind of the whole point. And honestly, I'd rather you felt weird and embarrassed by it instead of being completely calm and calculating. Those are the people I worry about, but you seem reasonably chill."

Chill wasn't exactly how Tessa would describe herself, but she was thankful her internal panics weren't entirely visible to everyone.

"You look a lot like your eomma. She's cute."

"Don't tell her that, her ego will inflate, but thank you."

Hwan tilted his head. "Just because you're a fan I'm compelled to say this, though I'm sure you've already realized. Eun Gi is not UpBeat. The same goes for the rest of us. What you see in videos and on stage is cultivated. It's not that it's necessarily inaccurate, but you have to remember there's no room for any unpleasant realities in a stage persona."

"I know."

She *did*. The difficulty was understanding where the differences were. She didn't know any of them well enough to properly separate, but she didn't want to put unreasonable expectations on them because of that.

"Good. Keep it in mind?"

Tessa nodded.

"I like you so far, and I'm hoping that continues. I'm going to make sure Sung Soo doesn't need help. You get back in there and wake them up." Hwan pushed her towards the bedroom and slipped away.

She popped back over to Eun Gi's room and tried to figure out the best way to wake them. She set a hand on his shoulder and he jolted upright, flinging Min Jae off the edge, who promptly yanked Eun Gi down with him. Tessa caught them both enough to save their heads from hitting the nightstand, but the combined weight pulled her to the floor.

Eun Gi hefted himself off and helped her up as well.

"Are you okay?" he asked.

"Yeah." She gave herself a little shake to clear her head. "Just a bit squished."

His eyebrows pinched together. "What is squished?"

Tessa lifted his hand and pressed it between both of hers.

"Ah."

Min Jae looked at them from his spot on the floor. "Why are we on the floor? Did you have another nightmare?"

Eun Gi shook his head and checked his phone. "Come on, let's go get breakfast. Tessa-ssi and I have a meeting to get to."

Eun Gi

"We're in luck!" Ha Yun's eyes were bright with excitement. "The fan forums have been exploding, and it's generating a lot of buzz for the drama now that people know it's based off Tessa-ssi's book. We wanted to discuss some covert promotion. It would be more interesting for the fans if you were involved with Brooks Lily, but she's married, and this is almost as good."

Eun Gi's lips pulled back in disgust, but he tucked it away and put a smile back on his face. "My involvements are not their concern."

He kept his voice placid, but there were several choice words poised on the tip of his tongue for everyone involved in this fiasco.

"Perhaps you've forgotten, Baek Eun Gi, but they definitely are. Your career is dependent upon the good will of the fans."

"Ha Yun-ssi, what do you mean by covert promotion?" Tessa asked.

"Releasing curated images. It helps give the best impression toward our goals. We'd like you to be seen together where we have cameras available. Tessa-ssi, you're not required on set every day, but those days you are here, we'd prefer if you spent Eun Gi-ssi's breaks with him. Be close. Be cute. For the photographs."

"We've agreed to this charade," Eun Gi snapped. "Why don't you all let us get comfortable with each other before you start making demands?"

Oh Jung Do, who had signed Eun Gi to the project, stood up from the table. "Baek Eun Gi, you are quickly proving to be a disappointment. Your company assured us you were quite capable of maintaining an appropriate façade, yet you resist these simple measures."

"It's fine," Tessa said, laying a hand on Eun Gi's forearm. "We'll do it and anything else you need."

He opened his mouth to protest. Her fingers squeezed gently, and he pressed his lips together.

"I'm sorry. This is all new, and we're still figuring out how to deal with it. I promise we'll be more cooperative."

Oh Jung Do nodded, apparently satisfied with Tessa's response.

Eun Gi rolled his eyes. Jung Do was always happy when you were doing exactly what he wanted.

"I'm glad to see at least one of you has some sense." Oh Jung Do clasped his hands together. "Now, Baek Eun Gi, report to makeup. Hale Tessa, stay close by."

"Of course, Oh Jung Do-nim," she said with a nod.

When they were dismissed, they rode the elevator down and Eun Gi tugged her into a quiet corner. "What was that?"

"I don't want you to get in trouble with the studio."

Eun Gi pinched the bridge of his nose. "You don't have to worry about that."

He hated seeing them try to turn her into a trained monkey for their benefit. She didn't deserve to have them meddling in her life like this.

"Um, yes I do? I agreed to this to protect you, and I'm not about to let you ruin it over a bad mood."

"I hate this."

"Well, being difficult won't make it any more enjoyable." She crossed her arms. "I am massively freaked out by this whole ordeal, and you promised you'd have my back and be my ally in this. I want to help, but you need to step up and do your part."

"You're right. I'm sorry. I'm just… It's exhausting." Eun Gi leaned against the wall, curling into himself. "They're never happy with how much you give. They always look for the next opportunity to take a little more. You lose so much of yourself in this industry that you start to wonder who you really are, whether you're you or your persona or whatever role they want you to play. I don't want you to end up feeling like I do. I don't want you to let them pick you apart and cut away the pieces they don't like until they're satisfied."

Tessa turned towards him. "I'm not going to let that happen."

It wasn't the first time he'd heard those words, and he wasn't able to tell if she genuinely meant it, or if it was an automatic reaction. He swallowed down his distress.

"Permission to hug?"

He startled. "What?"

"Can I hug you?" she asked. "I always feel like I need to hug people when they're upset, but it's not a thing here between people you're not close with, so I thought I'd ask."

Physical comfort tended to come from one of the other members since they were usually together, but here was this woman, a stranger, potentially his future wife, offering the same without even knowing how much it meant to him.

He opened his arms, and she slipped into them. She cupped the back of his head, and he let his cheek rest on her collarbone.

"This is all so weird, and you don't know me yet, but I'm here."

"Thank you." His whole body settled into her embrace. "I'm here too."

He rarely felt small around women, but she was a bit taller than him, and his hunching down had him easily nestling under her chin. Her fingers were gentle against him, and the sound of her heartbeat thrummed in his ear.

She was so soft.

"Eun Gi."

He liked how she said his name, with the slightest accent. "Hmm?"

"Do you feel like you have to perform for people? Off the stage I mean."

"Every day."

"You don't have to with me." She paused, and her heartbeat picked up beneath his cheek. "If the company gets their way, I'll be around a lot, and I want you to feel like you can be yourself."

The elevator pinged, and footsteps came closer to where they were tucked away. Tessa stepped back, and he nodded, both to acknowledge her words and his own desire to accept them.

Tessa slipped her hand into his as some of the staff with cameras came into view. He squeezed back gently when her hand trembled in his.

"Don't let them intimidate you," he said softly.

"I'm trying not to."

"Anything that gets published will have you looking amazing. It doesn't take off the pressure of having a lens in your face, but it's one less thing to worry about."

She puffed out a breath. "This is going to take some getting used to."

"You'll get the hang of it. I have no doubt of that. Want to grab dinner on the way home?"

"That sounds lovely."

The warmth of her hand disappeared as they diverted him to makeup. He let Hye Jin paint his face while he tried not to think about what the future might bring.

Chapter 8

Tessa

Tessa bit down a curse as she was forced into another sit-up. Joining the boys for their morning workout was a horrendous idea, but at least it left her little time to be awkward.

"How do you guys *do* this?"

She collapsed onto the mat, chest heaving, as Min Jae, Hwan, and Eun Gi hoisted their bodies next to her in rapid succession.

"Practice," Hwan said, puffing hard.

"I'm dying." Tessa whined and tried to wriggle away, but Sung Soo held fast to her ankles.

"Three more."

"Noooooo."

"Yes."

Tessa groaned and heaved herself upwards, once, twice, thrice, and collapsed again, holding her stomach. "Why do you hate me?"

Sung Soo laughed. "You said you wanted to participate. You're not even doing the full amount."

"There's a difference between participating and regretting my entire existence."

Min Jae snickered next to her and switched seamlessly into bicycle crunches. Hwan counted off his last few sit-ups and followed Min Jae into the next set. Eun Gi had his lips pressed together, but the upturned corners were obvious.

"Come on." Sung Soo tapped her ankle. "Time for crunches. Count them out yourself."

Tessa moved through the laziest crunches she could manage while Sung Soo dropped down and blasted through his sit ups. She bailed part way and sprawled on the mats.

Min Jae hopped up and pulled Tessa with him. "Race me."

"I can barely stand," she protested.

"Noona, you have legs like a gazelle, you can do it." He tugged at her again. "Come on!"

"Fine."

She trudged over to the treadmills.

"Whoever gets to two kilometers first wins, okay?"

"Yeah, yeah." She punched in the distance goal and jacked up the speed, determined not to embarrass herself in front of them like she had with the sit-ups. She ran until she couldn't breathe, and when her machine beeped signaling her goal was met a few seconds before Min Jae, she almost melted to the floor in delight.

The maknae stepped down. "You did so well, Noona!"

"Thank you." Tessa could have kissed Hwan when he handed her a bottle of water.

Tessa was convinced it was witchcraft for them to all be a sweaty mess and still look amazing, while she was likely bordering on train wreck appearance.

"It'll get easier," Sung Soo assured. "We've been doing things at high intensity for years. We don't expect you to keep up at the start. You should have seen Eun Gi complain when we were trainees."

"My complaints were reasonable. They were practically starving us, and I was so spindly. It was mean." Eun Gi glided off the treadmill as it slowed to a stop. "Do you need anything?"

"Food?" Tessa asked hopefully. "Water? Life support?"

"Soon," said Sung Soo. "Eun Gi, to the weights." The eldest member stopped and checked his beeping phone. "The moving company is coming tonight to transfer things between the units and also dropping off a new bed set for Tessa."

"That's not necessary," Tessa said.

"Trust me, it's necessary." Sung Soo laughed. "You don't want to use Hwan's mattress and sheets. There is no method of washing that can cleanse what has occurred on that bed."

"Hyung!" Hwan cried out. "Shut up!"

Sung Soo dodged a tackle. "I'm just being realistic."

Hwan's cheeks were flaming red as he slithered away behind the weight rack where they couldn't see him. Tessa tried and failed to contain herself, throwing her head back in laughter that had tears leaking out the corners of her eyes.

"Tessa-ssi, why are you so mean?" Hwan asked from behind the weights.

"I'm sorry. I didn't mean to laugh." Tessa hopped over to apologize. "Also, you don't have to call me Tessa-ssi. Tessa is fine, or Noona, like Min Jae if you wanted."

Hwan puffed out a breath. "I'm never going to regain my dignity around you."

"Consider it regained." Tessa winked.

Hwan slipped his glasses back on and picked up a set of weights. "Noona, please, I have delicate feelings."

Tessa pressed her fingers to her mouth to smother another giggle. "Of course, I'm sorry. I'll take more care in the future."

She glanced over at Eun Gi who was hoisting weights in biceps curls. A trail of sweat slid down his temple. A small sound escaped her mouth. Her eyes glued to that droplet as it glided over lean muscle and disappeared into the fabric of his tank top.

Holy sweet Jesus.

Tessa dragged her eyes away from his flexing muscles as her cheeks flooded with heat. She saw Hwan out of the corner of her eye, smirking like the devil. "What?"

His grin widened. "Nothing at all, Noona. Don't mind me."

Tessa sat out most of the remaining exercises. Part of her wanted to try to compete, but the other, larger and more sane part wanted to be able to move tomorrow. She stretched and watched them work themselves into a contented exhaustion.

Eun Gi

Eun Gi let her shower first and stopped in his tracks when she emerged, dressed with her damp hair curling around her face, cheeks pink. Seeing her like that felt strangely intimate, but he tried not to linger on the thought. He washed up quickly and disappeared to the other apartment at the earliest opportunity.

"You're leaving her there alone?" Sung Soo asked.

"She's a grown woman. She doesn't need anyone to babysit her while we work," Eun Gi retorted. "Besides, she'll be grateful to have a break away from us."

"Did Noona say that?" Min Jae asked. Eun Gi wasn't sure how he felt about both Min Jae and Hwan dubbing her noona this early in their acquaintance, but he supposed there was no real harm in it.

"No," he replied, "but we're a lot to handle. She doesn't even have her own room yet so there's no way for her to get away from us without leaving the apartment. I figured she could use the space. I doubt she's eager to spend all day with us."

"Anyone would be eager to spend all day with me," Min Jae said.

"That ego will inflate your head so much you'll float away," Hwan teased.

"Nah." Min Jae nudged Sung Soo. "Hyung would grab on to my ankles and drag me right back down."

Sung Soo rolled his eyes. "But think of how quiet our lives would be if I let you float away."

"Hyung!" Min Jae cried. "So mean."

The eldest sighed and looped an arm around the maknae, squeezing. "We'd be bored to tears inside a week if we didn't have you around."

They split off to different sections of the apartment to work. Hwan and Eun Gi sat at the dining room table with their laptops.

Hwan smiled at Eun Gi. "So, how's being engaged?"

"Are you actually asking me that question?"

Hwan nodded.

"It's weird."

"Weird how?" Hwan sat up, fully alert. "Has she done something?"

"I'm not used to her yet." Eun Gi shrugged. "She's there all the time, and so far neither of us hate each other, which means she's going to keep being there."

"Too true. Kyung Mi won't let you wiggle out of it unless you have a good reason. I like her though, she seems nice."

"She *is* nice," Eun Gi said. "Honestly, she's been way better about all of this than I ever expected. I feel a little guilty feeling weird about it. I don't want her dragged into the colossal mess that is my life."

"You could talk to her about this."

"Hwan, you say that like it's simple. You and I both know I'm terrible at confronting my problems."

"Can't argue with that," Hwan agreed.

A few hours later Sung Soo emerged from his room looking askew, but satisfied. "I think this song is ready for full production. Oh, also, the moving company is arriving in half an hour. Can you tell Tessa?"

"Sure."

Another one of them had lapsed into the informal, dropping the suffix so she was simply Tessa.

Maybe I should get on board.

When Eun Gi stepped into his apartment, he was greeted by the sound of their third album emanating from her laptop, the tail end of one of their most popular songs. It sat on the table next to a couple notebooks, handful of pens, and a glass of water. Tessa was in the kitchen humming along, hips swaying to the beat as she dug through the cupboards.

She was different from the women he was usually surrounded with; tall, golden, and leanly muscled, compared to the pale, petite, and sleek ladies of the industry. The song changed and she smiled. It was one of his solo songs, he noted.

She shook her head and dipped down to check one of the drawers.

His heart twinged.

"Why is there no tea?" she huffed.

"I'll get you some from Sung Soo's," he said.

Tessa jumped and whirled towards him, her dark curls flared around her face, and her hand leapt to her chest.

"Sorry," he apologized. "I came to let you know that the moving company will be here soon."

She leaned back against the counter to stabilize herself. "Thanks."

Eun Gi turned to the laptop as a new song began. It was the first one he'd helped write. The pulsing beat streamed out, and his younger, much higher voice crooned into the apartment. Her face paled. He didn't say a word about the music.

"What are you working on?"

"My next book. Deadlines don't stop for vacations or foreign companies taking over my life. I was about to wade through my emails for a bit of a break."

"What's the new one about? Another historical?"

"Mhmm. Set in Brazil this time, though I've been debating asking my publisher if they'd be willing to switch over to another one set in Korea. I figure if I'm here for a year, it would be prime research time. The last was popular enough that I highly doubt they'd refuse the request."

"I'm sorry." The words leapt out of his mouth before he could stop them.

Her face softened, head tilting. "For?"

"That you're going to be stuck here for a year."

She sighed, and he wondered if he'd offended her.

"You don't have to be sorry for anything. You're not personally strong-arming either of us into this situation."

"But your job."

"I can manage it. There are enough working hours between here and Vancouver that line up. My assistant can handle things there for the most part, and I'll address any travel issues or meetings as they come up."

"I guess that makes sense. I might not be useful for any of the stuff that you do, but please reach out if I can help."

"Sure, if you want me to."

"I do. Now, preference for tea? I think Sung Soo has green, chrysanthemum, and ginseng. Hwan and I don't drink it, so we don't keep it."

"Chrysanthemum, please," Tessa said. "I can buy my own. It's no trouble."

Eun Gi waved away the offer. She might only be a fake fiancée, but there was no way in hell he was making her buy her own supplies while she was staying with him.

"We'll get some with our next grocery order. I'll be right back."

He knew exactly where Sung Soo kept the tea because he knew where everyone kept everything. The others liked to refer to it as his superpower. He fished out the container of chrysanthemum tea and a steeper shaped liked a platypus that would hang on the edge of the cup.

"Developing an interest in tea?" Sung Soo asked.

"Tessa was looking for some, but we don't have any." He chewed his lip, uncertain what exactly he was feeling. "She's listening to our music."

Sung Soo raised an eyebrow. "Is that bad?"

"Isn't it weird?"

"Would you rather she hate it?"

"I... No, I suppose not."

Sung Soo shrugged. "Our international fans number in the millions. I'm not surprised she could be one of them."

Hwan perked up. "I already knew."

"And you decided to not say anything?" Eun Gi asked.

"Why would I say anything? It was cute, and I was keeping an eye on things. Her mom likes us too."

Eun Gi rolled his eyes. "You guys don't make it easy to complain."

"Oh, you can complain," Sung Soo said. "Just make it about something we can get behind. It's not like she's been stealing clippings of your hair in the night. She enjoys our music. We want people to do that. Now, get back to your fake fiancée with that tea."

Eun Gi grumbled on his way back to the apartment. The others weren't facing an impending marriage they wanted nothing to do with, so they couldn't understand. Last time he'd thought about marriage it had promptly exploded in his face.

He pushed the memory away. This wasn't the same situation, and the people involved were totally different. *He* was totally different too. When he stepped back inside, the music was off, and Tessa stood next to the bubbling kettle.

"You don't have to stop listening." He set down the tea implements and grabbed her a cup.

"I don't want you to be uncomfortable."

"If listening to my own music made me uncomfortable, I'd have a problem," he teased.

"Yeah, but you got this weird look on your face when *I* was listening."

"It's fine," he assured, though she still seemed skeptical.

"If you say so."

Tessa

The next night Tessa lay awake in her room. The moving company had cleared out Hwan's space after they'd boxed up the entirety of the three bedroom suite down the hall. Her walls were bare, and her closet was only half filled with the contents of her suitcases, but at least the bed was comfortable. They'd provided fresh sheets, pillows, and a quilt set. It was all pink and white, which she wasn't a huge fan of, but it was still pretty.

Tessa sat up, hearing a strange whimpering sound that resembled a dog.

Climbing out of bed, she shivered as her bare feet hit the floor. She stepped into the living room, ears perked for the sound, and her head whipped towards Eun Gi's bedroom as the whimper came again, quiet in the dark.

Tessa padded to the door and pressed an ear against it.

"Please, stop! Stop!"

Tessa bolted inside. It was too dark to see properly, and she cracked her foot on something hard, sending it skidding under the bed as she slammed both hands down on the mattress to catch her fall. Eun Gi jolted awake, his forehead smashing into hers.

"Motherfucking hell!" Pain burst through her, and Tessa wheeled backwards, hitting the floor. "Ow."

She clutched her head.

"What's going on?" Eun Gi climbed out of the bed, catching himself when he tripped over her, and slapped on his bedside lamp.

He knelt down in front of her. "Shit."

Tessa followed obediently as he carted her back across the living room to the bathroom. When he flicked on the light, Tessa caught her reflection in the mirror. Blood dripped down one side of her face from a gash under her eyebrow, leaving a trail of brilliant red. Eun Gi pressed a folded towel to the wound. She hissed away from the pressure, but he put a gentle hand behind her head to keep her in place.

"I'm sorry," he whispered.

"Are you okay?"

Their heads had collided, so he couldn't be feeling amazing.

"You're bleeding, so you're the priority."

Ordering her to hold the towel firmly, he went about the business of mopping up the droplets of blood that had followed them to the bathroom, then cleaned up the floor around her.

"How are you doing?" he asked.

Everything throbbed. Her toes hurt, but she could wiggle them, so she assumed none of them were broken, not that she knew how to check for certain. "Just peachy."

"I don't know what that means."

"Sorry." She winced. "I'm good. Well, mostly, but not dying?"

"I'll take it."

He sat down next to her and pulled the towel away, letting out a relieved breath. "The bleeding is slowing down."

Eun Gi fished the first aid kit out from under the sink and selected gauze, ointment, and medical tape. A fresh cloth was moistened to clean up her face, and Tessa melted into the smooth strokes of the soft fabric.

An ungodly sting throbbed against the wound when he tried to spread some ointment, and she rolled her head away. "That hurts!"

"Hold still."

"No." She turned away again, exhaustion and pain eroding good sense.

He grabbed her chin, fingers and thumb pressing against her cheeks so she couldn't wriggle away. She jerked back a little when he swiped over the injury, sending an electric bolt of pain through her.

His hold gentled while he scrutinized his work.

"I'm sorry. I had to, but that part's done. Hold still while I get the bandage on." Eun Gi methodically applied a thick piece of gauze over the wound and taped it down. He sat back to survey his work. "You're not supposed to struggle during medical procedures."

"It's four in the morning and I'm hurt. I should be excused."

He gazed skyward and sighed.

"I feel like a pirate." She poked at the gauze.

"An eyepatch would help if you insist on fussing with it." He snared her hand and lingered, keeping it contained in his. "Don't touch."

His hands were warm, but she was in too much pain to properly appreciate it.

Almost.

"So, why were you in my room?"

"Oh." Her cheeks burned. "You were yelling, and I got scared. I wanted to check on you."

His face turned pink. "Ah, sorry. I didn't mean to wake you with that."

"It's not your fault." She fidgeted awkwardly. "Do you want to talk about it?"

"Not really."

An arm looped around her waist as he helped her stand. She wondered vaguely if she was actually asleep and dreaming, hallucinating him touching her so intimately. She tested, leaning her weight against him a little more. His other arm came around her too, and he paused to check her face.

Definitely not hallucinating.

"Let me help you back to bed?" he asked.

"Painkillers?"

There was a small chance she'd be able to sleep through the pain, but she didn't want to risk it and then have to stumble around in the unfamiliar apartment searching for them herself.

After guiding them into the living room, he propped her against some couch pillows, then disappeared into the kitchen. He emerged with a bottle tucked under his arm and two glasses of orange juice, which he deposited onto the coffee table.

Tessa swallowed back the pills, slurping the juice. "Bleh, I hate pulp."

"With everything that just happened, that's what you're choosing to complain about?"

"The heart wants what it wants, and mine wants pulpless juice."

Eun Gi took his own painkillers and dug out a pair of soft ice packs from the freezer. He sat next to her, leaning his head back and setting one on his forehead before offering the other to her.

"I feel awake and tired at the same time," Eun Gi mused. "Adrenaline is a bitch."

"Mhmm," Tessa agreed, nursing her drink.

By the time the painkillers kicked in they were both drooping. He fell asleep slack-jawed, head resting on the back of the couch, his arm draped over her waist while she tumbled into sleep with her cheek pillowed on his thigh.

Tessa

"So, want to tell us what happened?"

Tessa cracked open her good eye. Sung Soo, Min Jae, and Hwan all stood in a line in front of her. Her toasty pillow shifted, and she froze as last night rushed back. She sat up gingerly. There was a steady throb in her skull, the weight and warmth of Eun Gi's arm across her, the sour taste in her mouth from the orange juice.

Only a groan came out when she went to speak.

Moving bad. So bad.

She inched back down and closed her eyes. She didn't even care that she'd fallen asleep on her idol. Other matters were far more pressing, like the gremlins burrowing out of her skull with jackhammers. Painkillers were needed to subdue them.

Eun Gi shifted beneath her. "Someone smother me. It hurts to exist."

"Well, I would," said Sung Soo, "but then you'd miss filming, and I don't think the studio would like that."

"Fuck." Eun Gi groaned. "I can't go to filming."

"You're welcome to phone and explain the situation to them, though I'd love to know exactly what it is first."

Eun Gi mumbled a brief explanation, but Tessa didn't pay much attention.

"I feel like we should take you two to the clinic," Sung Soo said. "You might have concussions."

"Need sleep," Tessa murmured. "And drugs."

"If you can't wake up properly, that's a bad sign." Sung Soo prodded her shoulder.

"I got three hours of sleep. There is no awake-Tessa on three hours of sleep."

"Tessa, I have to pee," Eun Gi whispered.

"Pillows don't pee."

Eun Gi hissed as he moved, and wrangled an actual pillow under her cheek as he did so.

"Oh shit," they heard from the bathroom. "I look like I've been hit in the face with a rock."

"Just my head." Tessa nuzzled her pillow.

Sung Soo laughed, deep and hearty, sinking onto the perpendicular couch. "You were only left alone for a few hours, and somehow you manage this."

"And you say I'm the one who shouldn't be unsupervised," Min Jae quipped.

"I still stand by that assessment." Sung Soo smiled indulgently. "You're no better than these two. How am I supposed to get anything done being hyung to this unruly batch of maknae? Where's the justice in the world?"

"Hyung, you're a millionaire with six best friends and millions of people around the world who love you," Min Jae pointed out.

"Way to ruin my dramatics." Sung Soo pouted and turned to Tessa. "Will you go to the doctor?"

Tessa nodded and immediately regretted it. "Fuck. Ow." She cradled her head in her hands pitifully.

"I'll call Kyung Mi to take you both over. Please stay awake for a little while, and you can sleep later," Sung Soo said.

"Hwan, can you go get the *dak juk* from my apartment for their breakfast? Jae, can you please find Eun Gi's phone so he can call the studio?"

"You got it, Hyung!" Min Jae disappeared into the bedroom and emerged triumphant with the phone while Hwan carted the steaming pot over.

Sung Soo gave them another dose of painkillers and settled them on the couches so they were easy to monitor. Eun Gi got off the hook with the studio, and Tessa nibbled at the savory porridge.

Kyung Mi arrived while they were eating. Entirely unimpressed, she sighed, absorbing their state.

"I'm starting to wonder if you need more supervision," Kyung Mi said. "How have things been progressing otherwise?"

"It's okay." Tessa shrugged. "We're still adjusting."

Kyung Mi prodded her charge. "Eun Gi?"

"It's fine. It's only been a couple days."

"But you're amiable?"

Both nodded.

"Good. I was a bit worried, but I have every confidence in you both. Now, go get dressed for the day, and I'll take you to get checked over."

The doctors they went to see worked in association with EchoPop, handling all their idols.

"You both have very minor concussions, so you'll need to rest for today, but you should otherwise have no concerns." The doctor ran down a list of potential symptoms with instructions for Kyung Mi to bring them back if needed. No broken toes were found on Tessa's x-ray and her cut was sealed up too.

"You two will have to wear makeup when you go out," Kyung Mi said as they drove back. "We don't want an abuse scandal on top of everything else."

Eun Gi's face scrunched up, altogether appalled. "I'd never hit her."

"We know that," Kyung Mi said, "but the media sees what it wants, as you've experienced. It's better to avoid giving them anything to run with."

Tessa glanced around the car. "I'm not great at doing makeup. Do you think we could hire someone to help for a bit?"

"No harm in asking," said Kyung Mi. "I'll check with the company."

"You don't have to do any of that," Eun Gi said. "I can do it."

Tessa turned to him skeptically. "Really?"

"Well, I'm not good with dramatic styles, but we all have a lot of experience with basic makeup."

Kyung Mi looked hard at him as they pulled into their parking stall outside the apartment building. "You do have the skill needed. I'd be comfortable letting you handle it."

Min Jae was already at the door when they punched in the code.

"Noona, you're alive!" Min Jae cried, pulling Tessa into a hug.

"Of course. It'll take a lot more than Eun Gi's head to get rid of me."

"Both of you get some rest. Stay out here so someone can keep an eye on you. I have some work to do at the studio, but call if me you need anything." Kyung Mi settled them in before heading off.

A throbbing pulse of pain broke through the haze of exhaustion. When she opened her eyes Eun Gi was stretched out on the other couch, and Hwan was sitting on the floor between them with his laptop. She made a sound of protest over her existence and Hwan glanced over.

"You're awake?" he asked.

"Yes? Mostly." She sat up gingerly, regretting every inch upwards.

He picked up his phone and read off a message from Sung Soo. "I'm supposed to ask if you have any nausea, ringing in your ears, or dizziness."

Tessa ran through her body and found nothing out of the ordinary besides the pain in her head. "No."

"Good. Eun Gi doesn't either. Are you feeling well enough to eat more? Do you need ice for your foot? Do y——?"

"Hwan, shhhhh." Tessa pressed a finger to his lips, and he startled like a baby deer at the contact, though he was wedged against the corner where the couches met and had nowhere to go. Tessa withdrew her hand guiltily, and Hwan puffed out a relieved breath. "Sorry."

Her phone buzzed.

Kelly:
Checking in. How's life with the idols?

Tessa rubbed her good eye and focused on her screen.

Tessa:
I'm minorly concussed, but no broken toes

A video call rang immediately, and Kelly's face filled the screen. "Oh my God, look at you! Tess, I'm coming to get you."

"Wait, what?" She blinked sleepily.

"Why are you concussed? What happened? Why didn't anyone call me?" Her expression shifted. "They'd better not be hiding anything. Did he hurt you? I'll kill him. I swear to God I will come over there right now and put his balls in a vise."

"Shhhh. It's fine." The ferocity in Kelly's voice renewed the throbbing in Tessa's head.

"It's *not* fine. You're hurt. What happened?"

"It was an accident."

"Tess, I don't want you to feel like you have to defend him if he did something. I'm here to help you. If he hurt you, I need to know."

"I promise it was an accident. I tripped."

There was silence for a few moments. "That sounds unconvincing."

"I'm safe. It's okay. He's probably concussed too. Our heads smashed together when it happened." Tessa turned the phone to show her a still-sleeping Eun Gi with a rapidly darkening bruise on his forehead.

"You're absolutely sure you're safe?" Kelly whispered.

"Yes, I swear on everything I love, and if that changes you'll be the first person to know."

Kelly let out a breath. "Okay. Keep me posted."

"I will I promise. I love you."

"I love you too, Tess. Take care of yourself. I'm going to kick Sung Soo's ass for not telling me what's up." Kelly huffed and hung up.

"Remind me never to upset your friend." Hwan sat with wide eyes. "I have no idea what she said, but she sounds scary."

"She's worried. I always believed her when she told me she'd fight a bear for me."

"She'd win."

"No argument here."

Her bladder made itself known, vying for attention over her viciously growling stomach.

She toed slowly across the living room and relieved herself before making the delicate journey back.

Hwan nudged Eun Gi. "Wake up."

"No." Eun Gi burrowed into the couch, hissing when his forehead made contact.

Hwan rolled his eyes. "Tessa is awake."

Eun Gi peeled open an eye. "I feel like I've been run over."

"You look it too." Hwan grinned cheekily. "Hye Jin will have her work cut out for her tomorrow."

"Hwan, please. It's too early to hear her name."

"It's not early. You slept in. Are we not allowed to talk about her at all even though you're working with her?"

"I don't want to talk about it."

"You'll have to someday."

"And today is not that day. Drop it."

"Fine, keep your secrets. It's not like I'm desperate to know anyway." Hwan huffed and left them to go heat up their breakfast in the kitchen.

"That's definitely a lie." Eun Gi sat up carefully. "Gossip is your lifeblood."

"Which means you know how much you're hurting me by not telling me."

Tessa watched the exchange with a warmth in her chest that almost distracted her from her head.

"Noona—" Hwan turned to her, "—tell Eun Gi he needs to share."

"No way am I helping fill your gossip quota. My head hurts too much for information weaseling."

Hwan shook his head. "Tsk, noona. No dedication to the cause."

Chapter 9

Tessa

"Hold still."

Tessa squirmed. "I'm trying. I don't like things coming at my eye."

Eun Gi braced his hand behind Tessa's head as he carefully applied her concealer. Only a few inches of air occupied the space between them. Heat radiated from his body, and she smothered the riot of feelings jumping around inside her.

His eyes, a ring of gold at the centre fading through warm brown to almost black at the outer edge, concentrated on his work.

He examined his work closely. The hand cupping her head was gentle and intimate, and her gaze helplessly drifted to his lips. There they were. Plump. Perfect.

Tessa ordered herself to focus.

Everything about him was inviting, and dammit all, she wanted him. She'd thought about what it would be like to kiss him more times than she was willing to admit.

It would be so easy to lean forward and find out what it was actually like.

The brush swept away the purple of the bruising, helping it disappear into her golden skin. She'd packed makeup, but had only the bare basics to be used with Kelly's assistance.

Eun Gi sat back. His brows pinched together, and he picked up the brush again, applying a little more to the other half of her face. He leaned closer, and Tessa's hands shot up to rest against his chest with a soft gasp.

"You're very close."

"Sorry." He backed up immediately. "I was trying to make sure it matched."

"Does it?" Her mouth went dry, and she licked her lips.

His eyes followed her tongue's path and drifted back up. "Hmm?"

"Match?" She sat frozen.

The brush swiped against her face, and she blinked sharply, jolting back, butt sliding into the basin.

"Yes."

"The sink was wet," Tessa lamented.

"You'll dry. Let me help you out."

He looped one of her arms around his neck and scooped under her legs to hoist her up. Tessa stopped breathing until her feet hit the floor. He lifted her like she was nothing. No one *ever* lifted her like she was nothing. She was nearly six feet tall, had been so since she was sixteen, and even the best-intentioned suitors had *struggled*. Eun Gi didn't even break a sweat.

Her heart did uncomfortable things, and she stepped away, running from the intimacy and into her bedroom to change. She closed the door and whimpered pitifully to herself. Tessa picked up her phone to bother Kelly with her nonsense.

Tessa:
I'm so stupid

Kelly:
How so?

Tessa:
I want to kiss him
I almost did

Kelly:
!!!!
TELL ME EVERYTHING!

Tessa groaned and dumped herself onto the bed. Rolling over, she clutched the phone like a lifeline, typing out a frantic word vomit.

Kelly:
Tess, you're the cutest goddamn thing in existence
Of course you want to kiss him
When have you ever NOT wanted to kiss UpBeat???

She was in the middle of thinking up a response when Kelly interrupted her thoughts.

Kelly:
Besides
You're fake engaged
That doesn't mean you can't eventually be real engaged

Tessa:
You sound like my mom

Kelly:
Well we're both right.
But seriously.
Kiss him.
Do it. DO IT!

Tessa:
But that could make it weird

Kelly:
Weirder than cohabitating with a fake fiancé?

Tessa:
Fair point. BUT STILL. I'm awkward af and I can't just kiss him

Kelly:
Well then give off vibes so that he thinks about kissing you

Tessa:
I'm ending this conversation

Kelly:
BUT I LOVE YOU

Tessa:
Still ending it <3

Tessa laughed and tossed the phone aside to pick out some dry pants. By the time she emerged Eun Gi was waiting for her by the door, his own bruise carefully concealed.

Eun Gi

"Eomeoni, no!" Eun Gi sat straight up in bed, covered in a cold sweat. He buried his face in his hands. "Fuck."

Climbing out of bed, away from the sheets that were strangling him, he pulled off his damp T-shirt and shook himself. His heart thundered and the darkness enveloped him. He took the familiar route to the kitchen to get some water and then slumped onto the couch with his glass, sipping slowly to calm the cloying panic.

You're fine. You're safe in Seoul.

He shuddered, and whipped his head up when a glow illuminated under Tessa's door. Silence descended as he waited. Her shadow blocked some of the light, and the door pulled open, revealing her, sleepy-eyed and in her pajamas.

"You're awake." Her hair was fuzzy all over, and it was clear she'd been woken up by his fussing.

Good going.

When he didn't respond she crossed the living room. "Are you okay?"

"Fine," he forced out.

Tessa flicked on a lamp, and her eyes went wide. She dropped to her knees in front of him, and he jerked back as her palm came to rest on his forehead. "You're clammy. Do you have a fever?"

"I'm fine," he said again, throat tight. He leaned away from her touch, goose bumps running down his arms.

"Hold still. I'm trying to help."

"You don't need to help."

He didn't *want* to want her help.

But he did.

She was looking at him like she cared, like he mattered to her.

"What can I do?" Her palm was back on his forehead, and this time he let it rest there. "Hmm, it's a little bit better. How do you feel?"

"Tessa, I'm fine. It was a... What's the word in English? A bad dream."

"A nightmare?"

"Yeah."

It was nearly two in the morning, and he dreaded being awake all night. She shifted, and he got distracted by her eyes, which were dark and welcoming in the low light.

"Mamãe always used to let me climb into her bed when I had nightmares," Tessa told him.

Eun Gi's heart thumped. If it had been Hwan in her room he'd have joined him, gotten a fitful couple hours of sleep, and been a surly beast the next day. Going to one of the others was an option, but it was so much less embarrassing when he only had to walk across the living room rather than slinking down the hall and into another apartment in the dead of night. What would it feel like to climb into the bed while she was there, soft and warm, arms open to him?

"Not that that's helpful right now," she amended. "But if you needed to, I mean, I'm just saying, you could. I'll shut up."

"Are you offering to let me spend the night in your bed?"

Her cheeks darkened, soft lips parting. "If it would help. Do you want to talk about your nightmare?"

He shook his head. "I just want to sleep."

Tessa rose to her feet, nodding. "Okay."

She moved like a robot, muscles taut.

"I can sleep in my own bed. You don't have to put yourself out for me."

"No." Her mouth snapped shut, and she blushed even harder before speaking again. "It's fine. I promise."

Finishing off his water, he followed her into her room. He hadn't been in it since Hwan moved out. Tessa climbed into bed, keeping near the edge to leave more room for him.

Eun Gi lay rigid, no matter how he willed his body to relax.

"What can I do?" Her voice was low and smooth. Soothing.

He shrugged.

Her hand settled on the bed between them. "Is it okay if I touch you?"

Sweat prickled his scalp, and his throat burned. The tension of his body pulled him taut as a bowstring. He lay frozen. The nod was almost imperceptible, but she noticed. Her palm settled atop his closed fist, and she brushed her thumb in soft strokes against his skin. The lingering adrenaline pounded like a drumbeat through him and the constricting pain that locked up his chest released bit by bit, subtle and slow until it no longer hurt to breathe.

"Permission to hug?" She opened her arms, an invitation that sent his heart into a fresh panic.

The compulsion to lean towards comfort clashed with the desire to withdraw, rendering him immobile. A flood of memory, of the warmth he'd found once before in her arms, rushed over him, and he let the heat of it tip him towards her.

Fuck it.

Her arms wrapped around him, a tender cocoon as he nestled into her embrace. His head rested under her chin, and he draped an arm over her waist, fingers curling into her pajamas. A tentative hand brushed over his hair, rubbing tiny circles on his scalp until his body finally relaxed.

Eun Gi woke disoriented. Tessa was fast asleep on her back, and he was sprawled over her, legs entangled, arm slung across her. Embarrassment burned his cheeks. Maybe he could slither off the bed and make it across the living room to his own bed without waking her so he could pretend last night hadn't happened.

She shifted and sighed contentedly under him. Eun Gi moved with all the stealth he could manage, lifting his leg and arm, rolling over to slink off the bed. After crawling like a criminal across the floor, he took off running the moment he was out of sight of her door. He dashed down the external hall to the other apartment, punching in the door code before hurling himself inside and directly into Sung Soo's room.

"Hyung! Wake up." Eun Gi launched into the bed like a rocket, jolting Sung Soo awake.

"Eun Gi? What the hell? What's going on?"

"I slept with Tessa!"

"You— Wait, what? You *slept* with Tessa?"

Eun Gi buried his face in the blankets. "Sleep, not sex, but yes."

Sung Soo huffed out a sigh of relief before picking up his pillow and walloping Eun Gi with it. "You brat. You scared me."

"What's going on?" Hwan asked as he shuffled into the bedroom, trailed by Min Jae.

"Eun Gi's giving me a heart attack before breakfast."

Min Jae flopped down right on top of Eun Gi, squishing him into the bed. "Hyung, why are you here? Not that I mind you being here, but it's so early."

"He slept with Tessa," Sung Soo supplied.

"*Excuse me?*" Hwan's eyes snapped to full alertness. "I thought you didn't even like her."

"Not like that." Sung Soo grinned. "I just needed someone else to feel that same panic."

"I had a nightmare, and you weren't there." Eun Gi's voice was muffled by the blankets.

"Ah." Hwan sat down next to the pile. "Are you okay?"

Eun Gi wriggled Min Jae off and lifted his head. "I guess. I mean, it was a little bit weird and I don't think she knew what to do with me, but it was...nice?"

"I'm glad you have someone else you can rely on when we're not around," Sung Soo said.

"You make me sound like a baby," Eun Gi protested.

Min Jae curled around Eun Gi, using a stolen pillow to prop himself.

"You're not a baby," Sung Soo assured. "Everyone needs comfort. I'm glad you have somewhere to turn. How did she react?"

Eun Gi settled into Min Jae's embrace. "Pretty well. She just held me once we actually got into the bed."

"And this morning?" Hwan asked.

Eun Gi blushed hard. "I don't know. I left before she woke up."

A chorus of protests erupted, followed immediately by Eun Gi being dog-piled.

"You idiot," Sung Soo admonished. "You can't bail on her like that. Get back to the apartment."

They collectively shoved him out of the bed until he landed with a squawk on the floor.

"Please don't make me go back. I'm awkward, and I'm bad at dealing with these things."

"Go." Sung Soo pointed to the door, and Eun Gi moped his way through it.

Tessa was still asleep when he arrived, and he thanked the universe for small miracles. He set the kettle to boil and prepared her some chrysanthemum tea from the stash he'd stolen from Sung Soo. The steeper hung cheerfully on the cup's edge, and he carried it to the bedroom, setting it on her bedside table.

The sound of the cup woke her. She blinked sleepily, and her cheeks flushed a charming shade of pink when she caught sight of him. "Good morning."

"Good morning." Heat warmed his face, and he hovered awkwardly. "I'm going to go shower."

Tessa

Tessa got dressed and took her tea into the living room. The front door opened, and the others flooded inside. She'd slept pretty well, all things considered, and felt reasonably awake to tackle Korean conversation first thing in the morning. Hwan parked himself right next to her.

"So," Hwan said.

"So?" Tessa blinked rapidly.

"How was last night?" He sipped at the coffee he'd brought with him.

She cringed, her cheeks warming, and she took a gulp of her tea to avoid answering. It scalded her tongue.

"It was...fine?"

"Hyung is the best nap partner," Min Jae commented. "He doesn't kick like Hwan or snore like Sung Soo."

Tessa struggled to maintain any form of eye contact.

"I'm not teasing you," Hwan said. "I genuinely want to know. If you were uncomfortable with what happened, then we can find an alternative, because his dreams aren't uncommon."

Tessa stared at the pale gold liquid in her cup, unable to meet his gaze. "I don't mind."

Sung Soo nodded. "If you change your mind just say the word. Okay?"

The eldest went off to start breakfast preparations. Min Jae and Hwan both looked far too inquisitive for her comfort.

"Noona," said Min Jae, "do you like Hyung?"

Hwan flicked Min Jae's ear. "Do you have zero experience talking to other humans?"

"Ow! I'm curious. Why aren't I allowed to ask?"

"You're allowed to ask, but she doesn't have to answer." Hwan turned to Tessa. "Don't answer that."

"Wasn't going to." Tessa took another sip of her tea.

A gleam flashed in Hwan's eyes. "That's not fair, now I want to know too. I was being gallant."

Sung Soo laughed from the kitchen. "Leave Tessa alone."

Eun Gi was taking his sweet time with his shower and morning prep, while she had to fend off the vultures.

"Noona." Hwan turned puppy dog eyes on her. "Please, I live for information. Give me this knowledge as a gift."

Min Jae and Hwan crowded her and Sung Soo hauled out the spray bottle from under the sink, firing shots. He nailed both boys in the back of the head.

"Hyung! I'm all wet now," Min Jae complained.

"I told you to leave her alone. Now, set the table for breakfast, and then you can bother Eun Gi when he gets out of the shower."

Tessa

Tessa had been dreading going to set. Ha Yun had mentioned wedding plans, and the whole thing set her on edge. She contemplated staying home, but that would be rude, and she didn't want Eun Gi to get in trouble for letting her stay behind.

Ha Yun zeroed in on her the moment she arrived. "Tessa-ssi. Have you had a chance to review the documents we sent you?"

"My lawyer checked over them, but I still have to read them once more."

"Please sign and return them at your earliest convenience." Ha Yun said. "The *sooner* the better."

"Of course."

"We need to be assured of everyone's protection so when we file the divorce after the drama's run ends there will be no barriers to separation."

"Leave her be, and let us work on the wedding." A middle-aged woman in a perfectly tailored blue dress approached. "Lovely to meet you. I'm Jeung Yuna, 24/7's stylist."

Another woman joined them, equally poised in a grey skirt suit. "And I'm Oh Mi Na. I'm the wedding coordinator for this event."

Tessa nodded a brief bow to each. "Nice to meet you."

"Come with us." Yuna shuffled her over to a table with three chairs.

"What are your thoughts?" Mi Na asked. "We propose a Western gown for the modern ceremony and a hanbok for the traditional Korean ceremony."

"Sure, that sounds fine. When should my parents come?"

"We're planning for April first," Mi Na said. "They're welcome to come at any point, but we'll only be covering their hotel for three days — before, during, and after the wedding. We'll also pay for two economy flights. If they wish to travel beyond that it will be their responsibility, as well as any other costs incurred during their stay."

Tessa passed on the information to her parents via text.

"What are your colour preferences?"

"Red is my favourite, but I can be flexible."

"Red is perfect for the hanbok. I think we'd like you in a more delicate colour for the gown." Yuna passed over a giant book filled with swatches of fabric. "Soft pink will be nice with your complexion, and won't draw too much attention."

"Isn't the point of the bride to draw attention?"

Mi Na waved her hand dismissively. "Trust us. Do you care about any particular styles, or do you want to leave it up to Yuna?"

"Do I *need* a stylist?"

Yuna's brows pinched. "Of course you do. You're marrying an idol and you're expected to look the part no matter what circumstances prompted the union."

"Right." Tessa wilted.

This wasn't an ordinary marriage, and even though she knew that, it still jolted her a little each time it came up. She sat with Mi Na and Yuna for a couple hours to go over fabrics, colours, flowers, and hairstyles. It would be small in comparison to any other wedding Tessa had attended. Parents were invited, and the other members of 24/7, plus Kelly would be present, but beyond that there would be few guests. There would be no dance, and only a short meal during the brief reception. Nothing else besides the ceremony. They only needed the photos, and then everyone would be sent on their way.

She was giving up her first wedding to be a half-assed project to appease the press. Every time the thought passed through her head, she had to pause and remind herself why she was doing this: Protect Eun Gi. Protect 24/7.

None of this was about her.

Tessa's phone buzzed, and she opened up Kelly's message while the stylist was debating pearls versus diamonds with the costume designer.

Kelly:
Are you still coming to dinner tonight? Joo's mom is excited :D

Tessa:
Absolutely
I'll head over as soon as I'm finished here

Kelly:
Is Eun Gi coming?

Tessa:

144

I don't know. I haven't asked. Should I?

Kelly:
Maybe
It might be weird if you show up without your fiancé

Tessa:
K. I'll ask

Three hours later Tessa was welcomed into the home of Min Joo's parents. She'd picked up a bouquet of sunflowers on her way to Kelly's apartment and handed them over to Min Joo's mother. So Mang's hair was curled softly and pinned back, complementing her round cheeks.

"Tessa-ya! How lovely to meet you again. Come in, come in. The meal will be ready shortly."

"Eomma." Min Joo greeted her with a kiss on the cheek, and she smiled like he'd handed her a million dollars. The three of them filtered into the beautiful hanok-style home. Min Joo's parents owned two of these ancient structures. One served as their home, and the other functioned as a bed-and-breakfast for tourists staying in the heart of the old district. The interiors were modernized for convenience, but the outside retained the shadows of ages past.

"Tessa-ya, where's your husband-to-be?" So Mang asked.

"Oh, he's running a bit late. They needed him longer on set than they needed me."

"Of course, dear." So Mang shuffled back to the kitchen, leaving the three of them in the doorway.

"Pyong Ho is coming for dinner too." Kelly held up a hand to stem Tessa's protest. "It's not because you're here. Pyong Ho doesn't have family nearby, and So Mang likes to invite all our wayward friends. She hasn't seen him for ages and told us to bring him over."

145

Tessa stared at her with wide eyes.

"Don't give me that look. You had two opportunities before this to deal with him. He's basically an adopted brother for me, and as much as I love you, I'm not letting you leave him hanging cuz you're being a chicken."

The doorbell buzzed, and So Mang bustled past them. "Pyong Ho-ya! Come in, we're almost ready to sit down."

Tessa stealthily slipped around the corner before he saw her. Min Joo's father was in the kitchen stirring a pan that smelled sinfully delicious. Tessa went to lean on the counter and greet Chang Mun whom she'd also met at the wedding a couple years ago.

"Hale Tessa, we thought you'd never get to Seoul. Welcome to our home." He grinned, a wide, toothy smile that made her feel instantly like family.

"Tessa-ya, have you met Pyong Ho?" So Mang asked as she joined them in the kitchen.

His cheeks coloured when they made eye contact.

"Yes, we went for dinner."

So Mang nodded and turned to her son. "Min Joo, please set the table while your father and I finish cooking."

"Can I help?" Tessa asked.

So Mang patted her cheek and set about depositing food across the table. "So sweet to offer, but we have everything under control."

Tessa gathered her courage. "Pyong Ho, could I talk to you in private?"

"Of course." He led her out to the courtyard where they were protected from the breeze, and away from the steaming heat of the kitchen.

Pyong Ho chewed his lip. "You stopped responding to my messages."

"I know. I'm sorry. Things have been weird lately, and I had no idea what to say. I should have though. You don't deserve to be blown off."

"I'm not upset for me. Noona's been a little strung out lately, and I worry about her worrying about you. I just wanted to make sure you were okay."

"I bet I strung her out extra when I kept avoiding talking to you. I'll do better." Tessa swallowed hard. "I'm not sure what to do now."

"What do you mean?"

"Well, we met for a date. I didn't think you'd want to be friends instead."

He shrugged. "It's not what I was aiming for when we met, but things have changed. You're in a relationship, as confusing as that is to me given how we met."

Tessa puffed up her cheeks. "Yeah, about that. I'm not under an NDA yet, but please, please don't say anything." She spilled out the entire story, every detail flooding out of her mouth until at last she ran out of information.

Pyong Ho stared wide-eyed. "Well…that's not what I expected."

"I know!" Tessa sank down onto one of the decorative benches. "And it sucks, because you're great, and I did have a wonderful time on our date, but it's way too complicated and then the company rolls up and it's like, fuck me, I guess?"

Pyong Ho sat down next to her. "I'm sorry you're stuck in all that. I'm going to look at your fiancé really weird now, but I promise I won't say a word. Is he treating you well?"

"Yeah, he's doing his best, and he's been very sweet. The others are great too. It's just a lot to adapt to."

He nodded. "Reach out if you need anything, okay? I know you have other people you can rely on here, but please consider me one of them."

The doorbell rang, and Tessa froze. They were only expecting one more guest.

"That'll be him. We should get back inside. Thank you for everything."

"It's no problem."

So Mang was already at the door when they got inside, and everyone else was crowded around to see. So Mang turned red as a beet when she swung it open and caught sight of who was on the other side. She dipped into a bow.

"Baek Eun Gi-ssi, welcome."

He bowed smoothly and handed her a bottle of *makgeolli*. "Thank you for your hospitality, *Ajumma*. I'm honoured to be in your home." He flashed a perfect smile, and then caught sight of Tessa and Pyong Ho walking down the hall together towards him. Eun Gi leaned through the crowd, and kissed Tessa's cheek. "I missed you."

Tessa's heart stuttered. *Just acting. It's not real.*

She glanced briefly back at Pyong Ho but didn't see what his reaction was before her attention was distracted again.

"Come in, come in!" So Mang recovered herself and ushered them farther inside, hooking her arm through Eun Gi's.

Eun Gi smiled brightly, obviously used to people reacting like this. "Please forgive my lateness. I was needed on set."

"Of course you were, no need to apologize," So Mang gushed and waved her hand at her husband who was already sitting. "Come, sit here by me. Chang Mun, scoot over."

Min Joo snickered. "Eomma, he should sit by Tessa."

"Baek Eun Gi-ssi, you'll indulge a mother, won't you?" So Mang asked.

Eun Gi looked to Tessa, who directed him back to Min Joo's exuberant mother. "Nothing would make me happier, Ajumma."

They crowded around the large table with a truly impressive array of dishes spread across it. Eun Gi was the picture of charm through the evening despite several of the guests unabashedly staring at him. He handled the invasive questions with poise and a smile, and when people asked about the wedding and Tessa slipped into blank-eyed terror, he handled that too. His powers of deflection were mind-boggling, and not a single person protested when he turned things around to inquire about them instead, keeping his privacy safely preserved.

Tessa was in awe. She hated being the centre of attention and was infinitely grateful that he was the more interesting one to the group so she got to avoid most of it.

They tucked into the makgeolli Eun Gi had brought, and both Min Joo's parents indulged heartily. They ended the meal with plates of fresh almond cookies and drinks passed around the table. So Mang laughed often, her fingertips constantly brushing Eun Gi's hand whenever it rested on the table. Tessa couldn't help her quiet laughter over how obvious So Mang's idol worship was. It was quickly revealed that she could name every album by 24/7, which was a shock to her son and a delight to her guests.

After they finished off the bottle Kelly tapped her husband's arm. "It's getting late. Should we head home?"

So Mang's smile dropped. "You're all welcome to stay the night. We have room."

"Eomma," said Min Joo, "the dinner was magnificent, but everyone needs to work tomorrow."

So Mang pouted her lip. Her husband laughed and patted her shoulder. Eun Gi indulged her with a kiss on the cheek before they left, and So Mang looked as if she could have ascended into heaven in that moment. Tessa didn't blame her one bit.

Eun Gi and Tessa were the first ones to leave. She slipped into the passenger side, and Eun Gi melted into the driver's seat.

"They loved you."

"Everyone loves UpBeat. That's kind of the point of the persona." He dropped his head back against the seat and closed his eyes. "I'm tired. I don't usually have to do that so late into the day."

"People love Eun Gi too," she said softly.

He rolled his head to face her. "I'm sorry if I overstepped with that kiss."

"Oh." Tessa's cheeks burned. "No, it was fine. We're supposed to be engaged after all."

"Even so, I don't want to feel entitled to anything from you because of the situation. I want you to be comfortable. We're in this together, right? Partners?"

Her whole body warmed, heart fluttering happily. She smiled. "Yes. Partners."

Chapter 10

Eun Gi

Eun Gi stuffed down his pride and climbed into her bed during the wee hours of the night for the fourth time that week. Tessa rolled over, bleary eyed.

"Why don't you just stay in here to begin with?"

"I don't want to intrude." His reply was soft, barely interrupting the quiet of the early morning.

"Eun Gi." She nestled closer to him as he settled. "You've never been an intrusion to me so don't think you'll start now. If you need me, I'm here."

The warmth was inviting, and he leaned into her touch, sighing against her body. She tucked him against her so his head rested in the curve of her throat, arm looped over her waist. Her fingers stilled in his hair, and her breathing became long and smooth as she fell asleep against him.

He toyed with the satin of her pajama top, feeling the gentle rise and fall of her chest. He'd been anticipating an awkward and reluctant roommate for a year, and instead he was met with someone who offered a haven.

Safe.

He snuggled closer. Frayed edges of the nightmare still clung to his fading thoughts. The happenings of the dreams weren't always the same, but he was always terrified, and he could *feel* danger everywhere. Every monster of his nightmares coalesced into gut-deep terror whenever he saw his mother's face. There was no escape until his frantic heart jolted him awake.

Tessa let out a squeak and opened her eyes. He hadn't realized he was squeezing her.

"It's okay," she murmured. "You're safe."

Her fingers brushed his cheek, pressing him closer.

Things were going far too well for either of them to back out of the upcoming arrangement, which meant in a month they'd be legally bound for a year. Not that long ago he'd wanted nothing more than to be married. That hadn't panned out and he'd accepted being a bachelor until his career tapered off, blunted by the compulsory military service and his growing despondency.

He laid there a long time, listening to the soothing lull of her heartbeat in his ear. At some point he fell asleep, waking in the morning to a knock on the door.

"Eun Gi-hyung, I think you slept through your alarm. Sung Soo says you're late for breakfast."

The words slipped through the sleep haze, but he only moved closer to Tessa, soaking in the warmth of her.

"Hyung." Min Jae cracked open Tessa's door. "You weren't in your room, so I thought you might be here, and I was right."

The maknae pushed them both over until Tessa almost fell off the bed and then flopped down next to Eun Gi. His hold on her waist kept her from tipping off the edge.

"Good morning, Noona."

Tessa sat up carefully, trying to avoid squishing Eun Gi. "Min Jae, why are you in my bed?"

"Hyung's allowed in," he protested.

"He was invited."

Min Jae turned wide eyes on her, his puppy dog expression beaming at her. "Does that mean you don't want me here?"

Eun Gi intervened, pinching Min Jae's waist, sending the maknae shooting off the bed.

"Hyung! We agreed not to touch the tickle spot anymore! I don't like it."

"And Tessa doesn't like unruly men rolling around in her bed," Eun Gi countered. "Personal boundaries exist, Jae. Learn them. Obey them."

"Noona, what are your boundaries?" Min Jae propped his chin on the bed from his spot on the floor.

"Can I be awake more than two minutes before I give you a list?" Tessa laid back down and pulled the blanket up to her chin. "Let's start with not jumping on my bed in the mornings."

A piece of hair fell across her forehead as she settled down. Eun Gi brushed it back, fingertips lingering over the silken strands like it was the most natural gesture in the world. He jerked back his hand, but she didn't open her eyes, already caught in a half-sleep. Min Jae, however, was giving him a knowing smile.

"Are you on set today?" Eun Gi steadfastly ignored the maknae, setting a gentle hand on Tessa's shoulder to rouse her enough to answer.

She shook her head and snuggled in a little more. "They only need me there to look pretty next to you, and I can do that on Monday."

Envy warmed his blood. He'd have happily burrowed back under himself if work wasn't dragging him away. Too few hours of sleep had elapsed, and he wasn't at all happy to be awake, but none of his day would wait for him.

"I'll make sure they save you some breakfast." He peeled himself away.

Getting too comfortable was a bad idea. Eun Gi reminded himself yet again to not get invested. She was only doing all of this to be nice, and he wasn't stupid enough to think otherwise.

He sent Min Jae on his way and slipped off to the bathroom to get ready for the day. His brain was altogether unhelpful with keeping inappropriate intrusive thoughts at bay. It kept wandering back to the soft warmth he'd been curled around all night. His forehead settled against the tile while he indulged, allowing his mind to summon her image, letting his hand distract him. The sharp edge of pleasure was blunted by his guilt and frustration.

By the time he emerged, he was well on his way to cranky. The others were busy eating when he arrived, and he tucked into his bowl in silence.

"Hyung is moody this morning," Min Jae announced.

"I am not," he snapped.

Sung Soo raised an eyebrow. "That's a very believable impression of not moody."

"I interrupted his cuddling."

Eun Gi rolled his eyes.

"Jae, you were only supposed to wake him up. Why did you have to get involved?" Sung Soo asked.

"Don't even pretend you didn't pick me to go over because you *knew* I'd get involved."

Eun Gi glared at Sung Soo, his eyes smoldering with betrayal. "Hyung?"

"Hey now, let's not get into a fight over breakfast. Hwan was in the shower, so Jae was the only one available to send. He'd have burned the food if I left him here."

Eun Gi's sour mood followed him to work, which turned out to be rather helpful since they were filming the altercation between Lee Do Yun and his parents over his desire to marry Bridie. As parents in many stories had done through the ages, they rejected the notion of their son marrying for love, especially when the girl in question was a foreigner with no family, no connections, and nothing to offer them. And, like many children in those stories, Lee Do Yun gave his parents the choice of gaining a daughter or losing a son. Eun Gi slipped into the role easily, allowing his anger and frustration to guide him, until he was no longer certain whether he was truly acting anymore. His jaw ached from his grinding teeth, and his shoulders were stiff with a tension that wouldn't release.

By the end of the day Eun Gi was worn out, repeating his uncomfortable emotions until the director got what he wanted. He'd exhausted his temper but still didn't feel right. Everything had felt off since he'd been rudely awakened. His cramping stomach begged for food, but he didn't feel like stopping anywhere, or facing the others to get whatever they'd put together.

This is so stupid.

Eun Gi sighed.

There's no reason to be in a mood.

24/7 was on the radio when he slipped into the car. He snapped the volume off.

Knowing it was stupid did nothing to alleviate it. In his younger days he'd have worn down his darker emotions by getting blackout drunk and waking up wishing his head would roll of his shoulders. He didn't want to do that though, didn't want to be that person who lapsed into self-destructive behaviour. Things had been getting better. The last time he'd drowned his sorrows in soju had been a few months ago after Ju Won and Jin had entered the military. His world had been collapsing around him, and he'd ended up in the hospital over it. The company told the media it was food poisoning.

Lack of control had always been a sore spot for him. He'd gone straight from an abusive home into an industry that had him running on a wheel like a trained animal. When it got too much he'd hurl himself in any direction to try to get off it. He hated himself when he did that and knew it wasn't healthy. Those blind, desperate grasps for control of *something* ended terribly every time.

Eun Gi pulled into the underground parking of their building and sat in the stall with his head on the steering wheel. In just over two weeks he was marrying a woman he hardly knew for the sake of his career. The complicated emotions surrounding that reality were an itch under his skin he couldn't reach. Ultimately, no matter how kind and understanding Tessa was, they were both being coerced.

If he were less of a coward, he could say no.

It wasn't the idea of losing his career that terrified him. What froze him to the bone was the realization that he would also lose his found family. They had come together because of shared goals, their hours of blood, sweat, and tears poured into the treacherous path to fame. What would happen to them if he was no longer a part of it? How long would it take to fade away? Until he was left alone.

Eun Gi gripped the steering wheel like a lifeline. He forced a deep breath through his aching throat. His eyes burned, and every muscle felt poised to snap at the slightest movement.

He didn't feel like he deserved to contact anyone.

Eun Gi sat and stewed until the cramping of his empty stomach began to hurt more than everything else and he was compelled to go upstairs. The others would worry if he took too long and already messages had popped up on his phone asking when he'd be home. He grimaced and left them unanswered.

Tessa

"There you a—" Tessa broke off as Eun Gi came through the door. Her heart dropped to her toes. "What happened?"

Eun Gi shook his head as she stepped toward him. He flung his shoes off his feet and beelined to his room. The door swung shut behind him, leaving Tessa frozen and staring after him.

She grabbed her phone and sent a message to Sung Soo.

Tessa:
Eun Gi is home. Something's wrong.
Please come over.

There was a knock a moment later. The boys filed in, and Sung Soo went straight to Eun Gi's door, knocking softly.

"What happened?" Min Jae asked Tessa.

"I don't know. He didn't say a word."

Hwan puffed out his cheeks. "I was hoping this wouldn't happen again."

"Again?"

"Eun Gi isn't great at recognizing when he's stressed. It compounds on him until he cracks over the tiniest thing. Honestly, we should have been on guard when all of this started." Hwan sighed. "He was doing so well."

Tessa's stomach twisted. "What can I do?"

Min Jae hooked an arm around her shoulders. "We usually just make sure he doesn't do anything stupid."

The three of them sat on the couch while Sung Soo disappeared into the room. Min Jae put on the TV, but none of them paid attention to it. Tessa wrung her hands, the voice of the newscaster blurring into the background. Her phone pinged about half an hour later, and she dropped it in her haste to see what was sent.

Sung Soo:
He hasn't had anything to eat or drink for hours. Can you find something for him?

Tessa and the boys fussed in the kitchen, settling on a *kimbap* stuffed with a random assortment from the fridge. Min Jae picked out banana milk to go along with it.

She tapped on the door with her foot and Sung Soo ushered her in, leaving her with Eun Gi. He was curled miserably around his pillow, eyes red-rimmed and uncomfortably blank as they stared past her.

She set down the food on the side table and got down to her knees. "Can I help?"

"Why are you here?"

She paused, unsure how to respond. "To help you."

"Why?" The word was so soft she barely heard it.

"I don't understand."

"Why do you care?" he continued. "It doesn't make sense."

"You're important to me. Why wouldn't I care?"

Eun Gi sat up, and she toppled backwards.

"You're giving up a year of your life. You've moved in with a stranger. You're putting yourself under scrutiny from the press. All for my sake. You're even giving up your first real wedding. You can't be happy about that."

"Well, it's not ideal—"

"Didn't you get mad?"

"Eun Gi, what do you want me to say? Do you want me to be upset?"

He let out a sound of frustration and curled his knees up to his chest. "No. I just don't want to be the only one who feels this way. You don't deserve to be trapped. You should be living your life and marrying someone you love. Not me."

She set a hand on his arm. He didn't pull away.

"I need you to trust that I don't resent you for what we're going through. We have to make the best of it."

He opened his mouth, but Tessa held up a hand for silence.

"I meant what I said. We're in this together and we can talk, but first you need to eat."

She parked herself on the bed, forcing him to scoot over. He took a few reluctant bites but then devoured it with ravenous hunger. The banana milk was consumed at a much more sedate pace.

The silence was heavy, words sitting on the tip of her tongue, waiting for release.

"You're sure you want to know why?"

He glanced up, eyes wide and curious, then nodded.

"Eun Gi." She paused to collect herself. "I owe my life to 24/7. I know it sounds overdramatic, but when I first heard your music I was not in a good place."

Tessa dropped her gaze, fidgeting with the sheets.

"I was nineteen, and Halmeoni had recently passed after a long battle with breast cancer. Appa was devastated. He'd already lost his dad, and then his eomma was gone too. She was a huge part of my life. She was there when I got home from school, taught me to cook, to speak Korean, and I struggled so much with losing her. Kelly had moved to Seoul recently too, and I wasn't good at coping. Technology wasn't the way it is now. It wasn't so easy to keep in contact with her, and I missed her so much. Then Halmeoni was gone, and I wondered if maybe it would be better if I was too."

Eun Gi made a sound of protest, and she realized she was sniffling. He opened his mouth to speak, but she held up her hand for silence.

"Kelly sent me your album that year for my birthday, and it connected somehow. She'd picked it out just for me, and it came from Halmeoni's homeland. I listened to it so often that I learned every word by heart. It made me feel less alone and gave me something happier to focus on. I know it's stupid. You weren't actually reaching out to *me* with the lyrics you sang, but it still felt that way."

He took her hand and squeezed gently. "I'm sorry you went through that."

"Thank you." She rubbed at her watery eyes. "You're being punished because you helped me when I was vulnerable. You took care of me when you didn't have to, and I'm never going to forget that. I might have freaked out when all of this was suggested, but there was no way I would turn my back on you. You were there when I needed you, now I'm here when you need me."

Eun Gi pulled her closer so he could loop his arm over her shoulders.

Tessa curled towards him. She hadn't meant to expose her history, but it felt good, or at least better, to have told him.

"We do write *for* people. We might not know their names or their faces or their stories, but I always thought the point of our music was to make a connection."

She nodded. He was so warm. She'd never told Kelly how hard it was for her when she'd moved away, hadn't wanted to put that burden on her. Kelly would have come home, and then she might never have gone back.

Silence stretched between them again.

"Would you rather I withdraw? I could tell the company that I changed my mind about the marriage and go back to Canada."

He tensed. "I don't want you to leave. I just..."

"It's okay to have mixed feelings. I have them too. You don't have to know how to deal with everything all the time. You have a devoted support system, and they love you. If you want to, consider me a part of it too. If you don't want to, or you don't know yet, that's okay too." She settled in, leaning her weight against him. "I'm sorry this is all so weird."

Eun Gi sighed. "It's not your fault."

A slow pulsing beat throbbed at the base of her skull, and the edge of her vision wavered. She didn't want to move, but she needed to. "I have to go grab my painkillers."

"Migraine?"

"Yep."

"Is that my fault?"

"Don't blame yourself for my body being uncooperative. It's treatable." She climbed off the bed. "Do you want me to come back?"

He hesitated and then nodded. "You can tell them I'll be okay. They can go to bed."

Tessa slipped into the living room, and three hopeful faces perked up.

"How is he?" Hwan asked.

"Better, I think. He says to send you all to bed."

Min Jae pouted. "Maybe I should stay with him."

Sung Soo pulled him toward the door. "Tessa can handle things. She'll let us know if they need anything, right, Tessa?"

"Of course."

Hwan snared her into an unexpected hug. "We're just down the hall. He gets kind of fragile when he's like this. Be gentle, okay?"

"I'll do my best."

Sung Soo paused before leaving. "Are *you* okay? We're here for you too, if you need us."

Her chest warmed. "Thank you. I'll be fine. I think we're going to sleep."

When they left she dosed herself with her painkillers and took a glass of water to Eun Gi before changing into her pajamas. Eun Gi had changed as well and moved over onto his side to make more room for her.

She laid flat, pressing a palm to her head.

He reached towards her, stopping a few inches shy. "Can I?"

"Yes," she whispered, and sighed contentedly as his arm draped over her stomach. Tessa turned over, and he nestled in, his breath tickling the back of her neck.

His arm squeezed her suddenly, firm but gentle. "Thank you."

Drowsiness crept through her, and she slipped away with him wrapped around her.

In the morning he was still there. Rolling over, mindful of her tender head, she tucked deeper into the blankets and under his chin. She wiggled around, getting comfortable in her new position, fingers latching on to his shirt.

"Hye Jin, quit squirming," Eun Gi mumbled.

Tessa pushed against him. "I am *not* Hye Jin."

He blinked sleepily. "What?"

"You called me Hye Jin."

"No I didn't." He sat up, rubbing his eyes.

"Eun Gi, you did." Tessa sat up and her expression hardened. "Would you rather it was her here?"

"No. I don't want her, I just—"

"Do you still love her?" She cringed, wishing the words back into her mouth.

He groaned and slithered back down to the mattress. "I don't think so. I don't like to talk about it much."

Well, that makes two of us.

"I'm not comfortable becoming your wife, fake or not, if you're in love with someone."

"Even if I was, she's not interested in anything."

Tessa frowned. "That's not the point."

"I know." Eun Gi pulled the blanket over his head. "I'm terrible at confronting this and I've managed to avoid the topic since we broke up."

"Why?"

"Please. It's embarrassing." He poked his face out of the blankets. "Didn't you ever have a relationship you didn't want to discuss?"

"Not really. I've only had one long-term relationship, and that ended when we graduated and she moved back home. Otherwise it was occasional dates, but nothing lasted very long."

"She?"

"Mhmm." Tessa reached for her phone and brought up a picture of a beautiful woman with deep umber skin and a halo of black curls. She held a baby in her arms, and both were grinning brightly. "This is Selena and her daughter Minnie."

She flipped through the online albums and found another picture, of Selena and an equally gorgeous woman with black twists down to her waist, both in white gowns. "This is her wedding to Kendra three years ago. We still talk once in a while, but I haven't actually seen her since graduation. I'm happy to talk about any of it if you're curious."

He was quiet a long moment, ruminating. "What about men?"

"What about them?"

"Do you like them too? Or just women?"

"Both, but I like any gender. I've had quite a few crushes, but I didn't pursue many because I don't enjoy dating in general."

Eun Gi squirmed.

"Is something wrong?" Tessa asked.

"No." He shook his head. "We tend not to talk about those things here. Lots of people pretend it doesn't exist."

"I noticed that."

"Is it easier to be open about that where you're from?"

"I think so. I mean, same-sex marriage has been legal for well over a decade, so it's nothing new, but there'll always be bigots." Tessa took in the pink flush of his cheeks. "Are you okay?"

He nodded and avoided eye contact.

"Eun Gi?"

"You can't say anything, okay?" He squeezed the blankets, and his knuckles turned white.

"Of course."

"I might be like you."

"Like me how?"

He groaned, burying his face in his hands. "Learn to read minds."

"Sorry." She burst into laughter. "Telepathy isn't one of my superpowers. Do you want me to try guessing?"

He made a vague, distressed sound that she took as agreement.

"Eun Gi, do you like men?"

His whole face flushed and he muttered, "Not just."

"Thank you for telling me." She nestled next to him and waited for him to speak, but he remained silent, hiding behind his hands. There was a slight tremor in his arms, and she settled her fingertips against his wrist. "Do you want to talk about it more?"

"No." He paused. "Yes. I don't know. I'm not the only one in the industry, or even the only one in the group, but it's still strange. It's so hard for any of us to be open about anything, so I've never gotten used to talking about it."

"Can I ask, do you have a history with men? Or have you never pursued?"

Eun Gi rolled face-first into the pillow and said something against the fabric.

"What?" She leaned closer.

"Hwan was my first kiss."

Tessa set a hand on his shoulder. "Are you embarrassed by that? Hwan's awesome."

His head popped up. "No, I mean, not exactly." His cheeks burned a steady hot pink.

"Kelly was mine. We were fourteen, at a weekend camp, and it was during truth or dare." She laughed and settled comfortably, turning towards him. "Friends are a safe place to experiment if you have the inclination to. I have to ask though, are you and Hwan a current thing?"

"We're not together, no." His head thwumped back against the pillow.

"Okay, good. Marrying you would be a little awkward if you were." She smoothed a hand over his hair. "As much as I'd love to keep talking, if you don't shower and eat, you'll be late to set."

He tilted his head and looked at her thoughtfully. "You don't think I'm weird?"

"What kind of hypocrite do you think I am? I support you and whoever you love."

Eun Gi laughed, relieved. "Thank you. You're the best fake future wife."

Tessa's heart swelled.

Maybe this would all be okay.

Chapter 11

Tessa

The phone buzzed frantically, puncturing the darkness with its glowing screen. Tessa blinked bleary eyes and yawned, reaching to answer it before Eun Gi woke.

"Hello?"

"Meu amor, I didn't mean to wake you." The slight tremble in her mother's voice had Tessa sitting up at full attention.

"What's wrong?"

A shuddering breath greeted her. Tessa climbed out of bed and moved into the living room, flicking on one of the lamps.

"Mamãe, you're freaking me out."

"I'm sorry. I'm a little worked up."

Tessa waited in agonizing silence for her mother to continue.

"Appa's in the hospital."

Tessa's stomach dropped, and she sank onto the couch. "What happened?"

"We were trying out a new medication to see if it might help, and he ended up having a bad reaction to it. He got woozy and fell down a few stairs. I'm at the hospital with him right now. They took him into surgery after finding a fracture on his hip."

Tessa's throat constricted. "I'm coming home."

"Meu amor, you don't have to. I didn't mean to worry you, I just, you're always the one I call." Her mother let out a quiet sound of distress.

"I want you to be able to call whenever you need me." A tremble crept into her lips, and she pressed her fingers against them to still it.

Her mother started crying then, a thank you pushed out somewhere amid the sobs.

"Mamãe, I love you." Tessa flipped open her laptop, squinting into the glaring light as she brought up the airline website.

"I love you too."

"I can be home tomorrow morning. The next flight out isn't until around dinner. I'll take a cab to the hospital as soon as I arrive."

"I'll text you the address. What time is it where you are?"

"Hmm." Tessa glanced at the laptop clock. "Not quite five in the morning."

"You should go back to sleep."

"I will." Instead, she got her mother to talk about every mundane topic and update she could think of until Tessa was assured she'd been able to relax a little. Her mother's voice was steadier by the time the conversation rolled to its end. "I'll see you soon. Give Appa my love."

"Always."

When they hung up, Tessa dropped her head into her hands, indulging in a few panicked tears before she got the flight booked. She ventured back into the bedroom, using the light of her phone to gather her things. Eun Gi appeared behind her as she was struggling to haul her suitcase out of the closet.

"What're you doing?"

Tessa slapped a hand to her hammering heart, dropping the suitcase to the floor where it just missed her foot. "Oh my God, you scared me."

"Sorry."

"I'm going home."

"What? Why?" He turned on the bedroom light and spun her towards him. "What happened? Did I do something?"

"No, you didn't do anything, I just, I have to go home for a while." The frantic edge of panic tinged her voice. A steady chorus of *get home, get home now* played on repeat in her brain, making it difficult to focus on anything else.

"I mean, you're allowed to go home, but can you at least tell me why?"

"Appa's in the hospital, and I need to be there."

"Oh. O-of course." He sidestepped as she splayed her suitcase over the floor and began shoveling her clothing into it, yanking outfits off hangers.

Her hands shook, and Eun Gi kneeled next to her, wrapping an arm around her. The tears came instantly, wracking sobs that dragged in her throat and shook her whole body. He hoisted her up and brought her back to the bed.

"Can you tell me what happened?"

She forced out an explanation, words chopped and halted.

"He has good doctors?"

Tessa nodded.

"I'm sure he's going to be fine. When's your flight?"

"About twelve hours from now."

His hand moved over her hair and down her back, long, smooth strokes meant to soothe. "You have lots of time. Let's get you some more sleep, and then I'll help you pack. Okay?"

"Okay." She allowed herself to be bundled under the covers and tucked up against him.

The soft hand on her hair continued its path, lulling her to sleep with the sound of his heartbeat in her ear.

Tessa woke a few hours later alone in bed. She sat up groggily and looked to the floor, expecting to see a mess, but instead her clothing had been neatly folded and her suitcase sat open and ready. Eun Gi peeked through the door.

He set a steaming cup of tea on the nightstand for her. "I was coming to wake you. Do you want some breakfast?"

She allowed herself to be herded into the other apartment, lost in her own thoughts. Conversation passed around her in a blur, only coming into focus when Eun Gi set a gentle hand onto her arm, returning her to reality. When it came time for everyone to depart for the day, Eun Gi pulled her aside.

"Will you be okay? I can call in and stay with you."

Tessa shook her head. "Kelly is already on her way over."

He hesitated and then snared her into a hug. "Call me, okay? Or text, or email or whatever. Let me know how you're doing, and what happens with your appa?"

Melting into his embrace, she soaked up the warmth and sweet coconut scent of his hair.

"I will."

The flight dragged on forever, and Tessa was painfully awake for most of it, unable to sleep through her worry. She stopped and started a half dozen movies, but none of them held her attention for more than a few minutes. Her knee bounced a constant rhythm, annoying the person next to her, but she couldn't stop the motion. Reading proved equally futile, the words blurring as tears snuck up on her. Brief dozes did nothing to relieve her exhaustion, and she struggled to stay awake as she moved at a snail's pace through customs. She sent a cursory text to Kelly, Eun Gi, and her mother to update them on her status and location.

The cab ride was blessedly short, and soon she was maneuvering her suitcase through the hospital where her father was resting post-surgery.

She rolled up to the nurses' station. "I'm looking for Jun Hale. Which room is he in?"

The nurse glanced up and tapped away at her keyboard before giving Tessa the room number and pointing her in the right direction. The small space was occupied with three people in scrubs with their backs to the door.

"One, two, three, and up!" one of the nurses said, and it was followed by a shout of pain.

The sound lanced straight through Tessa. "Appa!"

The occupants turned towards her, and she left her bag in the hall, shimmying through everyone.

Her father was leaning heavily on two of the nurses, brow sweating and furrowed. He peeled his eyes open, focusing on her slowly, as if he didn't quite realize who he was seeing.

Someone placed a hand on her shoulder, and she whirled to face a middle-aged woman with deep-brown skin and long straight hair held back in a ponytail.

"Who are you?" the woman asked.

"Tessa Hale. This is my father."

The woman nodded. "I'm Dr. Sanyal. Your mother stepped out for a moment, and we're assisting your father with his first movement post-surgery."

"But he's hurting. Isn't it too soon?" Tessa chewed her lip. There wasn't room to maneuver around to properly greet her father, so she stood awkward and immobile.

Dr. Sanyal shook her head. "It's important to encourage movement as soon as possible after a surgery like this so that his recovery will be easier. If we delay there could be difficulty in his regaining the ability to walk properly."

Tessa's stomach dropped to her toes. Tears welled instantly as her brain filled with the thoughts of what *could* have happened. She forced them away and concentrated on the doctor.

"Rest assured, the prognosis is very good. There were some minor complications during the surgery that will certainly prolong the recovery period, but I have every confidence that with proper care he will manage just fine. We'll be keeping him for observation for a few days to make sure there's no additional complications, but after that he should be able to go home." Dr. Sanyal turned back to her patient. "Ready to try again?"

"Can I help?" Tessa asked.

The doctor directed her around the bed. "Take the spot of Nurse Zhao."

The young Chinese woman smiled at Tessa and helped her get situated, supporting her father while he stood, sweating and shaking.

Tessa braced her hand on his chest. "Appa."

He set his temple against her forehead. "Hi, Peanut."

"Okay, Mr. Hale. Can you please take a step for me?" Dr. Sanyal asked.

Tessa's father took a single step, grunting with the movement, grinding his teeth.

"Appa, you're doing great." Tessa glanced to the doctor, who nodded, confirming her statement.

"One more step please."

Her father obeyed, slowly, leaning much of his weight on Tessa and the other nurse.

"Excellent. We'll let you rest and be back later to move again." Dr. Sanyal approached Tessa. "Your mother has been informed, but do you have any specific questions while I'm here?"

Emotion demolished most of her logic and left her brain feeling mushy. "Not at the moment, but thank you. I'm sure I'll think of something later."

Dr. Sanyal smiled, and the two nurses left with her. Tessa sank into the hard plastic chair placed next to her father's bedside.

"Appa." Her voice cracked. She scooped up the hand not occupied by his IV and kissed his knuckles. "I'm so sorry I wasn't here sooner."

He squeezed her fingers gently. "I'm sorry you had to come."

"Don't be silly." She let out a hiccup, pushing back at the climbing sob in vain. "I couldn't have stayed away knowing you were in here."

His thumb stroked over the back of her hand. "I'm glad you're here."

She lifted their joined hands and rested her cheek against them. He seemed smaller than when she'd left, though it was probably the hospital gown that tricked her eye. Seeing him somehow alleviated the weight of one worry while dumping another onto her shoulders.

"Meu amor?"

Tessa turned to the door where her mother stood, looking dead on her feet. Purple circles shadowed her eyes, and she moved as though her legs were made of lead. Tessa set down her father's hand and all but flew into her mother's arms.

"Mamãe."

Her mother tucked her head and burst into tears, which set Tessa off a moment later. They stood in the tiny entryway sobbing.

"I missed you so much." Her mother gave a hearty squeeze and stepped back, cupping Tessa's cheeks. A sigh melted out of her mother. "It's so good to see you. I'm sorry I wasn't here when you arrived. They ordered me to get food, so I was nursing a donut and coffee in the atrium."

"It's okay, Mamãe."

"Did you sleep at all on the plane?"

Tessa shook her head.

"I'll drive you home after you've had a visit. You can shower and have a rest."

"I didn't fly all the way here to not stay with you both."

Her mother smiled. "You still need to sleep."

Tessa eyeballed the chair in the corner.

"No. You are not sleeping in a chair here. You'll hurt yourself. Let me take you home."

For a moment it was the Seoul apartment that flitted through her head at the word, and not the house she'd grown up in. Tessa tucked that aside and allowed her mother to take her back to their house.

Eun Gi

"Earth to Eun Gi." Min Jae waved his hand in front of Eun Gi's face. "You okay?"

Eun Gi blinked. "Yeah, sorry. I'm a little distracted."

Min Jae's smile turned annoyingly self-satisfied. "Were you thinking about Noona?"

"So what if I was?"

Truthfully, he hadn't stopped thinking about her since she left. Recalling how she'd curled against him, fear in her gaze, made his gut twist.

"Hyung, don't be so cranky. You're allowed to think about her."

Hwan and Sung Soo exchanged a look.

"Has she said anything about her appa?" Hwan asked.

"Nothing yet. I only know she arrived. I'm worried."

Sung Soo refilled their coffees. "Send her a text?"

"I don't want to bother her."

Hwan snorted. "I don't think you've been paying enough attention to the situation if you think you're a bother to her."

"Let's all be nice to Eun Gi," said Sung Soo. "He's just figuring out he has a crush on the woman he's going to marry." The eldest of them propped a grinning face into his palm, watching Eun Gi's expression shift.

Min Jae burst out laughing and pulled Eun Gi into a squeezing hug. "Don't worry, Hyung, I'm pretty sure Noona likes you too."

Eun Gi groaned and dropped his forehead to the table. "I don't want this to be more complicated than it already is."

"Doesn't it make it less complicated if you have feelings for your wife?" Hwan asked.

"In any normal situation, maybe. Not so much in this one."

Tessa's panic in the wee hours, her easy surrender into his arms for comfort, her complete offer of trust, played on repeat in his head. He knew her now, had experienced her vulnerability, and seeing her hands shake as she tried to pack had triggered some deep need to protect. But now she was across the ocean, and there was nothing at all he could do.

"Hyung, can I be best man at the wedding?" Min Jae's voice snapped Eun Gi back to their conversation.

"Excuse you, best man is *my* right," Hwan insisted.

Sung Soo rolled his eyes.

"I already promised Hwan like five years ago that he could be," said Eun Gi

"That's no fair planning so far ahead!"

Sung Soo snared Min Jae away from Eun Gi.

"What am I supposed to do?" Eun Gi looked at each of them in turn. "What if she doesn't come back?"

"She's coming back," Sung Soo assured.

"But what if she *doesn't?*"

It was another thought that refused to leave his brain. She was back home now, and with an ill parent. There would be nothing he or the company could do if she chose to remain where she was. His stomach twisted when he contemplated it. They'd only just opened up to one another, and something between them had shifted.

"Eun Gi." Sung Soo nudged the phone closer to him. "Text her and save yourself the headache."

He avoided it long enough to give her time to settle, but eventually his curiosity got the better of him. He stared at the phone screen, willing it to conjure up a message without his involvement.

> Eun Gi:
> How's your appa?
> You've been so quiet, I hope everything is ok.

Relief swept through him when the typing dots appeared.

Tessa:
The doctors are hopeful he'll make a full recovery, but he has to stay in the hospital for a little while longer.

> Eun Gi:
> I'm glad he has a good prognosis. Does that mean you'll be
> coming back to Seoul soon?

His fingers felt clumsy, awkwardness fueling a growing tension in his limbs.

Tessa:
In a few days. I haven't booked the flight yet.

He typed and erased a half-dozen messages. Unable to discern the exact tone of her words, but unwilling to ask, he decided instead on another idea. She was stressed, he told himself, and exhausted. It would be too much to expect more from her right now.

Eun Gi:
Do you mind if I pick you up from the airport?

Tessa:
You want to brave the airport?
You can, if you want to.
No pressure though, I can take a cab if you change your mind.

Does that mean she doesn't want me to?
He stared at the screen.

Surely if she were opposed to the idea, she would say so. She had before, but now he wasn't sure what to think. He didn't want to pull back the offer in case he was misreading the situation. Forcing himself to roll with it, he typed out a response he hoped wasn't too stilted.

Eun Gi:
I won't.
See you soon :)
Let me know if anything changes or if you need anything

He was anxious to see her in person, but that made him even more confused.

Only a few more days. That was doable.

Probably.

Tessa

An ache through Tessa's body woke her several hours later. The sun was gone from the sky, leaving her home in a dismal twilight. Her mother had taken her home, and she'd fallen asleep on the couch under a fuzzy throw, too exhausted to make it any farther. She reached over in her sleep daze, expecting to find Eun Gi next to her, but there was only empty air. Disappointment sank in.

She climbed the stairs to shower away some of her fatigue and get dressed for the hospital. As she picked out her clothing it struck her that her bedroom had a foreign quality to it, like it didn't quite belong to her anymore. It had housed her for most of her life, but there was a certain level of detachment as she stood in it, knowing she was about to spend a year away.

"Meu amor." Her mother's voice carried from the front door. "I picked up Chinese on the way home. I hope you're hungry."

Tessa wandered to the entryway, damp hair curling around her face. "You're back early. I was just getting ready to head over."

"Appa's having a rest. We'll go back after we eat. Sound good?"

Tessa nodded and took the bags from her, depositing them onto the table before laying out the plethora of containers. Despite what had brought her home, she felt a little lighter being in their kitchen with her mother like everything was normal.

"So." Her mother plunked herself down at the table. "I need a distraction, which means I need you to tell me about this boy you're marrying. You've had a chance to get to know him a little bit. What do you think?"

Tessa's whole body warmed, cheeks flaming. "He's sweet. It's all so complicated, though."

"Feelings often are."

"I meant the situation, but I guess that also applies. I love spending time with him." Tessa twirled chow mein noodles on her chopsticks. Nostalgia rocked her hard. The scent was reminiscent of their Friday nights growing up when they would order in and watch a movie together. "It all feels different than what I'd expected."

"Different how?" Her mother dug into the sweet and sour pork.

"Hmm. More real? I'm not sure how to explain it. Before he was sort of this fantasy that existed, but didn't. If that makes sense?"

Her mother nodded.

"Now, he's this whole real person and I keep trying to not get attached, but I feel it happening anyway. He's clearly struggling with all of this too. It's hard for him."

"I would imagine it's hard for both of you. I'm not even part of it and I'm stressed. Do you think there's a possibility of something coming out of all this?"

Tessa's cheeks flushed deeper.

"I'm taking that as a yes. Do you trust him?"

"I think so. I'm not sure how far that goes this early on, but we seem to have an understanding. He was so great after you called. I cried all over him, and he just carried me back to bed and held me. He even tidied up the mess I'd made of my clothes when I was panic packing."

"Oho! You've shared a bed?" Her mother's face lit up. She scooched forward and stared expectantly at her daughter. "Was it a sexy bed sharing? I cannot believe it took you so long to tell me."

"Oh God. It's not like that. He stays with me because he has nightmares. I think he might have some PTSD from his parents."

Her mother's eyes widened, chopsticks paused halfway to her mouth. "Poor boy. I hope that's not the case. Does he have good people around him?"

"Mostly. The other members are amazing, but some of the company and studio staff kind of suck."

"Still, even if you only have a single person who truly has your back, that's more than many people have in this world. You should see how things go. You've got plenty of time to figure out if you want to have a relationship with him."

"But I'd have to live in Korea. There's no way he could leave. You'd be okay with that?"

"Meu amor, I love you so much—" she reached across the table, taking Tessa's hand in hers, "—and I need you to understand that I will support anything that makes you happy. If you find yourself in love and want to be with him, then I want you to do whatever you need to. We'll make things work, arrange for more permanent help if we have to, but Appa would never get over the guilt if you missed out because of him. Of course we want you to be close, but we're not so selfish that we'd tell you to stay if you think a move like this would be good for you. Besides, it's a direct flight, and I would talk your ear off on video calls."

"Have I mentioned lately that you're the best mom?"

Her mother grinned. "Feel free to remind me."

The next few days stretched into a sort of exhausted monotony. Tessa and her mother woke early and spent all day at the hospital with her father until visiting hours came to an end. The painkillers dulled some of his alertness, and he slept more than he was awake, but Tessa was grateful to be there regardless of his acuity.

"I snuck you a cookie," Tessa said, handing over the chocolate confection.

"I don't think it counts as sneaking if you ask the nurses for permission first." Her father laughed and nibbled at his treat.

Her mother slipped into the room. "I just got off the phone with homecare. They're sending a physiotherapist for the first while until he's moving easier. And at that point we can go to the clinic instead." She slumped down into one of the chairs.

"I can't wait to go home." Her father leaned against his pillows, setting the cookie on his rolling table.

"Soon." Tessa smiled.

Her father laid a gentle hand on her mother's cheek, thumb brushing softly over it. She smoothed his hair that had become a spiked disaster from lying in bed so long. They shared a kiss that in Tessa's youth would have had her scrunching up her nose in disgust. As an adult it was closer to heartwarming, knowing that sort of deep and attentive love was possible. She still averted her gaze, because no amount of sweetness made parents kissing comfortable.

Her mother glanced up and laughed. "We're done, you can look."

Tessa stole a bite of her father's cookie. "You're never done."

"Thirty years of habit, what can I say." Her mother settled her head on her husband's shoulder, watching Tessa from her snuggled post. "I'm sad Appa will have to miss your wedding."

"It's okay. It's mostly for show anyway."

"You should come back, and we'll do a party for you. Kelly's moms already offered to host," her father said.

"Appa, it's a temporary fake marriage. It would be silly to go to the trouble."

"But I can't come to it."

His wide-eyed gaze melted her, guilt swelling in her gut.

"I'll ask Eun Gi about it. I'm not sure what his schedule is like. I'm sure you two will get to Seoul before then either way. Kelly's moms will want to go all out, and they'll need time to plan."

"Too true. They throw quite the event." Her mother sat up and fished a small velvet box out of her purse. "I nearly forgot. They might not let you wear these, or you might not want to anyway, but if you do—"

Tessa grabbed the box and pried it open to reveal two pearl earrings. "Mamãe, these are gorgeous! Did you wear them at your wedding?"

"Actually, these were a gift Appa surprised me with when we found out about you. My wedding jewelry was stolen when someone broke into our first apartment, so I can't offer that to you, but we hoped that this might be almost as meaningful."

"It is." Tessa took her mother's hand.

"Olivia, Tessa, I'm so sorry to bother you." Nurse Zhao popped through the door. "You only have about five more minutes before I have to kick you out for the night."

Tessa's mother sighed dramatically. "We'll get going in a minute. Thank you, Nuan."

Nurse Zhao bobbed her head, smiling before she disappeared back into the hall.

"I love that you get to know all the nurses," Tessa said.

"I like to know the names of who's taking care of one of my favourite people." Her parents kissed again, soft and sweet, while her mother fussed and tucked him more comfortably into bed. "We'll see you in the morning."

Back at the house they sat on the couch, mother and daughter snuggled together. A sitcom rerun filled the silence until her mother muted it.

"I'm proud of you, meu amor. You've been so good through all of this, and I'm so grateful to have you as my daughter." Her mother's eyes shone in the lamplight. "You're doing such a big thing to help this boy back in Korea. I want to make sure that you take care of yourself too. Don't let yourself get lost in helping others and forget about you."

"I won't."

Her mother stroked a soothing hand over Tessa's hair. "You've always been a helper, ever since you were little. You say you won't, but you tend to set aside what you need to make sure others are cared for."

"Eun Gi is pretty good at not letting me do that. The others keep an eye on both of us. I think you'll like them."

"If you like them, I'm sure I will too. I'm glad he's looking out for you. That's important in a husband."

"Mamãe."

"I know, I know. Fake marriage, fake husband, but you like him, and he's kind to you. If I have to give you up for a year, it had better be to someone amazing." Her mother sighed, and a yawn cracked her jaw. "I'll fall asleep on the couch if I stay here any longer. Go on up to bed. I'll see you in the morning."

Tessa curled up on her bed, staring at the empty space next to her in the dark. A quiet ache burned in her chest. Her phone buzzed, and she rolled over to check it.

Eun Gi:
Sweet dreams :)

I miss you. She typed it out and erased it. Groaning into the pillow, she attempted a different message.

Tessa:
You too, when you get there

A <3 sat unsent. The phone slipped from her grasp, and she caught it before it smacked her in the face.

Tessa:
<3

"Oh, fuck my life."

Agonizing moments passed, and then those three dots appeared, taunting her.

Eun Gi:
<3

Tessa giggled, dragging her pillow over her face as the sound pitched louder. "Oh my God."

She stared at the screen for a long while before finally dipping into sleep, a smile tugging at her mouth.

The wee hours of the mornings were spent shoving a year's worth of clothing and assorted items into her two suitcases. It was a task that kept her firmly occupied whenever she wasn't at the hospital. Her remaining time in Vancouver disappeared with each heartbeat. As the end of the week drew closer, so did her return to Seoul and the beginning of a year apart from her parents. Her father was still in the hospital when the day of her flight arrived.

"I don't know if I can go." Tessa fidgeted in her seat. The healthier her father became, the more her thoughts drifted to Seoul. Eun Gi had been texting her with updates on the others, and she'd kept him apprised of the situation, but seeing his name on the screen wasn't the same as being there. Part of her felt guilty for how much she wanted to go back.

"Of course you can go," her mother insisted. "You've got less than two weeks until the wedding, and from the sounds of it that company is about to have a conniption if you stay away much longer."

Her father took Tessa by the hand. "Peanut, you don't have to stay here for me. Dr. Sanyal is sending me home tomorrow."

Tessa puffed up her cheeks. Two directions pulled at her. Family on one side, and a contractual obligation and the potential for something she wasn't quite ready to think about on the other.

"You have things to do in Korea that are important. We're not going anywhere." Tessa's mother pressed a kiss to each of her daughter's cheeks and sniffled. "I'm going to miss you so much."

"Mamãe, you're not supposed to cry until I get on the plane."

"I can cry whenever I want."

"Hey, hey, she's right, tears are for the airport." Tessa's father sat up a little more, wincing slightly at the movement.

"Appa, we're having a moment. Join the hug or shoo."

"I'm trying to keep myself together!" he complained even as he opened his arms to them.

Tessa indulged in a long embrace. "It's only a year, not forever."

Her mother scoffed. "I think children have a very different idea of forever than their parents."

All too familiar with the flight by now, Tessa firmly resolved to sleep, which ultimately meant that she greeted the sight of Seoul from above with burning eyes that hadn't slept a wink. When she shuffled into arrivals Eun Gi appeared out of the crowd, ball cap low on his brow. A blush warmed her face, her heart doing excitable flip flops. He pulled her straight into a hug, and she sank her weight into his arms with a contented hum.

The soft coconut scent of his shampoo slipped into her awareness, and her forehead tucked against his silken hair.

"How was the flight?"

Her breath caught at the sound of his voice. She'd missed it. "Long. Need sleep."

His laughter echoed in her ear. "Come on, then. Let's get you home."

Home.

She curled into him a little more. "I can't believe you braved the airport for me."

"You're worth the risk."

Something in her chest melted, tension releasing in a flood of warmth.

He managed to spirit her into their apartment without alerting the others to their arrival, and got her tucked into bed. His fingers brushed her cheek softly, and she could have sworn he kissed her hair, but the pull of sleep was too strong to know for certain.

Chapter 12

Tessa

"I have a problem." Tessa slumped onto Kelly's couch.

"With?" Kelly set two cups of tea on the coffee table.

"Eun Gi's been so sweet, and it's making me confused."

"You're gonna have to elaborate a wee bit."

"I just— I don't get it. It took me three months to kiss Selena, and I already want to kiss him. I used to frustrate the hell out of everyone I ever went out with because I didn't want to get physical early on."

"I mean, I'm not surprised that you want him."

"What do you mean?"

"Think about it. You've been invested in his life for years, and while that's not the same as having known him, he's familiar to you. Maybe your brain thinks you've been close all this time, and it's kicked into gear now that you're pushed into more intimate circumstances. It's like a demisexual shortcut."

"Maybe." Tessa sipped her tea and set it down with a groan. "I'm not comfortable feeling these things."

"Why not?"

"It's weird. I feel like I'm objectifying him when I think about kissing him, and…other things."

Kelly laughed so hard she choked on her tea.

"No dying, I need you alive to talk me through this." Tessa patted Kelly's back until the coughing subsided.

"He *is* very pretty."

"That is wildly unhelpful, Kel."

"Can't say that I was trying to be helpful. Seriously though, be honest with me. You've never done *any* bean flicking over him?"

"Oh my God." Tessa buried her face in her hands to block out the view of her best friend's face. "I can't believe you asked me that. This is worse than my parents' sex talk."

Kelly nudged her. "What? It's not bad. I've done it."

Tessa's head snapped up. "Over Eun Gi?"

"Sung Soo." Kelly poked at her. "You never did answer me."

"And I'm not going to. Why does the earth never open up and swallow me when I want it to?"

"If you can't talk to me about this, how can you talk to him? I'm the safe zone here. This is a big deal! When was the last time you had sexy feelings for someone? I'm betting it's been years."

Tessa nodded. "Close to five years I think."

"Exactly, and if you're having sexy feels, that means you've already got emotional ones, and if you're at the stage of panicking to me about them, then they're deeper than you're letting on."

Tessa let out a sound of protest.

"Girl, I know you way too well. Have you talked to him about *any* of this?"

"No. How do I even bring up the topic?" Tessa's cheeks burned and her insides twisted contemplating it.

"Well, how did people bring it up to you?"

"I am *not* asking Baek Eun Gi over text if he wants to have sex."

"So ask him in person."

"Kelly!"

"What?" She dodged a pillow Tessa hurled at her and grabbed it to hold as a shield. "We're opening the lines of communication. It's very important."

"Why did I think you'd take this seriously?"

"I'm sorry." Kelly set down the pillow. "I am, I promise, but you two are adults. You've got to talk about it. If you want to sleep with him and he's agreeable, then go right ahead. You have nothing to be ashamed of."

"I know." She groaned and reclaimed her pillow, squeezing it to her chest. "I'm just scared. It's more than all that."

"What do you mean?"

Tessa huffed. "If things keep on like they have been, how am I going to be able to manage it?"

"Well—" Kelly squeezed Tessa's arm, "—then that's all the more reason you need to talk. You're getting married soon, and you gotta be able to communicate with your partner. If he's a butt about it, then I'll have to punch him in the dick."

"Please don't dick punch. What if I need it later?"

Kelly snorted and dissolved into giggles until she was red-faced and crying.

Tessa flopped back onto the couch, arranging herself across Kelly's lap. "I feel so dumb about all of this."

"You're not dumb. Pretty much everything about sex is awkward. You gotta accept that. Feelings aren't easy." Kelly stroked a soothing hand over Tessa's hair. "It'll all be okay, one way or another."

"I want to believe that."

Tessa's phone rang.

"Hello?"

"Hale Tessa-ssi, it's Kyung Mi."

"Oh, hi. What can I do for you?" Apprehension buzzed through her. Any contact with the company didn't bode particularly well.

"I'm not sure if you've been updated on the situation yet, but Kim Hye Jin has spoken to the media. I'll send you a link so you can read it, if you want."

"Yes please."

"I cannot stress enough how important it is for you to not speak with them if approached. We don't need any more fuel on this fire."

"Of course. I'm not keen on it considering the last time they ambushed me."

There was silence for a moment. "Have you been harassed since then?"

"No, but I've been pretty careful about where I go."

"Good. I do apologize for the inconvenience. It's part of the lifestyle that can't be easily avoided. I hope your family is doing well? You left in such a rush we were concerned you wouldn't return."

"They're well enough. Appa's out of the hospital and back at home now."

"I'm glad. Though I do have to ask that you inform me next time, preferably prior to you getting on a plane. If I'm to do my best for you and Eun Gi, I need to be kept informed."

Guilt picked at Tessa's stomach. "Did you get in trouble because I left?"

"Don't worry about that. Let's just do better in the future, all right?"

"Okay." She was *definitely* going to worry about it, but Kyung Mi wasn't likely to spill the beans over what disciplinary actions she might've faced.

"I'm getting a handle on the Hye Jin situation, but I wanted to check in with you first to see if you'd been affected. I honestly thought my days of dealing with her were over, but the past never truly sleeps." Kyung Mi sighed. "I don't want either of you going through what happened then."

"What *did* happen? Eun Gi has been pretty quiet about it." Tessa sat up and turned the volume up full blast to assist Kelly with her eavesdropping.

"To be fair, he doesn't know everything." Kyung Mi hesitated. "Some of the fans were monstrous to her. She was still quite young at the time, only twenty, and she had to close down her entire social media presence. Her home address was leaked. It was an entire mess and the company washed their hands of her. It was far easier for them to let her go than to deal with it. I tried to keep an eye on her, but we were on tour and I had a million other things to attend to. She'd all but disappeared by the time we returned."

Each word piqued Tessa's anxiety. "Oh my God, that's awful."

"Yes. I should have intervened sooner. Idols don't have the luxury of a normal life, and I knew they would get in trouble with the company if they were caught. I never should have allowed their relationship to continue."

"You couldn't have known what would happen."

"It still happened on my watch, and I'm determined not to make those mistakes again." Kyung Mi's voice softened. "Your career wouldn't allow you to go on a blackout like she did, but the risk is there. I intend to keep the situation under control. As skeptical as I was at first, it seems like things are working out well, and I don't want Eun Gi to face the consequences of an irate EchoPop because you had to back out of the arrangement for your own safety."

"I'll follow whatever instructions you give me," Tessa promised.

"I'm happy to hear it."

When they hung up Tessa turned to Kelly, who was staring at her with wide eyes. "Wow, drama. Get the article, I want to read."

The message from Kyung Mi with the link popped up a moment later and Tessa clicked it.

Kim Hye Jin Speaks Out To The Press.

Previously outed to the public in a dating scandal with Baek Eun Gi of 24/7 fame four years ago, the makeup artist speaks out for the first time on the new scandal between Baek Eun Gi and Hale Tessa.

"You're all being horrible. Don't ruin things for them like you ruined it for us. Accept that he's happy and respect his privacy." The makeup artist eluded further commentary.

"Every time I think I understand what I'm getting myself into I get a whole new layer added on." Tessa downed the rest of her tea. "This is a lot."

"You're going to be fine. I've got your back." Kelly squeezed her tight. "If I have to mama-bear the entire fanbase, I will."

Chapter 13

Tessa

Tessa managed to chicken out of talking to Eun Gi about her feelings over a dozen times until she was staring down the day of her wedding. Her eyes burned and a mild ache prodded her forehead. She was tempted to roll over and scream into her pillow, but that might wake Eun Gi.

She could hardly marry him if she couldn't say a few simple words. What was so difficult about *"I'd like to pursue a proper relationship"*? She briefly wished telepathy upon him, but rescinded that a moment later when she realized that would mean he'd know *everything*.

She looked at his sleeping face. Her heart squeezed. Strands of dark hair swept over his brow, and his cheeks were soft and plump. It wasn't even fair how weak she was for him.

Surrendering to the intimacy their situation brought was too easy, but even so she kept reminding herself it wasn't real. They slept in the same bed at night as a preventative measure for his nightmares, not because he wanted to be there. They shared meals and went to set together because it was convenient. She knew she was being silly, but had no idea how to prevent it from happening. Logic was a terrible weapon when surrounded by the warmth of his body.

Eun Gi shifted and sighed against her skin, tugging her a little closer.

He was going to be the death of her if he kept that up.

She was marrying him today. Tessa suppressed the urge to cry and instead brushed his hair from his face.

She had a year. It would be best to enjoy this as it was and move along when the time came. How hard could it be?

Tessa jumped when someone knocked on the door.

Eun Gi lifted a sleepy head. "Hmm?"

"I need to speak with you." Tessa recognized the voice as Kyung Mi and slipped from Eun Gi's hold to open the door.

Kyung Mi glanced between Eun Gi, who had promptly fallen back asleep, and Tessa's sleep-worn hair. "I'm asking as a formality since I'm already quite certain of the answer given what I'm seeing, but am I to assume that the wedding will be going ahead as planned?"

"Um." Tessa backed away quickly and shook Eun Gi's shoulder.

"What's happening?" he asked groggily.

"You're getting married, is what's happening." Kyung Mi sighed. "This is your last opportunity to back out of the arrangement. Once you get on location, I won't be able to help you."

Eun Gi's cheeks paled, and Tessa's heart revved.

His gaze focused on Tessa, voice wavering. "If Tessa is comfortable with moving forward, I am too."

At least she wasn't the only one who was nervous. Neither of them had a reason to say no that the company would accept. Even worse, for all her internal panic, she didn't *want* to say no.

"Let's do this."

"Come on then, we've got to get you all to hair and makeup." Kyung Mi pulled the blanket off the bed, and Eun Gi contracted into a ball against the rush of cold air. "I have to check on the others. If you're not dressed and ready to go in thirty minutes, I'll sic Gyeong Suk on you."

The wedding coordinator kept a firm grip on Tessa's wrist, as if sensing her growing panic, thwarting any intrusive thoughts that might urge her to flee. Kelly and Hwan waited outside of the room where the guests, along with the film crew and photographers, sat in anticipation of Tessa's arrival. They'd managed to sneak the bride and groom into the building without being bothered, but she'd seen the lineup of cameras waiting to capture images of attendees.

Her fingers found her pearl earrings, and she rolled the smooth studs between thumb and forefinger to calm herself.

"You okay, Tess?" Kelly's dress matched the flowers they both wore in their hair, a pale pink that was almost lost amid her bubblegum-tinted curls.

"Um, sure?"

Hwan wrapped a tuxedo-clad arm over her shoulders. "You'll do fine. Just don't trip."

"Shouldn't be a problem." Tessa stuck her foot out from under the gown, revealing a bedazzled ballet flat. "They put me in these so Eun Gi isn't tiny next to me."

"I know what'll make you feel better." Kelly whipped out her phone, and a moment later the screen was filled with the face of Tessa's mother.

"Oh my goodness, meu amor, you're gorgeous! And they let you wear the earrings. I'm so glad." Her mother's face was paler than usual, hair unstyled, eyes glassy.

"How're you feeling, Mamãe?"

"Just peachy." Her mother held out a thumbs-up. "Food poisoning is still destroying me, but I haven't thrown up in two hours. I'm sorry I couldn't be there."

"Quit hogging." Her father's face nudged her mother over. "Look at you. Pretty as a peanut."

Tessa giggled. It was a ritual they'd had since she'd learned to speak. "Peanuts aren't pretty."

"But you are—" her father grinned, "—and you're my peanut."

The giggles wavered dangerously. "Oh God, don't make me cry, they already did the makeup."

"Let us see the whole look," her mother asked. Tessa stepped back and did a slow twirl. The full A-line skirt swept around her body, nipping in at her waist with a beaded silk belt over the lace bodice. They'd skipped a necklace since the scalloped edges of the off-shoulder neckline came up to her clavicle, but they did add pearl-studded pins to her hair, nestled amid the baby-pink roses to match her earrings.

"I wish I was there so I could see his face when you walk out in this. I'm glad they went with ivory for the gown. It's much softer against your skin."

Kelly turned the screen around. "I'll keep you guys on video call for the ceremony so you get to see. I have to mute you or the scary company people might steal my phone."

"Oh, is that my new son?"

Hwan awkwardly waved at the screen.

"Nah, that's just Hwan." Kelly grinned. "You'll see Eun Gi soon."

Mi Na swept over to them. "Why is your phone out? You're going down the aisle at any moment."

"Tessa's parents aren't here, so I'm being their eyes."

Mi Na sighed. "Fine, but as soon as the ceremony is over, the phone is off. Got it?"

"Roger that." Kelly opened the pop socket on her phone so she could hold it and her bouquet at the same time. "Can you guys still see?"

"Perfectly. Thank you, sweetie," Tessa's mother answered.

They'd done a short rehearsal the night before, but nerves melted the memories right out of Tessa's head. She squeezed her bouquet and tried to relax herself by inhaling the delicate scent of the roses. Eun Gi was waiting on the other side of the hall, but she wished that he was here with her, that they could walk in together.

The music began, and Mi Na ushered Hwan and Kelly through the doors. Tessa bit her lip to hold back the wobble. Her parents weren't here, and she was getting married. Sweat prickled her skin, and everything blurred out around her.

She ordered herself not to cry.

Mi Na and everyone invested in this event would roast her on a spit if she walked down that aisle sobbing. She stared up at the ceiling, willing back the tears.

Her heart hadn't stopped racing since they'd put her in the dress. She'd managed through hair and makeup reasonably well, but the gown made it so much more real.

"I can do this," she whispered to herself.

"Come on." Mi Na waved her over, and the ushers opened the double doors.

Every eye in the room turned to her, and her feet rooted to the carpet under the weight of their stares.

"Go!" Mi Na snapped.

Tessa took a step. Juice from the flower stalks leaked through the ribbons and onto her hands, but her fingers wouldn't relinquish their tight grip. One step, then another. Eun Gi was watching her too. He appeared completely unruffled in a crisp black tuxedo and pressed white shirt. His tie was the softest shade of pink to complement the flowers they'd woven into her hair. She put all of her attention on him, and responded in kind when he offered a tentative smile.

At the end of the aisle they faced one another. Eun Gi broke protocol to take her hand.

"*You look beautiful,*" he mouthed silently.

Heat rushed through her at the compliment. The officiant ran through the vows that in a year's time would be invalidated.

"Baek Eun Gi, you are becoming the husband of Tessa Juliana Hale. Do you promise to love her, respect her, and care for her in times of both joy and sorrow, health and sickness, until death parts you?"

"Yes."

They ran through the same for Tessa, and she replied, "Yes."

"You may now kiss the bride."

She stiffened, aware again of the multitude of eyes on them. This wasn't how it was supposed to be. The thought of a first kiss with him had glanced through her brain once or twice...or twenty times, but this was never how she'd imagined it. She wished she'd been brave enough to say something before this, so their first kiss wasn't happening right now.

"Ready?" he whispered, and she forced herself to nod, because she wasn't and didn't think she ever would be ready to kiss Baek Eun Gi.

He took a small step closer, releasing the hand he'd kept hold of through the ceremony to move it up to cradle her cheek. The other settled onto her waist, nudging her closer to him. Tessa raised trembling fingers to his shoulders as her pulse pounded like a kettledrum in her ears.

Then his mouth was on hers, a soft and tender heat that sent her heart into overdrive. The sweet, insistent pressure of his lips absorbed her quiet, desperate sound. Tessa swayed towards him, and just like that they were parted. The cheer of the attendants erupted around them.

She shoved down the feelings she was *not* supposed to be having for her fake fiancé—husband, she mentally corrected. He smiled at her, and her stomach flipped, a helpless grin taking over as she tucked against him, laughing, emotions flooding out. He squeezed her a little tighter and pressed a kiss to her hair.

Mi Na waved them over to sign the marriage documents.

They walked back up the aisle hand in hand, followed by Kelly and Hwan. When the double doors closed behind them all, relief smacked into Tessa like a brick.

Mi Na was already preparing to swoop in, but Eun Gi turned to her. "Do you mind if I borrow Tessa for a minute?"

It was obvious Mi Na did mind, but she relented. "Two minutes, and then I'm coming to find you."

Eun Gi nodded, pulling Tessa along with him and into one of the unused rooms. "How are you doing?"

"Um, okay, mostly. A little panicky, but I feel a bit better now."

He wrapped her in an unexpected hug, and she softened.

"I appreciate what you've done for me. I made a big fuss at the beginning because I didn't want either of us to be forced into anything. You're putting up with a lot to protect me, and I promise to do the same. I'll protect you too."

"Thank you." She sniffled, and he tucked her closer. "Do we have to go back out there?"

"Unfortunately."

Tessa stepped back, scrutinizing him. "How are you taller than me right now?"

Eun Gi groaned. "They put risers in my shoes."

A knock on the door had them both turning towards the sound. "Hurry up. The plate lunch is on schedule, and we can't start without you."

"Mi Na's a tyrant." Tessa giggled.

"We're coming." Eun Gi turned back to her. "Let me know if you need anything, okay? We have a few hours left before we can retreat, but I'll wrestle Mi Na to the ground so you can escape if need be."

Tessa laughed. "Hopefully that won't be necessary, but I appreciate the offer."

"Feel better?"

"Much."

"Good." He smiled softly and took her hand again. "Let's go face the mob."

Lunch put them on full display again, situated at a sweetheart table while the rest of the guests, most of whom Tessa could only guess at the identities of, were seated around the room. Much as she despised the many eyes on her once more, she was grateful to have the semi-quiet space with her now-husband, where she could breathe for a few moments.

When they finished eating they had to greet their guests before Mi Na would steal them away for photographs, as well as an outfit change for the Korean ceremony. Eun Gi kept a comforting hold on her hand as he introduced her to everyone. Every idol and trainee employed by the company was in attendance. Starstruck didn't quite cover the experience for Tessa, but she navigated without incident until they came up to an elegant couple.

Eun Gi's hand squeezed hers, and his body went rigid.

"The less we say the better," Eun Gi whispered. "I apologize in advance for anything she says."

"It'll be okay," Tessa whispered back.

"Eomeoni, *Abeoji*." He bowed sharply and Tessa followed suit. His mother had tightly permed, dyed-auburn curls and wore a form-fitting blue dress, cream-coloured nylons, and matching shoes. They complemented one another, with his father in a navy suit and blue tie the same shade as his wife's dress.

She took Eun Gi's face in her hands and pressed a kiss to each cheek. His hand shook in Tessa's grasp.

"I still can't believe you're married. I was starting to think it would never happen, given the things we caught you with when you were young." She patted his cheek and turned to Tessa. "And you, so sweet to take on my son. Heaven knows how much of a handful he can be, but I'm sure you'll be well compensated for any unpleasantness. I imagine it's quite the boost to your book sales."

Tessa bristled but kept quiet, pasting a smile on her face. She didn't need any help from Eun Gi to be a success, and the mere suggestion that that was why she was doing this had bile rising in her throat.

"Nice to meet you," she said in halting Korean, her tongue thick in her mouth.

Eun Gi's father looked her up and down, just slow enough to make her skin crawl. She shrank back against her husband, uncertain what to do. His father didn't speak and seemed entirely annoyed that he was there at all.

"Eomeoni." Eun Gi ground out the word, and his fingers twitched in Tessa's hand.

"Aren't you going to introduce me to all your friends?"

"I don't think that's a good idea. Abeoji seems tired. Maybe you should head back to the hotel."

His mother let out a laugh and returned her attention to Tessa. "We come all the way from Busan, and he wants us to leave. I thought I taught you better manners than that. Maybe I'll go introduce myself since you're being so rude."

"Don't."

Tessa set her palm on his shoulder in an attempt at comfort and stepped closer. Eun Gi sighed and shifted awkwardly.

"I'll introduce you, but...please don't talk to anyone else."

His mother smiled smugly.

If there were no cameras Tessa might have said something or simply stepped between her husband and his parents to give him space, but they had no such luxury. Eun Gi motioned to Hwan to come over, and the three other members of 24/7 crossed the ballroom along with Kelly and Min Joo.

Eun Gi glared at his parents, but nevertheless capitulated to her demand. "Eomeoni, this is Park Sung Soo, Lee Hyeong Hwan, and Jeon Min Jae." The three men bowed quickly, their movements robotic. "The others in the group are still doing their military service. This is Kelly Walsh and her husband, Lee Min Joo."

Kelly eyed Eun Gi's mother with a sharp gaze.

The details of why her husband was afraid of his parents eluded her, but the fact that he *was* afraid of them at all had Tessa on guard.

His mother patted Hwan's chest while looking at her son. "So tall and handsome. I always hoped *you'd* turn out like this."

Hwan coughed, cheeks flushing red.

"Oh," said his mother, "I was meaning to ask you. We could use some help with the rent. You're such a generous son, so I know you won't mind."

Eun Gi nodded.

Sung Soo stood tall, stepping between them. "Well, it's been lovely to meet you, but I do believe I see Mi Na summoning the bride and groom for their photos. Eun Gi, why don't you and Tessa go do that, and we'll keep your parents company."

Tessa and Eun Gi slipped away and into the room designated for the photography.

"Could you please give us a moment?" Tessa asked, and the photographer politely excused himself. She turned to her new husband. "Eun Gi, are you okay?"

His temples were damp with sweat.

"I'm fine." He stared down at his hands, and Tessa saw the crescent moon shapes dug into the palms where his mother had held them.

"It's okay if you're not. There's only me here."

Eun Gi shook himself head to toe and fidgeted in place, bouncing on the balls of his feet. "I just need a minute."

"Of course. Take your time."

Tessa grabbed him one of the water bottles from the case set against the wall. He swallowed the entire thing without taking a breath.

"Is there anything I can do? What do you need?"

"For my parents to go back to Busan." He let out a sharp laugh. "They don't even rent. She just wanted to put me on the spot."

Eun Gi paced the length of the room, back and forth, a tiger trapped in a cage.

"I'm sorry. They get me a little worked up." He looked at her for a long moment, but there was only curiosity in his gaze, not scrutiny. "Would it be okay if I hugged you before we go back out?"

"Absolutely." She stepped into his arms immediately and squeaked when he squeezed her tightly. He leaned on the wall and settled his chin on her shoulder. The tension in his body melted fractionally as he pulled the weight of her against him.

"Did they put perfume on you?"

"Oh probably. I zoned out part way through so I'm not sure what all they did." Tessa propped her forehead to his. "It might not need to be said, but your mom is clearly blind because you're tall *and* handsome. Hwan's cute and all, but I don't think he quite compares. I could be a little biased though."

Eun Gi laughed, and Tessa grinned, her mission accomplished.

"Well, I'm glad you think so."

"I do. I'm sorry they're here, and that you're upset. I wish my parents could have been here. I think you'd like them."

"I'd be more worried about whether or not they'd like me, but the fact that you wish they were here makes me feel a little better about the eventual prospect. I'm sorry that mine are...the way they are."

"It's okay."

He was so close, warm golden-brown gaze barely inches from hers. "Tessa."

"Hmm?"

He opened his mouth, but closed it again, shrinking into himself. "Never mind."

A knock on the door separated them, and Mi Na swept in, the photographer at her heels. "I need to keep you two on schedule. You can't be sneaking off constantly. Save it for the honeymoon."

"But we're not going on one," Tessa said.

Mi Na sighed and tapped away at her phone. Ha Yun appeared a moment later.

"I can't believe I forgot to tell you! The company has set up a gift for the two of you for being so cooperative with their measures. They're sending you to Jeju Island for four nights, all expenses paid."

"Oh, when do we leave?"

Ha Yun checked her phone. "In about two hours."

Panic lanced through Tessa. "But we haven't packed."

"Don't worry about that. Yuna's already packed a bag for each of you. We've had quite a few sponsor requests, so she's picked out all the items you'll need. Please do make sure to wear them all outside so they can be seen."

"O-of course."

Eun Gi slipped his hand into Tessa's and gave her a comforting squeeze.

"Once you're finished up with the photographs, you can change, and we'll have you off to the airport."

Mi Na shuffled them away for the costume change. They weren't able to do the full Korean ceremony without Tessa's parents, so the alternative was simply a photoshoot in the traditional clothing. Yuna had Tessa stripped down and transferred into a multi-layered exquisite *hwarot* in record time. White, red, and gold silk draped over her, embroidered with lotus and peonies. They'd painted red circles on her cheeks and forehead, somehow managing to arrange the headpiece without crushing her original style entirely.

"You look like a queen," Eun Gi whispered.

Tessa beamed. "You're so cute in hanbok!"

His face pinched. "Well, I'm glad you think so, because I kind of hate it. I feel like a doll."

The blue silk *jeogori* overcoat hung past his knees atop white *baji* that gathered at his ankles. A gold belt cinched his waist, matching the exquisite embroidery that wove across the outfit. The traditional *gat* hat had always made Tessa giggle, but she held it back, not wanting Eun Gi to feel even more self-conscious.

The photographer arranged them meticulously, for which Tessa was grateful. The hwarot was complicated and weighed a ton, requiring careful adjustments in each new position.

"Okay, you two get changed." Kyung Mi slipped into the room bearing two stacks of clothes. She shooed the photographer away. "I'm driving you to the airport after we sneak you out. The company wanted the press to get photos of you both leaving, but I think you've done quite enough to satisfy their desires for today."

The sudden urge to hug Kyung Mi surged through Tessa.

"Kyung Mi, have I mentioned before that you're awesome?"

A soft smile sprang onto the older woman's face. She passed over the outfits. "First time for everything. Hurry up now, we've got to get out before Mi Na finds out I'm stealing you."

Chapter 14

Tessa

They were checked into their hotel before dinner. Their suite was ornately decorated in shining cherry wood with gold features, and sleek cream fabrics adorned the furniture and king-sized bed. Tessa went straight to the windows where the sky was melting into shades of coral and gold, kissing the azure horizon. A small private pool sat on a covered terrace overlooking lush gardens, and beyond that the ocean stretched out before them.

"They went all out, didn't they?" Tessa pressed her nose to the glass. "Look at that view!"

It was easily the most expensive hotel room she'd ever set foot inside, and she was ready to soak up every second of the luxury. Their suite was expansive, with a dining room, living room, and bedroom, in addition to the terrace.

"They are impressively thorough when it comes to creating what they want people to see." He arranged their bags against the wall and locked the door behind them. "I don't see why we shouldn't take advantage of it though. Want to order obscenely expensive food and put it on their tab?"

"Absolutely." She flopped onto the bed to grab the menu on the nightstand.

"What would you get if you were in Canada after a wedding?"

"Hmm. Strawberries and champagne are the usual clichéd honeymoon treat."

He joined her on the bed, looking over her shoulder at the menu. Her skin prickled into goose bumps at the proximity, at the soft sensation of his breath on her bare skin.

"Beef, chicken, or seafood?" he asked.

"Any and all. I'm starving."

Eun Gi reached over to bring the menu a little closer. He scrolled through his phone. "The reviews all rave over the *ojingeo muchim*. Do you like squid?"

"I don't mind it, but I thought you didn't like it." It was a tidbit she'd remembered from when the group had done their own variety show. A cooking episode had included squid, and Eun Gi had looked green at the prospect.

"I don't, but I was willing to suffer through it if you did."

Tessa laughed. "Let's find something we both like."

Eun Gi scrolled some more, glancing at the menu between checking reviews. "They have a steak and lobster dish at one of the restaurants that sounds good, and a jumbo shrimp hot pot at the other."

She grinned. "Let's get it all."

A knock on the door heralded the arrival of a cart laden with food, including strawberries and champagne on ice. They set up on the terrace and sat with their feet in the pool. Candles flickered at the four corners, casting wavering images over the water. Eun Gi poured them each champagne.

"Being married to you has its perks." She held out the glass to him. "A toast to our sham marriage. May it be happy and free of drama."

The flutes clinked together.

Eun Gi sipped at the bubbly concoction and swung his arm over her shoulder. Tessa jumped.

"Thank you for everything," he whispered over the rim of his glass.

She sank against him, their temples resting together. "You're welcome."

The happenings of the day were one perceived impossibility after the next coming true. She was sitting in a hotel room with her idol on their honeymoon. If she could have told her younger self this would happen, she'd have gone into cardiac arrest.

Tessa chuckled to herself and shook her head when he raised a questioning eyebrow.

They worked their way through the cart of food, feet swishing in the pool and Eun Gi passing her the best pieces until the plates and bowls sat empty.

"Want to sit in the water?"

"Sure, if they thought to pack me a swimsuit."

She dug through her suitcase and found a sleek red one-piece. Tessa changed in the bathroom and came out to Eun Gi already in the pool. The champagne flutes had been refilled and awaited her.

She slipped in next to him and accepted the drink.

"You look cute," he said. "Red suits you."

A blush burned across her freckled cheeks. "Thank you."

The water was heated, drawing her in until she settled chest deep. She squirmed, self-conscious with his focus on her. The cool air had goose bumps springing up across her arms.

Tessa's curls were pinned to keep them out of the water, but one wayward coil escaped confinement. His fingers twirled around it, and goose bumps erupted for an entirely different reason.

Don't think about the kiss. Her breath turned shallow and her gaze flickered to his.

"I feel bad that you didn't get to experience all the usual wedding activities," Eun Gi said softly.

"It's okay."

His fingertips still toyed with that strand of hair, and she struggled to focus on anything else.

"I'm certain you're just saying that so I don't feel guilty." His thumb stroked her cheek, and she resisted the urge to lean into it. "You didn't get to plan it, choose your dress, have a first dance. You even got stuck with me at the altar instead of someone you wanted to kiss."

"Oh, I wanted to kiss you." She froze, and her thoughts ping-ponged through panicked curses.

Eun Gi bit his lip in a vain attempt to contain his laughter, but it was a battle he quickly lost.

"I'm sorry." She inched away awkwardly.

"You don't have to apologize for that."

Tessa groaned. "But it's weird."

"Well, then I'm weird too."

Her brain flew into maximum panic.

He wanted to kiss me? Holy shit. What do I do? What do I say?

"Do you still want to?"

Every muscle was taut as steel, her mind churning. *Oh God. Not that. You're not allowed to talk anymore.*

"Yes," he said, matter-of-factly, as if that confirmation didn't send her heart into overdrive.

"Oh," she managed. Her pulse was back to its kettledrum pounding in her ears. "Right now?"

His fingers curled around the back of her neck and he moved closer. "Yes. If you want to."

He searched her face. Her gaze kept dropping to his lips, helpless. She'd never wished for telepathy more than this moment.

"Please," she whispered.

A shudder twisted up her spine.

This time there were no cameras, no watching eyes, no pressure. The same gentle warmth from the wedding enveloped her. Her arms snaked around his shoulders, and he moved her closer, fingers spreading across her back. The space between them disappeared, mouths seeking the heat of one another. Tessa pressed forward and ended up in his lap, blood simmering.

A small sound escaped her mouth. He pulled back and fastened his lips against her throat, sparking ripples of sensation through her body. She gasped in his ear, and her hips rocked a sultry rhythm.

Her brain was screaming, mind abuzz with desire and panic.

"Yes," she growled.

She wanted a lot, but a voice in the back of her mind urged caution. Tessa braced her hands on the edge of the pool and pushed away.

"Wait."

He pulled back immediately. "What's wrong?"

"I don't..." her lungs burned like she'd run a marathon, "...want to rush."

"Then we won't." He traced his fingertips over her cheek and stayed still beneath her. "Should we go to bed?"

She sighed and sank against him. "Probably."

His mouth brushed hers, petal soft. "There's no rush."

Tessa's heart slammed hard against her ribs. Blaming the champagne for her choices would be convenient, but also a lie. She wanted him badly, but she was also afraid of how willing she was to fall face-first into whatever this was.

He covered a yawn. "Sorry. Our early morning tired me out. Want to sleep so we can explore early tomorrow?"

"Sure."

Summoning her last bit of boldness, she pressed a short, small kiss to his mouth and then climbed out of the pool.

Eun Gi

Sleep eluded Eun Gi for the better part of the night as he processed the day. Tessa slept peacefully next to him, and he was entranced by the rise and fall of her chest. He thought of their first kiss, then the others that had followed, and wriggled uncomfortably. The whole week she'd seemed like she was poised on the edge of something but was too nervous to step over it. Now he knew what it was.

Only moments before the ceremony Mi Na had drilled into his brain to make things look perfect for the cameras. He knew how to do that. It was ingrained into his being at this point in his life. There was no issue with understanding how to hold her for the best angles, but his nerves had blurred his thoughts and had his heart ready to beat right through his chest. Then he'd felt the tremble of her mouth before she melted against him, sweet and warm, and he'd forgotten about the cameras entirely. It was unexpected.

Falling asleep to the sound of her heartbeat, wrapped around her, night after night, had made him pliable and vulnerable. How was he supposed to resist getting attached to her?

Now they were married.

Do not *think about what married people do.* Eun Gi released his breath slowly.

The first kiss had made him curious, and when she'd spilled her own desires, he'd taken the opportunity to satisfy his curiosity. He hadn't expected all...that. His body had been taut as a bowstring, desperate for more, and then she'd called a halt to things scant moments after he'd surrendered to it entirely.

Another deep breath.

Stopping hadn't been a problem, but now, in the quiet dark, his memory kept taunting him. He considered getting up to take matters into his own hands, but when he tried to slither free, she only nestled closer.

Fuck.

He shifted away from the warmth of her pressed against him.

It's not fair. I was doing just fine lying next to her before all this.

Rolling carefully, he inched slowly away, waiting to see if she'd wake. She remained still and quiet, and he vacated the bed to indulge his errant desires in the shower.

It helped. A bit. The moment he returned, she wrapped around him and he settled comfortably. Hopefully sleep would take him before his body recovered enough to make things awkward.

Morning invaded with a knock at the door and a room service cart that they'd pre-ordered the night before. Eun Gi woke slowly, hair in every direction from his restless sleep. He took the cart from the staff and arranged it out on the terrace. Tessa was awake by then and sitting up in bed. He poured himself some coffee and indulged in the view of his sleepy-eyed bride and her fuzzed curls.

"Good morning," she mumbled. Her cheeks turned pink. "Oh God."

Eun Gi smiled into his coffee. "Good morning."

She scrubbed her hands over her face. "I shouldn't have done any of that."

"Notice you're not hearing any complaints from me."

Lifting the cover on the cart revealed small bowls of rice, eggs, seaweed soup, and *kimchi* alongside a plate of grilled snapper.

He looked up at her. "If you're uncomfortable with what happened, we can always pretend it didn't. I just need to know what direction you want things to go."

"That implies that I have any idea what I want," Tessa mused.

He sat down next to her and fixed his gaze on her face. Her mouth dropped open a fraction.

"Don't you?" His stomach squeezed.

"Well, I mean, um." Her eyes flitted to the ceiling. "I got a little scared, because I like you, and I don't want to fuck it up. Plus, I've always had kind of a difficult time with the physical side of relationships. Usually it takes me so long to feel *any* of this..." her hand gestured back and forth between them, "...if I ever do feel it at all. I tend to take a long while to warm up to people in every sense and I'm not sure how to process the fact that it happened so quickly with you."

Eun Gi nodded slowly. "Could you specify what exactly you're feeling?"

He liked the rush of pink that warmed her cheeks.

"Things."

"Very specific." Eun Gi smiled. He tugged her to stand in front of him, between his knees, and settled his palms on her hips. "Can I ask you a question?"

"Another one?"

He nodded.

"Okay."

"Do you think you'd still like me if I weren't UpBeat?"

"What do you mean?"

"If my persona wasn't real at all." He paused, both to collect his thoughts and to brace for her answer. "If it was just me, would you be disappointed?"

"Of course not."

It was likely an automatic reaction to spare his feelings, but then her hand was against his cheek, soft and gentle. He had millions of people across the world professing their love for him without knowing him. They knew a cultivated piece of him and loved that. It wasn't that UpBeat was a false projection, but his fears, concerns, and flaws were pruned away to create an easily digestible product for public consumption.

"I don't know you as well as I'd like to yet, but I like what I do know." She sank to her knees. "I missed you while I was gone. I wouldn't have missed a persona."

He couldn't quite manage to breathe past the knot in his chest. His face burned, gaze trapped by hers.

"I missed you too."

Tessa pressed a kiss to his cheek. "I want to brush my teeth before I kiss you properly, but I'm glad we're on the same page."

She disappeared into the bathroom, and the tension dissolved out of his body. He sat there staring after her. Their situation would be far less complicated and confusing if he'd resolved to treat her like a temporary houseguest, but it was too late for that now. Sung Soo was right. He *did* have a crush on his wife, and he didn't have a clue what to do about it.

When she emerged again, the tension zipped back. It didn't appear she was faring any better.

"I'm sorry if I'm awkward. I am *really* not good at this kind of thing. Honestly, it's a wonder anybody ever had the patience to date me." She shuffled forward and sat down with a sigh. "Actually, scratch that, only one person did."

"That just means only one person had any sense." He grinned at her. "Want some tea?"

"Please."

They'd sent up a selection of teas in a fancy cherrywood box. She chose the ginseng, and he prepared it for her. Summoning his courage, he forced out a suggestion he'd been contemplating.

"What do you think about dating?" He glanced over at her, and she was watching him over the rim of her cup. "This is a weird situation, but it's not like we'll get in trouble if we go out in public together. If you'd rather not, that's okay."

"This is going to sound stupid since we're married, but I'm kind of having a moment over you wanting to date me."

"It's just me," he reminded her.

"I'm sorry, but have you met you? Do you have any concept of how talented you are? Not to mention that you've been incredibly sweet, and you're unfairly pretty to the point it makes me insecure."

Eun Gi's chest warmed. He pulled her up, setting her cup down carefully before looping his arms around her waist.

"Well, if we're complimenting each other, then I'll catch up. You..." he dropped a kiss to the curve of her throat, and her fingers curled into his hair, "...are sweeter than I deserve, and..." he worked his way up her neck, "...I don't know if you've properly looked at yourself lately, but you also tend to be unfairly pretty."

She shivered in his grasp, fingers kneading his scalp.

"Also, full confession, but I may have teared up at several points when I read your book. And then I went and read your first and second books too."

He lifted his head, and Tessa's eyes gleamed with tears.

"You read them?"

"Should I not have?" he asked, suddenly worried.

The air came out of him in a whoosh when she threw herself fully against him, arms squeezing.

"God, no, you're absolutely allowed. I'm so self-conscious about my early work."

"Well that's something we share. I look at our debut photos sometimes, and I have this thing in my head like 'how did this infant ever get a career?'"

"You were so little." Tessa giggled, dropping her forehead to his shoulder. "I loved your debut stage, but then I loved every stage afterwards too, so I'm not very helpful."

He inched them both towards the terrace. "Breakfast is getting cold. I'm happy to shower my wife in compliments, but you have to eat first."

It felt incredibly weird to say 'my wife' but the way she blossomed when he did tempered a lot of the awkwardness.

"So," he said, "what's your favourite food?"

Tessa blinked in surprise and laughed. "Korean or otherwise?"

"Both," he said.

Over breakfast they covered most of the basics, absorbing bits of trivia about the other. Tessa told him she already knew some of it from various media, but she seemed pleased nonetheless to have him share the information. Favourite foods, colours, activities, and more passed between them. She shared about being neighbors and best friends with Kelly all through school and he shared about getting to know the other members in their early years. They talked all morning, picking their way through the food, until the lure of sunshine prompted them to get ready for the day.

"Yuna has a problem with me being taller than you, doesn't she?" Tessa rustled through the suitcase the stylist had packed for her. "Not that I'm crazy about heels, but am I not allowed at all? Every pair are flats."

"We can buy some while we're out if you want." The idea was almost *too* exciting and he crossed his legs when he sat down on the bed. "I don't mind that you're taller."

The boots wrapped shining black leather around her calves, and she wiggled back and forth in them. "I wish they'd have given us a heads-up to pack our own things. I hate breaking in new shoes. My feet are absolute babies about it."

"We don't have to walk far."

"I hope not. If my boots try to consume my flesh, you'll have to carry me back to the hotel." She snickered. "Could you imagine what Yuna would say if someone got pictures of me wearing comfy runners with this outfit?"

Tessa gestured to the sleeveless black knit dress that hugged her body from turtleneck halter to mid thigh. His attention flitted between her long legs and those amazing boots, to her golden bare arms, to the curls she'd barely managed to tame, with small gold hoops in her ears peeking between the ringlets.

"So what's the plan for today? I should have figured that out before getting dressed, but it's not like Yuna packed any hiking gear so all the nature stuff is out of the question."

Eun Gi flipped through one of the brochures provided by the hotel, cheeks bursting into flames when he got to one particular place that Jeju was known for. *Loveland.* Tessa dropped onto the bed next to him.

"What's with the face?" She turned the brochure towards her and burst out laughing. "Oh my God! Kelly and Min Joo went a few years ago, and the pics were hilarious. Did you want to go?"

"I don't *not* want to go." He fidgeted and avoided eye contact.

"I guess it doesn't hurt to check it out. We can always leave if we don't like it."

Eun Gi's first thought when they stepped through the gates of the park was that he definitely should not have agreed to this. Being an adult was supposed to offer some sort of immunization against the colossal embarrassment that consumed him...and yet. Standing hand in hand with his pretty wife, facing statues in every conceivable position and penises *everywhere*, he could barely make eye contact.

"Come on, we have to take a selfie so I can send it to Kelly." She tugged him over to a statue where a woman was hanging upside down in her lover's embrace, each partner pleasuring the other. Heat lanced through him as an image of Tessa in that exact position filled his head, and he'd never been more grateful for tight jeans in his life.

Every art piece brought a deeper blush until Eun Gi's face was permanently akin to a beet. Refusing to give in unless Tessa did, the two of them traipsed past the artistic and the obscene, taking pictures all over the park. Eun Gi snared his arms around her waist as they leaned against a metallic statue of a woman mid-orgasm.

Tessa snapped another picture and, giggling, sent it to Kelly. "I am definitely not mature enough for this place."

Her continuous embarrassed laughter reassured him that he wasn't the only one who descended into a teenage mentality when faced with a giant penis statue.

"I'm glad we came though. Mamãe will get a kick out of it."

The sweet flush of her cheeks had him nestling a little closer, settling his chin on her shoulder. "It's pretty fun if you can ignore the crippling awkwardness. I think I might be getting desensitized. How're your feet?"

"Surprisingly comfortable." Tessa's fingers laced into his hair, and he relaxed against her, tucking his face in the curve of her throat. She dropped her hand to rest on his arms where they crossed her stomach. "You okay?"

"Mhmm." The sun had taken its time warming the air, but now the light sweater he wore was making him sweat. "Want to go to Hyeopjae Beach?"

"Lead the way."

White sand spilled out of the turquoise ocean, draping the beach in sunlit crystals. A small island jutted out of the sea. It was too far to swim to but beautiful all the same. Tessa wiggled her toes in the sand, her flip-flops swallowed by it with each step. She wore her red swimsuit and a black sarong looped around her hips, while Eun Gi wore a black swim shirt and red swimming trunks. She kept distracting him from the view with her long golden legs peeking through the gap in the sarong with each step.

"I wonder if they coordinated all our outfits," Tessa mused.

"I wouldn't be surprised. Matching outfits is the thing couples do here. Is that not something people do in Canada?"

"Well, I think it's cute, but it's more of an old-people thing, in my experience."

"Huh." He'd always kind of liked couples clothing, a representation to the world that you were a team, but he supposed each country would have their own traditions surrounding romance.

"Everyone is staring at us."

"You stand out a lot," he said, as if he weren't also staring at her right along with them. "A tall, pretty foreigner usually gets some attention."

"Maybe they're staring at *you*. I bet you have fans who could pick you out of a crowd by the back of your head."

He snorted. "I don't doubt that."

They linked fingers and walked along the line where the surf met the sand. It swelled up around their ankles before slinking back into the wide blue sea. The sand was warm underfoot and sucked them in with each slurping step. The water was a cool contrast to the bliss of the sun baking their skin.

"I missed the ocean while I was in Seoul," Tessa said.

Eun Gi had fond memories of the ocean itself, but not so much the circumstances of when he'd lived so close to it. The drumbeat of the sea had been a lullaby whispering through the night, reaching past the sounds of the city as he'd cried himself to sleep as a child. He had mixed feelings about Busan and still dreaded the eventual return to finish filming the drama, but the sea at Jeju was sweeter than he remembered.

Tessa's fingers clenched his hand as a swell of water swept up her legs. She let out a squawk and leapt towards the dry shore. He spun her towards the sand and took the brunt of the next wave splashing up his legs.

Seawater clung like morning dewdrops in her hair, glinting bright as diamonds. He brushed the sprinkling of droplets from her face and smoothed down the wings of hair the wind had slicked upwards. She smiled at him, saltwater mingling with the dusting of freckles across her cheeks.

"Stop it," he whispered.

"Stop what?"

"Making me want to do this." He closed the distance, lips brushing softly over hers, the salt tang teasing his tongue. Tessa pressed back, mouth questing as the sea rippled around them and camera snaps filled the air.

Her body swayed towards his as he pulled away. She let out a small, pitiful sound, and he was tempted to ignore the cameras for another taste. The studio had warned them that people would be watching, but it dulled the enjoyment of being outdoors with her. Suggesting they go back to the hotel was an option, but he didn't want to be chased away.

Tessa looked at him, puzzled. "What's wrong?"

He gestured to the growing crowd of people and cameras pointed in their direction. "Apparently they have nothing better to do. I bet half of them have no idea who we are but didn't want to miss the opportunity to get a picture."

"Let's not let it spoil today," Tessa said. "Want to swim?"

"The water's cold."

"We'll get used to it."

Tessa dropped her sarong to the dry sand and kicked off her flip-flops, pulling him towards the ocean. It was warm enough to swim safely, but not enough to be particularly comfortable while doing so. They swayed with the water, hovering chest deep with toes skimming the sand. Eun Gi kept his hands planted at her waist, and she looped her arms behind his neck, keeping the warmth contained where their skin made contact.

Her eyes were fascinating; dark and liquid. His lungs constricted as he walked his fingertips down, watching those eyes focus on him, listening to the hitch of her breath. He traced the top of her thighs, and she moved with the next swell of water, legs following the surf until she was wrapped around him.

Her head tilted to the side, assessing him. "Okay?"

"Yeah." He squeaked, and his hands automatically cupped the underside of her thighs to support her position. She dipped her lips once, twice, just the lightest caress on his mouth. His heart rate climbed steadily. It was only the cold water that would let him get out of the sea without embarrassing himself.

He shuddered as she brushed against him.

"Fuck," came out as a single, hushed breath.

Tessa's mouth curved against his. "Want to go back to the room?"

Propriety be damned.

"Yes."

Chapter 15

Tessa

What the actual hell am I doing?

Tessa wrapped damp arms around Eun Gi in the elevator. Everything below her knees was covered in drying sand and the salt was starting to itch. It was so easy to stop thinking, to sink into the sensation of his mouth, of his hands spread over her waist. They'd taken the first available vehicle to the hotel, keeping a careful distance from one another in the back of the cab, but the heat of his gaze had kept her heart ping-ponging. Her whole body thrummed with the need to be touched.

It had been so many years since she'd had sex with anyone except herself. Every minute brush of his hands on her skin branded itself there, leaving each spot humming with sensation. The elevator doors pinged on their floor, and a thousand what-ifs flooded her head. Eun Gi wasn't her first lover, but he was the first with his particular anatomy.

He popped his head out of the elevator to check the halls. Finding it empty, he wrapped a hand around her wrist and tugged her towards their room. The key-card beeped in the slot, and he deposited them both inside.

"We should rinse off the sand." Eun Gi glanced toward the bathroom and then back to Tessa. "Together?"

"Uh, you go ahead." Panic rose in her throat. "I'll hop in after."

He gave her a long look before nodding, and disappeared into the bathroom.

Tessa grabbed her phone and sent a frantic text.

Tessa:
Kelly Kelly Kelly!

Kelly:
Tessa Tessa Tessa!

Tessa:
Help meeeeee I'm FREAKING OUT

Kelly:
What's going on?

Tessa:
Um, we might be dating?

Kelly:
Tess, you just married him...

Tessa:
I KNOW, but I mean like, proper dating. To see if we like being together.

Kelly:
But that's good, right??

Tessa:
YOU DON'T UNDERSTAND! I have permission to actually feel all
the things I'm feeling now and I CANNOT cope. I'm dying.

Kelly:
If by dying you mean living, then yes I agree

Kelly was no help at all. Tessa contemplated walking out of
the room and continuing until she stopped feeling so
overwhelmed. She'd have to keep going forever in that case
because her nerves would start all over again the moment she
turned back to the room.

Her phone pinged again.

Kelly:
Just roll with it.
If you want to be with him, be with him.
Have you kissed yet? I mean, outside of the wedding.

Tessa:
Yes

Kelly:
AND????

Tessa:
I'm doomed

Kelly:
Well we already knew that. Go get some!

Tessa:
That's the problem!!! He's showering right now and we
might...you know

Kelly:

Tessa...you're 27. You can say you're gonna fuck

Tessa:
Kelly!

Kelly:
Be safe. I'm not ready to be an auntie yet :P

Tessa groaned and briefly considered smothering herself with a pillow.

The bathroom door clicked open, and Eun Gi stepped out in a cloud of steam, towel wrapped around his waist.

Holy shit. Her gaze fastened on to the lean planes of his body. He was sleek, damp, and slightly pink from the hot water. Droplets coalesced and glided down his torso before disappearing into the fluffy white fabric. Desire coiled in her belly.

"All yours."

All mine. Tessa's mouth went dry. *Oh. He meant the shower.*

She slid off the bed and zipped into the bathroom, phone in tow. After peeling off her swimsuit, she stepped under the warm spray.

You're a grown-ass adult, and you've had sex before.

The indulgence of a good long shower helped calm her down a bit. She blow-dried her hair with the diffuser attachment Yuna had thankfully thought to provide, and it bought her a few more precious minutes. By the time she finished her routine she was almost ready to face him. It would be presumptuous to walk out naked, and Tessa didn't quite have the fortitude to attempt it. Instead, she opted for one of the hotel robes hanging on the back of the door.

The room was dimly lit, and music played when she opened the door—one of 24/7's earliest albums. A fresh bottle of champagne sat on ice, and Eun Gi was fully clothed.

Tessa blinked incomprehensibly.

There was a dress laid across the bed. Eun Gi smiled, stepping towards her. "You missed out on something important, and I want to fix it."

"Oh. I thought we were going to do...other things."

He snared her hands, lacing their fingers together. "Hmm, we were, but I could tell you were starting to panic."

Tessa cringed. "I wasn't panicking."

"Uh-huh. Sure could've fooled me." He slipped his arms around her waist. "I don't want you to have to push through your emotions to be with me. Nerves are one thing, but I've paid enough attention to you to be able to tell when it's more than that."

Tessa was so intent on his face that she jumped when his thumb brushed her cheek.

"I told you there's no rush, and I meant it. Whatever we do, and *whenever* you're ready, you let me know. Okay?"

She nodded, heart racing.

"It might be our honeymoon, but I promise I don't have any expectations. Would you mind putting on the dress I picked out?"

"What's all this for?"

"A surprise."

Red embroidered flowers adorned the hem of a white dress. She dug out undergarments to go with the dress, a matched set of black and gold lace.

He courteously looked away while she struggled inside of the robe to pull everything on, but she needed help with the zipper after getting it only halfway. Eun Gi swept her hair over her shoulder. Goose bumps raced down her arms, and she bit her lip against a gasp when his breath ghosted over the back of her neck. The zipper slid upwards, and his arms went around her again, his chin set on her shoulder. Her heart thrummed, and she settled her hands on his.

"What's your favourite song?"

"Is it weird if I say 'Lightning Dream'?"

It was Eun Gi's second solo piece, and the first he'd written all on his own.

"No. It means a lot to me. I'm glad you like it too."

Smooth, sultry notes poured out of his phone as a new song began. A hint of jazz mingled with the rippling music that saturated the air. He spun her in his arms, interlacing one hand with hers, and cradling her waist with the other.

"You didn't have a first dance at the wedding."

Tessa's lip wobbled. Wedding planning wasn't something she'd had much interest in growing up. She had never picked out the intricate details that some people did, and she'd convinced herself that she didn't need any of that, but now…

He twirled her and drew her back in, murmuring the words of the song in her ear.

"Come with me tonight, my love. The violet sky is calling. Your eyes light up like lightning. Your voice whispering from a dream."

A shiver raked up her spine, and her heart slammed into her ribs. This was a much more common fantasy than anything else that had ever wandered through her brain. To have him sing. For her.

"Come back, my love, and wait for me when you wake. The sunlight breaks the dream and leaves the lightning in the night."

When he pulled her back in from another twirl, she wrapped her arms around his neck and leaned in to kiss him. Surrendering to the sweetness of the moment, she indulged in the softness of his lips, in the steady way his hands pressed against the small of her back. She reveled in the heat of his skin through the thin fabric and dug in her nails when his mouth moved to her throat.

Tessa shivered. A whispered *yes* mingled with ragged breath and helpless sounds of pleasure.

"Bedroom," she gasped.

Stumbling steps took them through the suite, until her legs hit the edge of the bed. She leaned back, pulling him with her. Boundaries for how far she wanted this to go weren't firm in her mind yet, but she could have this.

The two of them inched up and settled onto the bed, the weight of him sinking down next to her. The heat in his eyes had her stomach clenching. Each heartbeat was a punch to her chest, and every inch of her body was hyper aware of his presence, eager to feel, yet afraid to do so. Tessa swallowed hard.

"Tell me what you want," he whispered against her ear.

The warmth of him sent fresh shivers rippling through her body. She wanted a lot. Too much.

"Touch me. Please." A low desperate sound escaped her throat when he inched closer.

One hand threaded into his hair, the other clung to his shirt. They kissed until she was melting into the mattress.

"Look at me," he said softly.

She peeled her eyelids open, not realizing how tightly she'd had them squeezed shut. He was *so* close.

"It's just us." His fingertips brushed over her hairline, ghosting over her cheek. "I promised to take care of you, right?"

Her voice was frozen in her throat, so she nodded instead.

Eun Gi propped himself up, putting her intimately on display. She stayed latched onto his shirt, keeping him at bay, but holding him close. He watched every shift of her features, dipping down to consume the hitch in her breath when his fingertips slid over the curve of her breast. Her stomach quivered under his hand.

Tessa wiggled closer, blood roaring in her ears. He toyed with the hem of her dress that pooled at her hips, slipping under the fabric, moving over bare skin, pressing her closer. Thoughts blurred and crashed together, whizzing through her brain too quickly to understand. All her senses focused down to him. Touching her.

She whimpered when he moved away from the waistband to settle on top of her thigh.

More.

"Please," she repeated.

Eun Gi's gaze flashed to hers. Her muscles twitched as he slid back down, hand curving over the inside of her thigh. When he sidestepped again, jumping to the other leg, she let out a whine. He buried his smile against her throat.

"Do you want me?" he whispered.

"Should I be *more* obvious?" She released a nervous giggle and unclenched her fingers from his shirt. Her lips brushed across his. "Yes, I want you. A lot. Please."

He slipped his hand into her underwear, giving her exactly what she'd been angling for. She shuddered desperately, and squeaked. His fingers glided through slick heat and Tessa's brain melted out her ears. Her nails dug into him and every rasping breath was accompanied by an uncontrolled gasp.

Tessa shifted her hips, rolling against his hand. Two fingers slipped in, and her back arched off the bed before slumping helplessly back down. The sounds she made no longer resembled anything coherent, as the heel of his palm pressed a slow grind against her, fingers moving in a steady rhythm that built an inferno in her belly.

He followed the guidance of her reactions, the pitching cadence of each moan leading him to focus on the exact spots that elicited the most desperate reactions. She shook with the waiting pleasure poised to burst.

"Eun Gi." His name left her mouth as a gasp.

"Hmm?" He nosed her throat and nipped, eliciting another helpless sound from her.

"Please, I'm so close."

"Your choice," he murmured against her skin. "I can finish you like this, or..." His tongue dragged over the curve of her throat.

"That," Tessa whimpered. "Definitely that."

He chuckled softly and withdrew his hand despite her fervent protests.

"I have to." Eun Gi crawled down the bed to situate himself between her legs. He tugged at the delicate swirls of black lace clinging to her lower half. Tessa hoisted her hips to assist and Eun Gi paused to look.

This was an expression she'd never seen on his face before, and nothing prepared her for how it turned her insides molten.

His mouth teased his way down one thigh and up the other. She clung to the blanket.

"Patience," he murmured.

"I am *beyond* patience." She laughed. "Please, for the love of God."

His tongue slid exactly where she wanted, and she cried out, hips bucking, body curving towards that one point of contact.

Eun Gi pressed a palm to each thigh, and dipped back down, gliding lips and tongue against her core.

A chorus of *please, please, please* poured out of her.

She swore as everything contracted into ripples of pleasure, shuddering as her hips moved frantically to chase his tongue. When he'd wrung every last spasm out of her, she collapsed into silence punctuated by the harsh drag of her breath.

Every limb was limp, and her eyelids weighed far too much to be open. The mattress dipped next to her, and she swung an arm, hooking him around the neck to pull him in. Their mouths collided, and Tessa lingered on the flavour of her that clung to his mouth.

Satisfaction lasted only a few moments before the curls of desire renewed.

"More."

Tessa pulled at his shirt, and he yanked it the rest of the way off, leaving her hands free to roam his skin. Her fingers kneaded him, and she gasped as his teeth nibbled her throat. She groaned and scratched her nails through his hair.

"Eun Gi?"

"Hmm?" he asked, not stopping in his quest to set her nerves aflame.

"Do we have protection?"

He froze and his weight sank onto her. "I forgot."

"You thought of a magical first dance, but forgot condoms?" Tessa giggled helplessly.

"Maybe."

She nipped away his pout. "I could still finish you other ways."

"Later," he promised. "I already did that in the shower so you wouldn't feel pressured and I'd have a clearer head."

"It's still early. Stores will be open if we want to pick up supplies. The hotel probably sells them too."

"I'd rather not let the entirety of the hotel staff know for certain what we're doing."

"They'll assume anyway, but we could get some food and stop on the way back. You can fuel up for later."

"I do like the sound of that," he mused, hand slinking down to rest on her thigh.

"Mhmm." She shifted, and dragged him back down. "You're going to need the energy."

Chapter 16

Eun Gi

Eun Gi couldn't stop looking at her or thinking about what had happened. Each time they made eye contact her cheeks flushed pink. Every fibre of his being wanted to get back on that bed, and yet here he was, on his way to a restaurant.

They wandered into a place that boasted the best *maeuntang* on the island. Eun Gi signed autographs for excited staff while Tessa sat down, until they brought out steaming bowls of the spicy fish soup.

When Tessa's hand touched his thigh to get his attention, he almost died. It was entirely possible he would combust by the time they made it back to the hotel. The food managed to remove the lingering flavour of her body from his tongue, but the heat in her gaze whenever she lifted her eyes to him was maddening. To make matters worse, she wasn't even doing it on purpose. Her expression would flicker between embarrassment and desire every few seconds, and it had him squirming in his seat.

Stop it. Just...think of something else.

He took a deep breath and watched the condensation slide down his glass. Their conversation that morning had prompted a million possibilities. What would it be like to be with someone like Tessa? Sweetness, a strong will, and more generosity than he had any right to were an alluring combination. She got along well with his closest friends too—those she'd met anyway—and he didn't mind the interactions he'd had with hers. They'd been functioning well as roommates, if a little more intimate than most cases. It wouldn't be difficult to slip into this new role as lovers.

Memories of her begging shot through him like an arrow, and he choked on his dinner. Tessa helpfully patted his back and passed him her glass of water, oblivious to his internal predicament.

"Are you okay?"

"Fine," he squeaked.

After dinner they located a convenience store.

Eun Gi picked out the first brand he recognized and the nearest bottle of lube, burying them in his arms under a variety of snacks as well as some bottles of orange juice, one with pulp and one without.

When they got back to the hotel room, she turned to him, suddenly serious. "So, full confession, but I've only slept with women before this. I might need some guidance."

He swallowed hard. "Okay."

Eun Gi stowed the drinks in the fridge and the treats on top for later. She pulled the box out of the bag, and the awkward tension became palpable. The tenderness that had given way to flame earlier had dispersed and now there was only anxious reality stretching between them.

"Nervous?" Tessa asked.

"Yes," he said frankly. "It's been a while for me too."

"Okay, we're grown people. This shouldn't be so weird."

"I think it usually takes time before most people are comfortable talking about all of this without it getting weird."

"Practice makes perfect?" She sat down on the bed. "I think we should be able to talk about things if we're going to have sex."

He raised an eyebrow. "I'm not opposed, but that's quite a change of opinion from a couple hours ago."

"Yes, well, you overwhelmed me with all..." she waved her arm, gesturing to him head to toe, "...that."

"Really?" The words triggered a smile, and he leaned closer. "You should tell me what I did, for research purposes, so I can avoid overwhelming you in the future."

"You're terrible." She hesitated a moment and then kissed his cheek. "Thank you, by the way. I didn't quite get a chance to say how sweet you were with the dance."

"You're welcome." He tucked one of her curls behind her ear. Her skin was warm under his fingertips, and he couldn't help but notice the hitch in her breath.

"Eun Gi."

The way she said his name was definitely growing on him.

"Tessa." He sat down by her side. "So, what are we talking about?"

She stared firmly at her fidgeting hands in her lap. "I'm about to get awkward for a second, so apologies in advance. I don't really have to worry about getting pregnant since I have an IUD, but I still want to use condoms."

His thoughts froze.

"And," she continued, still unable to look him in the eyes, "I got tested to be sure after my last partner, so no worries there either."

"Uh, good, I'm—I'm good there too," he stuttered out. Kyung Mi made sure they were all regularly tested when they had their blood work done, so he knew he was safe.

Tessa's face was bright red, but that didn't stop her from propelling the conversation forward.

"I don't need your full history or anything, but any hard limits or things you're not comfortable with? I'd rather know beforehand than accidentally do something you hate."

"I can't think of anything." His cheeks burned and he had a vague desire to lock himself in the bathroom. "You?"

Her cheeks got darker, though he wasn't certain how that was possible at this point.

"No, I've liked everything I've tried."

His stomach clenched, and his brain tipped into the gutter, rolling through filth as his blood rushed south. Tessa slid up the bed and patted the headboard. He settled himself next to her, unsure of what to expect now.

"Anything else?" he asked.

"Nope."

She swung her legs up and over, situating herself in his lap. The bottom of her dress inched up, and Eun Gi draped his hands over her thighs. Her dark eyes glittered, staring down at his face. He lifted a hand to her chest, feeling the hammering pulsebeat beneath his palm.

Sleek coils fell over her shoulders, her head tipping to the side, exposing the length of golden skin. He remembered the pool and dropped his mouth against her neck, teeth and tongue wringing a gasp from her. "Eun Gi."

Her nails bit into his scalp, hips rocking a steady rhythm. She was everywhere, heat enshrouding him. It got harder to think with each sultry grind of her body.

Everything she offered, he wanted. He fanned fingers over her thighs, gliding hands up her body. Her low, desperate sounds filled his ears, and he shifted again, exploring to see where else would elicit that hitch in her breathing he craved.

She leaned back to tug the skirt of her dress out of the way. Eun Gi took her face in his hands, thumbs brushing her cheeks as he tried to wrangle his own unsteady breath.

"I want to check in," Tessa said. "There can be pressure on men to go along with things when it's offered, but you absolutely don't have to."

He shook his head. "This is unexpected, but not unwanted." His hand slid behind her head and pulled her down for a brief, soft kiss. "I didn't give myself permission to think of you like this before this morning."

"I shouldn't have, but I thought about it a lot," she confessed. "The more time I spend with you, the more I like you. I mean, I already liked you, but I've enjoyed the opportunity to get to know the you behind what I've seen over the years."

His heartbeat picked up speed with each word. They were probably moving too fast, and he already knew he was tiptoeing in dangerous waters with his feelings. Everything was still so new.

"Maybe we should wait for a little while?"

"Of course." She moved to climb off, but his fingers pressed against her hips.

"I didn't mean you had to leave. Let's just move a bit slower." He settled back more comfortably against the headboard. "I got a bit ahead of myself earlier. Was it okay?"

Tessa giggled and nestled her face against his shoulder. "Should I be worried?"

"No, not at all." She hoisted back up, face etched into a grin. "I can't believe you had to ask. It was amazing."

He glowed with pride. He might be a bit rusty, but he knew how to pay attention. "Is it still okay if we sleep next to each other?"

"Well, there's only one bed," she mused. "I haven't minded sharing before."

"Yeah, but we weren't..." he searched for the word in English, "...sexually involved every other time we shared a bed. So, if you wanted new boundaries, I'd understand."

Tessa snuggled into his arms. "These ones are just fine."

Relief poured through him.

"Want to put on pajamas and watch a movie?"

"That sounds perfect." She slid off the bed. "Would it be out of line asking for help changing?"

He tugged the zipper down, and she lifted her arms to assist as he pulled the dress off. Then she stood there in the delicate swirls of black and gold lace. He traced his fingertips over the curve of her waist, fascinated by the goose bumps that decorated her skin following the path of his hands. Eun Gi pulled off his own shirt, and the tension built like a growling beast between them.

His gaze was rooted to her as she grabbed her pajamas from the suitcase and donned the nightgown before wrestling off her bra underneath it.

"Can I sleep in my underwear?" he asked.

"Okay." The word came out of her mouth barely louder than a whisper. She focused on him intently as he removed his pants. "Are we gluttons for punishment? We say take it slow and then tease ourselves instead."

He crossed the distance between them and brushed his thumb over her bottom lip. "Sometimes teasing is just as much fun."

Chapter 17

Tessa

Tessa was strangely placid when she woke. Her body was relaxed and her head clear as she stared at the ceiling. Eun Gi was curled around her, and she had to wiggle a little to get enough space to stretch her legs. He nestled closer and kissed her shoulder.

"Good morning," he mumbled.

Goose bumps prickled her skin. He nuzzled her face, pressing a soft kiss to her mouth, and Tessa melted into the affection, blood humming pleasantly.

This was definitely the best way to wake up.

A grin broke across her face and interrupted the kiss.

He opened sleepy eyes and snuggled contentedly into his pillow. "It's nice waking up to a pretty face. Last time I kissed someone in the morning it was Sung Soo by accident."

"How did that happen?"

His whole body went rigid. "I'd split from Hye Jin, and I forgot it was him there instead."

"I don't imagine Sung Soo appreciates that particular attention the way I do." She paused a moment before speaking the next thought that slammed into her brain. "You've never told me why you two split."

His face pinched, and he sighed, pulling the blankets up to his chin. "I asked her to marry me, and she said no."

Tessa's throat constricted. It wasn't the answer she expected, and she wasn't entirely sure how to proceed. "I'm so sorry."

He shrugged. "I was twenty-one. We'd been together for a year. Hye Jin was an apprentice then, and she'd helped at all our domestic shows. The guys were fond of her, so they were thrilled when we got together, and they helped cover for us. In the end it turned out I'd misread our relationship. I had a whole elaborate thing planned for the proposal, but as soon as she saw it, she knew. I asked anyway, thinking she was just nervous, and then she bailed."

"Why did she said no?"

His gaze dipped, and he fidgeted uncomfortably. "I didn't understand at the time, but I found out later that Yoon had talked to her about it. She wasn't interested in our lifestyle long term, and didn't want to deal with the press and the fans. She totally disappeared afterwards. I get it, and I don't blame her anymore. It's a lot to handle, and we weren't very old at the time. She liked me, but not enough to commit to all that."

Tessa's heart raced. She'd asked before, but she hadn't been invested then like she was now. "Do you still love her?"

He was quiet so long nausea crept up Tessa's throat.

"No."

Relief drained away the tension.

He lapsed back into silence, face closed off.

Unease picked at her gut as she waited for him to speak.

"Right after it happened we left on tour. Eomeoni leaked our relationship to the media, and between that and the proposal, Hye Jin wanted nothing to do with EchoPop anymore."

"Your mother leaked it?" Tessa snapped to attention. "Why?"

He puffed out a sigh and stared at the ceiling. "Eomeoni can be very controlling, and I was trying to push back at the time. I told her I was planning on proposing. Even though our relationship was so strained, I hoped that she might change and be happy for me. I knew telling her was a mistake, but I was still young enough to not entirely know better. Eomeoni doesn't like when people don't do what she says. I've learned to navigate that better now."

"God, I'm so sorry. That's awful." She nestled against him, pulling him into her arms. "You didn't deserve that, and neither did Hye Jin."

Heat filled her chest. She'd never truly hated anyone before, but Eun Gi's mother was quickly taking the honour of being the first.

"Anyway. Talking about Eomeoni stresses me out, and we were already talking about something else super uncomfortable, so take your pick between them, but I don't think I can handle both."

"Tell me about Hye Jin?"

"She got a job with Elite Studios, and I never took the time to process anything that had happened between us. I poured myself into my work and sort of pretended she didn't exist. By the time I got the job with the drama I'd entirely forgotten it was the same studio she'd gone to."

"I'm sorry it didn't go how you wanted. I couldn't imagine loving someone enough to propose and then have them say no."

He rolled onto his back, bringing her with him. Her cheek pressed against his chest, his heartbeat pounding in her ear.

"I was mad for a long time, not at her, but at myself. I'm glad now that she said no, even if I wasn't at the time."

Eun Gi toyed with Tessa's fingers, tracing over each one. She bit back a shiver.

He frowned. "I'm sorry I brought her up."

"No, it's fine. I was the one who asked. I figured she'd come up sooner or later, and I've definitely been curious."

"You constantly surprise me with how understanding you are." His tension leaked away like a deflating balloon. "Can I be honest for a second?"

"Of course."

"I was dreading what you'd be like when this whole idea was proposed. I'm not sure if I would say that I was afraid of you in particular, but I was definitely afraid in general. Sometimes I wonder if I've lost the ability to assume the best in people and started anticipating the worst. I'm glad to be proven wrong."

Tessa ruminated on his words, choosing her own carefully.

"I don't think I realized how difficult things were in your position. I'm not nearly as famous as you, but I've dealt with it on a much smaller scale. Like, people trying to befriend me because it could benefit them, but the expectations and restrictions on you are *a lot*."

"They are *so much*," he agreed.

"There's nothing wrong with being protective of yourself, because you don't know who to trust or who has your best interests at heart versus those who want to use your influence for their own gain."

"Well, I can't argue with that."

"It might not mean much to say it, but you can trust me. It's not an ideal situation that I came into this as a fan. You're not your persona, but you've still had a big impact." She brushed the back of his hand in soft sweeps. "I love your music and how you move because you can tell how much you love to dance. I love your smile and your laugh. Those are all things I got to know before I ever had a chance to meet you and it's weird having that history in my head when it's totally one sided."

"It's not entirely one sided," he countered. "I like a lot of things about you. I'm just a little behind and need some time to catch up."

He wriggled free and propped his head on his hand so he could look at her. "I like these..." he traced his fingertips over her freckles, "...and these." His thumb caressed her plump lower lip.

Her breath stuttered.

"I like listening to you speak Korean because you have a slight accent, and I love that you so readily accept the people that I love. You make it easy to fall."

"Stop it."

"Stop what?" He quirked his head.

"Being so charming." She laughed, covering her face with her hands. "I'm weak."

"Good." He slipped his hand into hers, pulling it away from her face and pressing it into the bed. "That makes two of us."

He kissed her then, slow, soft, and deep. She was so utterly doomed. Her free hand carded through his sleek black hair, bringing him closer.

Eventually she had to call a halt to things. "Okay, we're supposed to be going slow, so I need you to not be so perfect for a little bit."

"You're giving me such an ego." Laughing softly, he kissed her one more time. "Sung Soo will be so unimpressed when we get home. He tries to keep me grounded. You're undoing his years of hard work."

"Well, my apologies to him, but this is half your doing, so I'm going to insist he blame both of us."

"Noted. Now, since we need to do something less tempting than staying in bed, want to work out with me? I feel like I've been a slug lately."

"Does the hotel have a gym downstairs?"

"Mhmm. Come with me?"

"Maybe." She raised a suspicious eyebrow. "Are you nicer than Sung Soo about workouts?"

"Nope."

Tessa went anyway, complaining through the vigorous cardio session, and cursing him through the weights until she dropped to the floor, a pile of displeased noodle limbs. They did partner stretches, and it annoyed her all over again that he was so attractive while sweaty.

"My lungs hurt."

"Your lungs are weak." He smiled and pulled her deeper into the stretch.

"Excuse you, my lungs are regular. You all are just insane."

"But consider the many advantages to having a partner with this kind of stamina."

He let her out of the stretch and slipped into his own.

"Oh my God, you did *not*." Tessa got up off the mat and walked to the door on wobbly legs. "I'm leaving. I can't with you right now."

He looked so innocent, with his eyes wide and chin cradled in his palms between his outstretched legs. She was already flushed from the workout, and now her cheeks burned for a whole new reason.

Giggling to herself all the way to the elevator, she thumbed the button. He caught up to her by the time the doors pinged open.

"I can't believe you abandoned me like that. I could have been kidnapped." He hooked his arm around her waist and moved them both inside, elbowing the number for their floor. "Think of the scandal."

"World famous K-pop star with unrivalled stamina kidnapped on honeymoon because of wife's negligence?"

"The world would mourn my loss."

"I'd mourn it too."

"Good." He nudged her against the wall and took advantage of the solitude to press a kiss against the curve of her throat, nipping across her shoulder. Tessa's fingers dug into his waist.

"This isn't what elevators are for," she whispered.

"Do you want me to stop?"

"No."

His mouth toyed with the stretch of sensitive skin that was interrupted by the strap of her tank top, which he helpfully nudged to the side.

Her stomach growled. Loudly.

"I think there's a place around here that serves Western-style breakfast," he said. "Want to go?"

"That sounds perfect."

Back in the room they rinsed off in the shower separately, then changed into fresh clothes.

"What's the breakfast thing called that has all the pockets?" He swung their joined hands as they walked.

"Pockets?"

"Yeah, it's like a sweet bread thing. It has lots of little pockets in it."

"Uh, waffles?"

"Yes! I love them. I tried them on our last tour."

They found the restaurant and ended up with two plates of waffles loaded with cream, chocolate, and berries. Ravenous, Tessa cleaned her plate and briefly contemplated licking it, but couldn't quite bring herself to do so in public.

They wandered around Jeju for the rest of the day, dipping into restaurants whenever they got hungry, but otherwise just enjoying the shops and sunshine. After dinner Tessa's phone started buzzing frantically. When she retrieved it from her purse she stared at it in shock. Notification after notification poured in.

"What the fuck?"

He turned towards her. "What's going on?"

"I don't know."

She scrolled back up. Six hundred notifications in the last five minutes. Her phone rang, a number she didn't recognize flashing on the screen.

"Hello?"

A voice screamed at her, a barrage of words coming too fast to decipher. She hung up, but another call immediately came through. She didn't answer that one. Or the next.

Tessa turned it towards him and his eyes flared wide. "Shit."

She denied every call that came through, trying to sort through the onslaught to see what was going on. Her social media was backlogged, the apps crashed when she tried to open them, and her website wouldn't load.

"It looks like you've been breached. Let me see if they work on my end." Eun Gi pulled out his own phone. He frowned. "Your account has tweeted dozens of times while we were out. All of it is in Korean, and none of it is very flattering. Your website is down too."

"Fucking hell." The barrage of calls made it extremely difficult to navigate through her phone. Her hands trembled. "I wish I had my laptop. This isn't working. What do I do?"

"Figure out what's been compromised and we'll go from there." He scrolled through his phone. "We'll get it handled. I'll let Kyung Mi know what's going on."

Eun Gi scooted closer and tucked her against him while he continued checking her account activity. "It looks like only two of your accounts were breached. Your phone number has obviously been leaked."

"What is wrong with people?" Her voice shook, panic twisting frantically in her stomach. "This is my *career!*" Amid the notifications were texts from Kelly, but the calls made it next to impossible to read.

"Here, use my phone. Call whoever you need to." Eun Gi passed over his device. "Turn yours off for now. It won't be much use while they're doing a brute force attack."

She phoned her assistant first.

"Hello?"

"Amelia!"

"Tessa? It's three in the morning."

"The website is down, and my accounts have been hacked. I'm so sorry to wake you. I forgot about the time difference."

"What do you need me to do?"

"I'm not totally sure what all is happening yet. Can you call the website hosting company and see if they can get things under control?"

"Oh dear. Yes, let me grab a pen, and I'll make a list."

Tessa put the phone on speaker.

"Okay. Hosting company, then change my password on every social media account and make sure we have two-factor authentication properly set up. I'm getting too many calls to manage it on my end." She glanced to Eun Gi. "What else? I've never been attacked on this scale before."

"We'll get you a new phone number. See about contacting a security firm to investigate the breach. We can do that here, or your assistant can do it from Vancouver. Once you have the passwords changed, we can tighten up all the messaging, remove anonymous options, and block anyone involved."

Tessa nodded. "Contact my agent too so she's not blindsided by what's going on. We'll probably have to do a press release and public apology. I'll text my parents from Eun Gi's phone to let them know I'm okay."

"On it. I'll handle all that and get back to you when it's done," Amelia said.

"You're an angel."

When they hung up, Tessa pressed her hands to her face. Panic gripped her throat, and she let out a sound of distress.

"It'll be okay," Eun Gi assured.

"Or it'll be a disaster. I need my social media to sell books. These people are trying to ruin me!"

"Come with me." Eun Gi ordered a taxi that took them to the main shopping district in Jeju City. It stopped in front of the Samsung store. "Let's get you a laptop you can use for this until we get back to Seoul."

Tessa followed in a haze. Eun Gi spoke to the wide-eyed young woman who greeted them and listened to exactly what they needed. She zipped off to get everything prepared. Eun Gi glanced back over to Tessa.

"Take a deep breath."

She did so.

"They have some that are ready to go for what we need. The staff will meet us at customer service."

Tessa nodded and let him lead her there. Her vision blurred at the edges, a throb pulsating at the base of her skull.

"Oh, fuck me," she muttered.

Eun Gi paid while she fished through her purse for her medication. Then she paused. It would knock her out, and she *needed* to be awake to deal with all of this. But she wouldn't be able to read anything properly once the auras set in fully.

"Hey." He scooped her face into his hands. "Look at me for a second."

Her gaze darted to his, heart pounding.

"Are you getting sick?"

"Migraine."

"Okay." He stroked her cheek. "It's going to be fine. We'll get you back to the hotel and you can rest."

"But my accounts." Tension pulled her shoulders taut, and she winced at the renewed throbbing.

"Do you trust me to handle it?"

She stared at him for a long moment, focusing on the gold ring at the centre of his eyes. "Yes."

"Good. Then I'll handle it."

They picked up a bottle of water for Tessa to take her medication, and then he bundled her into another taxi with their new electronics, and back into their room when they arrived at the hotel. Eun Gi sat next to Tessa on the bed and popped open the laptop, signing into each account in turn.

She texted Kelly with her new number.

Kelly:
I saw the shitshow start up.
I've asked my followers to report anyone harassing you in your mentions.
I've got your back.

Tessa:
Have I told you lately that you're the BEST best friend?

Kelly:
You can never tell me too often :P
I'll do what I can from my side of things.
How're you feeling?

Tessa:
Migraine is kicking my ass.
Eun Gi is handling things.

Kelly:
Go to SLEEP!
I'll communicate with him while you rest.
Sweet dreams <3

Tessa watched with blurry eyes as Eun Gi pinned an explanatory tweet and then methodically went through and deleted every one that had been sent during the hack. There were hundreds of messages and even more notifications. She fell asleep when he was altering the settings to stem the flow.

A few hours later Tessa woke from a dead sleep to the sharp ache of gremlins chewing their way out of her uterus. This day couldn't get any worse. Groaning, she buried her face into the bed.

She shuffled bleary-eyed to the bathroom, searching through the toiletry bag Yuna had provided. There was plenty of obscenely expensive skin care and makeup products from sponsors, but no painkillers.

She slipped back into the room and peeled open the curtains to let in enough light to see her suitcase. Digging through it, she grew more frustrated. None of the available underwear was well suited to her situation, but it was better than nothing. There were no hygiene products anywhere.

"Super."

Grumbling her way to the bathroom, Tessa fashioned a pad from toilet paper to tide her over before climbing miserably back to bed. She curled into a ball and slipped into an uncomfortable half-sleep; too exhausted to stay awake, but in too much pain to truly sleep.

Eun Gi jostled her shoulder lightly. "What's wrong?"

Tessa peeled open the eye not currently pressed to the pillow. "I'm fine."

"You're clearly not fine." He flipped on the bedside lamp and sat up, hair spiked in every direction. "What's going on?"

"It's just that time. I'll be okay."

"That time?" He stared at her, confused. "It's four a.m."

"No, it's *that time*."

"Oh. *Oh*. What can I do?"

She rolled over to lie face-first into the pillow and mumbled, "Schedule me a hysterectomy?"

"I don't think I heard that."

She lifted her head. "That's probably for the best."

"I didn't know it hurt so much," he murmured awkwardly.

"Well, it wouldn't if I had any painkillers to deal with it."

"I'll go to the store. There's a twenty-four-hour one close by. What do you need?"

"All of it. Yuna somehow forgot I have a functional uterus, and I want to smother her with a pillow." She wrapped her arms around her stomach and groaned.

Eun Gi got out of bed, grabbed the small notepad provided by the hotel, and brought it back with a pen. "Give me a list so I can get what you need."

She rattled off what she could think of and closed her eyes, willing away the pain while Eun Gi got dressed to venture into the pre-dawn glow.

He returned a while later with two bags in tow. "I wasn't sure about the specifics from your list, so I got some of everything. The man at the store took pity on me and helped me find it all."

Eun Gi chattered away as he deposited bits and pieces from the bags around the room. Tessa sat up as he shook a couple pills from a container and handed them to her with a bottle of juice. She downed the painkillers and shuffled off to the bathroom without a word. Despite the pain, she cracked a smile when she noticed the three sizes of pads neatly lined up on the vanity.

When she came back out, there were enough treats on her nightstand to put an elephant into a diabetic coma.

"I didn't know which you'd like best when you said chocolate, so I got a bunch of options."

"I want to eat, but I might throw up right now."

He frowned. "Is this normal, or should I be worried?"

She sank onto the bed. "Normal. For me anyway. I'm down to three or four times a year with the IUD, but it still kicks my ass."

Tessa sipped at the chocolate milk he opened for her, and Eun Gi fussed with a sock and a bunch of hand warmers he'd stuffed inside, before offering her the makeshift hot pack.

"I looked up what might be helpful."

She curled around the warmth and settled against the pillows.

He set his elbows on the bed.

She blinked, confused. "What?"

"What should I do? Do you want to be alone? Should I stay quietly in your general proximity? Do you want to cuddle? Something else my five-in-the-morning brain hasn't thought of?"

"Cuddling is nice."

He climbed back in and sprawled out, letting her shift and adjust so he could lay along her back.

"Any news on the breach?"

"Not much yet. I cleaned out what I could. Blocked about eighty troll accounts. We'll keep managing it in the morning."

"Thank you for being such a good husband," she mumbled.

"I do what I can." He pressed a kiss to her shoulder. "I just want to be what you deserve."

Eun Gi

The morning disappeared while Tessa slept, head on his lap. He worked on his phone and waited for Amelia to update him. Tessa let out a soft sound of distress and curled up tighter. He stroked a soothing hand over her hair until she relaxed again, content. His heart squeezed uncomfortably. He was entirely too protective of her.

He made the mistake of checking on the fan forums. A small pocket were calling for his removal from 24/7, which was nothing new but still pissed him off. Sprinkled in amongst the ire against him were comments about Tessa that set his blood boiling. The words they used to describe her churned his stomach.

He shouldn't have looked. Kyung Mi was always telling him not to, but sometimes he was a slow learner. Most people were fairly supportive of him, but there would always be those who thought of him as property.

Tessa groaned and opened her eyes.

"Are you hungry?"

She shook her head. "I'm sorry I'm ruining our time in Jeju."

"You don't have to apologize. None of this is your fault. I'm happy to stay here and let you rest for as long as you need."

Tears beaded on her lashes, and panic jolted his chest.

"What's wrong?"

"Nothing," she whispered.

"Hey." He pulled her into his arms. "Talk to me."

"I'm scared for my career, and everything hurts. I get overwhelmed so easily when I'm in pain, and you're being so nice. It's hard to process it all right now."

"What can I do?"

"You've already done so much."

He smoothed a hand over her hair and tugged the blanket up to cover them. "You need to rest. We're doing all we can."

She hiccupped through another sob. "What will I do if I can't get it all back?"

"You'll rebuild. Losing your social media presence for a little while won't change the impact you've had on your fans. They'll find you, even if you have to restart. Why don't you have a shower and I'll find you something to wear to bed?"

"I don't think I can rest anymore. God, I wish tampons weren't so hard to find in this country. I don't like them, but I want to sit in the bath."

"All the more reason to shower. Maybe the hot water will help."

He bundled her off to the bathroom and spent too long staring at the closed door.

His phone buzzed in his hand.

Yuna:
Why haven't you been outside yet today?

Eun Gi:
Tessa is sick and we're dealing with some security issues. We're staying in.

Yuna:
Unless she's dying you need to go out

Eun Gi stared at the screen.

Eun Gi:
I'm not making her go out

Yuna:
Don't force me to get someone higher up involved. The sponsors paid for this exposure and you're going to give it to them whether you want to or not.

Eun Gi huffed and tossed the phone aside. Yuna wasn't his priority. Tessa emerged damp and miserable. Black underwear peeked beneath the hem of the towel wrapped around her torso. Her eyes were glazed with pain as she slumped towards him.

"Any better?"

She shrugged. "I guess. It's nice to be clean at least."

"Let me help with your hair?" Yuna had packed them a blow dryer, but not any extra clothes, he marveled. At least it would prove useful. "Do I have to do anything fancy for curls?"

"Use the diffuser attachment and don't brush them, or it'll poof."

Eun Gi nodded, sitting behind Tessa on the bed. Sodden strands dried under his careful attention, falling into silken coils. He'd always loved getting his hair done.

His phone buzzed insistently, but he ignored it after sparing a glance to see it was Yuna again.

When he finished with Tessa's hair, he applied firm pressure to her shoulders. She groaned and leaned into it, the knots in her muscles loosening under the onslaught. He eased her down onto the bed and fetched the hotel lotion from the bathroom. She melted in his hands. Eun Gi worked carefully down her body, digging into her hips.

Tessa's brow pinched.

"Okay?"

"It hurts so good. It's fine, keep going."

He shifted, and she gasped into the blankets.

"Oh my God, where did you learn this?"

"Trial and error mostly. Dance practice, workouts, and performances take their toll. The company doesn't exactly give trainees and fresh debut groups access to personal massage therapists. Sometimes we woke up with muscle spasms and relied on assistance from one another to get it under control."

She hissed and gripped the pillow fiercely as he released a stubborn knot. His touch gentled into long sweeps before moving to her neck. The muscles there stretched like steel under her skin.

"How do you live like this?" Eun Gi asked.

"I have a high pain tolerance."

When she called for a break, he laid down, and she plastered herself to him, head on his chest.

"Thank you." Her voice was soft as she traced little swirls over his skin.

"You're welcome. I just want you to feel better."

She released a heavy sigh. "I do."

Eun Gi swallowed hard, uncomfortable with the growing tenderness in his chest. He wasn't ready to face this quite yet. "I don't want to ask, but Yuna is insisting we go out today."

Tessa made a sound of disapproval.

"I know." He set his palm against her cheek. "We only have to be out long enough for pictures so the sponsors don't pitch a fit."

She pouted. "Do we have to?"

"I'm not forcing you to go. I'll go on my own while you rest."

She sighed, shoulders drooping. "No, it'll be weird if you're out alone. Can you do my makeup? I'm sure I look like a trash pile."

"You definitely do *not* look like a trash pile. I'm not convinced it's even possible for that to happen. You're just a little paler than usual."

She patted his cheek. "You're so sweet to lie to me like that. I saw myself in the mirror."

"And I'm looking at you right now, and I'm telling you you're beautiful."

Her mouth dropped into an O, and she leaned into the hand still cradling her face. His heart gave an uncomfortable squeeze.

"You don't have to do a thing. Sit here. I'll do your makeup and find what's most comfortable in your suitcase, which, let's be real, none of it is truly comfortable, *but* I propose we pick you up some soft pajamas while we're out."

Tessa pulled the pillow to her chest while he gathered supplies. She submitted patiently as he applied a fresh face on her.

"To be clear, I'm only putting this on you because the press is a bunch of assholes." He added some blush. "I am rather familiar with covering up sleep deprivation with makeup."

"You were always perfect." Tessa toyed with the pillow.

"I went out strategically." He smiled indulgently. "One time I got so much stress acne that I tried to hide at the dorm for a week. Kyung Mi taught me how to do my own makeup after that."

"How old were you?"

"Sixteen. It was not a good time." He swept blush over her cheeks. "Alright, should be good to go."

He dug through her suitcase, pulled out the softest item he could find, and handed it to her.

She stared at it with distaste before huffing and disappearing into the bathroom with it. Eun Gi pulled out his own sponsor clothing to match what he'd picked out for Tessa. Her expression of misery tempered how cute she looked in the short-sleeved red satin dress.

He gave Yuna two hours of their time. Long enough to get Tessa some street *tteokbokki*, and for the lurking cameras to capture some pictures. She hid behind her sunglasses and a broad-rimmed hat that protected her from the worst of the sun, but he still noticed her hiss whenever they stepped out of the shade. Determined to let her rest, he sent a text to Yuna.

Eun Gi:
We're going back to the hotel.
Whatever pictures they've gotten will have to be enough.

Tessa was asleep as soon as she hit the bed. He set her hat aside and put her sunglasses on the bedside table, smoothing back her hair before properly tucking her under the blanket. Eun Gi packed up the majority of their bags before allowing himself to lie down next to her. She reached out in her sleep, fingers curling against his shirt. The swell of emotion left him breathless. He fell asleep with their hands interlaced.

The next day they didn't have to be at the airport until early afternoon. Tessa felt mostly human, albeit stressed to capacity. She was on her phone constantly, blocking new trolls and checking in with her assistant as her website was brought under control again. Once it was time to get on the flight back to Seoul, Eun Gi encouraged her to take a break.

They were back in their apartment before it was dark.

"I'll check in with the guys so we don't have all three over here before you've had time to settle."

Tessa looked up from the tea she was steeping and smiled gratefully. "Sounds good. I'll be here."

The others launched from their resting places to ambush him the second he opened the door wide enough to fit a human. Min Jae hung off him like a koala, and Eun Gi grunted at the weight. Sung Soo and Hwan kept him upright, but only because they were desperately hugging him as well.

"I was only gone for four days."

"Hyung, four days is a long time," Min Jae protested. "Where's Noona?"

Eun Gi tried to wriggle free, but no one was ready to let go quite yet.

"She's resting. She's not feeling well."

He waddled the group farther into the apartment so they could spread out onto one of the couches.

"Is Noona coming for dinner?" Min Jae asked. "Hyung made extra."

"I'll check when I go back over."

"So, how was Jeju?" Sung Soo asked. "You didn't make a peep for days besides updating us about the security breach. Did something else happen?"

Even if he wanted to hide it from them, it would be obvious soon enough. "Yes."

Min Jae hurled himself onto Eun Gi's lap. "Tell us everything."

Eun Gi let out an *oomph*, and his eyes watered. "Jae, you're crushing me."

"Talk fast and I'll uncrush. What happened with Noona?"

Unsure how much to say, Eun Gi took a breath to stall. "We decided to try out an actual relationship."

"Damn, I owe Kelly fifty thousand *won*," Hwan lamented.

"What?"

They were all suddenly sheepish and avoiding eye contact.

"Did you bet on us?"

"Only a little," Sung Soo said. "Kelly guessed you'd get together a lot sooner than we did."

"I didn't expect it would happen at all," Eun Gi confessed.

"Oh, we know." Hwan grinned. "But we're not blind. She was into you from day one and you got along well enough. You're not subtle, even though you think you are. It was pretty obvious you two would step over that line eventually."

"We all approve," Sung Soo added. "We like Tessa and if you want to actually be with her, then we'll support you."

Eun Gi slumped back against the couch and Min Jae hopped off to take over the nearest spot.

"I wish I was good at this sort of thing," Eun Gi said.

"Well, it's not like the rest of us are any better," Hwan commented. "You're the most romantically experienced of the lot of us."

"That gives me no confidence at all." He stared up at the ceiling, the others exchanging a glance between them.

"Even if we had more experience, each relationship is different," Sung Soo pointed out. "Tessa is a whole new person, and you have to learn as you go. Figure out what works for the two of you."

Eun Gi pouted. He didn't want to mess things up because of something he hadn't figured out yet. Darker thoughts tugged at him. Min Jae thwapped him in the face with a pillow, and Eun Gi sat up like he'd been shot.

"Hyung, stop thinking so hard." Min Jae grinned. "You always get this weird look when you disappear into your head. It'll be fine. Noona is awesome. You just need to not be stupid."

Don't be stupid. That was easier said than done, but Eun Gi would certainly try.

He laughed. "I can't decide if it takes the pressure off or not that we're already married. I don't have to wonder where it's headed because we're already there."

"Well," Sung Soo said, "I guess the question instead will be if you want to stay that way."

Chapter 18

Tessa

The sound of the sea had been replaced by the ebb and flow of traffic outside the window. Tessa sat on the couch with her tea and sipped it while slogging through the mass of emails she'd left unattended during their honeymoon. Her whole system was a mess after the breach, but the worst of it had tapered off. The trolls still bombarded her accounts, but Amelia had done a good job of blocking them as they appeared, with Kelly's help flagging the ones commenting in Korean. Tessa's new phone number was so far secure.

She was glad to settle back into her work routine, and also to be in her own clothes again. Designer outfits were lovely, but they couldn't provide the same comfort as her well-worn pajamas. Luxuriating in bundling herself into the soft blankets on the couch, she was grateful it was an option because she didn't have the energy to pretend to not be in pain.

The door code beeped.

"Incoming maknae!" Eun Gi yelled a moment before Min Jae flew through the opening, launching himself at the opposite couch.

"Noona, you're home!" He moved to hug her and then stopped himself, frozen in midair. "Hyung said you're sick. Are hugs okay?"

"Hugs are fine." Tessa was enveloped as soon as the words left her mouth. His enthusiasm was infectious. She let out a little squeak. "You're squashing me."

Min Jae released her immediately. "Sorry, Noona. Do you want to come for dinner?"

"If you don't mind me in pajamas."

Jae's head whipped towards Eun Gi. "We could all wear pajamas so Noona doesn't feel left out."

Eun Gi laughed. "Sometimes I forget you're an actual adult."

"Hyung, that's rude." Min Jae pouted. "Who doesn't love wearing pajamas?"

"Ok, we'll do a pajama dinner. Go change and let the others know. We'll be over in a few minutes."

Min Jae crushed him in a hug on his way out the door. "I'm glad you're home."

Tessa pressed her hands to her cheeks, a smile overpowering her features. "He's so cute! He missed you a lot."

"You should have seen them when I first went in. It was like someone let loose a pack of golden retrievers at me."

She grinned helplessly. His brow were pinched with a slight hint of annoyance, but his tone was soft with affection. He loved it more than he was willing to admit.

"I love that you all have such a close relationship. It's so sweet."

His brow smoothed, a smile adorning his face. "I think so too."

He disappeared into the bedroom to change and emerged in a dark-blue pajama set with white polka dots.

"You look comfy."

"Oh, I am." He swished his hands over the fabric. "It's satin."

He moved close enough for her outstretched hand to touch. Her fingers slid up his arm. "Very silky."

Eun Gi dropped down in front of her. "We should go to dinner, or I might get distracted and kiss you."

"You could kiss me and *then* we could go to dinner?" Tessa suggested.

"I like this compromise."

Tessa had never considered herself to be touch-starved. She was an introvert by nature and loved her quiet time alone, but sitting snuggled up to Eun Gi on the couch while his best friends chattered happily had its appeal. They made it known she was welcome to join the conversation, but mostly she enjoyed listening to them. Eun Gi's fingers twirled randomly in her hair, brushing over her scalp in a haphazard, rhythmic fashion that had her drifting in and out of focus against him.

She closed her eyes and listened to the cadence of his voice. The words blurred into the sound of his excitement, his contemplation as he answered questions, punctuated by laughter.

Her chest bloomed with warmth when she woke in the morning and found herself in her bed. She must have dozed off and Eun Gi carried her back over. He was conked out and sprawled next to her.

He was so peaceful when he was asleep, or at least when he wasn't having nightmares. The stress of the day was gone from his face, leaving him looking soft and younger than his twenty-five years. She brushed at some unruly strands of his hair, just because she could.

Tessa snuggled into her pillow and watched the steady rise and fall of his chest. Three words danced on the tip of her tongue, but they were too much to say out loud. She'd been saying she loved him for years, but the crush she'd nursed seemed so silly now, pale in comparison to the emotions churning inside her.

His eyes peeked open.

"Good morning." She grinned.

He rolled towards her and snared her in his arms. "Did you want to go around Seoul today? I mentioned it last night, but you'd already nodded off. We could invite Kelly and Min Joo, all go together. I keep thinking it's a shame you've been here over a month and have hardly seen anything in the city."

"I'd love to. I'd planned on going with Kelly my first week here, but you know how that went."

"Perfectly?"

Tessa snort-laughed and buried her face in her hands. "Oh my God. You're such a cheeseball."

He nuzzled up to her. "I don't know what that means, but you're laughing so I'm assuming it's good."

"Yes." She smacked a kiss onto his lips. "It is."

They settled on Gyeongbokgung Palace. Sung Soo drove Tessa and the boys while Kelly and Min Joo took the train. They'd been having Pyong Ho over for breakfast so he joined them as well.

Gwanghwamun Gate loomed over them, a towering three-pathed entrance of white brick and a sloping decorative roof reaching into the sky. It opened onto a stone courtyard, and Tessa was struck immediately by the grandeur. They wore hats and sunglasses to blend in with the other attendees. Pyong Ho guided them through the courtyards and tucked them into the shade, where they stood among red pillars listening to his enthusiastic and intimate historical knowledge.

People wandered around the palace in hanbok and traditional hairstyles, lending an atmosphere of living history. Tessa was the only one of the group who hadn't been to the palace before, but no one made any fuss about waiting while she soaked in the details, snapping pictures to send home. The graceful sloping roof of each building ended with intricate carved floral patterns and brilliant colours. There were definite nods to ancient Chinese architecture, but the style was still uniquely Korean.

Despite the number of people visiting, they stumbled upon areas that didn't have a single soul present. The farther they went the more the palace grounds harmonized with nature.

Trees obscured the telltale signs of modern Seoul, leaving only a view of historic rooftops and mountains filling the horizon. Tessa was in awe at every turn. They settled in the shade of the trees, deep in the inner recesses of the palace grounds, away from potential prying eyes and tourists with cameras hung around their necks.

"The palace was destroyed in the late 1500s when the Japanese invaded during the Imjin War." Pyong Ho sat down between Tessa and Hwan. "They were rather fond of torching our important buildings and the palace was razed. Thankfully King Gojong had an interest in preserving our history and oversaw most of the reconstruction."

"It's a viable battle tactic," said Tessa, "but it's such a shame that wars take so much history from people. This place is beyond gorgeous. I hate to think of it ever having been gone."

Pyong Ho nodded. "Invaders care about resources and power. People are easier to conquer if you destroy their past and symbols of unity. Our country has had a rough time in that regard. Everyone wants a piece of Korea."

"We're not pie. Everyone should stop trying to eat us." Hwan pouted his lip, and Pyong Ho laughed so hard he snorted, cheeks turning pink.

"I guess that's one way of putting it." Pyong Ho grinned.

Tessa sighed wistfully as a girl in a pink and blue hanbok floated past. "Traditional clothing is so beautiful."

"And comfy as fuck. As long as you're not wearing the fancy version," Kelly said. "I haven't worn any since the wedding, but I could live in hanbok."

"You should," said Min Joo. "You look cute in it."

"I have to agree, but I already stand out so much being a foreigner. I'd have people gawking at me all day long if I was running around in a hanbok too."

"Everyone gather up for a selfie!" Min Jae herded them together into a cluster and held his phone aloft. "I need longer arms," he complained, angling the phone to get all the heads in.

He forwarded the picture onwards to the group.

"No one post it yet," Sung Soo said.

Pyong Ho quirked his head. "Why not?"

"If fans know where we are, they'll show up," Hwan said. "You have to wait until you've left the area, especially when the background of the image is so distinct."

"That's fair." Pyong Ho nodded. "I never thought about it before."

"You pick up lots of tricks to deal with the fame." Hwan shrugged. "If we didn't we'd never be able to go outside."

"It sounds exhausting."

Eun Gi leaned his chin on Tessa's shoulder. "It's not terrible. At least not if no one recognizes you."

Pyong Ho turned to Tessa. "How have things been since the breach? I reported as many as I could when it was happening."

"Thank you." Tessa sighed. "It's coming along. They're slow to tire, but it's being managed as best we can."

They wandered at their leisure, exploring the palace complex. Eun Gi, Tessa, Kelly, and Min Joo took photos with each other to send to Tessa's parents, and the members of 24/7 took a bunch together to share with the fan-sites.

Mamãe:
Meu amor, you look so beautiful!

Tessa:
Thanks Mamãe :)

Mamãe:

Your husband looks like he's having fun. You're both so cute! I showed Appa and he's jealous of you being at the palace. Maybe we'll plan a trip to come visit

Tessa:
!!!!
DO IT! Come visit me :D

Mamãe:
You shouldn't encourage me. I've already got the airline site open

Tessa:
Ooooh tragedy

Kelly peeked over her shoulder. "Your parents are coming to Seoul?"

"I hope so. I'm not sure when though. Appa should be okay to travel soon."

"I can't wait to see them!"

Eun Gi

Eun Gi flopped back onto the couch when they got home. "I'm afraid of meeting your parents." Nerves prickled his stomach.

"They're very nice, I promise."

"Yeah, to you, maybe. I'm the outlier, the wily man who stole their daughter."

Tessa started laughing and then couldn't stop, burying her face into a couch pillow as she dissolved into helpless giggles.

"What's so funny? Parents are terrifying. What if they hate me?"

Tessa pulled the pillow off her face. "Who could ever hate you?"

Panic raced through him. He hesitated, unsure how much he should say.

"My own parents managed to. I'm never certain that anyone else will like me because they don't."

Tessa sobered immediately. "I'm so sorry. That was insensitive of me. My parents are going to love you. I don't know what's wrong with yours that they would ever be anything but loving towards you."

He huffed out a sigh. "It's hard to shed the mentality. I know in theory that other people love me, but it doesn't quite seem real. I feel like I'm one stupid decision away from ruining it all."

His eyes burned.

No. You're grown now. You're fine.

Tessa's fingers brushed his cheek, slipping into his hair. "Lots of people love you, and even more will in the future. You're easy to love."

The words felt like lies—like a knife in his chest. He wanted it to be true, had always been desperate to feel that someone truly loved him. The other members expressed it often enough and without reservation, but still, he was *trying* to be loved. He put a lot of effort into stuffing down the unpleasant parts of himself so that he would be easier to love. It didn't always work, but he feared what would happen if he ever gave up trying.

The poisonous thoughts cycled around in his head, swirling down into his belly until the nausea forced him to head to the bathroom. He locked the door behind him.

He despised getting caught in these patterns, in letting the rising swell of self-loathing choke him. Memories of his parents shredded his self-confidence, stripping him away to a bare and broken foundation.

Tessa was saying his name, but the sound came from across a chasm too great for him to bridge. He hiccupped and tried desperately to get his breathing under control so he could stop embarrassing himself. It wasn't cooperating.

"Eun Gi!" Tessa called out to him and knocked on the door. "What's wrong?"

Don't let her in. The voice of self-loathing whispered to him.

He turned on the shower, stripping down to climb under the spray. The shock of the cold water broke through some of the haze, but all of the hatred directed at his parents, at himself, still roared in his ears.

He sat waging a quiet war against the monsters of his past, but eventually the door opened. Min Jae could always undo the locks. Sung Soo came in first and turned off the water. Shivers racked his entire body. Jolting forward, Eun Gi threw up into the basin before curling into himself.

Arms hoisted him out of the tub and wrapped him in a towel, hustling him back to his bedroom.

"I don't feel good."

"We've got you." Tessa draped a towel over his head, scrubbing at the dripping hair. The comforter from the bed sank over his shoulders, trapping what little heat his body was able to produce.

"What happened?" Sung Soo asked while they worked.

The voices were hazy.

Warm hands gripped his cheeks, and he tried to focus on Tessa's face. She looked so worried.

I did that. I always make everyone worry.

Tessa pressed a hand to his chest, and her voice reached to him through the haze.

"Follow me." She brought one of his hands to her chest and breathed deeply.

He inhaled once, then again, using the rise and fall of her chest to force his own to cooperate. Her forehead rested against his. He didn't know how long she kneeled in front of him, patiently coaxing him, when suddenly the grip on his lungs eased, and he sucked in a grating gulp of air.

Tessa's arms were around him instantly.

Sung Soo pressed against his side, cheek to his hair.

"I'm okay." Eun Gi's tongue felt thick and slow in his mouth.

"Panic attack?" Sung Soo asked.

"I think so."

They got him bundled onto the bed where he sank limply into the mattress. The others flooded into the room. Tessa stretched out on one side, Sung Soo on the other with Hwan and Min Jae draped over his legs. It was a tight squeeze, but they managed to fit without anyone falling off.

"We haven't had to cuddle pile for a while now," Min Jae said. "What set you off?"

"I think meeting my parents," Tessa said when Eun Gi didn't respond.

Sung Soo wrapped his arm over Eun Gi. "We're here, and we love you."

They stayed like that until Eun Gi's heartbeat finally calmed and he settled into a languid, half-sleep state. "You guys, this is embarrassing. I'm not a baby."

"Adults need care sometimes too," Hwan pointed out.

"We should order pizza and eat it in bed." Min Jae grinned.

"I'm not opposed," said Eun Gi, "but I definitely need to put on some clothes for that."

The boys vacated the room to order food, and Tessa waited while Eun Gi got dressed.

"Eun Gi, have you talked to a professional about all this?"

He pulled on a pair of sweatpants. "Like who?"

"A doctor or therapist? They can be helpful with anxiety and panic attacks."

He shook his head and slipped on a T-shirt. "I don't want to take drugs for that."

"They wouldn't force you, and even if it was recommended, it's no different than taking medicine for a cold. I take meds, and I've been to therapy before too. Sometimes your mind needs extra care just like your body, and there's nothing wrong with that. It's not so scary."

"Tessa, please."

"You could talk to someone with training for how to deal with this."

"Can you please drop the subject?"

She bit her lip, but nodded. "I'm worried about you."

"I'll be fine." He shrugged. "I always am."

Chapter 19

Eun Gi

"I don't want to go to Busan today," Eun Gi moaned.

Tessa kissed his cheek. "Good luck convincing the studio that you don't have to go."

Each day over the last two weeks had moved them closer to filming in Busan, and it was like a looming shadow that had Eun Gi becoming more anxious about his return to the city.

"If only. Couldn't you have set your book in the mountains?"

"I don't think Bridie's ship could have sailed into the mountains," Tessa remarked.

Eun Gi rolled over and crushed her. "Go back in time, make it a historical fantasy, and let the ships fly."

"I can't go back in time with you squishing me." She looped her arms around him.

He dropped a kiss to the curve of her throat, and she shivered, fingers tightening against his back. Her breath turned ragged in his ear, nails digging in a little more with each subtle movement. His name disappeared into a sigh.

"Hmm?"

"We have to get ready to leave."

He made a sound of protest and rolled off. "Who plans flights this early in the day?"

"Studios with no respect for sleep?" She pressed a kiss to his mouth and climbed off the bed. "We'll have some time to settle in before they need you on set. Maybe it'll rain and they'll have to postpone."

Eun Gi checked the weather on his phone. "It's not supposed to rain until tonight."

Indulging in one more kiss before gathering up her toiletries, she leaned into him, nipping his bottom lip.

"I'm trying to be good and pack all our things. You're being so distracting."

"Do you want me to stop?" She quirked her head to the side.

He backed her up until she met the wall and his arms moved to cage her. "No."

Shivers raced over her skin as she pulled him in, capturing his mouth. She inched closer until their hips touched. Her fingers kneaded the base of his skull, sliding through his hair, and he made another incomprehensible sound, diving down to nibble her throat just because he could.

His phone buzzed loudly on the nightstand, and he sighed, dragging himself away to answer it. The driver was waiting to take them to the airport. "We'll be right out. Give us five minutes."

Hwan was already in the hallway when they stepped out of their suite. Sung Soo was wrangling Min Jae who'd somehow managed to lose his wallet. Eun Gi stepped in and went straight to the couch, fishing it out from underneath one of the cushions.

"How'd you find it?" Jae asked, catching it out of the air as Eun Gi tossed it to him.

"I know you too well."

"Hyung," Min Jae turned to Sung Soo, "why don't you know me that well?"

Sung Soo rolled his eyes. "I know plenty else about you. I can't be expected to remember every single thing."

They hustled downstairs to the waiting vehicle.

"It's so early," Hwan whined. He leaned his head on Sung Soo. "Hyung, you have such bony shoulders."

Tessa sat on his other side and patted her lap. Hwan tipped over immediately, shoving Sung Soo with his hips until he could lay curled up on the limo seat. He was asleep immediately, lulled by the sway of the vehicle.

"You shouldn't spoil him like that," Eun Gi mused, propping an arm around her shoulders.

"Are you jealous you didn't claim the space first?"

"I shouldn't have to claim. Husbands should get first dibs."

Tessa stuck out her tongue at him.

"Noona." Min Jae pawed at her arm from across the way. "I don't know English yet. Can you speak Korean?"

"Of course. We didn't mean to exclude you."

"Speak for yourself," Eun Gi replied in English to make Min Jae pout.

"Noona, Hyung's being mean."

"It's too early for me to parent grown men." Tessa sighed. "Also, I refuse to do so. Work this out among yourselves. I'm closing my eyes until we get to the airport."

They made it to Busan without incident. Tessa and Eun Gi were swept off to set and the others settled into the hotel. Although his friends were only there for a few days of vacation, Eun Gi was glad to have them close while he settled into this new phase of the project.

"It's so beautiful here," Tessa said as they walked through the area cordoned off for filming. "It hasn't been that long since we were at the ocean, but I never stop missing the water when I'm away from it."

"I like the ocean, but I don't think I'll ever miss Busan. Seoul is where I learned to be happy."

Tessa slipped her hand into his and squeezed. "I'm here."

His fingers squeezed back. "Thank you."

Eun Gi was taken with Lily and some of the other cast to go over the set safety. The crew had been there a while already, transforming this section of the beach into Old Busan. People bustled like an ant nest, darting this way and that, putting the final touches in place. They'd be able to use some of the areas that had been restored to their original splendor, like the Haedong Yonggungsa Temple and the Chungnyeolsa Shrine, but most of the city was too modern to be of any use for their on-site work.

He was familiar with the process of blocking and set safety because of their music videos, though they weren't as intensive as a drama production.

Lunch called his name, his rumbling stomach serenading those around him.

When they let him go, he found Tessa perched on the edge of a stone wall watching the swish of the sea. A bank of pearl-grey clouds was encroaching quickly, warring with the wide blue for dominance of the sweeping vista. The colour of the ocean melted from aqua to green to grey as the light above faded, breeze pushing the clouds to engulf the sun. She looked so pretty sitting there with the sun to one side, setting her hair to gleaming, teasing out the strands of amber hidden there.

She glanced over as he got closer, a grin stretching over her features. "What're you smiling about?"

He sat down next to her and laced their fingers together. "You're so beautiful."

Her cheeks flared pink. "Want to go back to the hotel?"

His stomach growled obnoxiously.

"After we get food." She laughed.

Too hungry to wait for a restaurant, they ended up gorging themselves on street food the whole way back to the hotel.

"I'm so full," Eun Gi groaned as they stepped over the threshold into their room. "I need to digest for a decade."

"I'll check if the others want to go for dinner tonight and then I'm having a nap because that early morning flight is kicking my butt."

Eun Gi settled down on the bed, patting his food baby. She kissed his cheek before heading upstairs.

Eun Gi woke Tessa two hours later with soft fingertips brushing her forehead.

"Good morning," she murmured.

"It's afternoon." He leaned in for a kiss, smiling against her mouth.

"I have a surprise for you."

"Oh? What is it?"

Tessa giggled. "Well, if I told you, then it wouldn't be a surprise. Close your eyes and give me a minute."

He dutifully followed her instructions, listening to her suitcase unzip and her rustling around before the bathroom door closed. Minutes ticked by and he waited in impatient silence.

"Okay, you can open them."

His muscles froze in shock a moment before it melted under the heat that flooded his system. Red lace cupped her breasts, descending in delicate swirls over her ribs amid a criss-cross of satin ribbon until it joined up with the bottom piece that wrapped her hips in lace as well. Shining black heels adored each foot, elevating her already statuesque height. Each click of her shoes on the floor seemed to boost her confidence, a playful smile tugging at her lips.

"I know you weren't excited to come to Busan, so I figured I'd give you something a little more fun to focus on."

An animalistic sound escaped him. He was off the bed in an instant, staring up at her towering form in her four-inch heels, his hands on her lace-clad hips. She backed him towards the bed, dipping her head to kiss him as they maneuvered back onto the sheets. Tessa settled in, straddling his waist. His hands latched on to her again.

"Your eyes are so big right now." She grinned and stroked his cheek. "I like it."

Her fingertips slid up his arms, pressing the backs of his palms into the bed. She rotated her hips until a gasp spilled out.

"You like being on top?" Eun Gi asked, trying to sound casual while his insides churned and his heart thrummed.

"Mhmm." She kept up that maddening movement against him. "Is that okay?"

"Yes!"

Tessa giggled as his voice cracked. He coughed and died a little inside.

"It's very okay," he assured. "How do you be on top with another girl?"

"Strap-ons are a thing that exists."

A helpless sound escaped him, too many images filling his head.

"I'm wearing so many clothes."

"Well," said Tessa, "I imagine I could assist with that."

His stomach clenched, breathing shifting. She bit her perfect bottom lip and slid down. Every fractional movement of her body, her face, her hands, had him hyper focused on each infinitesimal touch.

Do not *embarrass yourself,* he ordered his body. Blood roared in his ears as she undid the button and zipper of his jeans.

A single raised eyebrow asked a silent question that threatened to melt his brain out his ears.

He nodded slowly, and she freed him easily from the confines of the fabric, planted a hand on each thigh and delivered a hot lick up the length of him. A gasp, groan and curse blurred together as his hips bucked.

She slid up his body and set her palm on his chest. "Guide me if you want something different, okay?"

He barely managed an "Mhmm" before she inched down and brushed her hair to one side. Eun Gi stared at the ceiling, trying to not move too much, to not simply explode when she put her mouth on him again.

Tessa wriggled his pants down and off, dropping them to the floor. Her nails scraped soft trails across his thighs. Goose bumps covered his skin and he couldn't control the shiver as she moved around him. Even the warmth of her breath set him off.

"Fuck," he whined. "How are you so good at this?"

Tessa's head popped up. "I did research."

"You did..." He paused, confused and amused.

"Research." She blushed hard. "Don't look at my search history."

Eun Gi laughed, burying his face in his hands. "I'm sorry, I don't mean to laugh. I wasn't expecting that answer."

"What did you think I'd say?"

"I don't know? Maybe that you were naturally gifted."

She closed her mouth over the tip and swirled her tongue. His voice evaporated into a shudder.

She lifted her head again. "Well, I am that too."

When he pawed at her helplessly, she took each hand in turn and pressed them palm down against the bed. His fingers clenched the sheets, and sweat coated his brow as her tongue worked in ruthless tandem with her hands.

He tried to stay still, met with the press of her nails on his thighs if he lost control of himself. Every breath dragged like sandpaper through his lungs while she pulled his taut, sensitized body to the edge of release before hurling him over it.

Sensation and awareness of the rest of the world slowly returned. Tessa stretched out next to him, her palm resting on his chest.

"How was that?"

"Good. It was..." he rubbed his face, "...so, so good."

Eun Gi rolled towards her and snared her in his arms.

"I was worried I'd do it wrong, so I spent most of the morning looking up some very questionable things."

"You didn't have to do that." He nuzzled her throat exactly how he'd learned she liked, loving the hitch in her breath and the clench of her fingers against him. "I'm not complaining that you did though."

"I think it's your turn now." He nipped her shoulder. "You'll have to let me recover a bit, but in the meantime, I can promise to give you my undivided attention."

"Oh? I do love attention."

Reverent fingertips slipped over lace and skin and satin. Tessa's eyes were luminous, mouth parted, tongue darting out to moisten her lips.

"Want to climb on top?"

Her pupils flared wide at the suggestion, expression shifting, even as her self-consciousness shrank her into herself. Cupping her cheek to draw her closer, he kissed her softly.

"Hey," he whispered. "You never have to do anything you're not excited about. I'm happy to be here regardless of what happens."

Tessa let out a laugh. "You're so sweet. I'm just awkward."

"You're doing great. You're intelligent, accomplished, and beautiful." Each word was punctuated with a kiss. "Be confident, and take whatever you want from me."

Eun Gi found himself flat on his back with Tessa's palms on his chest. The way she bit her lip had him squirming. Moving the pillow out of the way as she maneuvered up his body, he helped each thigh slip over his shoulders until she hovered above him. She braced her hands on the wall, and he pressed down against the top of her thighs until his tongue could reach.

Tessa jerked at the first contact, nails scraping the wall, hips shaking, curses pouring out of her mouth. A desperate sound prompted him to stroke soothing fingers up her waist. He stayed unrelenting at the crux of her thighs until she vibrated in his hands.

The moans and gasps she made saturated the air around them. He felt the exact moment she came, her weight sinking against him while she cried out. He looked up to a face twisted with the intoxicating dregs of pleasure. A spike of lust shot straight down his spine.

When the spasms retreated, she flopped to the side, nestled in the pillows. He moved to wipe off his mouth, but her hand stopped him a second before she devoured him. She was demanding, searching, and he surrendered happily to it.

"More," she growled against his lips.

He shivered head to toe at the fire in her eyes. Nudging him towards the headboard, she climbed straight into his lap, leaning to whisper in his ear, "I came prepared."

Reaching into the drawer of the side table, she pulled out the box of condoms they'd purchased in Jeju. Her eyes were dark and enthralled as he rolled on the latex.

Nervousness blended with obvious hunger on her face.

"Nothing you don't want," he reminded her. "You're in charge."

He groaned as she tentatively brushed their bodies together. Gazes locked, and she lowered herself, enveloping him in heat. His fingers dug into her hips.

Tessa paused, still and silent, save for her salacious breathing in his ear. Then she started to move, undulating a steady rhythm that stole his thoughts.

The sounds she made drove him crazy. Thoughts of anything except her body chasing its pleasure on his melted away. His mouth traced patterns on whatever skin it could reach and sometimes her fingers grazed through sweat-laden strands of his hair, guiding his mouth to other spots that had her gasping his name.

She pulled back a little, dropping her forehead to his. "Oh my God, this is so much more effort than I remember. I should have taken the work outs more seriously."

"I did tell you there would be advantages to a partner with stamina." He grinned, pressing a kiss to her shoulder as he helped her lie back onto the bed. "I've got you."

Tessa held the sheets in a vise grip while he ground their hips together.

"Please," she begged.

Eun Gi indulged in the intimacy of being so close, her body sinking beneath him, every inch of skin pressed together and slicked with sweat. He kissed her until they were both breathless.

Whimpers echoed in his ear as he slipped away, nudging her hips to the end of the bed before rejoining their bodies at a new angle. Her legs hooked his waist, shaking and insistent. His thumb moved in steady circles over her most sensitive point, coaxing her higher, even as his own body gave itself over in a surge of pleasure. He clung to her trembling thigh and kept his hand moving until she clenched around him, dropping over the edge to join him.

He collapsed to the bed and pulled her sweaty form against him.

"Sleep now," he murmured against her shoulder.

Tessa laughed and grabbed her phone. She nestled closer, and he could see a message from Sung Soo on her screen from ten minutes ago that Min Jae was ready for dinner.

"No sleep. It's time for dinner." She pushed his hair back from his brow, stealing another kiss. "You helped me work up an appetite, and I'm starving."

Showering together to save time was a mistake. Distractions happened. Tessa's phone buzzed incessantly with reminders from Min Jae that he was starting to wither away from hunger. It was only when Eun Gi accidentally hip checked the temperature knob, dousing them with cold water, that they actually finished washing and got out.

They were derailed again when Eun Gi helped her with lotion. By then Min Jae was calling, and Eun Gi snatched the phone to answer on Tessa's behalf.

"We're coming, calm down."

"Hyung, I'm starving. I ate all my snacks and my tummy has been growling for an hour."

"Go without us then and we'll meet you there."

There was silence for a moment.

"Soo-hyung said that's rude, so we're waiting and I'm dying."

Tessa took the phone out of Eun Gi's hand. "My favourite *dongsaeng* wouldn't be rushing his noona, would he?"

"Never ever," said Min Jae.

"Good. We'll be there in five minutes."

Tessa hung up and started to get ready in earnest.

Eun Gi smiled. "Accepting Min Jae as a little brother?"

"Hard to avoid." She grinned. "He's a sweetheart." When they got upstairs, Min Jae had his head poking out his door to watch for their arrival.

"They're here!" He called back into the room and was halfway down the hall by the time Hwan and Sung Soo joined them.

Min Jae looped an arm around Tessa and spun her in the other direction.

If the others noticed the increased proximity over dinner between Tessa and Eun Gi, they didn't say anything. Min Jae ate himself into a food coma, and the group got more than a little tipsy on soju.

It was dark by the time they left, but the moon glowed bright enough to navigate by. The beach was empty, and they opted for a slow meander across the rain-damp sand on their way back to the hotel. Min Jae kicked off his shoes and somehow managed a half-dozen cartwheels before collapsing regretfully onto his back.

"I'm going to throw up," he groaned.

Tessa plunked down onto the sand and used his shoulder as a pillow. "That's what happens when you're a toddler in a grown man's body."

"Noona, don't be mean. I'm dying."

"Is this what we're doing now?" Hwan flopped onto the sand next to Tessa. "I'm cold."

Tessa rolled over and snuggled up against him. "Better?"

"Absolutely."

"I'm supposed to get priority cuddles." Eun Gi pouted and sat down next to them. "Husbands get dibs."

"Husbands are inconveniently located. Liquor makes me touchy. Hwan is convenient for touchies."

"We can't stay on the beach all night." Sung Soo toed at Min Jae with his shoe.

"Join the pile," Tessa ordered.

Sung Soo sighed and settled in on Min Jae's other side. "Why are we doing this?"

"Do we need a reason?" Tessa asked.

Eun Gi curled up around her, using the curve of her waist as a pillow. "I like the beach. I used to come here a lot to get away."

Tessa grabbed his hand, planting a kiss on it before nestling his arm across her chest. Each heartbeat danced against his palm.

"I feel a little sick," she mumbled.

"Don't throw up on me!" Hwan wriggled away. "I'm a sympathy puker."

"Good to know." Tessa snuggled closer.

Eun Gi poked at her. "We should get back to the hotel."

"Too far. Carry me."

"Okay."

He hoisted her up, sand raining all over the others. Tessa laughed, delighted, and looped her arms around his neck. His heart thrummed hard as she rubbed their cheeks together. Eun Gi spun them, and she held on tighter, laughing until she started to hiccup.

Min Jae climbed on top of Sung Soo. "Hyung, carry me too."

"You're too heavy," Sung Soo wheezed as he was crushed into the sand. "I'm weak."

Hwan crawled over and squatted. "Climb on."

Min Jae lit up like a Christmas tree and jumped onto Hwan's back, toppling them both.

Halfway back, Eun Gi transferred Tessa to piggyback, and she clung happily, humming in his ear for the rest of their walk. Sung Soo, the only one of their group unladen, was in charge of doors.

Alone in their hotel room, Tessa's clinging turned amorous, and she nipped his earlobe as she slid down his back. A shiver raked up his spine and goose bumps erupted across his skin. Eun Gi turned in her grasp and kissed her cheek. When she dove in for more he took both her hands in his and stepped farther away.

"You've been drinking."

"And?"

"We're not doing anything until you're sober."

"But I'm needy. We already did stuff today. We can do more stuff now."

"Well, if you're still needy in the morning, I'll be more than happy to assist."

She puffed her cheeks and pouted.

He pulled her into a hug. "Sorry. I need you to give me the go-ahead when you're not full of soju, otherwise it doesn't count."

He scooped her up, and she latched on.

"Come on, let's go rinse off the beach."

"Why aren't you drunk too?" She held on to his shoulders on the way to the bathroom. He set her down on the vanity and arranged the small trash bin next to her.

"I'd wager I have significantly more drinking experience than you do."

When the water was warm, he transferred her to the edge of the tub and rinsed the sand off her feet. He helped her into pajamas too, though she was not helpful in the least with that endeavor.

Tessa squeezed his cheeks between her hands. "You are *so* cute. Why do I love you so much?"

She kissed him and then flopped back onto the bed. He was certain his face was a canvas of wide-eyed alarm. An invisible hand grabbed hold of his heart to give a sharp squeeze.

Calm was the furthest from how he felt, but he maintained the facade long enough to tuck her into the blankets. She nestled in contentedly and was asleep instantly while he was about two minutes off a full-blown panic.

Grabbing his phone, he slipped out into the hall and hit the call button, waiting for Sung Soo to answer while he swept towards the elevators.

"Hello?"

"Are you awake?" Eun Gi asked.

Sung Soo laughed. "Obviously."

"Can I talk to you?"

"Of course. Are you okay? You sound a little strung out."

"Uh, a bit. Can we go somewhere?"

"Sure. Let me get dressed. I'll come to you."

Eun Gi stepped off the elevator.

"I'm already outside your room."

Sung Soo answered the door half-dressed to let Eun Gi inside. "So, what's going on?"

Eun Gi opened and closed his mouth a half dozen times before finally spitting it out. "I slept with Tessa."

"Slept with, or *slept* with?"

His blush was answer enough. Sung Soo pursed his lips.

"She also kind of said she loves me."

Sung Soo's jaw dropped. He blinked, confused. "Kind of? Is that bad? What did you say? When did this happen?"

"About three minutes ago."

"Eun Gi." Sung Soo sighed. "Did you run away as soon as she said it?"

"She's asleep. She didn't even notice me leave." He wandered onto the terrace, looking out at the moon reflecting off the water. "I didn't say anything. She's a little drunk and didn't even mean it."

Sung Soo stared at him so long Eun Gi shifted uncomfortably.

"Why do you think she didn't mean it?"

Eun Gi shrugged.

"That's not an answer." Sung Soo frowned. "Some people get more honest when they've been drinking. Have you been around her before when she's been drunk?"

Eun Gi thought back to when they'd shared champagne on their wedding night, how easily what she'd wanted had come out after the liquor loosened her tongue.

"Yes, but that doesn't mean she meant it this time."

Sung Soo crossed his arms and sighed. He sat down in one of the patio chairs and used his gaze to order Eun Gi to do the same.

"Are you saying this because you don't want it to be true or because you do and you're afraid?"

Eun Gi tucked himself into the chair, wrapping his arms around himself. "Hyung, I—"

Sung Soo reached across the small distance between them and set a comforting hand on the back of Eun Gi's neck, smiling softly at him.

"It's okay to be nervous. I wouldn't be at all surprised if it were true. The important thing now is how you feel about it."

"I don't know."

"Don't you?"

"I'm not good at this sort of thing."

"Oh, trust me, I am well aware." Sung Soo chuckled. "You clearly feel something for her. You're protective, and you go out of your way to make sure she's taken care of. We've all watched you together. If you're not in love with her yet, then it sounds like you're not far off."

"Hyung, I'm scared."

"That's okay. Honestly, love is scary. I can't give you much in the way of advice about this because I haven't been there.

Even though you two had an unconventional start, you're building a pretty solid foundation."

"You think so?"

"I realize I only have an outsider's perspective on this," said Sung Soo, "but I've seen the change in you. You still struggle with the same things you always did, but you turn to her for comfort too. You would never be vulnerable with her like you have been if you didn't trust her. That's one of the most important things in any relationship, romantic or not. If you feel like you can trust her, and I think you can, then you have a good chunk of what you need to make it work."

"What do I do?"

"Talk to her?" Sung Soo shrugged. "This is a discussion that needs to happen while you're both sober. And in case you need someone to say it, Tessa is not Hye Jin."

Eun Gi tripped over the memories. The rush of young love, the absolute bliss prior to the proposal, followed by the crippling blow of her refusal, and the subsequent denial and detachment that carried him into their tour.

"Do you think her saying no has an impact on your fear with Tessa?"

"Maybe. I know now that I didn't love Hye Jin, at least not in any kind of sustainable way."

"Like how you love Tessa?"

"Hyung!" Eun Gi's gaze snapped towards Sung Soo.

"I'm just asking."

"You're supposed to tell me how I feel so I can move on."

"I can't do that. You're the only one who knows how you feel, but I can certainly speculate."

"Speculate away, then."

Sung Soo grinned and swung an arm around Eun Gi. "You've got it bad."

Chapter 20

Tessa

Tessa woke with a headache and a mouth like she'd been sucking on cotton. She sat up, bedraggled, and wandered over to the bathroom. The door was half open when she got there, and a damp but dressed Eun Gi stood at the vanity. He blushed when he caught sight of her in the mirror. His gaze darted away.

"Good morning," he said.

"Good morning." Tessa quirked her head. "You're up early."

"I didn't want to run late getting to set. Are you coming by today?"

She nodded. "I was going to. Are you okay?"

"Fine." He fussed with his hair.

"I have to call bullshit on that. Why won't you look at me?"

He sighed and put down the comb. "It's something you said last night."

"Oh God, what did I say? I'm not used to drinking. Min Jae kept pouring. What did I do?" Confusion gave way to clarity, and she cringed. "Eun Gi, please tell me I didn't say what I think I said."

"If what you think you said had anything to do with loving me, then I can't help you."

Tessa groaned, embarrassment flooding her system like wildfire. "I'm sorry. I never wanted to say it like that."

"But you did want to say it?" he asked, finally turning to face at her.

She chewed her lip. "Yes."

Tessa had no idea what his expression meant. Fear? Amazement?

"Really?"

"Really." He didn't speak for so long that Tessa shifted uncomfortably. "Can you please say something?"

His phone went off, and he checked the readout, cursed, and then denied the call. It went off again immediately. Irritation seeped across his face as he denied it again, slamming it down on the counter. When it rang a third time, he snatched it up and answered.

"What?" he snapped.

"Is that any way to greet your mother?"

Tessa could hear the other voice clearly from where she was standing. Her heart dropped to her toes.

"What do you want, Eomeoni?"

"You're in Busan. I want you to come home tonight."

"We have plans tonight."

"Cancel them."

"Eomeoni…"

"Cancel them, or I'll talk to some of the charming reporters hovering around your film set."

"Fine." He hung up and squeezed the phone, knuckles white.

He turned to Tessa with a sigh. His face was even more confusing than before. "I'm sorry. We need to talk, but I'm not in a good headspace for it right now. We have to go see my family tonight, or Eomeoni is going to pull some kind of bullshit, and I just...can't."

Anger flourished on his face, but a frantic edge of fear leaked through too.

"That's okay. We can talk later." She didn't *want* to talk later, but she wasn't about to push him while he was all riled up.

"Thank you." He slipped past her and gathered up his things for the day, then left without saying anything more.

Too distracted to work on her book, she plunged herself into emails and social media, sorting through business propositions and a million questions from readers. The alarm on her phone jolted her, signalling it was time to join Eun Gi on set.

When she arrived he caught sight of her. Surprise filled his expression, and he walked right past her. Tessa whirled around and saw him talking to a girl who looked to be in her early teens.

"Chun Hei, what are you doing here?" he asked in Korean.

She raised a manicured brow and popped her fists onto her hips. "I can't come because I missed you?"

"Why aren't you in school?"

She shrugged. "It's lunch time, *Oppa*. They won't care if I'm a bit late getting back."

Oppa?

Chun Hei inclined her head toward Tessa. "Is that her?"

Eun Gi's head whipped around. Panic flashed in his eyes before he waved her over.

"Tessa, this is Baek Chun Hei, my dongsaeng," Eun Gi said in English. "Chun Hei, this is my wife, Tessa."

Tessa couldn't remember having heard that he had a little sister, and she definitely hadn't been at the wedding with his parents.

"Nice to meet you, Chun Hei," Tessa replied in English, assuming Chun Hei would be able to understand.

"Don't you know how rude you were, getting married without coming to see us first?" Chun Hei snapped back.

"Chun Hei," Eun Gi bit out.

"What? I'm just stating facts." Chun Hei shrugged again, and switched back to Korean. "I should have been at the wedding, but I had exams, and Eomma wouldn't let me. She threw a fit when she found out everything."

Tessa placed a gentle hand on Eun Gi's forearm, a gesture of comfort to temper down the wildness rising in him.

"It was complicated. Drop it," Eun Gi told his sister.

Chun Hei surveyed her with a scrutiny that made Tessa want to shrink away. The girl gave a nod, declaring some finality to herself. Then she asked in English, "Did you marry Oppa for his money or his looks? Or are you pregnant and covering up the scandal?"

Tessa choked. "Neither. How could you say that?"

The shrug Chun Hei gave felt dismissive.

"I can say that because he's my oppa, and there are plenty of gold diggers out there. I haven't decided yet if you're one, but you're not very convincing."

Eun Gi stepped between his wife and sister. "Chun Hei, stop."

She leveled a glare that could melt glass. "I don't think you have any authority to order me around, Oppa. You might be older, but you're barely a brother," she snapped, returning to Korean.

"Chun Hei," Eun Gi growled. "You're being rude, and you need to stop. Now. Tessa didn't do anything wrong."

Chun Hei swept her hair over her shoulder. "Whatever. I have to get back to school. See you tonight, Oppa."

Stalking off, she left Eun Gi shaking in her wake.

He turned to Tessa immediately. "I'm sorry, she's—"

"Young. It's fine," Tessa answered. "You never said you had a sister."

Eun Gi drooped, suddenly sheepish. "I try not to let the world know too much about my family. For their sake and mine."

"Do I still count as part of the outside world?"

"I'm sorry. I didn't mean to not tell you, it just never came up." He rubbed his forehead. "We have a lot to talk about, and we will. I promise."

Being blindsided by a belligerent sister was something she'd have preferred to avoid.

"I have to use the bathroom." She turned and bolted. Resting against the vanity, she pulled out her phone and messaged Kelly.

Tessa:
Eun Gi has a sister

Kelly:
Since when??

Tessa:
I dunno. She looked about 14. She hates me.

Kelly:
I'm sure she doesn't hate you

Tessa:
We're having dinner with his family tonight and I'm not excited

Kelly:
Maybe it'll be fine?

Tessa:
I doubt it.

Kelly:
Well keep me posted. If you need me to fly to Busan to kick some ass you say the word

Tessa:
You're the best.
Love you <3

Kelly:
Love you too <3

Over lunch, Eun Gi was more anxious than Tessa had ever seen him outside of a panic attack. He was entirely unfocused, and he barely ate. Then they parted ways—Eun Gi to set, Tessa back to the hotel to finish her own workday.

When he arrived to pick her up, he was utterly deflated and miserable. She was still a little miffed, but stuffed it down. They would deal with that later.

His family lived close enough for them to walk and they passed the distance in awkward silence.

"I'm sorry," he said when they stopped in front of an apartment building. "I've been a bit of an ass today. It's not your fault I have these issues, and I should have told you, even if I couldn't go into details."

"Eun Gi, I've said that I'm here for you, and I am. You might not be able to accept that yet, but it doesn't change it. I know this is hard for you."

"Quit stalling, Oppa!" Chun Hei yelled at them from the balcony several floors up.

"Let's get this over with. I can only guess at what Eomeoni wants, but please try not to respond to her baiting. I don't need her to have any more ammunition against me." Eun Gi sighed. "Maybe they'll get bored, and we can get out early."

They were both on edge when Chun Hei opened the door for them. The apartment was spacious, with gleaming floors, a wide sweep of windows overlooking the sea, and expensive furniture arranged just so. It smelled heavily of stale cigarette smoke, and there was a vague haze in the air. Articles over the years had informed her that Eun Gi didn't come from money, but a home this large, next to the ocean, and in such a densely populated city would be beyond the means of most people. How much of Eun Gi's money had gone into it?

His mother stepped out of the kitchen dressed in sleek cream trousers and an embroidered blouse. Eun Gi's hand leapt into Tessa's and squeezed, tension radiating through his body the moment he saw his mother.

Moving like a cat, she approached him, a predator cornering her prey. She pulled her son into a stiff hug and ignored Tessa entirely.

"He's here," she called out, striding into the dining room.

Eun Gi's father emerged. Thin wire glasses almost disappeared on his brow, and a frown marred what was otherwise a handsome face. He scanned Tessa head to toe, the same uncomfortable leer he'd forced on her at the wedding.

"He brought the foreign tramp with him."

Tessa's mouth dropped open.

305

"Abeoji!" Eun Gi snapped.

The man shrugged. "What? Look at her. She can't understand a word I'm saying."

Tessa's heart hammered. She'd never been spoken to or about like this before. Chun Hei was bad enough, but Eun Gi's father was an adult.

Chun Hei sauntered past. "She's pregnant."

"Chun Hei!"

Tessa stood frozen, unsure of what to say or do.

"She's not pregnant," Eun Gi insisted. "Can't you all be pleasant for a single meal?"

His mother shrugged. "I don't think we have any obligation to be pleasant to a son who can't be bothered to visit us."

Tessa squeezed Eun Gi's hand.

They all sat at the dining room table where an array of dishes were spread out. No one spoke to Tessa, continuing on the assumption she couldn't participate in their conversation. Dissuading them of such a notion wasn't appealing.

"Why couldn't you find a Korean girl for this nonsense?" his mother asked. "Or will none of them have you?"

"Gold digger," Chun Hei muttered under her breath while she helped herself to food.

"You all need to stop speaking about my wife like this."

His mother laughed, reaching across the table to pat his cheek. "She can't understand anyway. Besides, if you think you can order your Eomma around, then clearly living in Seoul has addled your brain."

They picked at him through the meal. Tessa's stomach pitched, and nausea roiled in her throat. She reminded herself of the rules: be cordial for his sake, and don't give his mother a reason to go on the attack.

Tessa didn't say a word. She kept hold of his hand under the table, absorbing the desperate squeeze of his fingers in hers.

Finally he stood. "We have to be going."

"I didn't say you could leave yet," his mother said.

"I don't need your permission to leave, Eomeoni." His hand clutched Tessa's painfully.

His mother twisted the stem of her wine glass. "Think of all the things we could leak to the press. If your dating scandals don't destroy your career, I wonder what a family scandal could do? Or I could tell them this whole arrangement is a sham, meant to fool your fans because you think they're all idiots. I don't care whether that's true or not, but I expect this marriage to not interfere with our arrangement."

Tessa's breath came out in a whoosh. "What kind of miserable bitch are you?"

Everyone turned to her, mouths dropped open.

"You speak Korean?" Chun Hei asked.

"Fluently."

Chun Hei blushed, but the parents looked almost amused.

Tessa's heart raced. "He is your *son*, and you're being so horrible to him. I would be absolutely sick if my parents ever spoke to me that way."

His mother smiled, and Tessa checked the urge to step back.

"Eun Gi, does your wife know what a pathetic child you were?"

"Eomeoni."

"He paid us a lot of money to keep quiet." She waved a dismissive hand at her son. "He didn't want anyone to know about us. Made such a fuss. You can imagine how hurt we were that he would turn his back on his family that way."

Tessa bristled. "I'd turn my back on you all too."

"You're making this worse. We should leave." Eun Gi let out a sound of distress.

Tessa stayed focused on his mother. "It doesn't matter if you tell them our relationship is a lie, because it's not."

"You poor delusional girl." His mother's expression sharpened, brows drawing together. "He only cares about his career. He doesn't love anyone except himself."

"Eomeoni, *please.*"

The edge of tears was audible in his voice, and it put Tessa's hackles up. "How can you speak so hatefully about your own child?"

"I can say anything I like," she snapped. "He was an ungrateful boy who never appreciated anything we gave him. Then he left."

"I left because I would have died if I stayed here!" Eun Gi's face was red, his eyes wild. "You might hate me and my career, but it's what bought you this apartment. It puts food on your table and sends Chun Hei to a good school because you can't be bothered to do it yourself."

His mother sneered. "You wouldn't have died, you stupid boy. Don't be so dramatic."

"Eomeoni, you locked me in a fucking cupboard!"

The bile rose in Tessa's throat.

Chun Hei's eyes widened, and she jolted away from the table. "Eomma, what the hell?"

"You hated me." Eun Gi's voice broke. "Blamed me for everything. I thought every day about walking into the ocean to drown so I didn't have to go home."

His mother laughed and reached for him again, but Tessa's hand clamped around her wrist.

"Don't you fucking touch him." She threw her hand back towards her and grabbed Eun Gi's arm. "We're leaving. I don't care what you do about this. I'll protect him. You don't deserve to be his mother, and I hope one day you realize what a piece of garbage you've been."

Shouting erupted behind them, Chun Hei's and her mother's voices suddenly damped by the slamming door.

Eun Gi

"I can't believe you did that." Eun Gi bounced on his toes outside of the apartment building, desperate to release some of the energy that snarled inside him.

"She deserved it," Tessa insisted.

"She's going to destroy my career. Fuck." He sank into a squat, breathing hard, arms wrapped around himself. "She'll ruin 24/7 if she has the chance. She hates me. The company is going to fire me, and I'll die in poverty because Eomeoni's taken all my money. No one will hire me for anything after she gets through with me."

Tessa knelt in front of him. "You don't have to face her alone."

"I do," he insisted. "She's going to come after me. I give her money to make her leave me alone, but now she's mad."

"Maybe she won't do anything. I mean, if she ruins your career she's killing her own income."

"She's taken almost everything I've ever made and she just demands more and more. I hardly keep anything. There's probably millions stored away somewhere I'll never see again."

They had to have planned for the day when he stopped being their cash cow. His level of fame, of energy needed to create and tour at such an intense calibre, wasn't sustainable in the long run. Eventually it would taper off.

"Sometimes I think it would be a relief to have nothing left for her to take from me." His voice was barely above a whisper. "But at the same time, I don't want to give up what I've worked so hard for."

"You should talk to a lawyer. There's no way what she's done is legal. Fight back."

Eun Gi cast a withering look at her. "I can't litigate my own mother."

"Eun Gi, you deserve justice. You're so talented, you could rebuild things if it became necessary."

"Family is too important here. There's no way I could recover if this all exploded. Even if the fans eventually forgave me, no company would ever hire me again. I'd be a *problem,* and they don't want that on payroll. If I move against her, it would ruin me."

He grabbed at his chest, the crush of panic squeezing him. His heart was trying to beat right through his ribs

"I can't breathe," he gasped. "I can't—I can't breathe."

Tessa dropped to her knees and wrapped her arms around him.

"It's going to be okay. I promise."

"You don't understand. You don't know her, what she's capable of."

No one knew all of it. The cupboard was her favourite punishment. They'd shove a broom through the handles and sometimes forget about him until the next day. Before he'd moved them into their current apartment, he used to descend into panic when he walked through the door.

His lungs constricted. Numbness climbed up from his fingertips, stealing sensation from his limbs.

"Whatever she does we'll handle it. We're a team, and I won't let her hurt you."

Her voice sounded so far away. He curled into himself.

"I can't," he choked out.

Sweat beaded on his brow. His hands shook as he clung to his arms, trying to hold himself together.

"Talk to a professional then. If you won't do anything legal against her, then you should at least work through some of this in a safe environment."

He shot to his feet, almost stumbling back down. "Please don't. I can't deal with this right now."

"I know that, because you keep charging at it alone. You need help."

He trembled, and anger twisted his gut. "I don't need to talk to a stranger about my problems!"

"Well, you need to do something."

"I *am*." He stepped back, tension vibrating through him.

"I just want you to be safe and happy."

"Then leave me alone."

Tessa stared at him, eyes shining. "I'm sorry. I didn't mean to say anything to her. I didn't mean—" She broke off, a tear slipping past her lashes.

He didn't look at her. Didn't *deserve* to look at her. He hated that he'd made her cry, but the overwhelming urge to retreat pushed him beyond that. "I need to go."

"I don't think you should be alone right now," Tessa pleaded. "Come back to the hotel. Be with your friends."

"I don't want to be around anyone." He stuffed his hands into his pockets and turned his back on her. His internal panic screamed at him as he drifted further from rationality. He needed to get away.

"When will you come back?"

He shrugged and kept walking.

She followed him. "I don't feel right letting you leave like this. Please talk to me."

"Tessa, this isn't your problem."

"We're married. Your problems are my problems. I want to help."

"I don't want you to help." He walked faster, and she hurried to follow. "I want you to leave."

Her breath hitched, but he didn't turn around. He kept walking, hand over his mouth to push down the urge to throw up. Then he ran.

Eun Gi traced streets and alleys, winding deeper into Busan, running until his lungs burned and his legs threatened to cramp. When he couldn't manage the pace any longer, he stumbled to the ground. He ignored the persistent pings and buzzing from his phone, holding down the power until the screen went black.

Hours passed and the sun left the sky behind. He found his way to his old school. The schoolyard was empty, eerie in the growing darkness. Dew-slick grass soaked his shoes as he crossed to stand in front of the building. It had been one of the few places in Busan he'd felt safe, where his love of music and dance had blossomed, encouraged by teachers who saw the potential in him.

At some point he ended up on the beach, ravenous and exhausted. The moon slashed a glint of silver across the water, the reflection wavering as the sea swelled up against the sand over and over. It wasn't the first time he'd run here. The ocean had been a lullaby to him many times when he couldn't be at home anymore.

Eun Gi's body ached when he woke the next morning with the sunrise. He'd hardly slept, shivering, tossing and turning through the night. The battery on his phone was almost drained when he turned it on, but not enough to prevent him from seeing how many messages he'd missed. He despised the person he became because of his mother. She triggered his worst instincts, seemed to take pleasure in breaking him down.

He typed out a message to Sung Soo.

> Eun Gi:
> I'm ok

Sung Soo:
Where are you?

> Eun Gi:
> If I tell you you'll come get me

His phone rang, and he sighed before answering it.

"Hyung, I'm fine."

"I'm glad, but we're not."

"What do you mean?" Eun Gi's heart raced.

Sung Soo cursed quietly. "Eun Gi, we've been up all night trying to find you. Tessa came back in tears, and you've ignored every attempt at contact."

"I didn't want to be around people."

"Then you should have sent Tessa up to us and stewed in your hotel room. We were worried you might be dead. How could you pull this kind of bullshit after everything that happened with your eomeoni?" Sung Soo was silent for a moment. "We love you, and we've always tried to be supportive of you, but this isn't okay. You fucked up. Come back to the hotel so we can all get some food and talk this through."

Eun Gi's hackles rose. He didn't *want* to talk it through. He wanted to deal with it in his own way.

Alone.

He reasoned that if he didn't go back, they wouldn't be able to find him, and he could avoid the inevitable for a while yet. There were still a few hours before he had to be on set, and the idea of skipping that particular conversation until tonight was appealing. He started walking towards the city to hunt down breakfast.

"You all go to bed or eat or whatever. I'll be back tonight."

He hung up and turned off his phone again before Sung Soo could call back.

Somehow he made it through the day. None of them came to set. Part of him wished they had, but another part was dreading seeing everyone.

He gathered up his things to head back to the hotel, turning on his phone to check if he'd missed anything important. His phone buzzed. Kyung Mi's number flashed on the screen, and he thought hard about ignoring it, but she wouldn't call if it wasn't important.

Eun Gi answered. "Kyung Mi?"

"I'm so sorry, my boy. I tried to stop it."

"I don't understand. Stop what?"

"EchoPop is cancelling your contract."

The world dropped out from under his feet, and he sank to his knees.

On the third attempt his mouth finally pushed out a single word. "Why?"

"Your mother released a statement to the press. She's charging you with assault. EchoPop doesn't want to deal with the backlash, so you're being let go."

"They can't do that! She's lying."

"Your father corroborated the story. There will be an investigation. I tried to get them to wait until it was complete, but they refused."

"Kyung Mi, I never— I didn't— I've never hurt her. Please."

She sniffled. "I'm so sorry. I don't have any power to reverse their decision. I know you can't leave Busan right now because of filming so you'll have to send Tessa to handle the move out of your suite. I did manage to get them to agree to let you retain it until the end of the month."

"Please," he begged, his voice cracking and pitiful.

"My boy." Kyung Mi dropped into silence, but he heard the quiver in her breath. "I want to help, but there's nothing I can do. I'm as much at the mercy of the company as you are. Take care of yourself."

The silence that followed her hanging up was stifling. He stumbled behind a building and crashed down with a sob. His throat swelled against the tears until breathing was agony.

Everything was wrong. His mother had found a way to win. She was never satisfied until she'd stripped him down to this quaking and terrified child under her thumb.

He curled into himself, letting the weight of his mother's victory crush him.

Chapter 21

Eun Gi

After hours spent in a numb haze, Eun Gi returned to some level of clarity. He knew on the surface that he had to go to the hotel, start figuring out what he was going to do, but that seemed on par with scaling Everest. Drained and broken, Eun Gi dragged his feet, the thought of another night on the street still more appealing than facing the people who mattered most.

Then there was the drama to consider. He *needed* this job, assuming they kept him on once they caught wind of his mother speaking to the media. They were unlikely to fire him this far into filming, but he wouldn't put it past the studio. If they decided it was better to boot him and hire someone new rather than risk the bad press, he'd be utterly screwed. No one would hire him again and all of his mother's bullshit would follow him for years.

He walked as slowly as he could manage back towards the hotel, trying to keep his courage high enough to continue moving forward. Every cell in his body felt wrong, and a litany of insults flowed through his mind, condemning him for being so stupid.

A uniformed officer was waiting for him when he arrived. Eun Gi cursed. His phone was dead when he pulled it out of his pocket. If he was taken away, no one would find out until it hit the news.

"Baek Eun Gi?" The officer rose from his position against his vehicle and crossed the short distance between them.

Eun Gi swallowed back nausea. "Yes."

"My name is Detective Cheon. You've been charged with assault and I need to take you into custody while we investigate. Please enter the vehicle voluntarily."

Panic lanced up Eun Gi's spine and rooted him to the spot. His vision blurred.

"Get in the vehicle."

Move! Eun Gi's body ignored the mental command. *Movemovemovemove.*

The detective's hand latched onto Eun Gi's arm and swung him around until his chest was pressed against the vehicle. Every attempt at words failed. He stared at the hotel doors. He'd been so close.

Cold metal wrapped around his wrists and he sank into his despair.

Tessa

Tessa stared at the readout on her phone. It wasn't familiar, but it was definitely a local number.

"Hello?"

"Tessa."

"Eun Gi!" She leapt out of bed and grabbed her shoes at the door. "Where are you? We've all been so worried."

His voice broke, lost amid sharp catches of breath. "I'm sorry. I don't know what to do."

"Tell me where you are." Bile climbed up her throat. "Please."

"Prison."

"Prison? What?" She ran out of the room, pulling her shoes on while she waited for the elevator. Time slowed down, molasses in winter, and Tessa fought back the urge to kick the elevator doors or turn and attempt running up the stairs before it arrived. She was staring indecisively down the hall when the doors pinged open.

"I tried—" he let out a low sound of distress, "—I tried to come back. Can you have someone contact my lawyer?"

She pressed the door close button repeatedly, but the elevator continued at its sedate pace.

"I'm going to the others right now." Her heart raced, and she clung to the metal bar in the elevator for balance.

"I ruined everything."

"Please tell me what happened."

Tessa flew out of the elevator, slamming her hand against each of 24/7's doors until she reached Sung Soo's, hitting it until he swung it open.

Sung Soo's hair was askew, and his eyes were barely open. "Tessa, what?"

She dipped right past him and put the call on speaker.

"Eomeoni," Eun Gi said. "She did something. The police were waiting for me."

Sung Soo cursed. "Eun Gi, tell us where you are."

A disheveled and confused Hwan and Min Jae slipped into the room.

"I don't know the name. Hyung—" Eun Gi broke off again. "I only have two minutes."

The call went dead.

Tessa's stomach heaved, and she clapped a hand over her mouth.

"What the hell is going on?" Hwan asked. Tessa swayed, and he looped an arm around her waist, pulling her close. "Noona, are you okay?"

Her whole body shook, and she latched on to Hwan's T-shirt.

"Noona?" Hwan took her face in his hands and forced her to look at him. "Take a deep breath."

Her stomach rebelled, and she pushed away from him, reaching the bathroom in time for that morning's tea to come back up.

When she finally lifted her head, Min Jae passed her a glass of water and wrapped his arms around her. "Noona, it'll be okay."

"How?" The question came out as a whisper. She sipped the cold water and leaned into him. Her head throbbed.

"I haven't figured that part out yet." Min Jae smoothed back her hair and let his hand rest on her shoulder. When she sat back on the floor, he gathered her into his arms. "Feel any better?"

Sung Soo and Hwan hovered at the bathroom door.

Tessa leaned into Min Jae, letting her weight sink against him, a pink-haired anchor. "I feel gross."

She didn't know what to do or how to fix anything. Eun Gi had hidden from all of them, ignoring calls and texts as he retreated into himself. She'd questioned her actions a hundred times since the dinner. Wanting only to defend him, she'd done exactly what he said not to and managed to provoke his mother. Now she'd lost him.

"Someone needs to call his lawyer." Tessa pinched the bridge of her nose. "He asked me to tell you."

"I'll do it." Sung Soo disappeared onto the terrace, his voice muffled through the pounding of Tessa's pulse in her ears.

"Come on, Noona." Min Jae helped her stand, and he and Hwan carted her over to the bed.

"What's going to happen?" She looked from one to the other. Kyung Mi had phoned them after she spoke to Eun Gi to tell them the company was cancelling his contract, and then he had never come back. "How do we find him?"

"We'll call the police station and ask where he's being kept," Hwan said. "You're his wife, so they'll tell you."

They propped her up with pillows and took up a position on either side of her. She kept her eyes closed, willing the nausea away. Hwan tucked his hand into hers, and she squeezed it gently. His hand shook, and Tessa moved a little closer, lacing their fingers together. She wanted to tell him it would be okay, but the words never made it past her lips. They sat together in silence. Hwan's bottom lip trembled even as he sucked it between his teeth to still it.

Min Jae draped across their laps. "Hyung, we're going to get him back."

Hwan nodded but remained quiet.

Min Jae rolled over them and snared Hwan into a hug. Tessa squeezed his hand a little tighter, leaning her temple against his.

Sung Soo returned from the balcony a few minutes later. He paused at the sight of them and blinked back the shine in his eyes. "His lawyer will review the case as soon as possible."

He filled the kettle and pressed the button, staring at the blue glow until the water bubbled and it clicked off. The delicate scent of green tea wafted as he poured the steaming liquid over the tea bag provided by the hotel.

"Hyung, do you need to join the pile?" Min Jae asked.

Sung Soo shook his head. "I'm okay. I can't believe his eomeoni would do this. Eun Gi never gets violent. It's not how he responds to things."

His brow was furrowed, deep lines between his eyes. He sipped at his tea and tapped away on his phone, frowning.

"What do we do?" Tessa asked.

"Wait?" said Sung Soo. "There's nothing much we can do while he's in custody. The lawyer will have to deal with it now that he's been notified. I'll update Kyung Mi. She'd want to be kept informed even if she's no longer his manager."

"*Hyung.*" Min Jae stared hard at Sung Soo. "Join the pile."

Sung Soo sighed but put up no resistance, moving to settle next to Tessa. "Joined."

"Good." Min Jae tugged on Tessa's arm. "Noona, do you need anything?"

Her stomach churned. "Could one of you grab my purse and toiletry bag from the hotel room?"

"I'll get it." Min Jae hopped off the bed. "Where's your room key?"

Tessa fished it out of her pocket and passed it to him. He returned barely a minute later, out of breath, tossing the procured items into her lap.

"Did you run the whole way?"

"Maybe." He grinned.

Tessa dug out her medication, a steady throb building at the base of her skull. Hwan fetched her fresh water and resumed his position next to her. She dosed herself with the painkillers and snuggled against the pillows.

Sung Soo quickly grew restless and hopped off the bed to pace the floor.

"This is so stupid," Sung Soo snapped. "We know he's innocent. EchoPop doesn't even care, and I'd bet you anything Elite is going to drop him too."

"I don't want to do music without Eun Gi-hyung," said Min Jae. "It's not his fault."

"We shouldn't have to. The company would flip if we all threatened to quit if he's not reinstated once this is all over," Hwan suggested.

"Or they might fire all of us and decide 24/7 isn't worth the trouble." Sung Soo stopped dead and sank back onto the bed. "I wish he'd have come straight back here afterwards. Tessa works as a witness only up to a point. If he hadn't run off, he'd have a proper alibi for the whole night, but none of us can account for him after that. We should have all gone to that dinner and carried him back here ourselves if that's what it took."

Every word piqued Tessa's nerves.

Sung Soo threw his phone onto the pillows. "Fuck."

Tessa's vision swam as the migraine progressed and her medication kicked in, bringing a wave of exhaustion that turned her limbs to lead. She settled a hand over her eyes to block out the light.

"Noona, are you okay?" Min Jae asked.

"No, but I will be."

They wrangled her under the blanket and went out to the terrace to talk, turning off the lights as they left. The delicate ocean breeze filled the room with the scent of salt and the sound of waves brushing over sand. Their voices blurred and blended with the sea. Silence engulfed the room when the terrace door slid shut, and Tessa let the exhaustion drag her under.

Tessa woke the next morning groggy and aching. Min Jae was plastered to her side, face down in the gap between the pillows. Yesterday hit her like a truck, and she groaned.

Min Jae lifted his head. "What's happening?" He settled back against the pillows, one eye peering at her.

Sung Soo lifted a sleepy head from his pillow on the other bed.

"How're you feeling, Noona?" Min Jae asked.

"Not great." She rolled over to face him. "What'll happen to him? All I know about Korean prisons is from dramas."

"They won't keep him in a regular prison," Sung Soo said. "He'll have to stay in a detention centre until he's either released or convicted."

"Are those better?"

"I've never been in one, but I would imagine so since the people there haven't been found guilty. They have to treat them as innocent. It's not great, but better than the alternative, I guess." Sung Soo tapped away at his phone. "This is the number for the local police station. If you call, they should give us the address for where he's being kept. We can go over as soon as we're ready."

When someone answered Tessa explained the situation, who she was, and what she needed.

"We can't release that information without proof of your legal relationship. In cases with celebrities we have to be increasingly stringent. You can come to the station with a copy of your marriage license and identification."

"I don't just carry it around with me."

"I'm sorry, there's nothing we can do without proof. You're already the eleventh person this morning who's called to find out where he is. Have a good day."

They hung up, and Tessa let out a growl. "They want me to come down to the station to prove we're married before they'll give me the location."

Sung Soo sighed. "I'll contact Kyung Mi to send you a digital copy of the marriage license."

"Thank you." Tessa put a hand to her throbbing head. She couldn't take any more medication until tonight, but her migraine didn't care.

Min Jae nestled closer. "Noona, you should have breakfast. Want to order room service?"

"I'm not hungry."

"Meal skipping isn't allowed." Sung Soo handed her the menu.

She settled on a bowl of yachae juk since it would be the easiest on her stomach. A cart laden with food arrived, and she picked at her porridge, taking a bite whenever one of them focused on her.

Her phone buzzed in her lap.

"Hello?" She brushed her hair back from her face, trying to focus through her headache.

"Hale Tessa-ssi? This is Kim Ha Yun from Elite Studios."

"Hi Ha Yun-ssi. What can I do for you?"

The voice on the other end of the line hesitated, and anxiety rippled through Tessa's belly, disturbing her breakfast.

"In light of the recent allegations, Elite Studios has decided to cancel their contract with Baek Eun Gi. I'm sorry to ask given the circumstances, but we'll need you to remove your things from the hotel room and check out, or purchase another room for yourself before ten this morning."

Tessa sat in stunned silence. "You're making me move out of the room?"

Min Jae, who had been eavesdropping, tapped her shoulder. "Why would they kick you out? Aren't you part of the drama too?"

She said as much to Ha Yun.

"Your presence for on site filming was a courtesy, easily allowable since you were sharing space with someone being paid for already. I'm only passing along the instructions I've received, but you are welcome to take it up with our finance department. In the meantime, you will need to vacate the room or pay for it yourself. I'm sorry."

"You don't see anything wrong with that?" How could they kick her out when Eun Gi had just been arrested? Tessa shook her head and wrapped her free arm around herself. Cool fury simmered through her blood. On some level she wasn't even surprised, but that didn't make it hurt any less.

"It's not my call, Tessa-ssi."

"I see." Tessa tapped her fingertips on her arm to work out some of the nervous energy. "What happens now?"

"What do you mean?"

"With the drama. If you're canceling the contract of one of the leads, what happens to everyone else? Are they all out of work?"

"That remains to be seen. Publicity like this could shut down production, but we have been in contact with other potential actors to replace Baek Eun Gi."

Tessa curled her legs up. This was entirely too much to deal with, and the edges of her calm cracked. All of her excitement over the drama turned to dread.

"Ha Yun, please. Talk to whoever you need to talk to, but please don't replace him. He's innocent."

"Tessa-ssi, I have no control over casting, or any other measures being taken. Thank you for your cooperation in vacating the hotel room. Please let me know if you have any further questions." Ha Yun hung up.

"What the hell is wrong with people?" Tessa stared at the black screen. She bit back a sound of distress, her throat aching with the effort. Her stomach churned, and she set aside the remaining food in her bowl.

Sung Soo pushed a hand through his hair. "Was that the studio?"

"Yeah, they…" she swallowed hard, "…they work fast. They're dropping him and want me to move our things out of the hotel room. I have to go pack and check out, see if I can find somewhere closer to where Eun Gi will be kept."

Min Jae sidled up next to her. "Take a deep breath."

She did so, but her mind kept whirring. "I can't believe they're replacing him. Why can't they put things on a hiatus until he's cleared?"

"A hiatus would likely be as damaging as the route they're choosing," Sung Soo said. "The longer a project is shut down, the more likely it won't come back."

Tessa clenched her fists, nails digging half-moons into her palms. "This isn't fair. What am I supposed to do? I don't think I can handle staying here on my own."

"Noona, you're not on your own. You can stay with us," Min Jae told her.

"I thought you were only staying for a few days? Aren't you just here on vacation?"

"We're not leaving either of you here," said Hwan.

"Oh, fuck." Sung Soo dropped his head into his hands. "I forgot Kyung Mi mentioned you and Eun Gi have to move out of the suite before the month is over."

Tessa's shoulders slumped. "I'll have to go back and pack up."

"Let's all take a moment." Hwan turned to Tessa. "Noona, you don't have to do any of this by yourself. Eun Gi is our family, and we'll help with everything."

Sung Soo nodded. "Hwan's right. It'll take some time before they go to trial. We'll go visit Eun Gi at the detention centre, and then we'll sort out Seoul. Tessa, you don't have to worry about anything. We've got you covered for whatever you need during all of this, I promise. If you want to stay in Seoul or Busan, or even go back to Canada, that's entirely up to you."

"Well, I'm not leaving the country. I'll go to Seoul to sort out this nonsense with the suite, and I'd like to come back to Busan for as long as he needs someone here. If he's convicted..." She trailed off.

"If that happens, we'll figure out a new plan," said Sung Soo.

Tessa was still in her clothes from yesterday and not in a great state—emotionally or physically—to be handling any of this. Splashing her face in the bathroom sink helped a little bit. She took a few minutes to herself, borrowing from the plethora of bottles along the counter to wash up. When she emerged, they were all dressed.

Sung Soo passed her a cup of tea. "Rest for a minute."

"I'm fine."

"Tessa." Sung Soo's voice was unyielding. "You're not well. What would Eun Gi say if he knew you weren't taking care of yourself?"

Her lip wobbled, and she accepted the cup. There was a hint of sweetness to the steaming liquid, a light floral flavour sliding over her tongue. Sung Soo brought her onto the terrace and sat with her in the soft morning sun.

"Thank you," she whispered.

"Family takes care of each other." Sung Soo set a comforting hand on her shoulder.

"I'll help you grab Eun Gi's things, Noona." Hwan joined them on the terrace. "I'll go back to Seoul with you too."

They made her rest long enough to finish her tea and relax a little bit with the ocean view. After that Tessa and Hwan went to the room she'd been sharing with Eun Gi. They were quiet as they packed up the bags. He paused in his packing, catching sight of the box of condoms sitting on the nightstand. She didn't have the energy to be embarrassed. Hwan set it in the suitcase and zipped it up, turning to her.

"I guess things have been progressing?"

Tessa nodded, shoving her toiletries into her bag.

Hwan opened his mouth and closed it again.

"Noona." He paused. "Do you love Eun Gi?"

She hesitated, thoughts blurring and heart racing.

"I think so. I mean—" She sighed. "Yes. It feels weird to say it so soon, but I do. Is that bad?"

"It's never a bad thing for Eun Gi to have more love in his life." Hwan's face softened. "Does he know?"

She hoisted her bag off the bed. "Sort of? We got derailed by his eomeoni, and we never got to talk. I said something while I was a little drunk and half asleep, but I don't think it counts."

"Not so much," Hwan agreed. "I've told him a million times before, but I'm never certain that he actually believes me. I won't stop saying it though. You should tell him when we go to see him today. If you want."

"You don't think that would be in poor taste? Hey, you've lost everything and you're locked up, but by the way I love you?"

Hwan smiled, sweet and understanding. "He hasn't lost *everything*. Remind him what he still has and what he has to look forward to when he gets free."

"I want to." She groaned and slumped onto the bed. "I just want him to be happy."

Hwan kneeled down and took her hand in his. "I promise we'll do whatever needs doing to fix this."

"I kno—" She broke off, voice catching.

He laced their fingers together and helped her stand. "Come on, let's get back upstairs. You can shower and finish your breakfast."

"You're being awfully calm about all of this."

"Oh, trust me, I'm not." He looped an arm through hers and led them towards the door. "I'm trying to put on a brave face. I love him so much, and it's literally making me sick to think about him being locked up."

Tessa pulled Hwan into a hug. The squeeze activated his tears, and he clutched her like a lifeline. His breath hitched in her ear, and it triggered her own emotions to rise, overwhelming her defenses.

"It's okay to be scared," Tessa whispered.

Hwan's whole body shook. "She can't take him from us."

What would happen to her relationship with the others if Eun Gi wasn't freed? She'd become so fond of all of them, and the thought of that all disappearing...

Tessa hiccupped. "She won't. He's innocent, and we have to prove it."

Hwan pulled back, swiping at his tears as he put on a wobbly smile. "Come on. The others will worry if we're gone too long."

They stopped at the nearest precinct, presenting the marriage license and Tessa's passport to get the address for where Eun Gi was being kept. Tessa's heart broke all over again when they finally arrived at the detention centre. Eun Gi was utterly deflated. He was dressed in the same plain uniform as all the other prisoners they saw. His eyes were red-rimmed, hair askew, and he looked like he hadn't slept in days. Eun Gi caught sight of them, and relief, excitement, and despair flashed over his face. They packed into a visitation booth where he sat disconnected from them by a set of bars.

The others asked about how he was doing while Tessa struggled with her tears. Exhaustion weighed down his shoulders, and hopelessness glazed his bloodshot eyes.

"They're moving me to the pre-trial detention centre in Ulsan this afternoon," he told them. "I'd prefer Seoul, but it's not like I have a choice."

"Probably better to avoid Seoul for now," Sung Soo said. "Less eyes watching you in Ulsan."

Eun Gi nodded slowly. "I guess that's true. You're all going back to Seoul?"

"Tessa and Hwan are," Sung Soo replied. "Jae and I are staying with you, and they'll meet us in Ulsan once everything back home is handled."

Eun Gi focused on each person in turn. "Guys, could I talk to Tessa for a second? Alone."

"Of course." Sung Soo shuffled them off, and Tessa sat quietly, waiting for him to speak.

His breath flowed out, shuddering and weak. "You don't have to stay. If you want to go back home, I would understand. There's nothing to protect anymore."

She flinched. "You don't mean that."

He pressed his lips together.

Tessa scooted forward on the seat and reached her hand through the bars to grab his, despite the disapproving stare of one of the guards, until he came over and ordered them apart.

"Eun Gi, I'm not leaving. I told you before, I'm here." She glanced at the guard, who was staring down some people farther up the line, then reached through again, lacing their fingers together. "We're all going to fight for you."

He chewed his bottom lip. "You're sure you wouldn't rather file for divorce? No one would blame you if you did. I wouldn't want to be married to me right now, and I might be in a place like this for a long time."

"Try not to think that far ahead. It's innocent until proven guilty, and you're innocent."

His hand squeezed hers. "Thank you."

"We'll all be here when you get out. I promise I'm not going to Seoul to run away. I'm only staying long enough to figure out our living situation. I'm coming back." She smiled softly. "I don't want you to get in trouble, so I won't suggest a dramatic kiss through the bars."

The corners of his mouth lifted slightly.

"I do love you though. We never had a chance to talk, but I wanted you to know."

He opened his mouth to reply, but she held up a hand.

"Don't say anything now. Tell me how you feel when you get out of here. However long that takes, I'll be here when it happens."

The guard's baton slammed down on the table next to them, jolting Eun Gi backwards.

"No touching!"

Chapter 22

Tessa

Word of Eun Gi's arrest had already spread through the news and the fan forums. Everyone was talking about it, and while a small portion were skeptical, a lot more had turned on him. Tessa tried not to look at any of it, but her social media was bombarded by thousands of questions and people either spewing hatred or pledging their unwavering support. Some blamed her for what happened, and others seemed to just find her a convenient target. She turned off her notifications, unable to keep up with them while she hovered on the edge of near-constant panic.

She stared out the plane window. The clouds blocked her view of the ground below. Her fingers tapped a steady rhythm against her knee while Hwan napped on her shoulder. More than once she pressed a hand to her mouth, willing back the rise of hysteria that left her utterly breathless. She kept her gaze firmly out the window, regardless of what little there was to see. A couple people on the flight recognized Hwan, and if they had seen the news, it was only logical to draw conclusions about who she might be with him so close.

Hwan woke as they started the descent into Incheon International Airport and tucked his hand into hers. "Did I sleep through anything interesting?"

Tessa shook her head. She turned on her phone when the plane pulled to a stop and sent a text to Kelly.

Tessa:
We've landed.
Going to pick up supplies before we get to the apartment.

Kelly:
We'll head over soon.
If you want an extra set of hands, Pyong Ho offered to help move boxes. Or are you getting movers?

Tessa turned to Hwan and asked.

"We won't be moving anything big. The company keeps ownership of most of the furniture. We just need to get all the personal items out. Pyong Ho can come if he wants. It's not like all of this is a secret anymore."

The doorman looked at them with pity when they stepped through the door bearing boxes and bubble wrap they'd picked up on the way. Tessa paused in the doorway. Everything was still and silent. Hwan nudged her inside and diverted straight to the kitchen for some water, chugging down a glass before forcing another into her hands.

"This place feels weird with everyone gone," Hwan murmured, sipping at a fresh glass. "I don't think I've experienced complete silence here before."

Hwan poked at his phone, and music flowed out to break through the quiet. He left it on the counter, and they did a quick perusal of the space to see what had to be done. Tessa didn't have much of her own that she hadn't already packed off to Busan, so most of what needed to be dealt with were Eun Gi's personal possessions.

She was folding the flattened boxes into shape when Hwan buzzed in Kelly, Min Joo, and Pyong Ho. Kelly went immediately to Tessa and snared her into a hug.

"You've said you're okay, but are you?"

No.

"As okay as I can be, I guess." She sank against Kelly. "I just want it all to be done with."

Kelly gave her a squeeze and smoothed a hand over Tessa's curls.

"I know. If you need a place to stay in Seoul, you can absolutely stay with us," Kelly assured her.

"Or with us," Hwan offered. "I don't really care what the company has to say about it. Jae and I can double up so you can have your own room."

"Thank you." Tessa sighed. "Let's get this finished."

They fell into their tasks. Kelly followed Tessa into her bedroom with a stack of boxes.

"Talk to me, Tess." Kelly stood next to her, tugging items off hangers and tucking them into boxes.

"I don't know what to say." She bit her lip and folded a sweater, hugging it to her chest. "I hate what's happening and have no idea how to stop it."

"It's going to be okay."

"Will it? I'm not so sure. I want to be positive, but I don't feel it."

Tessa let out an *oof* when Kelly attached herself in a hug.

"I can't fix it, but I'm here and I love you. Joo and I will do everything we can to help."

Tessa set a hand on Kelly's head and wrapped her other arm around her shoulders. Min Joo found them like that when he came in to check on their progress. Tessa's vision blurred, and she sniffed back fresh tears.

"I'll finish up the closet for you." Min Joo guided them both to the bed where Tessa curled up with a pillow, and Kelly kept a steady hand stroking her hair.

"You rest so you don't stress yourself into a migraine," Kelly murmured.

"Tessa-ssi, I assume your husband already has a lawyer, but in case he does not, I have some competent people in mind from the university who could assist."

"Thank you." Tessa squeezed her pillow. "He has someone. I would have to ask Sung Soo about the details."

"I'll confirm with him." Min Joo tucked the last of the closet into a box and taped it shut. "I would offer to pack your dresser, but I imagine there are items in there you wouldn't be comfortable with me touching."

"I can do it. Thank you for your help."

The two women sat on the floor emptying out drawers while Min Joo rejoined the men.

Kelly nudged her. "You never said how the lingerie went over. Did he like it?"

Tessa's cheeks flared pink. She nodded.

"I knew it. You look killer in red. We should get something new and celebratory for when your man is freed."

Tessa smiled despite herself.

"Yes! I knew I could get a smile out of you." Kelly grinned and pressed a kiss to Tessa's cheek. "When did you last eat?"

"Um, at breakfast."

Kelly's brows pinched together. "Come on, let's check on the boys, and then you and Hwan need to have some food."

Tessa obliged when Kelly dragged them all out to dinner, allowing herself to be distracted from the stress and guilt over her part in what was happening. Eun Gi was locked up in Ulsan by now. Kelly kept hawk eyes on Tessa to ensure she was eating, and Min Joo checked in on how she was feeling whenever she let a lip tremble slip. Pyong Ho helped keep Hwan distracted. It was an utter relief to be managed.

"Do you want me to stay tonight?" Kelly asked. "I have a meeting in the morning, so I'd have to be out by six, but if you want some extra company, I can make it work."

Tessa squeezed her. "I'll be okay, but thank you for offering."

Hwan turned to Kelly and Min Joo, then focused on Pyong Ho. "Thank you for coming. I know Noona and I have both been a little out of it, but your help hasn't gone unnoticed."

When everyone left, Tessa took over Sung Soo's bed for the night, trying to stem all the what-ifs that flooded her brain.

A soft cough drew her attention to the door, and she sat up to see Hwan standing sheepishly in the doorway.

"What's wrong?" she asked.

Hwan opened his mouth, then closed it. He inched into the room. "Noona, would it be weird if...Could I...?"

"Hwan, do you want to stay in here tonight?"

He nodded.

Erin Kinsella

Tessa scooched over and pulled back the blankets on the side nearest the door. Hwan slipped in next to her, keeping a careful distance between them, and stared at the ceiling.

He was quiet so long she thought he'd fallen asleep, but then his voice broke the silence. "I wasn't sure what to expect when you came into the picture."

Tessa froze, muscles taut, eyes focused on Hwan in the dark. His tone was too ambiguous to judge how he was feeling and it put her on edge. She tried three times before her mouth cooperated with her. "And now?"

He didn't answer right away, still staring upwards. "I've loved him in a lot of different ways over the years and I'd be lying if I said you two getting together wasn't extremely weird for me." Hwan sighed. "I'm glad you're here, though."

"Pretty sure it was extremely weird for all of us." Tessa nestled into her pillow. "He told me you were his first kiss."

"He was mine too. Young Hwan was hopelessly in love with Eun Gi."

"I don't blame you."

Hwan laughed and turned towards her. "Part of me was a little jealous when it got obvious that he liked you. It was a stupid part, I know that. We hadn't been together in any sort of romantic capacity for a long time, but I was still uncomfortable watching the future chance of anything get snuffed out."

Hwan accepted the tentative hand she held out.

"I'm sorry you struggled. Are you okay?" she asked.

"I am. Mostly. It made it easier that you were you."

"What do you mean?"

"You're good for him. I wasn't so blind that I couldn't see it, even when I was confused about the whole situation."

Hwan went quiet again and closed his eyes. His fingers squeezed hers.

"Do you think he's okay?" His voice was soft.

"I hope so."

"Do you think they'll let him go?"

She hesitated. "I have to believe they will."

"Me too." He laced their fingers together. "Noona, you still belong with us, even if Eun Gi isn't here for a while."

Tessa pressed a hand to her mouth, unable to smother the sob that broke free.

The flight to Ulsan in the morning was short and sombre. Sung Soo had managed to procure a rental home on short notice. It was sparsely furnished, and cramped with all four of them, but there was little choice if they wanted to stay close to Eun Gi. Tessa took one of the two bedrooms at their insistence, too tired to argue, and dropped her bags at the foot of the bed.

Melancholy tension thickened the air and made it difficult to breathe.

Afternoon rolled around, and a knock at the front door startled Tessa out of her nap. She opened the door and Kyung Mi burst inside.

"All of you get out here," she ordered. "Now."

Sung Soo, Min Jae, and Hwan all filtered into the foyer.

"What on earth do you think you're doing? You're all supposed to be back in Seoul."

"We can work from here as well as there." Sung Soo crossed his arms.

Kyung Mi pinched the bridge of her nose. "Are you trying to give me an aneurysm? Eun Gi in prison and the lot of you up and move to Ulsan. Do you have any idea what the company will say when they find out?"

"We don't mean to make things harder for you," Min Jae said. "We just want to be there for Hyung. He's family."

Sighing, Kyung Mi dropped her bag and rubbed her face. "I want to be there for him too, but that doesn't mean the rest of your obligations stop." She turned to Tessa. "I'm sorry for how the situation has gone."

Tessa drooped. "It's not your fault."

"You cannot stay in Ulsan," Kyung Mi insisted, turning back to the men. "The company is going to roast us all on a spit."

"We work remotely on tour all the time. I don't see why we can't do it from here for a little while," Hwan said.

Kyung Mi looked skyward. "You're not on tour. None of this is authorized."

"So make it authorized," Min Jae crossed his arms.

"Make it—" Kyung Mi sputtered. "You *cannot* stay here."

Bemused, Tessa watched the exchange, waiting for one side or the other to cave.

"I understand this compulsion to be here for Eun Gi, but you are doing nothing for him. You are taking unnecessary risks with your own careers, including mine and that of your other three bandmates who cannot be here to weigh in on the situation. What would Eun Gi say if he were the reason you lost your contracts? What if the fans found out you were here with no security to speak of? There are consequences to impulsive decisions like this."

All three men stared at the floor, sheepish.

"I'll stay in Ulsan." Tessa didn't want them to go, didn't want to be alone here with her guilt, but she knew they would have to leave. "He would understand if you needed to go back. I've already had to uproot, and I can work from here as easily as I can from Seoul."

Kyung Mi nodded. "Tessa is right. Come back with me. It's a short flight, and if you desperately need to, you can come back on *authorized* trips."

Tessa set a soft hand on Kyung Mi's arm. "Do you want to go see him?"

Kyung Mi's expression shifted, the veneer cracking, her mask of strength slipping. It lasted for only a second before her face returned to normal.

"I would like to, yes." Her voice was softer.

"It's almost time for visiting hours. We could go together, unless you want to see him alone?"

"I appreciate the offer. I'll come with you to see him, but I won't stay long."

They all hung back at the detention centre while Kyung Mi spoke with Eun Gi privately. Her eyes were glossy and her shoulders drooped when she turned to the group. "Thank you. I need to get some lunch and find myself a hotel."

"Stay with us," said Tessa.

"I think they'll need some time without me." Kyung Mi took in their displeased faces. "It's the unfortunate side of having to enforce rules. I'll stay overnight at a hotel, and come by in the morning."

The group eventually capitulated, returning to Seoul with Kyung Mi the following morning. Tessa blasted music to fill the silence, but more than once the emptiness overwhelmed her, leaving her curled on the couch, tears sliding over her cheeks. The not-knowing ate at her. How long would she be in Ulsan? How many times would she have to see her husband only through bars?

As much as she had always enjoyed her quiet time, there had usually been the background comfort of another human existing in the same space. Being entirely alone in a strange place made her jumpy, her nerves spiking at every unfamiliar sound. She wasn't particularly unsafe, but her anxiety wasn't one to listen to logic.

Giving in, she video called her parents as soon as it was late enough in Vancouver for them to be awake.

"Meu amor, what's wrong?" The screen shifted, her parents' heads tilting together to both be visible.

The story spilled out, a tumble of words amid hiccupping sobs, until her parents knew everything from the dinner to the arrest to the others going unwillingly back to their lives.

"You're sure he's innocent, Peanut?" her father asked.

"Yes." Tessa nodded. "That might sound ridiculous given how long I've known him, but he runs when he panics, and he's terrified of his mother. He wanted to get away. There's no way he'd have gone back there after we left."

"Do you have a date for the trial, meu amor?"

"Not yet."

Her mother's mouth pursed. "I want you to come home."

"Mamãe, I can't."

Even the thought of leaving paralyzed her with guilt and filled her eyes with fresh tears.

"I know, but it doesn't stop me from wanting it. Please think about it? I hate seeing you hurting and being so far away. Do you want me to come there?"

"You don't have to do that." Her voice broke into a sob. "I just needed to hear your voices."

They talked for hours, taking her well into the night while they updated her on every person they could think of. Tessa's chest ached. She missed her parents more than she'd let herself realize, but it had been made bearable having Eun Gi and Kelly and the others around. Now that she was alone, there were no distractions dampening the ache in her chest.

Come morning and for days afterwards, she poured herself into her work, writing until her arms burned and her back stiffened. It was a story of separation, a lover gone to war while a young woman stayed behind and tried to keep her home and family from collapsing during the advancing occupation.

Her alarm startled her, ordering her to eat before going to the visiting hours at the detention centre.

Eun Gi's eyes were glazed when she arrived. Heavy, dark circles had become more prominent, his lips were cracked, his skin flaked from dehydration, and his hair grew increasingly unkempt with every visit. He was a mirror to her in many ways, as she allowed self-care to fall to the wayside in the depths of her distress. The visitation allotments blurred past.

She cast a glance at the guard and stealthily slipped her hands through the bars, giving his a squeeze. His face was etched with anxiety.

"I don't want you to leave," he whispered.

Tessa's heart broke. "I don't want to go. I'll be back tomorrow."

In less than a week the press had discovered where Eun Gi was being held and had shown up, eager for a story. Others joined them, fans and locals, curious for a glimpse at her. Tessa braced herself, weaving through them, never veering from her path. There was no one to protect her from the press this time. Their voices howled in her ears.

"Please stop," she whispered.

Hands grabbed at her.

"Hale Tessa-ssi. Tell us what you know about the case!"

"Do you believe he's guilty?"

"How can you support someone who assaulted his own mother?"

"Stop!" The word flew out of her mouth, and the questions halted for a brief moment.

"Did you witness the assault?"

"Does he have a history of violence?"

Another hand reached out, grabbed her by the back of the neck, and turned her face to one of the cameras.

Gasping as her heart raced, she pushed away from the crowd to run inside.

An officer approached her. "Hale Tessa-ssi. We wanted to discuss with you if you'd be willing to avoid coming to the centre for a while."

"What? Why?"

"The reporters and fans are extremely disruptive. We're doing what we can to remove them, but they're here to see you since they can't see Baek Eun Gi. If you're not visiting, they might be more cooperative."

"For—for how long?"

The officer shrugged. "For as long as it takes. We can have someone contact you when they've been cleared out entirely."

Tessa's stomach dropped to her toes. "That's not fair. I can't just not see him. He needs me to be here. *I* need to be here."

"The press will likely exhaust themselves in a few days. It's not a large ask to give us that time."

Her throat squeezed as her anger built. "Not a large ask? You're not the one with a family member locked away. Do you understand what you're asking me? You can see for yourself what this place is doing to him. I have to be here."

"It's a reasonable reques—"

"No, it's not. You have no idea how many things have been presented to me that people think are reasonable only because they don't care about me, and I can't keep bowing down to each one because *you* think it's *reasonable*. My husband is in a detention centre for a crime he didn't commit, and you want to stop me from seeing him."

The officer's face hardened. "If you won't agree to stop coming on your own, then we'll ban you from the premises."

Tessa deflated, her surge of righteous indignation and conviction crumbling under her. She wrapped her arms around herself, and her voice fell to a whisper. "You can't do that."

"We can, and we will if you don't cooperate. The choice is yours, but the outcome is the same."

She hesitated, mind churning. "Can I still see him now?"

"You're already here, so yes you may. I'm sure he'll understand that the measures are required for the safety of all our visitors."

Numbness slowed her walk to where Eun Gi was waiting for her. She slumped into the chair.

"What's wrong?" He leaned up to the bars. "What happened?"

"The reporters are scaring people. The staff wants me to stop coming until they can get them to leave."

Eun Gi paled, the dark circles under his eyes all the more apparent.

"Please," he whispered.

"I don't know what to do." Tessa dropped her head into her hands. "I don't want to stop coming. If I ignore them and keep showing up, I'll get banned, and they might not lift it. If I stay away on my own it's just until the reporters can be handled."

"Please don't leave me here alone." His gaze went unfocused.

"I don't want to, I swear. I want to be here with you, but if I get banned then I can't. If I don't listen, what if they take it out on you?"

Eun Gi pressed a hand to his chest, white-knuckling the fabric.

Tessa reached through the bars. "I'll talk to your lawyer and see if there's a way around it."

Tears climbed up her throat.

The patrolling guard smacked his baton on the table, and Eun Gi jumped away. "No. Touching."

Tessa turned on her webcam the moment she arrived at the rental home, flipping on various lights until she wasn't a shapeless blob on the camera. Anger and grief simmered through her body. She clicked the button to go live to her platform.

"Hey, everyone," she began in clear, quiet Korean. "I'm sure by now most of you are aware that Baek Eun Gi is being kept in a detention centre. A lot of people have been reaching out to me and I wish I had more time to answer, and more information that I could provide. Please know I appreciate your support, and that the rest of 24/7 appreciates it too. I see you, and I'm grateful."

She paused and hugged herself, rubbing away the goose bumps prickling her skin.

"If you're one of the people encamped outside of the centre, please go home. I know you want to be there for him, or get a story, or whatever, but I *don't* deserve to be harassed for going to see my husband. The people visiting their families should feel safe, and they don't. This is the only statement I'm willing to make, so if you're part of the press, I'm telling you now that I won't speak with you. Please let us be while we figure things out".

Tears slipped over her cheeks. She stared up at the ceiling, willing them away, but gave up and wiped at them with her sleeve.

"There are people who won't believe me, but I'm not saying this for them. Baek Eun Gi is a good person. Please keep showing him your support, and please be patient with me during this time. I'm doing the best I can.

"I want to be okay—" her voice broke, "—but I'm not. I'm trying—I'm trying so hard to keep going. My husband is locked away for a crime he didn't commit. I have no way to prove it, and I'm so afraid I'm going to lose him."

She pressed her hand to her mouth to hide the quivering of her lips. Tears blurred her vision. Comments poured in too quickly for her to read. She ended the feed and buried her face in her hands before the sobs overwhelmed her. Her phone rang, first Kelly, then Sung Soo, and when she failed to answer those calls, more from Min Jae and Hwan came in right after. Her parents would be asleep, but come morning she expected they would be calling as well. She sent a text to all of them.

Tessa:
I'm ok.

She wasn't, but it was all the assurance she could give them right now. Tessa curled up on the couch and let her tears drag her into exhaustion and sleep.

Eun Gi

I'm going to die in here.

Eun Gi stared at the blank walls of his cell. Sleep had eluded him to the point where he saw figures moving in the shadows, hallucinations tricking his eyes. His stomach roiled, and his anxiety kept his heart racing. His nights, when he did manage to fall asleep, were plagued by nightmares. He hadn't seen Tessa for days. His time was long hours of nothing, interrupted by meals. None of the other people in custody tried to talk to him, and headaches had become a constant companion. Minutes marched by with agonizing slowness, prolonging his isolation.

He let out a helpless sound, resting against the wall as he tried to reconcile this as his future. Every time he blinked he fell into a doze, too exhausted to process anything properly. His knee bounced a steady rhythm, burning off what little energy he had.

Sleep. Please.

He closed his eyes and curled onto his mat. The craving for the warmth of another human body had him itching for contact. He was the only one in his cell, and although he wasn't in solitary, the idea of approaching a complete stranger for comfort was unimaginable to him. All his thoughts turned toward Tessa, summoning the memory of her touch, the way she would soothe him and hold him close. Eun Gi woke in tears with the sun at the same spot in the sky. His head throbbed viciously.

It had only been two weeks, and the prospect of surviving years of this seemed unfathomable.

The bolt on the door slid open.

"Baek Eun Gi, come with me. Bring your effects." A guard stood, arms crossed, in the doorway.

Eun Gi moved in a haze. Maybe they were putting him in a new cell? He picked up the few items the centre had provided— blanket, toothbrush, extra uniform— and followed the guard. He was led to an empty room and sat at a table with a glass of water. A man in a suit came in, and Eun Gi stared at him for a long moment before his brain connected the face with the identity.

"Baek Eun Gi, I have news." His lawyer sat down across from him.

"News?" The word was thick on Eun Gi's tongue, and he struggled to focus.

"You're being released. The police captain is filling out the paperwork now."

His mind absorbed the information, but no matter how he thought of it, it didn't make sense.

A man in a police uniform stepped into the room. "Baek Eun Gi, I am Police Captain Kim."

Eun Gi bowed his head sharply.

"There have been complications with your case."

"Complications?"

The captain turned to the guard. "Please bring them in."

Frozen, Eun Gi held his breath as his sister walked in, accompanied by a middle-aged woman in a grey skirt suit.

Tears coated Chun Hei's cheeks as she slammed against his chest. Eun Gi's arms locked around her, and he turned to the captain, not comprehending what was happening.

"Baek Chun Hei went to the Busan police with evidence on your behalf. I've reviewed it myself and that, in addition to her testimony, clears you of wrongdoing. I have the authority to release you. That being said, we do request that you don't leave the country and are accessible during the continuing investigation."

Eun Gi stared down at his sister. She cried into his shirt, fingers latched on to the fabric. Unsure what else to do, he simply held her, mind churning.

"The complication is that I'm released?"

His first thought was that he would get to go back to Seoul, but then he remembered EchoPop had cancelled his contract, and he had no home or job to go back to.

"Your parents have both been arrested," the captain clarified. "They're currently in custody in Busan."

"My— What?" Eun Gi's heart slammed against his ribs. Questions bounced through his head, but the words froze on his tongue.

"There are multiple charges and the investigation is still ongoing. Unfortunately, this leaves Baek Chun Hei without a legal guardian."

Eun Gi's thoughts stuttered. He opened his mouth to ask what the charges were, but was immediately interrupted by the woman who'd entered with Chun Hei.

"That's where I come in. My name is Kim Seo Yun. I'm the social worker assigned to this case file. Your sister has requested to be placed with you as her first choice before seeking out other family members or foster homes."

Chun Hei pulled back and watched her brother. Her lip wobbled. He'd never seen her like this before, but that could also be because he could count on one hand the number of times he'd seen her over the last decade.

"For now," Seo Yun continued, "we only require you to agree to temporary custody until such a time as your parents are convicted or cleared. At that point you would either be relieved of guardianship or we would discuss you becoming a permanent legal guardian until Baek Chun Hei reaches the age of majority. Are you interested in providing temporary guardianship?"

His thoughts blurred and melted, exhaustion bolstering his growing confusion. "I...I'm... This is a lot right now."

Chun Hei went rigid, and she snapped a tearful gaze to the floor. Her arms fell to her sides.

Guilt leaked past the exhausted haze, but was quickly snuffed out as his mind lost focus again. The desire for sleep was so intense he could scarcely remain standing.

Eun Gi knelt next to his sister. "I'm sorry I can't answer yet. This is a decision I have to make with Tessa."

"Let me come for the night. I promise I'll be good." She bit her lip. "Please. I'll be nice to her this time."

Eun Gi's lawyer stepped up. "I think perhaps that aspect can be dealt with tomorrow. Kim Seo Yun-ssi, why don't you keep your charge for the night? Let's give him more than five minutes before he has to make a decision of this magnitude. I'll get my client situated, and we can address this at a more opportune time."

Seo Yun frowned. "That's not fair to my charge."

"And your insistence isn't fair to mine," the lawyer countered. "He needs to rest, and his wife needs to be informed before anything can be decided."

Seo Yun eventually nodded. She acquired an address from the lawyer and turned to Eun Gi. "We'll be by at nine tomorrow."

Time slowed and warped as Eun Gi moved through a daze. He cringed as he got dressed. His clothing was disgusting from his night spent on the beach and being stored in plastic for two weeks. His stomach churned when he tugged on his shirt. He returned everything he'd used during his stay, grateful to be rid of it. His phone battery was still dead, so he shoved it into his pocket before allowing his lawyer to guide him out to the vehicle.

Dread slowed his step the entire walk through the facility and into the parking lot where a car waited. He was convinced a mistake had been made, that someone would come screaming out of the building and put him back in that cell.

Breathing came a little easier as the Taehwa River appeared out the window. Somehow crossing the water made him feel safer. His phone beeped, charging en route. So many calls and emails waited for him, but one in particular caught his eye. Elite Studios had emailed a contract cancellation. His heart dropped to his toes. Eun Gi groaned as his last hope disintegrated.

He was free now, but his career had been demolished. Emptiness stretched out before him. What was left for him?

The car pulled to a stop outside a building he didn't recognize. His lawyer beeped the horn and a face appeared in the window nearest the door. Tessa blazed outside before he made it to the front steps.

The warmth and weight of her was an anchor. Her voice blurred in his ear, but the familiarity leaked through. The sweet, floral scent from her shampoo invaded his nose, and he buried his face in her hair, clinging desperately.

Home.

Once inside, his legs turned to jelly, and he sank to the floor in the hallway. Tessa slid down next to him and settled his head in her lap. He had no music career, no acting career, no money, no home, and his reputation was in shambles.

Tessa stroked his hair and spoke softly, but the words were lost to his churning mind. She offered food, and a shower, but what he wanted most was to sleep. Stripped naked, he climbed into bed and tucked himself around his wife. He fell asleep like that, entering an exhausted, dreamless sleep, making it through the night for the first time in two long weeks.

Chapter 23

Eun Gi

Tessa's warm weight pressed Eun Gi into the mattress. She slept peacefully against him, breath smooth and gentle, fingers curled into his hair. He drew swirls over her back, memorizing the dips and curves of her body. The sun wasn't quite over the horizon, draping the room in a pearlescent glow.

Untethered, his mind ping-ponged between all the things he had lost, and the few bleak possibilities that might await him. There was so much he and Tessa had to talk about, but he was reluctant to disturb the stillness of the early hours. He turned his face into Tessa's hair, inhaling the sweetness of her shampoo, shoving back the worry that daylight would come and she would be taken away from him too.

Tessa stirred, blinking away the sleep-glaze from her eyes. When she recognized him a second later, she squeezed him tightly.

"I thought I'd dreamed that you came home."

His arms tucked around her. "I'm here."

A shuddering breath betrayed the sudden swell of emotions within him. He blinked back the burn in his eyes, overwhelmed.

"I don't want you to go," he whispered.

"I won't."

She clung tighter, resting her forehead on his temple.

"I don't know what to do. Everything you signed up to protect is gone, and I'm afraid I'm going to lose what I have left. Nobody wants me anymore."

"I want you." Her lips were soft against his. "I'm not going anywhere."

She led him to the shower where she scrubbed his hair clean and soaped his body with a tenderness he'd grown unaccustomed to. He melted under the attention. The ragged, fragile state of his whole being was soothed by her presence.

Reality felt surreal. An unfamiliar house in an unfamiliar city, and now that he was free he was devoid of purpose. The pressures that had driven him daily for more than a decade were gone.

They moved to the kitchen after dressing him in the most comfortable clothing left in his suitcase. A cup of tea sat between his hands, elbows resting on the table.

He whispered her name, half hoping she wouldn't hear it.

"Hmm?" She turned from the stove where she was stirring their *ramyeon*.

He waited until she'd brought the pot to the table before completing his thought. "I wanted to tell you at the centre, but you told me to wait until I was free." His gaze dropped to his food. "I have nothing to offer but myself and no idea what the future will bring. Before I say anything, I need to know, if you— if you wanted to go home, I would understand."

The touch of her hand on his prompted him to look at her.

"I am home." The certainty in her tone was a balm to the fear that ravaged him. "I missed you. A lot."

Eun Gi left the ramyeon untouched. His fingers threaded through her hair, urging her closer. Her palm pressed to his chest, met with his frantic heart striking the ribs beneath. He took every second of contact into his soul, memorizing the taste and texture of her mouth, the heat and pressure of her hands, and the thrum in his blood. Every day in the detention centre he'd relied on her visits, when she would hold his hands for those brief moments. He'd craved being able to touch her so easily like this, desperate for more than he was allowed. She didn't even know how much he needed the comfort of her nearness.

"Tessa." Their lips brushed together once more as she settled onto his lap, his arms looping around her waist.

"Yeah?"

Guilt gnawed at him. Was he being selfish? Trapping her somehow despite her assurances? He pushed past it. The words needed to be said.

"I love you."

Her mouth was on his again, fingers cradling his head. Tension discharged like a pressure valve released.

She dropped her forehead to his. "I love you too."

"There's something else." He'd considered it a lot over the past few days when the exhaustion hadn't turned his thoughts to mush.

"Oh?"

"I want to be better."

"Eun Gi—"

"Please let me finish." He paused. "I want to be better, for you, but also for me. Neither of us deserves what I've put us through with my inability to cope. I want to get help when we get settled again. Would you help me find a therapist? I don't know where to start."

"Of course. I'll help with whatever you need."

"Thank you." He nestled closer, pressing a kiss to the curve of her throat.

She shifted uncomfortably in his lap. "Eun Gi, I'm sorry. I should never have provoked your mother the way I did, and then afterward... You were so upset and I handled it badly." Her thumb brushed over his cheek. "I'll do better."

The doorbell rang, yanking their attention towards it. Eun Gi went rigid.

Shit.

Kim Seo Yun and Chun Hei stood on the other side when he opened the door. Eun Gi swallowed hard, glancing at his wife, who was staring at the two women, thoroughly confused.

Seo Yun bowed to each of them. "Baek Eun Gi, Hale Tessa, thank you for having us."

Tessa nodded, looking curiously to Eun Gi.

"Could we possibly have a few minutes?" Eun Gi asked.

Seo Yun frowned.

"Just a few. Please come in. Have some water, we'll only be a moment." Eun Gi dashed away with Tessa, closing the bedroom door behind him. "I'm sorry. I'm not even free for a day, and I've already fucked up."

"What's going on?"

"My parents were arrested, and Chun Hei has nowhere to go."

"Holy shit." Tessa sank down on the edge of the bed. "Okay. So, what do you want to do?"

"I have no idea. If I don't take her, what happens to her? If I do, what happens to me? I don't know how to be around her." He sat next to her. "What do you think we should do?"

"Taking in a teenager won't be easy. She doesn't seem especially fond of me, but she's family. If you want to take her, then I'll support it. We can figure it all out somehow."

"What did I do to deserve you?" He snared her into a hug, kissing her temple. "I guess we have to go back out?"

"Yes. Your sister has to be scared. It's a lot of upheaval for a kid."

Anxiety locked up his muscles, but he kept his hand in Tessa's when they went to face Chun Hei and Seo Yun.

"Chun Hei, how are you doing?" he asked.

His sister shrugged, her usual vigor gone, replaced by a deflated countenance.

Eun Gi directed them towards the living room.

"Before we get too deeply into this," Seo Yun said, "I have to ask if you're interested in taking over the guardianship of your sister? I understand you're newlyweds and that things have been... complicated, but the matter is pressing. If you're not willing to take this on, we'll have to contact other relatives, or foster care."

"Oppa. *Please.*" Chun Hei's voice cracked. She dropped to her knees in the hallway, tears streaking down her red face. "I didn't mean to! I didn't know—"

Eun Gi sank down. "Didn't mean to what?"

"I thought they'd be fined. I didn't know they'd be arrested. I just wanted you to get free." She hurled herself into his arms. "Please don't hate me."

"I could never hate you." Eun Gi gathered his sister into a hug, letting her cry. What he would have given for someone to have done the same to him when he'd been young.

Tessa led Seo Yun away to give them some space.

"I didn't know what they'd done to you," Chun Hei whispered. "Eomma always said that you didn't care about us and sent money to keep us from embarrassing you. I was mad at you for so long."

"Chun Hei, I—" He choked. "I'm so sorry. I could never handle being around them. The panic was always too much. I'm not surprised you believed her when she said I didn't care."

She hiccupped and lifted her tear-streaked face. "Please don't send me away."

"I won't." Eun Gi squeezed her tightly. "We'll get this all sorted, okay?"

"Okay." Chun Hei sniffled.

Eun Gi showed her to the bathroom so she could wash up, then he joined Tessa and Seo Yun, pulling out a seat that he dropped into like a stone. His wife slipped her hand into his, lacing their fingers together.

The ramyeon had gone cold.

"I'd like to pursue guardianship."

Seo Yun nodded, turning to Tessa.

"If Eun Gi wants to, then I'm absolutely supportive."

"Where would you be living?" Seo Yun asked.

"That's up in the air," Eun Gi said. "Truthfully, everything is going to be. The false charges cost me both of my jobs, and our home."

"But," Tessa added, "we have a network of friends in Seoul that would help if we moved back there, and I have more than enough money to cover any expenses until Eun Gi gets established again."

Seo Yun scribbled down her notes. "What about moving to Busan so Chun Hei has some consistency with friends and schooling? Chun Hei will still have access to the apartment once they've swept it for evidence."

Eun Gi cringed. Busan was the last place he wanted to be, but he nodded anyway. "If that's what you think would be best."

Chun Hei emerged from the bathroom and sat on the last free chair.

"Where would you prefer to live?" Seo Yun asked her.

Chun Hei shrugged.

"I think Busan would be best," Seo Yun said. "Until a verdict is reached, staying in a familiar place would offer the most stability."

They discussed options, though there were few, and by the time afternoon rolled around they more or less had a plan.

Seo Yun nodded. "I'll need to do a home visit and check ins to be sure this is working out to Chun Hei's benefit, but I'm willing to let this be attempted."

After dinner that night Eun Gi sat with his sister while Tessa went to work in her room to give them some time together.

"Chun Hei," he began, "if you didn't know about what they'd done to me, does that mean they never did anything to you?"

Curiosity warred with dread as her face shifted. She wrung her hands.

"Not like they did to you, I don't think anyway. When we moved into the apartment after you'd started sending even more money, then Eomma got a little better. She'd go out all the time and mostly ignored me. She— One time she left me in the car when she went shopping. I almost died."

"What?" Eun Gi snapped to attention.

"It was summer. She said she wouldn't be long, but she ran into a friend and didn't come back for so long. The child locks were on, and I couldn't open the doors. Someone broke the window to get me out. Eomma cried and begged them not to phone the police. They didn't. She used to forget me a lot. They'd go away for days, and I wouldn't find out until I got home from school, and they weren't there."

"How old were you?"

"I was six with the car, but they've been going away since your first big cheque, so I guess I was about nine? I got good at doing things on my own. I'd come home expecting them to be gone. That made it easier." Chun Hei tucked her knees up, wrapping her arms around them. "Eomma is mean when she's around. She picks at me all the time. My hair, my skin, my clothes. She's never happy. I started hating myself as much as I hated her."

"You're perfect as you are." Eun Gi draped a tentative arm around her and she leaned against him. "I should have helped you. I should've checked in to make sure you were okay. Can you ever forgive me?"

"Maybe." She rubbed her hands over misty eyes. "I hope so. I don't want to hate you. I didn't know what to think when you never came around. You were always so weird when you came to visit, and I never knew why."

Guilt struck him. He hadn't expected forgiveness so soon, or at all, but the answer still stung.

Chun Hei sighed and scraped her fingers through her hair. "Oppa, what do I do? I don't know you."

He let out an exasperated laugh. "Well, that makes two of us."

"Was it Eomma and Appa you didn't want to see? Or did you want to avoid me too?"

The words lodged in his throat, and he sipped at his water to loosen the knot in his chest. "Truthfully, once Eomeoni got under my skin, I hardly noticed you or Abeoji. All I wanted was to get away, and I did my best to not think about any of you because it made me miserable. It's not an excuse, just an explanation."

She stared at him, eyes wide, waiting.

"When I first left, it was easy to not think about home. None of us got to see our families for years, but then there were breaks in our schedules, and every time I came back here I'd have my head shoved so far up my own ass trying not to have a breakdown that I hardly let myself have a second to consider that you might be in the same situation. I'm so sorry I wasn't the brother you deserved."

He'd never seen any bruises when he'd come to visit, and she'd always been snarky with a serious attitude. He should have talked to her, gotten over his own issues long enough to make sure she was safe beyond a cursory glance. She'd been so young when he left, still a toddler when he'd fled for Seoul at thirteen, and he'd been home so infrequently since.

"Oppa, you're looking at me really weird."

"It's the guilt," he said, giving a small, chagrined smile.

"You don't have to take me if you don't want to."

"Chun Hei, of course I want you. We're family. I've been absolute shit in that regard, but I'll do better." He took her hand in his. "I promise."

Eun Gi settled into bed for the night after setting Chun Hei up in her own room. Tessa nestled next to him, and he tucked himself against her warmth.

"I have no idea what to do for a job now. I'll have to figure out a sustainable way to support us all, unless they give Chun Hei and I access to the accounts where my parents hoarded my money."

"Hmm, I don't know if you've noticed, but I'm not exactly destitute. I could certainly help with any expenses that show up."

His eyes widened in the dark. "I can't ask you to do that."

"You're not asking." Tessa cradled his cheeks. "Chun Hei is my sister-in-law, and she needs us. I have absolutely no issue helping out. We're all family, and family is important to me. We can find a new place to live, she can go to school, and we can be here for her."

"You wouldn't mind moving to Busan?"

"I want to be wherever you are. Whether that's Busan or Seoul or anywhere else. I'd suggest moving to Canada because my parents would adore both of you, but all our best friends are here." She kissed him, sweet and slow. "We have each other, and we can handle this. I have every faith. Take some time and figure out what you'd like to do. I promise there's no need to rush. You're so talented, and even with the hiccups I'm sure you could become a producer or whatever you want. We'll find what's best for everyone."

He nodded and squeezed her tightly. "For the first time in my life I'm properly grateful that the media is so intrusive. I'd never have gotten the best wife in the world without them."

Tessa giggled helplessly and squeezed him back. "What did you plan on doing when you retired from performing?"

"I was considering choreography. I wouldn't mind teaching some of the new generation."

Her face lit up. "You'd be amazing at that!"

A small knock had them both sitting up.

"Chun Hei?" Eun Gi called.

The door cracked open, and Chun Hei shuffled inside. "Can I sit with you for a bit?"

Eun Gi patted the space between them, both sliding over to make room.

"Are you okay?" Tessa asked.

Chun Hei shrugged and settled in. "I guess. I mean, I miss them, but I also don't. Am I a bad person?"

"Not at all. It's normal to feel conflicted. Your parents weren't good people, but they were still your parents."

Chun Hei curled onto her side and nestled into her pillow facing Tessa. "They suck, but if they get convicted, they won't see me graduate or get my license. Maybe I'll get married young, and they won't be around to see it. They're awful, and I'm so mad that they're going to miss everything. Maybe this is my punishment for waiting so long to come forward."

"I don't think that's true," said Eun Gi. "Why *did* you come forward?"

"I saw Tessa's video."

Eun Gi perked up. "Video?"

"I may have been a little upset after they told me not to visit," Tessa confessed. "I didn't intend to get quite so emotional, but it all just came out."

"She cried," said Chun Hei, rolling over to face Eun Gi. "I felt really bad. My friends and I watched it on our lunch break, and I went to the police after school that same day. I was afraid of what Eomma and Appa might do to me if they found out, but you didn't deserve what Eomma had done to you."

"What evidence did you have to give them?" Eun Gi asked. "They wouldn't release me on your testimony alone."

"It was an app." Chun Hei pursed her lips. "I've had it on my phone for ages. If you're ever in danger it'll start recording once you trigger it. I turned it on when Eomma went after you, and I kept it going. Eomma told Appa to hit her, that it didn't matter if you were ruined because they had enough money. I think Appa kind of liked it." Chun Hei shuddered. "Eomma was black and blue by morning and went down to the police station. I didn't understand what her plan was until I heard my friends talking about the news after you were arrested."

"What the fuck," Tessa murmured.

"Thank you." Eun Gi reached out to his sister. "I've done nothing to deserve your sacrifice, but I promise I'll do my best for you. We're going to do whatever we can to be there."

"I'm going to be in the way." She curled into herself.

"You won't be. You'll be part of the family," Tessa assured.

"Plus you'll have Sung Soo, Hwan, and Min Jae, and the others when they're back. Tessa's best friend, Kelly, and her husband, too," said Eun Gi. "If we move back to Seoul, you'll have more family than you know what to do with."

"I don't belong in Seoul. I don't belong anywhere anymore."

"You belong with us," Tessa insisted. "We're sisters now, and I've always wanted a sister."

"Really?"

"Really."

Chun Hei tucked into Tessa's arms, sniffling quietly until her breathing finally evened out and she fell asleep.

Eun Gi looked at Tessa over his sleeping sister. "So, tell me more about the video?"

"I don't think I've ever been quite so angry before," she said softly. "It was selfish and indulgent to pour out my feelings online, but I needed to say it. I wanted to be with you, and I couldn't. I've tried so hard to be patient, and I just couldn't be anymore. It got ten million views. I never expected it would take off like it did. I wasn't even thinking straight when I went live."

"I'm glad you were selfish. It ended up getting me free." He took Tessa's hand in his, lacing their fingers together. "I'm sorry you were hurting so much"

"That's not your fault."

"Still. Be selfish more often. You deserve it."

She bit her lip. "Can I be selfish right now?"

"Of course."

"I want my parents to come to Korea. I know that idea freaks you out, but I miss them, and they'll love you."

"It freaks me out a lot less than it used to. I don't think I have enough energy left to panic. Let's plan it. I'll meet them, and if they're anything like you, I'm sure I'll love them."

"Yeah?"

"I want you to be happy, and having your parents around will do that."

"You're so sweet. I'll tell them tomorrow. We can plan for a visit after we get settled." She stroked her thumb over his hand. "I love you."

"I love you too."

Tessa woke up sandwiched and sweating the next morning. Chun Hei had rolled over her sometime in the night, and she was trapped between the Baek siblings. She tried to wiggle free, but Eun Gi and Chun Hei snuggled in tighter. If she didn't have to pee rather desperately, she might have basked over how precious the two of them were, but her bladder allowed no such sentimentality.

She inched down the bed until she could melt off the end and dashed to the bathroom. Relieved, she returned to check on the sleeping beauties. Asleep, and without a perpetual frown, Chun Hei resembled her brother a fair bit. They had the same soft cheeks, strong brow and defined jaw. Their parents might be monsters, but they had damn good genes.

Tessa leaned over Eun Gi and kissed his cheek. "Good morning, my love."

Her insides got all squishy as a little smile spread over his lips before he blinked awake. "Good morning."

He tugged her down for another kiss.

"Gross."

They looked over at a sleepy-eyed Chun Hei.

"Good morning to you too." Tessa snared her into a hug and while Chun Hei wriggled away, there was no mistaking the contentment on her face when she slid off the bed.

Chapter 24

Eun Gi

Eun Gi was wide awake, sitting in the kitchen, when Tessa flicked on the bedroom lamp, illuminating the darkness. He'd given up halfway through the night and made himself some coffee. It was only their first night in his parents' Busan apartment, but he could hardly imagine staying here. If it was what Chun Hei needed, then he would find a way to manage it, but he was already eyeballing apartments to rent so he could get away from his parents' space. His mother's perfume clung to everything, mixed with the cigarettes his father chain-smoked. No matter where he looked he was reminded of them.

"What're you doing up?" She sat down on the edge of the table.

"I couldn't sleep." He nudged a piece of paper towards her. "I wrote a song."

"A song?" Her eyes flickered over the scrawled Hangul. "Eun Gi, this is beautiful. Are you going to record it?"

His heart swelled with warmth. "Maybe. It's not like I have anywhere to record anymore, but I miss music."

"What if we record it here and release it to the public? Kelly is coming tomorrow. I could ask her to bring some of her equipment."

"You think I should? What if everyone hates it?"

"I think people would love it." She settled onto the chair next to him. "If you want to try to pursue music on your own, I'll support you one hundred percent. There's no reason for you to lose it just because you're not part of the group anymore."

His voice caught in his throat. "I miss them."

"I know." She wrapped her arms around him, and he allowed her to cradle him. "We'll plan a visit to Seoul, and they're coming to Busan as soon as they can."

It wasn't the same. Visiting his friends could never compare with the ease they'd always had living on top of one another, working together, spending so much time in one another's company. He was trying so hard to reconcile the fact that he was no longer a part of their world, but it still didn't seem real.

"We'll go when Chun Hei is done with school. Maybe we can spend the summer."

"That sounds perfect." Tessa traced soft fingertips over his cheek. "Do you need anything besides the microphone and filming equipment for the song?"

He glanced over to the grand piano that sat in the corner. As far as he knew none of his family could even play it. "I don't think so. I'll use the piano. I thought I'd figure out the full tune tomorrow."

Tessa made a small squeak of delight.

"What?" Her blush was so charming he tugged her closer and kissed each flaming cheek. "Tell me."

"Sorry. I'm having a moment over being the first to hear one of your songs." She laughed. "I'm forewarning you now I will probably cry."

He pulled her onto his lap and indulged in the taste of her mouth until she shivered in his hands, her fingers curling into his pajama top.

"If you're interested," he said, "we could burn off some of the energy keeping me awake."

She giggled against his mouth. "Come to bed. I'll tire you out."

Tessa

Tessa stood on the other side of the camera with Kelly, vibrating with nervous energy as she waited for Eun Gi to begin. Her bestie had arrived that morning with the supplies they needed in tow. Eun Gi plunked away at the piano keys and then nodded to Kelly. She pressed record.

Mournful notes filled the apartment, a smooth, flowing melody before his voice joined in. Tessa squeezed Kelly's arm, utter joy rendering her wide-eyed and speechless watching him sing.

"Lost in the mist, climbing out of the darkness. I'm finding my way back home." The song moved through a delicate cadence of

melancholy and despair, into a final hopeful crest. "*I don't know where I belong, but I'm making my way. I'm finding the light once more.*"

The soft Korean words faded into silence with the last note and Kelly turned off the recording. Tessa leapt across the room, tears streaking down her face, and pulled him into a hug.

Kelly crouched behind the camera and played back the piece, glancing up at Eun Gi. "Do you want any edits, or do you want to upload the raw footage?"

"The raw was gorgeous," Tessa said.

"Raw it is." Eun Gi smiled and looped his arm around his wife's waist.

Kelly started the upload to her computer. "Alright, let's get you in front of people."

"Are you nervous?" Tessa draped her arms over his shoulders.

"Mildly petrified. What if everyone hates it?"

"People will love it." Kelly grinned. "I'm not your wife so I'm not obligated to love it, but I still do. In a few minutes you'll be in front of my seven hundred thousand subs. I have your new channel linked in the description so you can start growing your own social media."

"I might need a drink." Eun Gi puffed out a nervous breath, but Tessa only nestled closer.

"You did amazing." She kissed his cheek. "I'm so proud of you."

His cheeks flushed pink. "Thank you."

"He's at twenty million views, and my sub count has quadrupled. You guys!" Kelly stared at the screen in her lap. "Twenty. Million. In less than twenty-four hours."

Kelly had been keeping an eye on the analytics, updating them when they hit each new milestone to prevent Eun Gi from obsessively watching the count in real time.

Eun Gi sat wide eyed and shaking. "Holy shit. How?"

"I mean, between my platform and Tessa's we got a lot of eyeballs on it, but I *may* have texted Sung Soo to let him know when it went live. It was up on all the official 24/7 accounts for a while before the company noticed and deleted their posts." She scrolled through her phone. "People are losing their minds. It has over one-hundred-thousand comments, and from what I can see they're majority positive. I saw a few assholes, but they were immediately trounced by the Eun Gi stans."

"What's going on?" Chun Hei wandered in with her bedhead and pajamas.

"We're jumpstarting your oppa's career." Kelly waved her over and turned the phone screen towards Chun Hei.

"Holy shit."

Tessa giggled at their identical reactions.

"Oppa, that's a lot. Are you going solo?"

"Maybe? I haven't gotten that far yet."

"Well, figure it out so I know if we're moving or not." She crossed her arms over her chest.

"Do you want to move?" Tessa asked.

Chun Hei shrugged. "All my friends are in Busan, but Oppa hates it here. As long as I don't have to change schools before the semester is over, I could be persuaded."

"We're planning on spending a few weeks in Seoul when you're done with school. We could check out some apartments while we're there." Tessa smiled softly.

It was far too early to be awake on a Saturday morning, but they all settled in for breakfast since no one was going to go back to bed. The news played in the background while they ate. A reporter was talking about the case, and images of Eun Gi's parents being removed from their apartment flashed across the screen. Tessa turned up the volume. His mugshot appeared as well, paired with a picture of him from one of their concerts as they explained he'd been cleared of charges. Both his parents had been arrested for a laundry list of crimes— perjury, fabrication of evidence, slander, and fraud.

"They're investigating them for fraud too?" Kelly asked.

"Oh yeah, Eomma and Appa were screwing over a bunch of businesses," Chun Hei said between bites.

Kelly whistled low. "Well, that'll go over like a lead balloon. Why aren't they being charged with child abuse too?"

"I would have to agree to testify, and I just want to move on," Chun Hei whispered. "Even if they hurt me before, I don't feel right going after them. I don't have proof anyway."

"Part of me wants justice, but I'd rather let it go too. I don't want to relive it all in a lengthy court case." Eun Gi took Chun Hei's hand. "We can move on together."

"We'll support whatever you want to do," Tessa said. "Once we're out of limbo on whether or not they're convicted, we can sort out something more permanent."

Chun Hei fidgeted at the table. "Um."

"Hmm?" Tessa turned to her.

"Even if they're not, do you think I could still stay with you guys?"

Tessa blinked. "You want to stay?"

Chun Hei dipped her gaze. "Only if you want me."

Eun Gi and Tessa made eye contact across the table. Eun Gi nodded.

"Of course we want you." Tessa took Chun Hei's hand in hers. "It's a little more complicated if your parents aren't convicted since they're your legal guardians."

"Apply for one of the fancy schools up in Seoul," suggested Kelly. "If you get in and they let you go, you'd be able to get away."

"If you want to be with us and they walk free, I'll take them to court for custody," Eun Gi said.

Chun Hei perked up. "You'd do that for me?"

"Between the two of us we stand a good chance." Tessa spooned some food into her mouth. "We're married, we have money, and soon we'll have a stable home too. You're fourteen, so the judge might be swayed by what you want."

Chun Hei burst into tears at the table, burying her face in her hands. Tessa dropped to her knees next to Chun Hei and pulled the girl into her arms. Eun Gi was at their side in an instant.

"No one's ever wanted me before." Chun Hei held on to Tessa.

Tessa's heart broke. "We're going to fight for you."

That only made Chun Hei cry harder.

By the time she recovered, Kelly had made her a cup of tea. "You've got good people on your side now who will step up to protect you."

Chun Hei wiped her tears and sniffled. "I hate crying. It's so dumb. I haven't been yelled at for days, and I forgot what that was like. I don't know any of you, but you're already way nicer to be around than Eomma and Appa."

Tessa gave her a hearty squeeze and helped her stand. "You have a place with us as long as you want it."

Chapter 25

Tessa

"Hyung!" Min Jae leapt straight into Eun Gi's arms, latching arms and legs around him as soon as Eun Gi opened the door of their Busan rental home. Tessa caught them both as they staggered back. "Hey, Noona!"

Eun Gi's face lit up, and it warmed Tessa down to her toes. Grinning, Min Jae dropped to the floor and snared Tessa into his arms.

"How was your flight?" Tessa asked.

"Short, but also too long because I'm impatient."

"Impatient? You? Never."

Hwan and Sung Soo came up the walkway.

"Jae, you couldn't wait an extra five seconds and bring your own bag?" Sung Soo rolled his eyes.

"Nope."

Eun Gi dashed down the yard, and Hwan dropped his bag on the grass, hoisting Eun Gi right off the ground.

Hwan swung him around. "It has been way too long since I've hugged you."

When Hwan didn't let go after setting Eun Gi back on his feet Eun Gi looked at him speculatively. "Are we just going to keep hugging?"

"Yes. I have to catch up on lost time."

"So, I don't get to hug at all?" Sung Soo stood with his hands on his hips.

"You can have a group hug now and a personal hug later." Hwan gave Eun Gi another squeeze. "He's mine right now."

Sung Soo sighed and enveloped Eun Gi from behind. "It's good to see you. These two have been underfoot the last two days getting too excited to come visit."

Min Jae hung off Tessa. "Don't even pretend you weren't excited, Hyung."

"I didn't say I wasn't. I just don't start bouncing off the walls like you do."

"Come on inside," Tessa said. "We'll order some food, and Chun Hei will be home from school soon."

Hwan and Eun Gi waddled in as a unit. Tessa took up Hwan's bag, and Min Jae collected his own after a stare down from Sung Soo.

They filled up the small two-bedroom home Tessa and Eun Gi had rented only a few minutes from Chun Hei's school. It was small but private, barely large enough for the three of them to live comfortably. It had come mostly furnished, the dregs left over from the landlord after they'd moved out.

"So, update us. We've been texting, but that's less fun than in person." Sung Soo tucked all their bags against the wall in the living room and parked himself on the couch.

"I got a call from K-One Entertainment this morning," Eun Gi said. "They're interested in signing me as a solo artist."

Hwan's head snapped up, jolting Eun Gi. "That's great! I mean, the awful, selfish part of me wants to yell at you to not take it, but I'm proud of you, and I'm telling that part to shut up."

"I told them I would think about it, but I don't know that I want to sign with them. All I want is to be back with you guys, and if I sign with another company, then I can't ever do that." The Eun Gi and Hwan unit slumped onto the couch. "I'm not delusional. EchoPop doesn't want me back, but I can't bring myself to let go of the hope quite yet."

"We want you back," Hwan insisted. "Maybe the company will pull its head out of its ass."

Eun Gi laughed. "I can dream. I don't think this opportunity is right in either case. I want to get Chun Hei properly settled, and I promised to let her finish out the semester here at least. If I sign with K-One, they'd have me working back in Seoul immediately. That's not fair to her. There's too much up in the air for me to make a commitment like that, and I can't leave Tessa to handle things here alone."

"If you did sign with them or anyone else," Sung Soo said, "and I'm not trying to sway you one way or the other, we could still do collaborations. Would you forgive EchoPop for what they've done?"

"I want to be with you guys. The company can shove it up their ass, but I can't have you without them."

Min Jae draped himself across both of their laps. "Hyung, you always have us."

The door code beeped, and it swung open to reveal Chun Hei. Her cheeks flared pink when she caught sight of everyone, and she let out a little squeak. Curious faces peeked in behind her, a half-dozen other young girls crowding around her. Realization dawned on them one by one, cheeks turning pink. They clung together.

"Holy shit, she wasn't making it up." They whispered frantically, voices jumping over one another.

Tessa brought Chun Hei inside. "Give us one minute, girls." She closed the door gently. "I take it your friends would like to meet everyone?"

Chun Hei stared at her feet. "None of them knew I was actually related to Oppa. I got too excited that everyone else was going to be here, and they all wanted proof, but I didn't have any pictures on my phone, and anyway they're here now."

Min Jae leapt off the couch and headed for Chun Hei. She looked ready to implode at any second. "Nice to meet you. I'm Min Jae."

"I—I know."

"Do you like 24/7?"

Chun Hei nodded hastily, hair bouncing as she backed into Tessa. She went rigid at the contact. "I have all the albums on my phone."

Eun Gi perked up. "You never told me that."

"I didn't want you to get a big head."

Tessa laughed. "If everyone is ready, I'll let the girls in."

Hwan released Eun Gi from their hug and scooted over a few inches.

Tessa glanced down at Chun Hei. "Just for a few minutes, okay?"

"Okay, Eonni."

Tessa paused, eyes wide. "Did you call me Eonni?"

Chun Hei's cheeks flared again. "I don't have to if you don't want me to."

"Oh my goodness! Yes, you can absolutely call me Eonni."
Tessa crushed the girl in a hug. "I'm honoured that you want to
call me your sister."

Chun Hei wriggled free. "I can't tell either of you anything
without you getting egos. It's just a word."

"An important word." Tessa's eyes shone. "I'm glad you're
feeling comfortable."

Chun Hei rolled her eyes, but the smile on her lips revealed
the truth. "Don't embarrass me in front of my friends."

"I'll do my best." Tessa opened the door and spread out her
arms. "Welcome to our home, girls."

They moved like a flock of flamingos, tucked up against one
another, heads swiveling around to take in the home and the
idols scattered across the living room. The girls clustered
together even tighter when Min Jae approached them. One of
them seemed like she was about to burst into tears.

"Jaybird!" she squawked.

Min Jae beamed. "That's me."

One of the girls nudged Chun Hei. "I can't believe it took
you this long to tell us UpBeat is your oppa!"

"Oh, like you would've believed me if I had. You still didn't
believe me even when Eomma and Appa were on the news."
Chun Hei stuck out her tongue. "He was never around for
proof. Now he is."

One brave soul left the flock and bowed sharply in front of
Eun Gi. "I'm glad you're not in prison."

Eun Gi laughed awkwardly. "I appreciate that."

She schooled her features and thrust out a notebook. "Could
you please sign this?"

"Sure. Let me grab a pen."

She held one out before he could even stand up and he
chuckled, taking both and signing his stage name with a

flourish. She looked meaningfully towards Hwan, and Eun Gi passed the notebook to him.

She grinned brightly. "Thank you!"

Tessa gathered pens for the others, and the girls made their rounds, getting autographs from all the men. They chattered among themselves, as disbelieving as Tessa had once been to be surrounded by the idols.

One of the girls tugged a case of banana milk out of her backpack and held it out to Tessa. "We stopped and got a host gift on the way."

Min Jae's eyes lit up, and he slithered over, yoinking one before Tessa could take it to the fridge. He sipped happily, and the girl beamed at him like he'd hung the stars.

"Eonni, can you take a group photo?" Chun Hei held out her phone.

Tessa snapped a picture, and approached the girls. "Make sure not to tell anyone that they're here, or they won't be able to come visit again, and this will be the only time you ever meet them."

They nodded dutifully.

"You heard Eonni." Chun Hei crossed her arms. "If you screw this up for me and the school finds out, I'm never forgiving you."

"Yeah, yeah. We know it's a secret."

"Thank you for coming over." Tessa nudged the group to the door. "24/7 just arrived, and we should let them rest."

The girls' heads bobbed reverently.

"Thank you for having us." They bowed as a group and slipped, giggling, out the door. Their excited screams echoed as they ran across the grass and off the property.

Chun Hei tucked next to Tessa when her friends were gone, eyeballing their guests.

"I know you know them, but I'll introduce you anyway. This is Sung Soo, Hwan, and Min Jae." Tessa pointed to each in turn. "Guys, this is Chun Hei."

Her cheeks were back to flaming pink, and she inched closer to Tessa. Chun Hei waved. She turned to Tessa and whispered in her ear. "They're so pretty, what do I do?"

Tessa smothered a laugh. "They're just people."

"But *Hwan*."

Tessa smiled to herself when Chun Hei's fingers latched onto the back of her shirt. A safety anchor.

"What would you like for dinner?"

"Could we make *budae jjigae*?"

"Seconded!" Min Jae thrust his hand into the air.

"Sure we can do that. I've never made it before, and I don't think we have everything but you and I can go to the market and give the boys some time to catch up. Go change and I'll meet you at the door."

"I'll help you with it when you're back," Sung Soo offered.

Chun Hei zipped off to her room and Tessa finally got to indulge in her welcome hugs.

Eun Gi and the others were piled on the couch together watching a movie when Tessa and Chun Hei arrived back at the house. Sung Soo peeled himself away to help Tessa prepare the food. She set out the ingredients—Spam, hot dogs, noodles, mushrooms, tofu, kimchi, and green onions—and set about digging the sauce ingredients out of the cupboard.

"How's he been?" Sung Soo whispered as he sidled up next to her and snared the *gochugaru* off the shelf.

"Fragile," she answered honestly. "Better now that we're out of his parents' apartment. We've contacted a few therapists recently, so hopefully one will be a good fit for him."

"Is there anything else we can do to help?"

"Your being here is more than enough. He needs to feel connected again." She stirred the sauce ingredients to give herself time to push down her worry. "He's so isolated here. It's not like he can just introduce himself to people safely, and I think the lack of interaction outside of the home is getting to him."

"I want to help more." Sung Soo looked contemplative as he sliced the Spam and set it into the waiting pot. "I'll transfer some money to your account when I have a chance."

"You don't have to do that."

"Tessa, you were there for him when we couldn't be, and that means more to us than you'll ever know. I want you all to be comfortable, and I know you have money, but so do I. Eun Gi is family, and whatever happens in the future he'll stay family. You're supporting him and Chun Hei, plus you're helping out your parents. I don't want you to run into a position where you have to start picking and choosing what to spend your money on. A bigger nest egg can't hurt, right?"

"I suppose not." Tessa set a bundle of enoki mushrooms into the pot. "I'm not used to accepting money from people."

"Eun Gi never got the opportunity to save the way the rest of us did. I can't undo what they've done to him, but I can help correct this part. The three of us have already discussed it, and we're all comfortable helping. We don't have the flexibility to be here as much as any of us would like, but it's one thing we can do from Seoul. Eun Gi won't be happy about it either, but

I imagine he'll feel a little less guilt taking it from us than he will from you. Five people on your income puts a lot of pressure on you even if you're successful."

Tessa frowned. She hadn't wanted to say anything, but she'd begun thinking about it. Her mother usually made enough to handle the basics, while Tessa covered any shortfalls, and now she was the breadwinner for Eun Gi and Chun Hei. It wouldn't be a problem immediately, but if something didn't change they'd run into issues.

She nodded. "I appreciate the help. Thank you. It's such a shame you guys can't stay longer."

"I know. Kyung Mi barely wrangled us an overnight."

"I'll stay with Chun Hei. You all sleep wherever you're most comfortable tonight."

Tessa and Sung Soo watched the maknae line bundled up together on the couch, grins across their faces.

Sung Soo let out a relieved sigh. "Those two have been stuck together since we went back to Seoul. I've had them both in my bed more nights than not. They've been way worse than when the others left for their military service. I'm glad to see them so happy again."

"God, me too. We've been managing, but I can tell it's killing him to be here. He's trying so hard, but there's only so much I can do. I'm still only one person when he's used to a network of support. We'll be coming up for the summer at least. It'll be good for everyone to be closer."

Sung Soo nodded. "How have *you* been doing?"

Tessa paused her slicing. "I haven't stopped too long to think about it."

"Stop now then."

She fussed with the green onions to give herself time to think. "I'm adjusting. I'm so happy to have him back, but it's hard being here. Eun Gi and Chun Hei are the only ones I know in Busan, and I miss Kelly, I miss my parents, I miss all of you. It's selfish of me because it's so much worse for them, but—"

"Tessa. It's not selfish to admit you're struggling or that you want to have your support network close. We miss you too."

Tears threatened, and she turned to move the pot onto the stove so no one would see. Sung Soo followed with the sauce.

"I don't want to make him feel guilty when things are still so fresh. We're making the best of the situation right now."

"He can't support you if he doesn't know."

"I'll talk to him. It'll get better in time, but I'm impatient to be back in Seoul."

They crowded around the table when the budae jjigae was ready, shoveling it into their mouths from the communal pot.

Chun Hei wrinkled her nose. "Watching you guys eat is a good way to get over being starstruck. You're like vacuums."

Min Jae looked up, cheeks filled with noodles. He swallowed them. "There is no way to eat budae jjigae gracefully. I refuse to try."

Chun Hei rolled her eyes and slurped up her own bite.

Eun Gi hadn't stopped smiling since they'd arrived, and it relieved some of the worry Tessa kept tucked inside. She allowed herself to soak in the contentment of the day. Eun Gi had his family back, even if only for a while.

A one-night visit in Busan wasn't long enough for any of them.

When Tessa woke the next morning she slipped out of bed, leaving Chun Hei to have a few more minutes of sleep. She put on coffee for their guests, and popped the kettle on for herself and Sung Soo before cracking enough eggs to feed the six of them. Once they were scrambled and poured into a pan, she peeked into the bedroom to see all four of the idols tucked together like sardines on the queen-sized bed. She stood there for a moment watching them, her heart soft. She pushed back the dread that pricked her chest, reminding her how temporary this all was. They still had more than a month left in Busan before Eun Gi could have his friends back for the summer.

She finished preparing a simple breakfast of scrambled eggs with sides of steamed rice and kimchi while everyone else slept. They'd have to be woken soon in order to get ready for their flight back to Seoul, but she could let them indulge for a little while yet. Kyung Mi sent Tessa a text to make sure everyone was up since none of them had responded to her messages. She ventured into the bedroom and toyed with Eun Gi's hair until he woke. His face wrinkled in confusion when he couldn't move, and then a contented smile broke over his features. He tucked back in for a moment and then stretched luxuriously, waking Hwan and Min Jae in the process. Sung Soo lifted his head when the youngest three shifted and sat up.

"Good morning, sleeping beauties. Breakfast is ready."

Min Jae slid off the bed and dashed away to claim the bathroom. The other three climbed out at a much more leisurely pace. Eun Gi tugged Tessa into his arms and pressed a kiss to her cheek.

"Good morning."

"How did you sleep?"

"Like the dead. I feel great." Tucking his hand into hers, he followed her out to the dining area and got the table set by the time everyone else was finished with the bathroom.

Chun Hei wandered out, still in her pajamas and half asleep. The idols sat together along one side of the table, Eun Gi in the middle. Breakfast started off jubilant—they laughed a little too hard at jokes, smiled a little too wide—but then Sung Soo's phone alarm sounded, giving them a ten-minute warning to head to the airport. Eun Gi went pale.

"We'll be back soon," Hwan said.

"I know." Eun Gi's lip wobbled.

"And you'll be with us for the summer." Sung Soo reached past Min Jae and took Eun Gi's hand.

Eun Gi nodded.

Chun Hei watched them all with a speculative look, but kept diverting her focus onto her food.

Eun Gi insisted on taking them to the airport to get those few extra moments with them before they were separated again.

Min Jae squeezed Tessa when they all gathered at the door. "Aren't you coming, Noona?"

"I'm taking Chun Hei to school." She hugged back fiercely. "Have a safe flight."

Hwan hugged her from behind before Min Jae let go. "We love you."

Tessa blinked back tears. "I love you all too."

Sung Soo and Eun Gi joined the hug, and Tessa wriggled free before she lost all composure. "Text us when you're home safe."

Eun Gi kissed her cheek and hugged his sister before he left. Tessa waited until they were in the car before turning back to Chun Hei.

She stood in her uniform. "Ready, Eonni?"

Tessa nodded, and the two of them set off on the short walk to the school.

"Oppa hates it here, doesn't he?" Chun Hei stared down at her shoes.

"Busan isn't an easy place for him to be," Tessa acknowledged. "It's too soon for us to go back to Seoul. There's too much left unknown."

"I know." Chun Hei sucked in a breath. "I feel bad for saying it, but I hope Eomma and Appa go to jail."

Tessa took Chun Hei's hand. "We have to wait and see. Remember that you're safe with us."

"Oppa could go back to Seoul if it weren't for me." Chun Hei paused, pulling Tessa to a halt.

"Don't say that."

"Can I stay home from school today?"

Tessa pressed a hand to Chun Hei's forehead. "Do you not feel well?"

"Does feeling like a burden count?"

Tessa squeezed Chun Hei's hand and looped an arm around her shoulders. "You're not a burden. We love you, and none of this is your fault. You can stay home if you want to."

Chun Hei sighed and let her cheek rest on Tessa's shoulder. "I'll go. My friends will want an update anyway. See you tonight, Eonni."

Tessa dragged her feet on the way back, stopping to get herself a fancy coffee at the cafe down the street before she returned to the house. It was silent inside, and she sat on the couch to wait.

The door clicked open, and Tessa was halfway there by the time Eun Gi walked through. He slipped straight into Tessa's arms and broke down. She held him tight as he cried against her.

"I know," she whispered. "I know."

Chapter 26

Eun Gi

Eun Gi's phone rang while he was helping Tessa prepare lunch.
His lawyer's number flashed on the screen. He put the phone
on speaker.

"Hello?"

"Baek Eun Gi, more evidence of fraud has almost assured a
conviction against your parents, and I managed to prove that
you paid for your parents' home. The courts have awarded you
ownership of the property. You're free to rent, sell, or use it at
your leisure once I get all the paperwork completed for the
transfer."

"Thank you so much." Relief loosened one of the many
knots in his chest. Selling the luxury apartment would free up
much-needed funds to support their eventual move, and secure
them until Eun Gi had some form of employment again. It

would give him the perfect excuse to never set foot in that apartment again.

"Sell it!" Chun Hei yelled from her perch at the kitchen table.

"If you're interested, I can put you in contact with a discreet realtor to handle the sale," his lawyer said.

"Yes, please."

"I'm still working on getting the accounts released, but I'm hopeful."

"Thank you." Eun Gi paused. "For everything."

"You don't have to thank me for doing my job." The lawyer's voice was friendly and soft.

"I know, but still. Thank you."

"You're welcome. I'll be in contact if anything changes. I hope once this is all over you don't need to make use of me anytime soon. Good luck."

The lawyer hung up.

Eun Gi's phone rang again, startling them.

"You're popular today." Tessa added sliced tofu to a simmering pot.

The screen showed *Kim Ha Yun - Elite Studios*.

"Baek Eun Gi?" Ha Yun's voice came over the line, clear but sheepish.

"Yes?"

"I'm so sorry to bother you. I just left a meeting with the executives, and they wanted me to get into contact with you."

"What can I do for you, Ha Yun-ssi?"

Tessa and Chun Hei perked up. He turned up the call volume, and Tessa scooted closer to listen. Dread and excitement churned in his gut as he imagined all the possibilities that could come out of Ha Yun's mouth.

"Are you still in Busan?"

"I am."

"Things have been complicated regarding your relationship with Elite Studios, but we were wondering if you might be interested in renewing your contract and continuing filming? Our analysts have determined that the outcome of the drama should still be positive, especially considering the swell of fan support your release has prompted. Your video is up to fifty-million views and it's gone a long way to placating the worries of the company."

It was on the tip of his tongue to refuse, but realistically it would serve no one if he turned them down. Tessa deserved to have the drama completed, and he needed to get his life back on track. If he was filming then he had another substantial reason to stay in Busan, keep Chun Hei in her comfort zone while they adjusted, *and* he'd have the income from the drama as well. His first real paycheck without his parents interfering in how much he would get to keep.

"Give me one moment." He muted the phone. "Family vote?"

"Part of me wants to tell them where they can stick it." Tessa glared at the phone. "*But*, I would also love for the drama to be finished, so I completely support you if you want to return. You're Lee Do Yun in my head now, and I can't see anyone else playing the role."

"I'll be way cooler to my friends if you're an idol *and* an actor," Chun Hei supplied. "Ask for a pay bump. Emotional damages!"

"Let's not push our luck. I need a few more popular videos before I can negotiate for anything."

"Well, get on that." Chun Hei puffed up her cheeks.

"I'm working on it. I have two more songs written. We're picking up recording supplies this week to film them. Are we agreed on the drama?"

Tessa and Chun Hei nodded.

Eun Gi turned back to the phone. "Ha Yun-ssi. I'm happy to see the project to the end."

She let out a relieved breath. "Excellent. I'm sorry for how everything went. I hope you know there was no personal ill-will?"

Business had no loyalty when it came to money, and he was lucky they were considering him at all, rather than scrapping the project entirely or replacing him outright. Individuals might care, but as a whole, the companies were only interested in their bottom line. He accepted this. Mostly.

"I know. Thank you for the opportunity."

"I'll email you the paperwork."

Eun Gi

"Okay, first video on your channel is going live!" Kelly grinned and pressed the button. "Nervous?"

"I don't have your subs to bolster this one." Eun Gi held Tessa's hand between his.

"I'm still going to share it. I'm not leaving you hanging like that." She fiddled with the laptop for a minute. "There, it's spread across all my accounts."

Tessa looked up from her phone. "And mine."

"I texted Sung Soo the link too." Kelly flipped through the tabs. "You're up on the official 24/7 accounts, for however long that lasts before the company pulls them down."

Eun Gi's leg bounced, anxiety ticking upwards. Tessa squeezed his hand. Kelly opened up the analytics and turned the screen towards them. He stared wide-eyed as the numbers climbed.

"Thoughts?" Kelly asked.

"I could actually do this." His voice shook. "I could have a music career without the company."

"Totally. Lots of people do. I'd help you with anything you needed. I've got access to a ton of kickass video editors who would help if you want to do some more complex things. People seem to be enjoying this raw and vulnerable stuff you've got going on right now, but you can evolve as we go."

He turned to Tessa. A smile illuminated her whole face.

"I'm so proud of you." She kissed his cheek.

"Ah! We hit the first hundred thousand views!" Kelly bounced in her seat.

The doorbell buzzed, and Tessa went to collect the dinner they'd ordered. She returned with fried chicken, plated it up with side dishes from the fridge, and passed out the meal. Eun Gi picked at his, staring at his subscriber and view counts.

"Holy shit." Two hundred thousand. Three hundred thousand... The numbers kept rising.

By the time they finished eating he'd hit a million views. His phone pinged, and he glanced down to see an email from ARH Entertainment. He clicked it, curious.

"Tessa!"

She jumped next to him. "What?"

"I got a contract offer." He turned the phone towards her. She and Kelly crowded together to read it.

"I bet you'll have a bunch of the small-timers trying to crawl up your butt with offers to snap you up before the big names realize how valuable you are." Kelly scrolled down. "What do you want to do?"

"I kind of like the idea of working for myself. I'll still check out the companies making offers, but I don't want to close any doors this early on. What do you think?" he asked Tessa.

"I support whatever direction you want your career to take."

If he could keep up this trajectory, other offers were likely to come in. Other offers like… He pushed away the thought. It was useless to hope to get back with 24/7 when EchoPop had already slammed that door in his face. People liked what he did now, and it had been too long since he'd been able to channel his full creativity into his music. He glanced back at the analytics, the burgeoning knowledge that he could do this settling over him.

"I like this direction. I want to try."

"Hell yes!" Kelly threw her fist in the air. "I'm on board. If those companies want you, they can grovel."

"Should we film the other song now?"

Kelly's eyes gleamed. "Fuck yeah. Let's show the world what Baek Eun Gi is made of!"

Tessa

June melted into July, and the stifling heat of the Korean summer brought Chun Hei's school semester to an end, and the drama's filming to its completion.

The last scene they were filming was Lee Do Yun convincing Bridie to stay in Joseon, having defied his family to marry her. Eun Gi stood on the recreated docks in his traditional hanbok, holding Lily, who was dressed in her Georgian attire, ready to turn away to get on the ship that would take her back onto the trade routes. Tessa wasn't close enough to hear the lines, but she knew them by heart.

The sun slashed across the water, casting diamond refractions that made the ocean glow. Tessa wrapped her arms around herself, tears slipping over her cheeks. Her story was going to be on TV soon, open to a fresh audience who might love her characters the way she did. Who could have known when she'd sat down to start writing that it would have brought her here and given her so much more than she'd realized was possible?

Her husband came back down the docks grinning until he saw her face. "What's wrong?"

"I'm a little emotional." She stepped into his arms. "It's finally done, and I just feel like this huge worry is falling off my shoulders."

Eun Gi stroked his thumb over her cheek. "I love you."

His mouth was soft against hers, and then he pulled her close.

"I love you too." She savoured the warmth even as the heat of the day clung to her skin. Tessa grinned. "We get to go to Seoul soon. Are you excited?"

"God, yes. I am so sick of Busan."

"Why are you two always being gross?" Chun Hei marched up to them.

Tessa giggled. "Why are you here to see it?"

"I got bored at home."

Eun Gi opened his arms to let Chun Hei join their hug. "Eonni, were you crying?"

"Only a little." Tessa smoothed a hand over the girl's sleek hair. "Who knows if I'll ever get another book picked up for a drama? I'm trying to savour all the parts that didn't make me want to pull my hair out."

Chun Hei snickered. "Oppa, you look like a dork."

"Excuse you, I look good."

"I thought you didn't like traditional clothing?" Tessa quirked her head.

"That was before you told me I was cute in it. I've grown attached to it."

"You are *so* cute in hanbok." She pressed a kiss to his cheek.

"Hello! I am *right* here." Chun Hei pushed away from them, but the smile was clear on her face.

"Let me go get changed, and then we can head home." Eun Gi wandered off and left Tessa and Chun Hei together.

That night Eun Gi's phone rang while they were crowded together on the couch watching a movie. Tessa perked up.

"Hello?" Eun Gi put the phone on speaker.

"Baek Eun Gi." His lawyer's voice came over the line. "I wanted to update you on your parents. Has anyone else called to inform you?"

Eun Gi glanced to Tessa, who shook her head.

"No, not yet. What's going on?"

"Your parents have been convicted. They found sufficient evidence to charge them on all counts. EchoPop and Elite

Studios also both tacked on defamation lawsuits. Unfortunately that means I won't be able to free up your parents' accounts for you. I imagine the companies will be demanding enough to drain them, but if there's any remaining at the end of this, I'll see about transferring it to your name."

Chun Hei pressed a hand to her mouth, and Eun Gi had gone rigid.

"I—I see. Thank you." Eun Gi stumbled over his words.

"How long will their sentence be?" Tessa asked.

"Ah, Hale Tessa-ssi, I didn't realize you were on the call as well. As far as I'm aware the sentences will last six years. I would imagine Kim Seo Yun will be in contact to discuss a more permanent arrangement for Baek Chun Hei's guardianship. I'll email you any necessary paperwork from my end. Do you need anything else in the meantime?"

"No, but thank you. I appreciate it."

"Best of luck to you all."

The call disconnected, and Tessa hopped off the couch. "What're we feeling?"

The siblings shared twinned expressions of disbelief.

"I get to stay?" Chun Hei whispered.

"You get to stay!" Tessa pulled her into a hug, squeezing her until Eun Gi joined them.

The lingering spectre of their parents evaporated, and both Chun Hei and Eun Gi dissolved into laughter blended with sobs, emotion pouring out of them as they leaned on Tessa. She held them close, hands tucked protectively against their heads.

Eun Gi wiped at his face. "We get to be a real family."

"We do." Tessa kissed his forehead.

"You're *really* sure you want to keep me?" Chun Hei asked.

"Absolutely," Eun Gi said.

"I finally got the little sister I always wanted. There's no way I'm letting anyone take you from us." Tessa smacked a kiss on Chun Hei's cheek.

"As long as you're sure."

"One hundred percent."

Chapter 27

Tessa

"Hurry up, let's go!" Tessa herded Chun Hei and Eun Gi out to the car to tackle the six-hour drive to Seoul. They'd decided to forgo the flight so they'd have ready access to a vehicle during their month-long stay to visit everyone. Tessa's parents were already in the air, and they would all meet up around dinner at the airport.

They followed the route from Busan up through Daegu, Daejeon, and into Seoul. Tessa stared out the window at the undulating mountains enrobed with trees, and glittering rivers that wound past charming towns and thriving metropolitan centres. Daejeon offered them a respite when they stopped for a leisurely lunch, inhaling barbeque and rice until they could hardly move. Chun Hei still picked up a box of chocopies and nibbled them through the rest of the drive.

"We should do a proper tour of the country sometime," Tessa said. "I always forget how beautiful the countryside is. We're taking my parents a few places, but I bet there are hidden gems all over."

"Oppa, can we?" Chun Hei leaned through the seats.

"Pick the destination, and we'll make a plan."

Tessa admired him as he drove. His shoulders were relaxed, face soft with a smile curving up the corners of his mouth. Going back to Seoul was exactly what he needed.

The turn off to Incheon brought them to the international airport with an extra hour to spare before Tessa's parents were due to land.

"Oppa, can I get some *bingsu*?"

"How are you still hungry?" Eun Gi pulled into a parking spot.

"I'm growing." Chun Hei turned to Tessa. "Eonni, can I have some?"

"We'll get some after we pick up my parents. I'm sure they'll need a little pick-me-up." Tessa wiggled in her seat. "Now I'm hungry too. Bingsu will be amazing with this heat."

Eun Gi

"Mamãe! Appa!" Tessa dashed towards her parents as they emerged into the arrivals lounge pushing their luggage cart.

Her mother lifted Tessa right off her feet with a sound of absolute delight. Her father joined them at a far more sedate pace, wrapping his arms around them both. Eun Gi hung back, watching the strange and wonderful family dynamic he'd never known. Warmth bloomed through him at seeing his wife so happy.

Tessa's mother popped up her head, and Eun Gi paused in place as her gaze locked on to him.

"You must be Eun Gi." Her face was so similar to her daughter's. "I say that as if I don't already have you memorized from Tessa's posters. You've grown up so well. My name's Olivia, but I don't mind at all if you want to call me Mamãe too."

She snared his face in her hands and delivered a kiss onto each cheek.

"Mamãe, please, you're embarrassing me." Tessa poked at her mother's ribs.

Her mother ignored her entirely and pulled him into a hug. He checked the urge to flinch and tried to just absorb her exuberance. She reminded him of Min Jae, a puppy with new people, and he knew how to handle that.

Tessa's father stood with his arm looped around his daughter's shoulders. Eun Gi bowed. "It's nice to meet you, Hale Jun-ssi. I'm sorry it wasn't able to happen sooner."

Her father grinned. "No need to be so formal. We're family and not so fussy with all that in Canada. I hope Olivia didn't startle you. She comes on a bit strong sometimes."

"Not at all," Eun Gi lied.

"Who's this cutie tucked behind you?" Tessa's mother asked, urging Chun Hei to come to the front.

"My little sister, Baek Chun Hei."

Tessa's mother scooped her into a hug before any protest could be made. "Another daughter! Is that the whole set? Biological, honorary, and in-law? I don't know exactly how the in-law part works, but I'm claiming you as a daughter. If that's okay?"

Chun Hei blinked rapidly. "Um, sure. I'm down an eomma, so I could use an extra."

"We did warn you that you'd have more family than you knew what to do with." Tessa laughed.

Her father's brow pinched. "Peanut, would you mind popping open my wheelchair? The flight didn't agree with me."

"Of course." Tessa lifted it off the cart and pressed the seat down until it clicked into place, wheeling it up behind him. He settled in, and his wife took over pushing the wheelchair.

Tessa and Eun Gi pulled their luggage.

"Thank you for taking such good care of our girl." Tessa's father reached for Eun Gi's hand and gave it a grateful squeeze.

"We've been taking care of each other," Eun Gi replied. Tessa smiled out of the corner of his eye.

Her mother squished his cheeks in her hands again. "You're a good boy. I knew it from the beginning."

"Um, thank you?"

"Mamãe, no." Tessa tried to pry her away, but she had an astonishingly strong grip.

"I'm expressing my affection for your husband, meu amor. Let me be."

Tessa's father looked chagrined from his seat. "Sorry. She's been over the moon for weeks about meeting you."

"It's okay," said Eun Gi. "I'm just not used to it."

Tessa's mother looped her arm through Eun Gi's. "So, meu filho, are you going to show us around Seoul?"

"Of course, but what does *meu filho* mean?"

"Oh, it means my son. Would you rather I not call you that?"

She said it so casually, but the simple use of it left him breathless.

"No, it's fine."

He listened with a stunned but delighted ear as Tessa's mother chatted the entire drive from Incheon into Gangnam. They stopped for bingsu, at Chun Hei's insistence, and spent a quiet hour overlooking the Han river while they ate their treats.

"I haven't been here in so long," Tessa's father remarked. "Not that we ever got into the city all that much. Eomeoni always had us going straight to Seongnam to visit relatives when I was younger."

"How long ago did you come?" Eun Gi asked.

"When Olivia and I got engaged so she could meet the family over here. That would be, what? Thirty-three years now?"

Olivia nodded. "Tessa went with her Halmeoni when she was about four, but I don't imagine you remember much of it, do you?"

"Not a bit." Tessa shoveled another bite of her strawberry bingsu into her mouth. "I've seen all the pictures a million times though, so it almost counts."

"I want to visit where you're from, Eonni." Chun Hei tugged on Tessa's sleeve. "Can I?"

"Absolutely!" Olivia answered in her daughter's stead. "Everyone's been dying to meet Eun Gi, and they'll adore you too."

Stress melted out of Eun Gi's body, leaving him pliable and content, watching his wife and her family envelop his own.

Tessa's mother sidled over to him. "You look contemplative."

"I'm not used to parents. Nice ones, I mean. Mine are..."

"I've seen the news. I'm fully aware of what kind of people they are. We're your family now too, and you can take all the time you need." She smiled. "My girl adores you, and I'm ready to do the same."

Eun Gi softened. "Thank you. I adore her too."

Olivia grinned, squeezing her cheeks between her hands. "I'm sorry, you're just so cute."

"Mamãe." Tessa plunked down on the other side of Eun Gi. "You wouldn't be overwhelming my husband, would you?"

Olivia pouted. "Not at all. You're not overwhelmed, are you?"

Eun Gi blinked rapidly, glancing between his wife and her mother. "Um. No?"

"Oh, alright. I'll give you some time to get used to me." Olivia polished off the rest of her bingsu and stretched out comfortably. She turned to Tessa. "Why isn't my other girl here?"

"Kelly is helping Min Joo and Sung Soo cook, but she's definitely hanging out with us while you're in town."

"Sounds perfect."

When the sun edged towards the mountaintops, they crowded into the car and headed to the apartment where 24/7 was waiting for them.

Tessa turned to her parents in the backseat when they pulled to a stop. "Ready to meet everyone?"

"I was born ready." Her mother's eyes were sparkling with mischief and mirth.

Sung Soo greeted them at the door to the building, a smile bright on his face.

"It's good to have you back in Seoul." He hugged Eun Gi first before Tessa's mother could visit upon him the same level of affection she'd given Eun Gi.

Sung Soo pushed the elevator button.

"That's not the right floor," Eun Gi said.

"You've been in Busan too long. It's definitely the right floor.'"

Eun Gi's brow furrowed, but he didn't press the issue. All the outsides of the suites looked the same in the building, but he hadn't forgotten the suite number he'd lived in for years.

Sung Soo knocked when they arrived, and Hwan swung the door open with a grin. "Welcome home!"

"Home? What's going on?"

Min Jae, Sung Soo, and Hwan gathered together. Hwan couldn't keep the smile from his face. "We got you a gift."

Baffled, Eun Gi could only stare at them blankly, heart pounding. "A gift?"

"We bought you this suite. The company wouldn't let us buy the one you were in before, but this is only one floor up," Sung Soo explained. "We wanted to surprise you."

The shock drained away, heat rising from his toes, heart racing.

"You guys," his voice broke. He dove into the group. "Thank you!" He chanted the words over and over again, squeezing his friends before he spun around to gather his wife into his arms, then his sister.

"You like it?" Tessa asked.

"I love it, and you. All of you. How did you do it?"

Tessa grinned and looped her arms around his waist. "Coordinated effort between the realtor, moving company, and everyone here."

"We bought you new furniture, dishes, the works, and it all arrived yesterday. The rest of your things just had to be transported," Sung Soo said.

Tessa nodded. "We took as long as we could over lunch and snacks to make sure there would be time to get everything moved."

"You're amazing." Eun Gi kissed her cheek. "I feel like I don't tell you that enough."

Kelly chattered away with Tessa's mother, and Min Joo occupied her father.

"You guys are going to love Seoul. We have tons of stuff planned." Kelly swept Tessa's parents over to the kitchen, where she plied them with samples.

Hwan hadn't left Eun Gi's side since they'd arrived.

"Busan is way too far away." Hwan snared him in a sudden hug. "I'm glad you're back."

"Can't get rid of me that easily."

"I'd never want to."

"I know." Eun Gi's smile softened. "I think it's finally starting to click."

"About time." Hwan laughed. "I've only been telling you for a decade."

"I'm a slow learner about these things."

"Well that's an understatement if I've ever heard one."

A knock on the door drew everyone's attention. Eun Gi pulled it open.

"Kyung Mi?"

"You're back!" She sounded happier than he'd ever heard her. "I was so worried about you."

"Give him your present!" Min Jae hopped over, leaning over Kyung Mi's shoulder.

"Can I be here more than a moment before you start badgering me?"

Min Jae slumped away, but only to the table where he stared impatiently at her.

Kyung Mi sighed. "First, I'm checking to make sure that you've been informed EchoPop is pursuing charges against your parents."

"My lawyer mentioned it, but I'm not sure why."

"Defamation costs them money. This whole scandal has affected their bottom line."

Bitterness rolled over his tongue. "Of course that would be what upsets them."

"My boy, I know it's not ideal that money is what forces their hand, but this is a good thing right now."

"I appreciate that you're keeping me informed." Eun Gi nodded.

Kyung Mi pulled out her phone, tapping away at it. "I'm here." She thrust the phone at Eun Gi.

"Hello?"

"Baek Eun Gi, this is Kim Gyeong Suk." Her voice came over the line, clear and crisp, as always. "I want to apologize on behalf of the company."

"I— Wait, what?"

"We were hasty in our actions, and you have some tireless advocates who fought for you."

"What do you mean?"

"The remaining active members of 24/7 all demanded release from their contracts if you were not reinstated upon being declared innocent of wrongdoing."

Eun Gi's gaze snapped to the others who were all watching him anxiously.

He mouthed, *I love you, but what the fuck?*

"You may consider yourself employed once more by EchoPop. We've already drafted up a contract renewal, and Kyung Mi will handle everything from there." She was quiet for a moment. "Baek Eun Gi?"

"Yeah?"

"Welcome back."

He hung up in a daze.

Min Jae thrust his hands into the air. "We did it! I knew they'd back down. We're too awesome for them to risk losing us."

"I can't believe you guys risked your entire careers for me." Eun Gi's lip wobbled. "Have I mentioned how incredibly amazing all of you are?"

"Once or twice." Sung Soo grinned, eyes misty. "But we always like to hear it."

Kyung Mi held out a manila envelope. "If you're interested in returning, I have the contract here for you to sign."

Eun Gi stared at the envelope. The key to his old life. Exactly as it had been...filled with restrictions and control.

Kyung Mi nudged him. "I have it on good authority that if you want to negotiate they'll agree to an additional fifteen percent payment increase."

His eyes flared wide. He glanced at the others, but they were all nodding enthusiastically.

"You deserve the increase after your parents stealing from you," Sung Soo said. "It'll help you rebuild faster."

"I'd also negotiate having clause thirty-five and forty-two struck from the contract," said Kyung Mi. She glanced over to where Chun Hei was perched on the dining room table. "It'll give you more freedom now that you have a family. And perhaps have a lawyer add in a stipulation that allows you to retain control of your own channel to produce your own music at your leisure?"

Eun Gi couldn't quite manage to breathe.

Kyung Mi handed him a pen and showed him exactly where to make the changes, then bundled it back into the envelope and tucked it into her bag. "If I thought they'd go higher I would suggest it, but from what I overheard, that's as much as they're willing to bend."

"Kyung Mi, thank you."

"You're welcome. I don't often get a chance to hit back at the company when they do things I disagree with. Gyeong Suk got very tired of me during these past few months, but I consider it her penance for going along with your removal. You deserved so much more than was given to you. I'm sorry for how you've suffered."

Tessa slipped her hand into Eun Gi's.

Kyung Mi turned to her. "I admit I was not entirely convinced of the company's idea when this marriage was proposed, but I'm pleased it's worked out. Thank you, Tessa, for taking care of him when I could not."

Kyung Mi squeaked when Tessa hugged her. "I always knew you were awesome."

"Come on, everyone. I'm starving!" Tessa's mother flagged them all towards the dining area. "I spent way too many hours on a plane, and Kelly has been tempting me with samples. Someone please feed me."

They filtered towards the table that was laden with extra chairs. Tessa glowed when surrounded by her parents and Kelly. She pulled him along with her, fingers entwined with his. "I'm glad you liked the surprise. It was hard to not ruin it."

Tessa's mother tapped her chopsticks against her glass, then her father joined, followed by Kelly.

"I didn't get to clink at your wedding!" Tessa's mom grinned.

"Clink?" Eun Gi turned to Tessa for explanation, but instead she pressed her mouth to his and leaned back smiling.

"Wedding tradition. You have to kiss when the guests clink their glasses and cutlery."

Chun Hei whacked her glass with a chopstick and grinned. "I want to clink too."

Eun Gi laughed and kissed his wife again.

Voices climbed over one another, conversation moving in a swirling flow between everyone crowded around the table. Eun Gi looked at them all in turn. His wife, his sister, found brothers, friends, and in-laws. He was surrounded by people who loved him, and it was everything he'd ever wanted.

"You okay?" Tessa asked, squeezing his hand.

"Yeah." He tucked his hand into her hair and drew her closer for a kiss. "Just happy."

Glossary

In alphabetical order:

-nim (님) - a Korean honorific suffix. It is typically used for those of a higher rank (including family members).

-ssi (씨)- a Korean honorific suffix similar to Mr., Ms., Mx.

Abeoji (아버지) - "Father" in Korean.

Ajumma (아줌마) - a Korean term that can be used to respectfully refer to any woman who is married, or of an age to be married.

Appa (아빠) - "Dad" in Korean.

Baji (바지) - the lower garment component of a hanbok. Men typically wear it as an outer garment, while women wear baji under the chima (skirt) of the hanbok.

Banchan (반찬) - small side dishes that are typically served alongside Korean cuisine.

Bingsu (빙수) - a summer treat made of shaved ice with toppings such as fruit, chocolate, red beans, and nuts.

Budae jjigae (부대찌개) - Korean army base stew. It is an amalgamation of Korean and American cuisine developed during the Korean War. It uses ingredients commonly found at the American army bases, such as Spam, hot dogs, American cheese, and baked beans, all mixed with traditional Korean ingredients such as kimchi and gochujang (Korean red pepper paste).

Busan (부산시) - the second most populated city in the Republic of Korea.

Canjica - a Brazilian porridge made with maize, milk, sugar, and cinnamon.

Dak juk (닭죽) - a Korean chicken and rice porridge.

Dongsaeng (동생) - "younger sibling" in Korean. It is used for any older sibling to a younger one, regardless of gender. This term is not exclusive to blood relatives but is also used among people you are close with.

Eomeoni (어머니)- "Mother" in Korean.

Eomma (엄마) - "Mom" in Korean.

Eonni (언니)- "older sister" in Korean. It is used by younger women to older women. This term is not exclusive to blood relatives but is also used among people you are close with.

Gangnam (강남구) - a district of Seoul. It is one of the most expensive districts in the city.

Gat (갇) - the hat component of hanbok worn by men.

Gochugaru (고추가루) - Korean red pepper powder.

Gwanghwamun Gate (광화문) - the main gate of Gyeongbokgung Palace.

Gyeongbokgung Palace (경복궁) - the main royal palace of the Joseon dynasty. Today it functions as a museum.

Hanbok (한복) - Korean traditional clothing. It typically refers to clothing worn during the Joseon dynasty. Most people today wear it for festivals and ceremonies.

Hangul (한글) - the Korean alphabet.

Hanok (한옥) - a traditional Korean house.

Hwarot (활옷) - Korean traditional clothing. This elaborate garment was once only worn by royal women, but commoners adopted it for weddings. They are extremely expensive and tended to be passed down through families.

Hyung (형) - "older brother" in Korean. It is used by younger men to older men. This term is not exclusive to blood relatives but is also used among people you are close with.

Imjin War (임진왜란) - the Japanese invasion of Korea from 1592-1598.

Itaewon (이태원) - a district of Seoul that is popular with expats and tourists.

Japchae (잡채) - Korean "glass noodles" made from sweet potato starch. The dish is often served with vegetables and meat.

Jeju Island (제주도) - an island in the Jeju Province. It's a popular place for vacations and is sometimes referred to as "the Hawai'i of Korea".

Jeogori (저고리) - the upper garment component of hanbok.

Joseon (조선) - the Joseon dynasty ruled the Korean peninsula from 1392-1897.

Kimbap (김밥) - a Korean dish of rice and other ingredients rolled in seaweed. It is similar to a sushi roll.

King Gojong (고종 광무제) - King of Joseon from 1863-1897 who restored Gyeongbokgung Palace.

Maeuntang (매운탕) - a Korean spicy fish stew.

Makgeolli (막걸리) - a Korean milky rice wine.

Maknae (막내) - a Korean term meaning the youngest person in a group.

Mamãe - "Mom" in Portuguese.

Meu amor - a Portuguese endearment meaning "my love".

Meu filho - "my son" in Portuguese.

Mukbang (먹방) - videos in which the host binge-eats on camera. Sometimes the host will prepare the food on camera, and they will talk to the audience while eating.

Noona (누나)- "older sister" in Korean. It is used by younger men to older women. This term is not exclusive to blood relatives but is also used among people you are close with.

Ojingeo muchim (오징어 무침) - a Korean dish made of boiled squid and vegetables, served with a sweet, spicy, and tangy sauce.

Oppa (오빠) - "older brother" in Korean. It is used by younger women to older men. This term is not exclusive to blood relatives but is also used among people you are close with.

Ramyeon (라면) - Korean instant noodles.

Sasaeng (사생팬) - a Korean term for obsessive fans who stalk, and/or invade the privacy of public figures.

Seoul (서울) - the capital city of the Republic of Korea.

Soju (소주) - Korea's national drink. Soju is a clear and colourless distilled liquor, and is extremely popular in Korea.

Tteokbokki (떡볶이) - a Korean dish made of rice cakes, and a spicy sauce.

Won (원) - the currency of the Korean Republic. ₩1,000 is roughly equivalent to $1USD.

Yachae juk (야채죽) - a Korean vegetable rice porridge.

Gratitude

There are so many people involved in getting a book from idea to publication, and I want to give a shout out those incredible humans for helping me!

To my husband: Chad, you're the ultimate enabler of my dreams, and the best husband I could possibly ask for. Thank you for supporting my many late nights and for getting me out of the house to interact with humanity so I don't become a hermit during this whole process. And for publishing my book, obviously. :P

To my critique partners: Jenna and Cat, you two are incredible. You helped make this story blossom, and I am forever grateful to have friends as amazing as you.

To my editor: Sasha, you're literally the best. I had the absolute best time working with you. Thank you for making my book baby shine. Cheers to a long and wonderful partnership with many more sparkly books between us.

To my artist: Odette, I admired your beautiful art for ages before I finally had an excuse to get some for myself. Thank you for bringing my characters to life so everyone can see them like I do.

To Eight Little Pages: Thank you all for bringing my book into its final form so it can meet the world looking its best.

To my inspirations: Deanna and Joanna, you two introduced me to K-pop and patiently fostered that love. Without you, even the idea for this book wouldn't exist. Alek, you suggested that the book be a series instead of a stand-alone. Thank you for turning this book into the beginning instead of the end.

To all my beta readers and street team members: Every single one of you is an awesome person. Thank you for taking the time to polish this book with me, and helping to introduce it to the world.

I am more grateful to all of you than I can ever express. Thank you for everything.

CPSIA information can be obtained
at www.ICGtesting.com
Printed in the USA
LVHW051521210120
644287LV00001B/55